Bleeding Hearts

Not a Creature Was Stirring

Precious Blood

Act of Darkness

A Great Day for the Deadly

"A novel full of lore, as of suspense . . .
bound to satisfy any reader who likes multiple
murders mixed with miraculous apparitions and a
perfectly damnable puzzle."
—*Chicago Tribune*

A Stillness in Bethlehem

"A high-quality puzzler."
—*Publishers Weekly*

A Feast of Murder

"Haddam offers up a devilishly intricate whodunit
for fans of the classic puzzler."
—*Tower Books Mystery
Newsletter*

Fountain of
Death

Jane Haddam

BANTAM BOOKS
New York Toronto London Sydney Auckland

Fountain of Death
A Bantam Book/December 1995

ISBN 0-553-56449-8

Published simultaneously in the United States and Canada

Bantam Books are published by Bantam Books, a division of Bantam Doubleday
Dell Publishing Group, Inc. Its trademark, consisting of the words "Bantam
Books" and the portrayal of a rooster, is Registered in U.S. Patent and Trademark
Office and in other countries. Marca Registrada. Bantam Books, 1540 Broadway,
New York, New York 10036.

PRINTED IN THE UNITED STATES OF AMERICA

OPM   0 9 8 7 6 5 4 3

Fountain of
Death

❧

Prologue

"America is a place where everybody is supposed to get a second chance."

—HOUSEWIFE,
USA Today

— 1 —

It was nine o'clock on the night of Monday, December 6, and all across the New Haven Green the bums were getting ready for the weather. It was bad weather to have to get ready for. All last week, the new weatherman on WTNH had been predicting a serious winter storm. Now the storm was here, piled up in black clouds that stretched from one end of the horizon to the other, hidden in the dark of a moonless night. There were little needles of rain turning to ice coming down everywhere. The three tall Protestant churches that always seemed to be just empty in the daytime had begun to look haunted. Over in the Old College at Yale, all the freshmen with rooms that faced into the quadrangle had their lamps on. On the steps of the old New Haven Library building, a bag lady searched through a bright red Saks Fifth Avenue tote to find a scarf to wrap around her mouth and nose. It was that kind of cold. The bums were in trouble. The ones who had newspapers could pretend they had some kind of protection. The ones who didn't drank a little harder, if they could afford it, and got themselves a little more dead.

For Frannie Jay, standing on the corner of Church and Chapel streets with her duffel bag at her feet, the scene was like something out of a science fiction movie Stanley Kubrick might have been making about her life. Stanley Kubrick was dead, but Frannie knew what she meant. She had been born and brought up in New Haven. She had gone to high school at Saint Mary's out on Orange Street. She had spent every afternoon of her teenage life in a booth at Clark's Dairy, arguing the existence of God and the merits of affirmative action with a girl who eventually went on to become a nun. Frannie's mother had said something, the last time they talked, about Saint Mary's being closed and New Haven being changed—but Frannie hadn't expected anything like this. Her mother was always talking about how things had changed. She lived out in West Haven now, in a triple-decker house with her sister, Frannie's Aunt Irene, and neither one of them went for a walk on their own, even just down the block to the candy store.

The wind was picking up. The rain-turning-to-ice was getting harder. Frannie nudged her duffel bag with the toes of her lace-up boots and stuck her bare hands into the pockets of her pea coat. She was a tall young woman, thin but strong, and she was getting nervous. Her pale blond hair was folded into one long braid and wrapped into a chignon at the nape of her neck. Her ears were cold. This scene was eerie and she didn't like it. Macy's and Malley's both seemed to be closed, and one of them—Frannie was never sure which was which—was boarded up. The little arcade mall that now stood across the street from the Green near the old bus stop looked vacant. There was dirt and garbage everywhere, on the sidewalks, in the gutters. There were almost no cars on the road. What had happened to this place? Every once in a while, somebody seemed to be whispering in her ear. Frannie could hear the music of words in her ears and the heat of breath on her neck. Somebody was dancing just out of sight behind her. Someone was creeping up to her while she strained her eyes to see farther up the road. It was dark and getting darker. Frannie wanted to grab her duffel bag and run.

You're getting spooked, Frannie told herself severely, picking up her duffel bag all the same. There was the sound of a car coming in from somewhere. When Frannie finally caught sight of it, it was the wrong shape and the wrong color and going in the wrong direction.

A car came by that she did recognize, a silver-gray Mercedes sedan. A boy stuck his head out of the front passenger-seat window as it passed and screamed at her. "Great tits," he yelled, making Frannie rock back and forth on her heels, but the car didn't slow up or stop. In a moment, it was gone. Frannie was sure the boy couldn't have seen her breasts, not under the pea coat and the sweater and the turtleneck she was wearing. Frannie was sure, but she buttoned the top button of her coat anyway, and wound her scarf more tightly around her throat.

I don't know enough about New Haven any more to know if I'm safe or not, Frannie thought. That's the problem. When Frannie was growing up here, New Haven was almost a country place. There was a slum, but nobody ever went there. There was crime, but it was the kind of crime that held very little interest for the media. Once, when Frannie was small, there was a corruption scandal in city government. Once, when she was in high school, a boy killed his girlfriend and left her body near the tracks behind the New Haven Railroad station. It all happened to people she didn't know, who had nothing to do with her. Frannie and her mother lived in a big old Victorian house on Prospect Street. Frannie went back and forth across town on city buses, always in a crowd of girls in Saint Mary's uniforms, always dreaming what she would do when she finally Got Out. Getting Out was the only real ambition of Frannie's adolescent life, and now, back on the corner of Church and Chapel, she couldn't even say whether she had ever achieved it.

There were car sounds in the distance again, coming from the right direction this time, Frannie was sure of it. She turned to look up the road, toward Yale. The streetlights seemed too dim to her, straining to shine through filthy glass globes. Something like rain was coming down on her head and stinging her ears. She was colder than she could ever remember being before in her life.

That's what comes of spending twenty years in California, Frannie told herself, and then she saw it, the little blue station wagon, stopped for a light two blocks up. Frannie readjusted her duffel bag on her shoulders and leaned out into the road. The lights changed and the little blue station wagon came toward her, moving very slowly. The station wagon's headlights looked like they were straining to shine through filthy glass globes, too. Maybe it was something in the air. Maybe, instead of being the place to come for good libraries and good museums and interesting theater, New Haven was now the place to come to collect free-floating dirt.

As the little blue station wagon reached Frannie's corner, it pulled into the curb and rolled to a stop. Frannie took a deep breath. There was a man in the car, blonder than she was and very young and muscular. He could be the man she was waiting for, or he could be some jerk looking for a little action. Frannie had run into jerks looking for action before.

The driver's side window came sliding down. The young man stuck his head out into the cold and asked, "Frances Jakumbowski? Is that you? Frances—"

"Frannie Jay," Frannie said. "I don't use the Jakumbowski. Nobody can spell it."

"Right," the young blond man said.

He fiddled with something inside the car, and Frannie heard a sharp click. It took her a moment to realize that the car's doors were now unlocked. Back in California, a woman Frannie worked for had an entire apartment rigged up like that. Push a button near the front door, and every door and window in the place locked up. Frannie got a more comfortable grip on her duffel bag and went around to the car's passenger side, out into the street. There were no other cars coming anyway. Frannie opened the back door on the passenger side and threw her duffel bag in. Then she opened the front door on that side and got in herself. At the last minute, she realized that the front door had letters painted on it in gold, nearly impossible to see in this bad light.

"The Fountain of Youth Work-Out," the gold letters on the door read. Then, when Frannie was safely inside, she found more gold letters on the dashboard. These were printed on a plaque that had been fixed to the glove compartment door. They said, "Bring Your Body to the Fountain of Youth." Frannie closed her eyes.

"It's weird out here," Frannie told the blond man, as the car pulled out into the street again. "Doesn't New Haven celebrate Christmas anymore?"

"Of course New Haven celebrates Christmas," the blond man said. "It's weeks before Christmas."

"Every other town in America has had its Christmas decorations up since the day after Thanksgiving. Why aren't there any Christmas decorations here?"

"There are Christmas decorations here. You just didn't notice them."

Frannie peered through the windshield. There were no Christmas decorations that she could see. There were no people, either.

"It's so deserted here," she said. "When I was growing up, New Haven was always full of people. Even at night. Especially this close to Christmas."

"When you were growing up here, there probably wasn't this much crime. I come from Massachusetts myself. I hate this place. I want to go out to California, but there never seems to be a place. Not with Fountain of Youth. Maybe I should just take off."

"Maybe you should."

"My name is Tim Bradbury, by the way. I do the weight training out here. Magda said you were going to be the new step aerobics specialist. We need a step aerobics specialist out here. We haven't had one since Debbie North left, and people are always asking for it. It's the big thing this year. I guess they can get anybody they need out in California. I guess that's why they never need a weight trainer when I want to go."

Frannie closed her eyes again. The street seemed to be full of potholes. All the streets seemed to be full of potholes. They were going around the Green in a big circle. Frannie tried to remember what Magda Hale had told her about the location of the Fountain of Youth Work-Out Studio, but all she came up with was something about its being "up past Albertus on Prospect," which told her everything and nothing. It told her everything, because that was her old stomping ground, the part of town where her mother's house had been, the part of town she had once known better than any other. It told her nothing, because with the way things had changed, the neighborhood might easily be unrecognizable.

The car made a turn and another turn. Tim Bradbury pushed a few buttons on the dashboard and music began coming out of the tape deck. It was surprisingly soft stuff, old Joni Mitchell, and not the driving heavy metal Frannie would have expected.

"Listen," Tim Bradbury said, "are you really hyped on Christmas? Is Christmas your thing?"

"Is it my thing? I don't know. I like it. Why? Don't we celebrate Christmas at Fountain of Youth on the East Coast?"

"Oh, we celebrate it," Tim said. He made another turn, onto a well-lit block this time. The houses were bigger here and more neatly kept. "The thing is, we're not making a big deal about it this year. I mean, not as big a deal as we used to. It wasn't working out."

"What wasn't working out?"

"The promotions. Magda said it was too much like vacuum cleaners. You know, women don't like their husbands to give them vacuum cleaners for Christmas. It's kind of an insult. Like the husbands see the wives as just maids."

"Oh."

"Magda said it was the same way with the work-out memberships," Tim went on. "It was like the husbands were telling the wives they had big butts and better do something about them. It was a kind of insult."

"Oh," Frannie said again.

"So we're not doing Christmas this year," Tim said. "We're doing New Year's instead. We had a whole campaign made up at an advertising agency in New York. 'A New You for the New Year,' Simon says it's going to be the key to taking us really national. What do you think?"

What Frannie thought was that maybe she shouldn't have come back here. Maybe she should have stayed out in California and let her life fall apart. "A New You for the New Year." As a slogan, it had a lot to be said for it. Frannie could certainly use a new Frannie, for the New Year or any other time. She could use a whole new universe, with none of the people she already knew left in it.

"That's Prospect Street up there, isn't it?" she asked Tim Bradbury, and when he nodded, she settled down a little. Prospect didn't look all that much different from the way she remembered it. More of it seemed to belong to Yale, but the Yale it belonged to was being very good about Christmas decorations. A building with a sign out in front of it that identified it as the Charles A. Hamilton Anthropological Laboratory had a pine tree in its front yard decked out in hundreds of colored lights. Frannie didn't know if the Charles A. Hamilton Anthropological Laboratory belonged to Yale or not.

"The thing about New Year's," Tim said, as they drove up the steep hill toward Albertus Magnus College, "is that it's the perfect holiday for a work-out studio. Everybody's always making New Year's resolutions. Everybody's always trying to change their life. Simon says there aren't a dozen people in any hundred thousand who really like the way they are. Do you know Simon?"

"I know who Simon is," Frannie replied.

"Everybody is going to know who Simon is pretty soon," Tim said. "They're doing a profile on him in *Forbes* magazine. 'The Selling of a Way of Life,' it's called. We've got an advance copy up at the house. It's the only thing that makes me feel okay about not being able to get out to California. I mean, everything that's really happening for the studio is happening out here."

"It sounds like it," Frannie said.

"I like the whole concept anyway," Tim said. "Changing your life. Changing yourself. So many people are stuck in really destructive patterns. It's nice to know you can always have a second chance if you want to do a little work for it."

"Mmm," Frannie said, and then she noticed that Albertus, being a Catholic college, was really done up for Christmas. There were colored lights everywhere. There was a life-size crèche on the grass at the front just inside the gate, with a life-size Mary and Joseph inside it.

Sometimes, Frannie thought, you don't get a second chance. Some things come without second chances built into them. The way the world worked, these were always the things you most wanted to be able to take back and do over again.

Out on the street, the asphalt was wet and shiny under streetlights whose globes were grease free and clear. The houses were getting larger and more elaborately gingerbread. College girls were walking in groups, dressed from head to toe out of J. Crew and L.L. Bean catalogs.

Time ought to make things better, Frannie thought, and distance ought to make them fainter, and after a while she should be able to look out on a street or a day or a woman walking in a park without feeling that her stomach was full of glass and iron shavings, that she wanted to double over and die. That was what ought to be happening, but it wasn't happening. She had come three thousand miles across the country, and it had done her no good at all.

What would happen to her if nothing did any good? she wondered. How would she get along? She had accepted this job. She didn't know if she was going to be able to do it. She couldn't imagine standing up in front of a couple of dozen women, bouncing on and off a little plastic step and making it look like it mattered.

"We're just up the hill here and to the right." Tim's determinedly cheerful voice filled the car the way helium filled a balloon.

Frannie had to stifle the impulse to break his neck, and wreck the car, and take off on her own again.

— 2 —

Magda Hale had not been named Magda when she was born. She had been named Margaret Jean, after her father's two sisters, and from the beginning she had known what that was supposed to mean for her.

"Margaret is a good plain name," Magda's mother always said. "Jean is much too French. She's never going to know what kind of person she's destined to be."

Actually, Magda Hale had always known quite well what kind of person she was destined to be. She knew everything there was to know about destiny by the time she was five, because her mother was addicted to the idea. Susan Burnham Hale was a True Believer without a True Religion to anchor her. She drifted from spiritualism to mesmerism to Theosophy to astrology the way the other women on their block drifted from one brand to another of dishwashing detergent. This was back in 1942, in Kettleman, New York, where Magda grew up. The men were all away in the War and the women and children were wedded to their radio sets, hoping for a scrap of cheerleading or news. Susan Hale had been a Seeker long before this. She had worn a little net sack around her neck under her wedding dress, containing two slivers of garlic, a sprig of rosemary, and a half-drowned nettle plant. She had attended the christening of her own daughter with a juju bag stuffed inside her purse. She had bought the juju bag from a lady she had gone to in New York, who claimed to be a gypsy fortune-teller and a voodoo expert as well. If Susan had known anything at all about voodoo, she would have known that the woman had to be lying. Magda didn't think her mother would really have cared. What mattered to Susan was not the efficacy of the magic. Susan didn't believe that anything was truly effective against Fate. What mattered to Susan was the rigid, unyielding nature of the universe itself. Everything was set in eternity and in advance. No amount of effort or talent or will or hope or prayer had any effect at all against the blind force of the universal will. If Susan had been a Christian, she would have been a Calvinist. She would have believed that God destines the great majority of people to hell before they are ever born and that nothing on earth was strong enough to thwart His omnipotent destructiveness.

Magda Hale's universe was not rigid, or unyielding, or controlled by destiny. It was a very fluid place where actions very seldom had consequences and no deed was so irreversible that it could not be undone. Magda Hale had a horror of all things final. The idea of death made her sick to her stomach—not because it meant the end of consciousness, but because there didn't seem to be any way to escape from it. Escape, to Magda, was the key. Life and death, good and evil, health and disease, none of it mattered in itself to Magda. All that mattered was the extent to which any part of it was inevitable.

"You're going to be a plain woman when you grow up," Susan Hale had told her daughter. "You're just going to have to learn to live with it."

Standing in the middle of this large room with its formal bar on one side and its collection of mock–French empire chairs on the other, Magda didn't think there was anyone left on earth who would have called her plain. She was a small woman, but she was very slender and very delicate. She looked, her husband Simon Roveter sometimes said, like a high-fashion line drawing from the 1920s come to life. In spite of the fact that she didn't have the stature, she had the composition. Everything about her was elongated and tapering. Even her face was long and thin. Magda made it look longer and thinner by wearing her hair piled on top of her head. She made her eyes look wider and bluer by ringing them with eyeliner and highlighting them with pastel powders. She made her lips look fuller by painting them past their natural outlines. She left nothing to chance, and because she didn't, she never had to bend to the will of her mother's all-powerful nature.

Until now. The room Magda Hale was standing in was the formal living room of a house on Edge Hill Road in New Haven, Connecticut. The house belonged to one of the minor investors in the Fountain of Youth Work-Out Studio, whose wife had decided to give a supper party for no good reason Magda could tell. Magda Hale was not a party animal. She did not entertain or allow herself to be entertained unless there was a business reason for it. She didn't understand why so many people wanted to waste their time standing around in stuffy rooms drinking bad wine with people who bored them. She only knew that people did want to, and that sometimes she had to keep them company to keep them from getting unhappy.

She had been standing in this same place in this same room for almost half an hour when it started, a pain in her left leg that felt like a needle traveling jaggedly through a vein. She was holding onto a glass of mineral water that she had barely touched. She was talking to three middle-aged women—two lawyers and an academic in Yale's English department—who looked frumpy and big bottomed and definitely annoyed at her. All three of these women had once been members of the Fountain of Youth Work-Out Studio. All three of them had quit the Studio and stopped working out at least a year before. All three of them looked it. That's what happens when you let yourself go, Magda told herself, shifting from one leg to the other to try to get rid of the pain. That's what happens when you let nature take its course. Even the clothes these women were wearing had been affected. The lawyers were wearing beige evening suits that looked like they could have come off the rack at K mart. The academic was wearing one of those drop-waisted dresses that were supposed to disguise oversize hips, but never did.

"What I can't understand," the academic was saying, "is why you don't realize what effect institutions like Fountain of Youth have on the lives of women in America."

"I don't think Fountain of Youth has that kind of effect yet," Magda said pleasantly, shifting legs again. The pain was getting worse instead of better. "Maybe after this new campaign, when we go aggressively national—"

"Magda thinks the effect Fountain of Youth has on the women of America is positive," one of the lawyers said.

"I don't see what's supposed to be positive about being told we're supposed to look seventeen for the rest of our lives," the other lawyer said. "And all those bean sprouts and steamed vegetables on rice. I don't see what's so wonderful about making six figures a year and eating like a graduate student."

"I didn't eat like that when I was a graduate student," the academic said. "I drank twelve cups of coffee and smoked two packs of cigarettes a day."

"I slept with a lot of people I didn't like very much," the first lawyer said. "I thought I was supposed to."

The pain in Magda's leg had settled in, a long thin line of it that seemed to be bolted to Magda's ankle, knee and hip, like a crepe paper banner held to a wall by carefully spaced thumbtacks. Magda put all her weight on her other leg and lifted the one that hurt off the ground.

"It's the attitude I'm interested in," Magda said, thinking that these three women were all at least fifteen years younger than she was, and that they all looked older. "You can go about your life just accepting things as they come, or you can take charge of yourself. I prefer to take charge of myself."

"But you can't take charge of everything," the second lawyer objected. "We all have limitations. There isn't anything any of us can do about getting old."

"I think there is," Magda said.

"Magda has very good genes." The first lawyer made a face. "Most of us get wrinkles in our forties. Magda just sails on through."

"That may be all well and good for Magda," the academic said sharply, "but what do you think happens to all those women out there who are trying to be just like her? They probably don't have very good genes. The only way they're going to save themselves from having wrinkles in their forties is to resort to surgery."

"I have never advocated resorting to surgery," Magda said. "You know that."

"I know that women are never really going to be equal until they are allowed to get old just like men," the academic said. "I know that every organization like Fountain of Youth that is successful enough to 'go national,' as you put it, puts equality back another twenty years."

"It makes all the young women feel they were right about us all along," the first lawyer said. "We're old and over the hill. They don't have to listen to us."

"But you don't have to be old and over the hill," Magda said. "That's the whole point of Fountain of Youth. You don't have to be old unless you want to be."

The pain was now so bad, Magda was having a hard time trying to see—and it didn't matter at all that she was putting no weight on the leg that hurt. The leg that didn't hurt was getting tired. Magda looked around for something to lean against and couldn't find anything. There was a green leather couch and a matching club chair in front of the fireplace, and all those chairs along the wall, but nothing close enough for her to grab.

"I think you ought to consider the implications of the fact that all the people who belong to Fountain of Youth are female," the academic said. "I think you ought to spend at least some time examining your responsibility, your personal responsibility, for the epidemic of eating disorders that is sweeping this nation."

Magda was having a hard time accepting personal responsibility for standing upright. The pain was now so bad, she wanted to cry. The three women were looking at her expectantly. They expected her to come up with an argument they could counter with sociological studies or statistics. She couldn't think past the point of finding some place to sit down. But what good would sitting down do? If taking the weight off her leg didn't help when she was standing, why should it help when she was sitting?

"Excuse me," she told the women. "I think I need to find the ladies room."

The three women looked at each other, and then at her. Magda thought they thought she was probably having a hot flash. At any other time, Magda would have countered this assumption. She had never had a hot flash in her life. She didn't think she was close to menopause, in spite of the fact that she was nearly sixty years old. Everything she had ever told these women about the Fountain of Youth Work-Out was true. It really did keep you young. It really did mean you didn't have to get old unless you wanted to.

With her leg feeling the way it did, Magda couldn't move very quickly. She had a hard time moving at all without limping, and she didn't want to limp. Simon was standing with a group of men at the bar. Magda caught his eye and gestured toward the wall of French doors that led out to the terrace. It had to be wretchedly cold out there, but people had been making the trip all evening. Maybe there was a winter garden or a Christmas light display or something else that was supposed to be beautiful to look at.

Magda found the door in the wall of French doors that was open. She slipped through it and found herself looking at a dead black sky over a dead black yard, all the gracelessness of winter without snow. She limped over to the low balustrade and sat down on it, glad that nobody could see her as she hobbled. The balustrade was even colder than she had expected it to be. She winced.

"Are you all right?" Simon asked as he came through the door.

Magda waved her left leg in the air. "I've got a pain in my leg," she said. "I haven't got the faintest idea what it's from. It's really incredible."

Simon frowned. In his white dinner jacket, Magda thought he looked like a character in a novel by W. Somerset Maugham or Graham Greene. Even his hair, which was gray and thinning, was thinning in just the right way.

"What *kind* of a pain is it?" he asked her. "The kind of a pain you get when you bruise yourself? The kind you get when you break a bone? What?"

"I've never broken a bone," Magda said. "It's not the kind of pain you get when you bruise yourself. I don't know what it is, Simon. Maybe I pulled a muscle."

"Is that the kind of a pain it is?"

Magda shrugged. "If it hasn't gone away by tomorrow morning, maybe I'll see a doctor. That'll make you feel better. But I think I'm all right, Simon, I really do. I think I was just standing around in one place for too long."

"I think you've got a tour to do in just a couple of weeks." Simon was still frowning. "And the television appearances. And the ad campaign. We can't afford to have you out of commission right this minute."

"I know that, Simon. I'm not out of commission."

"We can't afford to have you out of commission permanently, either. Maybe you ought to see a doctor tomorrow even if your leg doesn't hurt."

"Don't be ridiculous." Magda stood up and leaned against the leg again. It felt a little better, except when she put all her weight on it. Then the pain started up all over again. She sat back down on the balustrade and tried to do some calf flexes. Those hurt, too.

"I wonder what it is," she said absently. And then she laughed. "Maybe those awful women put a hex on me. Maybe that's the only thing that's wrong with me. They kept saying they thought I ought to quit."

"Do you think you ought to quit?" Simon asked her.

Magda was surprised. "Of course I don't," she said. "I'd never want to quit. You're never going to have to worry about that with me."

Simon didn't look like he was worrying about her. He wasn't even looking at her. He was looking away from the house and into the cold black sky. Magda swung her painful leg in the air and stared at the back of his neck, at that place where the barber's razor had cut too close and left the skin looking raw and red.

Funny, Magda thought. You'd almost think he wanted to get rid of me.

Why would he want to get rid of her when they were so close to getting everything they wanted, to going national, to being really important in the field? They had been together for over thirty years. Ideas like that simply made no sense at all.

Funny, Magda thought again, and then she found herself forcing herself to get up, to stand straight, to move without limping. For some reason she couldn't fully understand, it now seemed more important to walk without limping in front of Simon than it had to walk that way in front of all those strangers at the party.

In all the years they had been together, Magda had never seen Simon as dangerous to her, or as a threat, or as someone she needed to protect herself from. Suddenly, he was all those things, and she didn't think he would ever go back to being anything else. He still looked like a character out of W. Somerset Maugham or Graham Greene, but now he looked like the wrong one, the one that would be played by Sidney Greenstreet in the movie.

"Are you feeling better?" he asked her, turning away from his contemplation of the sky.

Magda gave him a big grin and told him she most definitely was.

— 3 —

By the time Dessa Carter was able to leave work, it was so late she almost forgot about stopping in at Fountain of Youth to pick up the material she needed. If her way home had been in the other direction, she *would* have forgotten about it. She came out into the parking lot with her head pounding. Even after she was safely behind the wheel of her car, she could feel the grunt and whine of the machines from her neck to her ankles, like a pulse. Her car was a Pontiac Grand Prix that had been old on the day she bought it. Lately, it had developed radiator problems that kicked in whenever the heat or the air-conditioning was on. Dessa put her big cloth bag into the passenger bucket to her left and her forehead down on the steering wheel. She had started work at eight o'clock that morning and gone straight through, except for half an hour for lunch, all day. She had racked up enough overtime to pay for another week of having Mrs. O'Reilly in and a full-scale shop at the grocery store. She had started on the needle assembly line and ended up with stamping, because stamping didn't take any skill and could be done when you were tired. Her shoulders ached and her fingers were raw and bloody. It was going to take three days just like this one to pay for what she wanted at Fountain of Youth.

I ought to give it up and just forget about it, Dessa told herself as she eased her car out of the lot and onto the darkened access road. Everybody always said there ought to be more lights on this road, but nobody ever did anything about it. There was a big sign at the entrance to the parking lot that said, "The Braxton Corporation—Better Medicine for a Better Future," making it sound as if Braxton were a pharmaceuticals company, which it wasn't. Braxton made "medical supplies," like hypodermic needles and blood pressure cuffs. Dessa spent her life sitting in a small chair at a small table, wearing a surgical mask and surgical gloves and a surgical hair cap, trying to be sterile for $6.10 an hour.

The access road could take you straight to the Wilbur Cross Highway, or into New Haven itself. Dessa shifted her bulk nervously in the bucket seat and made her choice. She had been listening to the ads for a month now, on the radio and sometimes on very late night TV. "A New You for the New Year," some of them said—or maybe it was "A New Body for the New Year." Dessa never listened to radio or television with her full attention anymore. Whatever the ads said, they made her happy. Sometimes, in the still early hours of Sunday morning, when her father was tucked safely away in bed with the bedroom door locked and she had eaten her way through two pounds of Lay's potato chips and eleven cans of Old El Paso guacamole dip, the ads almost made her feel as if she could do something to change her life.

In New Haven, Dessa drove carefully from stoplight to stoplight. She looked at the big Victorian houses on one street and the triple-deckers on the other and the gothic stone piles that belonged to Yale. Then she pulled into the driveway at Fountain of Youth and felt nothing.

Nothing.

Dessa cut her engine and got out of the car. She stood under the hot light of the security lamp that hung over the side door. She looked through the small window there and saw a tall young woman sitting at a tiny desk, typing something into a computer. The exercise rooms at Fountain of Youth were open to members every weeknight until eleven o'clock. That was in the ads Dessa had been listening to, too. That was how she knew it would be safe to stop in after work. I ought to learn to use a computer, Dessa told herself. And then she giggled. Learning to use a computer would get her just as much as learning to type had gotten her. Dessa could type very well, over ninety words a minute, but no one would hire her to do it. No one hired five-foot-six-inch, 340-pound women to do anything if they could help it, but especially not to sit in an office. The only reason Dessa had the job at Braxton was that her mother had had a job there before her. When Dessa had graduated from high school, her mother had gotten her right in.

Sometimes, when Dessa tried to talk to normal-size women in offices and stores, they either ignored her or looked her up and down the way cattle traders would have examined a mess of spoiled meat. Dessa was ready for this one to do something worse, like claim that there were no places left in the Fountain of Youth Work-Out workshop for the week between Chistmas and New Year's. Dessa knew there were places, because the last thing she had done at the end of her workday was to call Fountain of Youth and ask.

To get in, Dessa had to ring a buzzer and show herself to a security camera. She held her big cloth bag up protectively in front of her body and wondered what she was doing that for. When the door clicked open, she pushed herself through it and squinted against the bright light. The tall young woman was looking straight at her without flinching. Nobody else seemed to be around.

"I called before," Dessa said, wishing she didn't sound so defensive. "About the beginner's workshop? For the week between Christmas and New Year's?"

"Oh, right," the tall young woman said. The name on her little wood nameplate said Traci Cardinale. She opened the long center drawer of her desk and came up with a little packet full of papers in a brightly colored plastic folder. The folder had pictures of balloons all over it and the words

"BRING YOUR BODY TO THE FOUNTAIN OF YOUTH" splashed bannerlike from corner to corner across the front.

"There you are," Traci Cardinale told her. "Do you want to just take those home to read or do you want to sign up?"

"I thought I needed these to sign up."

"If you've got a check for the fifty-dollar deposit, I can sign you up right now. I can just write you down in the book and your place will be reserved, and all you'll have to do is show up bright and early on the Monday after Christmas, with exercise clothes and a pair of good running shoes. We always recommend running shoes. They have special aerobics shoes now, but as far as we can tell, they cost a lot of extra money and don't do any extra good."

Running shoes. Dessa hadn't given a thought before this to what she was going to wear to a week of Fountain of Youth workshops. Exercise clothes. That meant leotards and tights. Maybe she should buy a Richard Simmons tape instead. Maybe she should just forget this whole thing.

"I'll put the deposit down now," Dessa heard herself say. "Do you have to have a check? Would you be willing to take cash?"

"We'd love to take cash," Traci Cardinale said. "I'll just have to give you a receipt. Oh, and you've got to tell me how you want to schedule the work-out classes. Buildup or smorgasbord."

"I don't understand . . ."

"With buildup, you do the same thing every day, but it keeps getting a little harder. Like five days of aerobic dance, say, or five days of step aerobics. With smorgasbord, you do something different every day, so you can check out all the different options and see what it is you like."

"I'll take that one," Dessa said.

Traci dug into her desk again and came out with a thick ledger book. She opened it to a page Dessa could see was clearly marked in red felt pen, "C-to-NY-NH" and looked up expectantly.

"I didn't get your name," Traci said. "And I need your address and phone number. Do you live in New Haven?"

"I live in Derby," Dessa said.

Traci looked sympathetic. "Nobody lives in New Haven

anymore, do they? Unless they go to Yale. It's terrible what's happened to this city."

It probably was terrible what had happened to this city, Dessa thought a few minutes later, sitting out in her car again, but she hadn't really noticed it. She had had too many other things going on in her life. And since her mother had died, she'd had her father.

Dessa got her car back onto Prospect Street and then down the hill. She made the twists and turns automatically, knowing exactly where she was going in spite of the fact that she didn't know the names of any of the streets she was traveling on. She went past the Yale Bowl and saw that it was not lit up. She went through the intersection that would get her to Orange if she turned left and onto the Derby Road. If she remembered correctly, there used to be an International House of Pancakes near this intersection when she was still in high school. She and her two best friends used to spend half of every Friday night in it, eating waffles with hot fudge sundaes and talking about which of the girls who wouldn't talk to them was sleeping with which of the boys who called them names.

The Derby Road was dark and punctuated by cross-streets and filling stations. When Dessa got to Derby itself, she had to pass that big brick complex—parish church, parish school, convent—that sat on the hill right next to her turn. When she was growing up, that group of buildings had always made her think that Catholics were better than other people, since they were able to build big buildings like that and put them high up where everyone else was forced to see them. Once she made the turn and went over the bridge into Derby proper, the night seemed to get darker and the weather seemed to get worse.

The house where Dessa lived with her father was a triple-decker one, just like the triple deckers that filled up so much of New Haven, but smaller. It sat on a bad twist in a narrow street near the center of town, surrounded by houses just like it that had started to come apart. Dessa's house had started to come apart, too. The paint was peeling. The porch sagged. Dessa eased her car up the narrow driveway and cut her lights. This house belonged to her father. It had been paid for, free and clear, when Dessa was fourteen years old. Now the neighborhood had disintegrated and Dessa's father had disintegrated along with it. Mrs. O'Reilly had the apartment on the second floor, but nobody had the apartment on the third. Dessa had tried to rent the apartment once or twice, but she had been afraid of the people who showed up asking to look at it.

The ground floor back door opened, and Mrs. O'Reilly came out. She turned on the back porch light and stood in the open doorway, her arms folded across her chest. Dessa bit her lip.

"Mrs. O'Reilly?" she asked, getting out of the car.

Mrs. O'Reilly swayed from leg to leg. "You're back later than you ought to be," she said. "You told me you were getting off work at eight."

Dessa thought of the Fountain of Youth folder in her cloth bag, the fifty dollars in tens laid down on Traci Cardinale's desk. "I ran into a little traffic," she said. "I'm sorry to inconvenience you, Mrs. O'Reilly, but I need the overtime."

"You ought to be glad to have a job at all, from what I hear," Mrs. O'Reilly said. "All this unemployment. There was nothing else on the news tonight. Pratt and Whitney laying off. Electric Boat laying off. I thought we were going to be finished with all that as soon as we got rid of the Republicans."

"Yes," Dessa said. "Well."

"I think it's Governor Weicker's fault myself," Mrs. O'Reilly said. "I never did like that man. Bringing in an income tax. He's from rich people down in Greenwich, you know."

"I know."

"I never did like Greenwich," Mrs. O'Reilly continued. "They're a lot of snobs down there, if you ask me. They think they're better than the rest of us."

Dessa pushed Mrs. O'Reilly gently out of the way and went through the pantry into the kitchen. The kitchen was empty and she went through that into the living room. The living room was dark, but she could hear her father snoring. She went over to the chair he always sat in and touched his arm.

"Daddy?" she asked him.

No answer. No answer, no answer, no answer. He was wearing one of the flannel shirts she bought him at Sears. It was an old one that had been washed many times and felt soft and smooth against the palm of her hand. Dessa patted the old man on the shoulder and walked away from him.

"Torpedoes," he said in his sleep. "Torpedoes *first*."

Mrs. O'Reilly was in the kitchen, wrapping a scarf around her throat. She only had to go up a single flight on inside stairs, but she always complained the landings were cold.

"He was all right today," Mrs. O'Reilly said. "Nothing serious going on. He soiled himself a couple of times. I cleaned him up."

"Thank you."

"You should get those diapers they have these days for people like him. It would make things easier. Easier on all three of us, if you ask me. And he's not ever going to get it back, not anymore. He's not ever going to be able to go on his own after this."

"No," Dessa said numbly. "Of course not."

"What you really ought to do is find him a nursing home. It's crazy, what you're putting up with here. It's crazy what we're both putting up with. We're not doing him any good."

"I didn't get a chance to go to the bank today," Dessa said. "I'll have to get your money out tomorrow. Do you mind? Or would you like to have a check?"

"Don't know what I'd do with a check," Mrs. O'Reilly said. "I can wait until tomorrow."

Mrs. O'Reilly had the scarf wound around her neck now, just the way she liked it. It made Dessa think of a bright yellow neck brace. Mrs. O'Reilly left the kitchen and went through the living room to the stairway at the front.

"Torpedoes," Dessa's father said again.

Mrs. O'Reilly ignored him. "I'll be down at ten minutes after seven in the morning," she told Dessa. "I think I'm going to try to make tomato jelly, if he's having a good day. He doesn't have a lot of good days any more. You ought to try to remember that."

"I do," Dessa said.

Mrs. O'Reilly went out the living room door to the ves-

tibule at the front and then up the stairs. Dessa closed up behind her and listened to the sound of her feet moving heavily
from step to step in their thick-soled rubber shoes.

I shouldn't have spent the fifty dollars at Fountain of
Youth, Dessa told herself. I shouldn't be thinking of spending
four hundred and fifty more.

"Torpedoes," Dessa's father said.

Dessa sat down at the kitchen table. She opened her cloth
bag and got out the folder from Fountain of Youth. Her father was never quiet the whole night through. He couldn't be
trusted to sleep. Later, she would have to clean up what he
had done and get him into his pajamas and tie him to the
bed. If she didn't do that, he got out and wandered around
and broke things.

Dessa opened the folder and looked at the first of the
things in it, a little flyer advertising the wonders of diet and
exercise as purveyed by Magda Hale and the Fountain of
Youth. "A New You for the New Year," the flyer promised.

Dessa desperately hoped so.

— 4 —

Virginia Hanley could have understood it if her husband had
left her for a younger woman. She was fifty-two years old,
and she had been expecting something like that to happen
for more than a decade. Steve being Steve, she had been expecting it sooner rather than later. Even when she and Steve
had been in college together, at Gettysburg, Steve had been
famous for his roving eye. There had even been some sort of
comment about it in their college yearbook. Virginia had
been surprised at the time that Steve had finally settled on
her. He'd had better looking girls to go out with, and richer
ones, too. Virginia could only explain it by saying that Steve
found her safe. Since she wasn't a beauty queen, she was impressed with him and grateful for his attention. Since she
wasn't rolling in money, she was respectful of the money he
was able to make. Since she wasn't used to being popular,
she wouldn't find herself bored and frustrated in her subur-
ban ranch house, eager to find a partner and start an affair.

She was the perfect candidate for a corporate wife, the way corporate wives were defined in those days—but even in those days she had been smarter than most of her friends, and she hadn't expected it to last. That was why she wasn't surprised to find herself sitting here, in the living room of her house in Orange, while Steve told her why he was going to pack his bags and leave.

The living room of Virginia's house in Orange was a beautiful thing, with a cathedral ceiling and a wall of windows and a masonry fireplace with a chimney that rose two and a half stories to a beamed ceiling. The carpet on the floor was a thick blue pile, expensive and impractical. It cost an arm and a leg and had to be replaced every three years, because it faded quickly in the sun. The built-in wet bar that had been constructed along one of the lower walls was made of western red cedar that had had to be imported to Connecticut from Oregon. The glassware on its shelves was real Lalique crystal. The liquor in the cabinets was all first-rate and premium brand, right down to the clear, unblended Scotch whiskey Virginia could never help mistaking for vodka. There was a glass of this Scotch whiskey sitting on the coffee table now, with an ice cube in it, half drunk.

"I don't understand," Virginia could hear herself saying. "This doesn't make any sense."

Steve was standing by the wall of windows, nowhere near his glass of Scotch. He was as tall and trim as the first day Virginia had ever seen him, standing over a pile of luggage outside a Gettysburg College dorm. Virginia was surprised to realize that she couldn't remember what dorm it was or what dorm she had lived in that same year. She could remember that Steve's hair had been darker and shorter and less well cut. We were more formal then, Virginia thought. Steve is more relaxed now, in his jeans and turtleneck sweater, than he would ever have allowed himself to be when we were both at school.

Virginia herself was not a relaxed woman. She was wearing good wool trousers and a good silk shirt and a set of matching gold jewelry: earrings, necklace, bracelet, ring. Her hair had been done at a hairdresser's, curled and shaped and slightly touched up. Her nails had been done by a manicurist, cut a little bluntly at the tips, so that she didn't look as if she had claws. She was drinking diet Pepsi from a Steuben glass goblet, crammed with lots and lots of shaved ice.

"I don't understand," she said again. "You can't possibly be talking about the Linda Bonnard we know. Linda Bonnard is—three years older than I am."

"Is she?" Steve asked. "I didn't know."

"Linda Bonnard *looks* three years older than I am," Virginia said more firmly, feeling on surer ground, "but it isn't just the way she looks. I know how old she is. I've seen her driver's license."

"I don't see what age has to do with it," Steve said. "I'm not talking about age here. I'm talking about love. And exhaustion."

"You love Linda Bonnard," Virginia said.

"Yes, I do."

"And I exhaust you," Virginia went on.

Steven crossed the room and got his Scotch off the coffee table. "It's not that you exhaust me by yourself," he said. "It's everything together that exhausts me. With me and you it's just—nothing, I guess. We don't seem to have anything to say to each other."

"Husbands and wives never have anything to say to each other," Virginia said sharply. "What do you say to Linda Bonnard?"

"We talk about horses."

"Horses," Virginia repeated.

"Linda bought a horse place up in Litchfield. She's leaving work after the first of the year and going to live there. She's selling her place in Milford. She's just—getting out."

"Turn on, tune in, drop out," Virginia said.

"It isn't like that, Virginia, for God's sake. It's just that we're all fifty years old now. We ought to know what we want to do with our lives. We ought to have come to some conclusions."

"What kind of conclusions have you come to?" Virginia asked him.

"Maybe it's just that when I talk to Linda, everything we say doesn't turn into a fight. Or worse yet, into a nonfight. Maybe it's just that Linda is never polite."

"You're not making any sense," Virginia said. "You're contradicting yourself."

"I don't really care."

"Linda Bonnard is a frumpy middle-aged woman who doesn't wear any makeup and buys all her clothes from L.L. Bean. Her own husband left her for a bimbo. She hasn't had a promotion at work for three years."

"I don't really care about any of that, either."

"Then what do you care about?" Virginia demanded. "What's the point of Linda Bonnard? What do you get by leaving me for her?"

"Maybe I get a horse farm," Steve said. "Maybe I get some peace and quiet. Maybe I get to retire a decade early. Maybe I get nothing at all."

"Maybe I'll go out to this horse farm of Linda's and blow it to pieces," Virginia said pleasantly. "Maybe I'll send her a bomb in the mail. Do you think I'm too polite to do any of those things?"

"I think this is a ridiculous conversation, and we ought to cut it off," Steve said. "I think I ought to pack up and get out of here before you do something really crazy. Trust me, Virginia. You won't even notice that I've gone."

"If you leave here now," Virginia said, "I'll call the cops and say you left here driving drunk, and they'll pick you up. That ought to be enough to ruin your day."

Steve was standing over at the wet bar now, pouring himself more of that clear Scotch whiskey. He found a piece of paper on the bar counter and picked it up.

"Here," he said, holding the paper out to her. "This is yours. This is what sums you up. This is what I get so tired of living with. Bring your body to the Fountain of Youth. Get a New Body for the New Year. It makes me nuts."

"I don't exercise hardly at all," Virginia said. "I don't even belong to a health club."

"It's not the exercise I'm objecting to, Virginia. It's the attitude."

I could object to your attitude, too, Virginia thought. I could object to this whole lecture you've been giving me, from start to finish. There's no reason I have to sit here listening to this.

Steve had his back to her now. He was pouring Scotch over another single ice cube. Virginia took a long swig of diet Pepsi and stood up. Steve had put the flyer from Fountain of Youth down on the bar counter. Virginia crossed the room and picked it up.

"I'm not the one who needs Fountain of Youth," she said. "Linda is the one who could use it."

Steve didn't answer. Virginia put the flyer back down on the bar and walked out of the living room. This house was full of long, cool hallways, their blank walls dotted with framed and glass-fronted prints. The prints were all pen-and-ink life studies, picked up on the streets of Athens and Vienna for a dollar or two American apiece. That was one of the things she and Steve had done for a while, in the days when she was supposed to be trying to get pregnant. Go to Europe. Buy street art. Come back pretending that you'd stumbled over a real find. It was all crap, as far as Virginia could see, just like that business about trying to have a baby. If Steve had really wanted her to have a baby, she would have had one. She knew Steve.

The kitchen was large and spotless and full of too many pieces of equipment. It had two refrigerators and three sinks. It had metal mold pans hanging from the beams and stainless-steel baskets full of specialty items—corn huskers, apple corers, hamburger shapers—on all the counters. There was a machine that did nothing but make heart-shaped waffles. There was another machine that did nothing but roll six different sizes of meatballs. The doors of one of the refrigerators were covered with snapshots held up by plastic novelty magnets. A snapshot of Steve and Virginia in front of the Plaza Hotel in New York was held up by a bright yellow plastic banana. A snapshot of Steve and Virginia in the Virgin Islands was held up by a plastic tomato with glasses and a mustache and a pork pie hat. Virginia opened the knife drawer and looked through it until she found the small onion chopper with its honed tip and brown wood handle. It was hardly as long as her own small hand. She put the onion chopper in the pocket of her trousers and shut the drawer. She heard Steve moving along the carpet in the hallway and went out into the center of the room, so that when he came in he wouldn't know where she had been.

"I just thought I'd check up on you," he said, when he found her standing at the center island, looking through the vegetable bins in its side for a carrot to munch on. "I just wanted to make sure you weren't about to pull something."

"I'm just getting myself something to eat," Virginia said. "Low fat, low calorie. Once I don't have you around to cook for, maybe I'll adopt the Fountain of Youth way of life."

"I'll be out of here in half an hour."

"That's nice. Will you be leaving me any money in the bank account? Will you be covering the credit card bills?"

"I've got the finances all worked out. I've got a lawyer. You can have the house."

"There's a mortgage on the house," Virginia said. "And it would be impossible to sell in this market. Nobody's buying houses like this in New England these days."

"We'll work it out. You're not going to starve, Virginia. We're not poor. And I won't be leaving my job for at least another year."

"Leaving your job," Virginia said. "To go out and live with Linda on her horse farm."

"I think so, yes."

"How nice for you."

Steve was finally angry. "I don't need this sarcasm, Virginia. I don't need this bullshit. All I'm trying to do is give myself a second chance. After all the work I've put in around here over the years, I think I'm due."

"Maybe I think I'm due a little something, too," Virginia said.

Steve turned his back to her. "Maybe I don't think I have to stand here and put up with this. I'm going to pack. I'll be out of here before you know it."

The kitchen door swung on its hinges. The sound of footsteps on the carpet in the hall was heavy and blunt. Virginia waited until she was sure that Steve was gone and not coming back. Then she let herself out the kitchen door into their attached garage. It was a big garage, big enough for four cars, although they only had three. The little blue Ferrari was supposed to belong to Steve. The Mercedes two-door was supposed to belong to Virginia. The Lincoln Town Car was supposed to belong to the two of them together.

Virginia would have liked to spare her own little Mercedes, but she knew that would never work. Once she set out to do a thing, she always made sure to do it absolutely right.

First she got the door to the kitchen locked firmly behind her. Then she got the onion chopper out of her trouser's pocket. Then she walked over to the Ferrari and went to work on the tires.

Virginia Hanley didn't know what she was going to do about this situation in the long run, but she did know this: her husband wasn't leaving this house until she was damned good and ready to see him go.

— 5 —

Right up until the time he walked into the SuperHour Grocery on Tamsonville and Howe, Nick Bannerman was having a good day. In fact, he was having a great day, one of those days when everything had gone so perfectly, it seemed only a matter of time before he was able to fly, or walk on water, or live forever. Even being back in New Haven hadn't made him depressed, and being back in New Haven almost always made him depressed. Nick Bannerman believed in burning bridges. He had been a student here, six years ago. Now he was supposed to be out in the great world, not hanging around the university as if life would never be any better than it had been the night before he graduated. Nick barely remembered the night before graduation, because he, like everybody else he knew, had been dead drunk. He did remember the guys who had come up every weekend or so for a year after they were supposed to be gone, hanging around looking like they couldn't find anybody new to talk to. Nick wanted to be remembered on the quad at Timothy Dwight College as a winner: an affirmative action baby who had *made* it. The underground word at Timothy Dwight, and at all the other residential colleges at Yale, was that affirmative action babies only made it if they learned to suck the federal teat and went to work for EEOC.

Nick Bannerman went into the SuperHour Grocery because he was close to starving, and it was the only place he could see in Tom Levardi's dark and frightening neighborhood where he might get something to eat. There weren't any restaurants in screaming distance and he couldn't find a pizza place in the yellow pages that was willing to deliver. Tom Levardi had been one of Nick Bannerman's' suitemates at Timothy Dwight, and the first one Nick thought of when he got the call yesterday to come out and audition. Tom Levardi was still at Yale, in the graduate school now. He had been a scholarship student with no money to speak of when Nick had first known him. He was a scholarship student with no money to speak of still.

"I'll tell you the truth," Nick had said on the phone last night. "I'm not expecting to get this thing. I'm not even expecting to get taken seriously. I thought I'd buy us a bottle of wine and come pass out on your floor when this was all over."

"I've got a late class," Tom had said. "You'll have to pass out on my floor after ten o'clock."

The only real problem here was the time. Nick had been due at his audition at ten forty-five in the morning. That had meant he'd had to take a train out of New York at just after eight o'clock. He thought he was going to have a long day in New Haven before he was able to settle down in Tom's living room and lick his wounds. In the end, he had decided to go about it as aggressively as possible. Being aggressive would at least take his mind off just how dire his circumstances were, which meant at least as dire as every other nonworking actor's in New York, black or white. Nick didn't have any money. He didn't have any prospects of getting any money. He didn't have a job and he didn't have a part. It was all par for the course.

The first he realized that his luck was going to change was at the station in New Haven, just after he got off the train. He was dressed up in his usual preppy-go-to-Yale style—necessary for the audition, he thought—but since that rarely made any difference to what other people saw when they looked at him, he was wearing comfortable rubber-soled shoes for what he was sure was going to be a very long walk uptown. He could have tried to take a bus, but it had been years since he rode the buses in New Haven. He didn't have the ambition to look up the schedules. He went out onto the sidewalk with his plastic Delta Airlines flight bag under his arm and turned in the direction he thought would take him up past the Knights of Columbus headquarters building, although he wasn't sure. His grasp of the geography in this part of town was hazy. He started to cross the street in the middle of the block and was stopped by the blast of a car horn. He was jaywalking. The landscape down here was forbidding and bleak, all concrete and dirt and ancient advertising. It was the kind of place where it would be too easy to end up dead, in spite of the fact that it seemed to be inhabited by nobody at all.

The car that was honking at him was a cab. It was still parked at the curb in front of the train station, and the driver was leaning out his window, waving his hand.

"Hey," the driver said, when Nick turned around. "Hey. You going up there? You going to Yale?"

The words made sense but the context didn't. The driver was white. White cabdrivers did not offer to pick up young black men, not even when "young" meant "twenty-something" and the young black men had bought their sports jackets at J. Press. Hell, Nick thought, black cabdrivers didn't offer to pick up young *black* men, not with the way things were these days, not in New York. Things might be different in New Haven, but that difference wouldn't explain this. Nick felt a tingle in his spine, the way he did when he thought there was somebody following him down the street back on the Upper West Side. Maybe this guy was a nut. Maybe he had a Colt automatic in the glove compartment, and he was itching to use it.

"Hey," the driver called again.

Nick recrossed the street. The driver was youngish, maybe younger than Nick himself. He had thick dark hair and the rounded face of someone who was already spending too much time drinking too many beers in front of too many televised football games. Clipped to the visor over the steering wheel, Nick could see a bumper sticker that read: "*Not the Bills, Not Again.*"

Nick stopped a good foot from the car. "I'm not going to Yale. I'm going to the Carlisle Theater."

"On foot?" the driver asked.

"I thought it would be a nice day for a walk."

The driver didn't respond to this. It was a terrible day for a walk. It was dark and cold and damp. This neighborhood was not one of those places sane people wanted to walk in.

"The thing is," the driver said, "I'm supposed to go off, but I'm supposed to have a fare before I go uptown, and I haven't got a fare. I've been here twenty-five minutes, I still don't have a fare. You looked like you could be going to Yale."

Nick explained where the Carlisle Theater was. Out past the Old College and the art museum, toward the Bowl but not that far. Turn left. Turn right. The place with the pink marquee and the mime cutouts out front. The driver consulted his city map and nodded.

"I remember that place," the driver said. "They did that play there last year, supposed to be about AIDS, all the actors on the stage were naked. Actresses, too. Supposed to be experimental theater."

"Right," Nick said. He'd heard about that one, too.

"I could take you up there," the driver said. "I mean, it's close enough, you know? I wouldn't have to get another fare from there. And I'm beat to hell, if you get my drift."

Nick got his drift. He also got something else. As much as he might want a cab—and he did want one; oh, he definitely did—he had only fifty dollars and a return trip ticket to New York to his name. He really shouldn't spend the money.

"You could even smoke if you wanted to," the driver said. "I mean, I don't smoke, but I'm not one of those health Nazis. You get me?"

What Nick got was this: there were other people coming out of the train station, white men in business suits, white women in long skirts and thin belts over their sweaters. This driver had not had to settle his hopes on Nick Bannerman. What was even more surprising was that the decision to settle on Nick Bannerman had, as far as Nick could tell, nothing at all to do with race. Nothing. Being black had not worked in Nick's favor in this case. It had not worked to Nick's disadvantage. It had simply been irrelevant. The driver was looking for somebody who looked like he might be on his way to Yale. Nick was dressed like somebody who might be on his way to Yale. That was it.

Never scorn a miracle, Nick's grandmother used to say—

and Nick's grandmother was no high cracker chewing tobacco on the porch of a shanty in South Carolina. She had graduated first in her class at Howard University and gone on to be the first black woman ever to take a medical degree from Johns Hopkins. She was a power and a personality and a principled atheist. But miracles were miracles.

Nick opened the door behind the driver's seat and climbed into the cab. That millennium called the race-blind society was not likely to come to fruition in Nick's lifetime, but he saw nothing wrong with enjoying little pieces of it when they happened to show up.

"The Carlisle Theater," Nick said solemnly.

The driver pulled out onto the road. "They're going to do it again," he said morosely. "The Buffalo Bills, I mean. Five times to the Superbowl. Five times to the pits. Wait and see."

After that, the day had been one miracle after another, a domino theory of miracles all the way down the line. First there was the Carlisle Theater, which was one of those places every actor in New York wanted a piece of, but most of them never got. The Carlisle didn't pay much, and it was all the way out in Connecticut, but it had prestige. "New" and "experimental" and "important" plays were staged first at the Carlisle. Critics came out from New York in droves. The list of actors and actresses who had gone on from Carlisle productions to win Tonys and Emmys and Academy Awards was as long as a small telephone book. The list of those who had gone on to make money was as long as a decent dictionary. Getting a significant part in a play being put on at the Carlisle, even a bad play, was like picking up a little winner in the lottery. The dividends went on paying out for twenty years.

The reason Nick hadn't expected to get the part at the Carlisle, or even to be taken seriously there, was because he knew perfectly well that his agent hadn't told the Carlisle's director that Nick was black.

"Telling him you're black," Sherry had said, "would just make an issue out of it. I've read this script, Nick. And he asked me to send him someone I thought would work for it, someone new, without a big reputation. The part isn't black. The part isn't white. The part is a psychiatrist."

In Nick's experience, when the part was "a psychiatrist," everybody on earth read that to mean "a white psychiatrist." He got out of the cab prepared to be told he would have to go back to New York without ever being given a chance to read. He checked in at the box office—half an hour early, a bad move in and of itself—and went to sit in the theater to wait. It was too dark for him to read his copy of *Time* magazine. He was too tired to do anything serious like balance his checkbook or sort through the little stack of mail that had piled up in his apartment over the past week and that he hadn't bothered to open yet. Most of it was past-due notices on bills, anyway. The Carlisle was a small theater with plush seats set into a steep incline. The stage was a jutting semicircular thrust that felt too big for the rest of the room.

The director was a fat man who seemed to be dressing in imitation of Wolfman Jack. He came out onto the middle of the stage, looked Nick up and down and said, "Interesting."

"Interesting?" Nick asked him.

"Sherry is an interesting woman," the director said. "You agree with me?"

"Sure," Nick didn't think of Sherry as an interesting woman. Sherry was his agent.

"Read for me," the director said.

The director's name was Hammer Wade. It probably hadn't been, in the beginning, but Nick wasn't going to bring that up. He got his copy of the script out of the flight bag and climbed onto the stage. He found the page Hammer Wade wanted him to read from and plunged right in. Under ordinary circumstances, Nick was something of a method actor. He liked to think about his motivation and have somebody cue him when he felt ready to gear up. This time, since he really didn't think there was any chance, he just read what was on the page with as much emotion as he could manage and got it over with.

When Nick was done, Hammer Wade sat in the first row of audience seats, drumming his fingers against his knees and looking thoughtful. Nick felt like an asshole, or a prize cow. He always did when he had to wait up on a stage while somebody stared at him. The wait went on long enough so that Nick started to get angry. He wanted to climb down into the audience and tell Hammer Wade to stuff his precious experimental script up his precious experimental ass.

"Okay," Hammer Wade said finally.

"Okay, what?" Nick asked.

"Okay you'll do," Hammer Wade said. "We start work in three weeks. Maybe it's four. Right after New Year's—"

"It's four," Nick said, feeling a little dazed. "I'll do?"

"—We pay like shit and we don't start paying until rehearsals get into gear," Hammer Wade was going on, "so you're probably going to need a job if you're going to stay around New Haven, and I want you to stay around New Haven because I want you to do some publicity. We're going to get great publicity. You know how to dance?"

Nick knew how to dance. He'd taken lessons. He'd taken millions of lessons. "I didn't think there was any dancing in this part," he said stiffly.

"It's not for the part," Hammer Wade explained. "It's for the job. If you need a job to tide you over for the next month. It's for Fountain of Youth."

Nick was feeling very dizzy. He was happy, yes, but he was definitely dizzy. He wanted to sit down and put his head between his legs.

"Is 'Fountain of Youth' a play?" he asked.

"Nah," Hammer Wade said. "It's one of those exercise studio places. Big deal, got branches out in California. Woman who owns the business is a friend of mine. They've got some deal going with a tour and special introductory classes and that kind of shit. It's capitalist bourgois as hell. They're looking for an aerobics instructor."

"Oh," Nick said.

Hammer Wade was on his feet. He had produced a small notebook and a pencil out of thin air. Maybe he had been holding them both all along, and Nick hadn't noticed them. He scribbled something down with elaborate slowness, tore the page off the top of the pad and handed it to Nick.

"Here," he said. "That's the address. I'll call on ahead for you. If you need a job."

In the SuperHour Grocery, frozen food was limited to brands Nick had never heard of in boxes that looked old. He passed into the aisle with the potato chips in it and looked over what was there. That was better. There were Lay's and

Wise and State Line. There were Doritos tortilla chips and Fritos corn chips and the first bag of Cheese Waffies Nick had seen in years. He had gotten the job at Fountain of Youth, of course. Like everything else in this perfect day, his interview there had gone perfectly. Now his pockets were stuffed with brochures and business cards and his airline bag back at Tom's apartment was full of scheme drawings for aerobic dance choreographies. Bring your body to the Fountain of Youth, Nick thought, and nearly started to laugh.

He had a bag of pretzels in his hand and his mind on exercise clothes outlets—did he know where to find a Foot Locker in New Haven? Should he pick up some things when he went back to arrange his life in New York?—when he noticed the man in the aisle behind him, standing a foot away with his hands in his pockets and not doing anything at all. At first, Nick thought it was a jump. Some kid had seen him wandering around among the cholesterol killers, checked out the J. Press jacket, and decided he'd found an easy mark. Then Nick realized that the man was, in fact, a man, not a kid, and that he looked a lot like the man who had been at the checkout counter when Nick came in. Brothers, Nick thought absently. Nick looked back over his shoulder and saw the other one, still standing at the checkout counter. He was older than this one, and shorter.

Nick put the bag of pretzels back on the shelf, very carefully. "Do you want something?" he asked the man standing behind him, very pleasantly, very calmly.

The man looked away, toward the ceiling, toward the floor, gone. "You going to buy something?" he asked finally.

"I'm thinking about it," Nick said.

"You don't find what you're looking for, I can help you."

"I don't need any help."

"I help you, you'll find what you're looking for faster than you do it on your own."

"I don't need any help," Nick said again. "If I find something I want to eat, I'll bring it up to the counter."

"You could be hours, looking for something you want to eat," the man said. "You could leave without paying for anything. That wouldn't be a good idea."

In the big stores, they were subtler than this, Nick thought. The store detectives followed you at a distance. The saleswomen hovered inches away from your elbow, but they were smart enough never to actually accuse. They had been trained in the ins and outs of lawsuits. Nick was hungry to the point where his stomach hurt. He hadn't had a chance to eat anything substantial all day. He wasn't hungry enough for this. He looked at the bags of Lay's potato chips and sighed.

"Forget it," he said. "I think I'll just get out of here."

"No," the man at the counter said. "No, Jerry, don't let him out of here until you see what's under his coat."

The one called Jerry looked to the counter and then back to Nick. "Yeah," he said finally. "Maybe that's not a bad idea. Maybe I want to see what's under your coat."

"Of course," Nick said, still calm, still pleasant. "And if there doesn't happen to be anything under my coat, anything that belongs to you, that is, I think I'll just go see my lawyer."

"Don't listen to him," the man at the counter said. "Those people don't have lawyers. They only got drug lawyers."

"I want to see what's under your coat," Jerry said.

"No."

Move. Countermove. Impasse. Nobody knew what to do next. Nick put his hands in the pocket of his jacket—it really was only a jacket; where did these two jerks think he was supposed to be hiding a lot of bulky packages of snack food?—and started to walk toward the front door. When he got to the counter, he nodded to the man who was standing there, he didn't know why. The man reached under the cash register and came out with a gun.

It happened that fast. Move. Countermove. Impasse. Gun. The man behind the counter was hysterical and shaking. Nick Bannerman was scared to death.

"Jesus Christ," Nick said.

"I want to see what's under your coat," the man behind the counter said. "Make him take his coat off, Jerry. I want to see what's under his coat."

"Calm down," Nick said. "I'm taking off my coat."

Nick unzipped his jacket and opened the flaps, so that the man could see. Then he took the jacket all the way off and laid it down on the counter.

"There," he said. "There's nothing to see."

Jerry picked up the jacket and searched through it, feeling the pockets, feeling the lining. Then he put the coat down and turned away.

"There's nothing in it," he told the man behind the counter.

The man behind the counter got a mulish, angry look on his face. Nick thought he might be borderline mentally retarded. He was definitely dangerous.

"There has to be something in it," he insisted. "He's been in here for five minutes. He has to have taken something."

"No," Jerry said. "No, he didn't."

"Search his pants," the man behind the counter said.

Nick picked up his jacket and put it back on again. "These pants are tight as hell," he said. "I couldn't hide a piece of Saran Wrap in them."

"Search his pants," the man behind the counter repeated.

Jerry reached across and grabbed the gun by the butt. He pushed at his brother's hand until the gun was pointing at the ceiling. "Get out of here," he told Nick. "We don't want no niggers in here."

"The neighborhood is full of them," the man behind the counter said. "They're taking over. There isn't going to be anybody else left."

Fighting this would only mean getting shot by the man behind the counter. The man behind the counter wanted to shoot something. He wanted to do it right away. Nick didn't think he'd ever heard anybody call him that name before, never in his life. He'd heard about black people being called that name. He'd just never heard anybody actually use it.

Nick walked out of the store. He was still hungry as hell. He was still tired. There wasn't enough light out here and he was afraid of the dark.

"Nigger nigger jungle bunny," the man behind the counter screamed out after him.

The words went bounding around the brick and concrete and old dry wood, getting bigger and bigger, louder and louder, until no other sound seemed to be possible in the universe.

Nick Bannerman was standing alone on a street corner at the end of his perfect day, feeling like he wanted to get his hands around the neck of the next white person he saw, and squeeze and squeeze and squeeze until he heard the neck bones snap.

— 6 —

Christie Mulligan had begun to develop a phobia for her telephone. It had started one week ago today, and now—at nine thirty on the night of Monday, December 6—it had grown into legendary whackiness, so that she couldn't even pick up the receiver when she knew that the voice on the other end was going to be somebody she wanted to hear. Nine thirty on Monday nights was when Christie's boyfriend called her from his dorm at the University of Chicago. That was the time they had both decided would be optimal, since it was a time when neither one of them expected ever to have anything else they wanted to do. Monday nights were dead boring in New Haven. Everybody had gotten over their weekend hangovers and gone back to work. Out in the common room, Christie Mulligan's suitemates were quizzing each other for an anthropology test that was supposed to take place at the end of the week. Christie was taking the same anthropology course. She ought to be out there with them, instead of lying here on her bed listening to the phone ring and ring and ring but not answering it.

"Christie?" Tara's voice, coming through the door, muffled. "Christie, are you all right? Your phone's ringing."

"I'm fine," Christie said. "I don't want to answer it."

Consultation out in the common room. More muffled words, so muffled they were indecipherable. "Okay," Tara said finally. "As long as we know you're all right."

"I'm fine," Christie said again.

Her hand went to her chest, under her sweater, under her turtleneck, under the skimpy little bra she wore because she was so small-breasted she didn't really need a bra at all. The lump was still there, in her left breast, just where it had been two weeks ago when she had gone in to see the doctor. It was less like a lump than a marble, planted just underneath the skin. It was a hard round ball that seemed to move when Christie touched it, but never went away.

"This does not have to be the end of the world," Dr. Hornig had said, one week ago, when the biopsy results came back. "Breast cancer is a curable condition as long as you catch it early enough to do something about it right away."

"Did we catch it early enough?" Christie asked.

"Yes," Dr. Hornig said. "We're going to have to put you on radiation after the operation, but yes. But Christie, we have to do something about this *right away*."

Breast cancer.

I can't have breast cancer, Christie thought now. I'm too young to have it. Breast cancer happens to women who have been through menopause.

The phone was sitting on a big black steamer trunk Christie had brought to Yale from her room at home in Bellmare, Ohio. The steamer trunk had belonged to Christie's mother when she was a student at Vassar in the early 1970s. Christie's mother had died of breast cancer at the age of twenty-seven, when Christie was five.

The phone stopped ringing. Christie thought of David out there in Chicago, feeling half annoyed and half anxious because Christie had broken their covenant. That was what David always called what was going on between them. A covenant. David's family were very religious Jews, and David like to give a biblical perspective to everything he could.

Now that the phone was quiet, it was too quiet. Christie sat up and wondered if she should call David back. Then she wondered what she would talk to him about. It had been bad enough last week, when she had just found out and didn't really believe it yet. It had been bad enough before she started to hide from the doctor.

The doctor is only lying to me anyway, Christie told herself. The doctor made a mistake. The doctor only wants to make a lot of money out of cutting me up. This thing is not really happening to me, and I won't let them panic me into believing it is.

Christie got off the bed and walked over to the phone. She tried to touch it and couldn't. She walked over to the window and looked out at the quad. This was Jonathan

Edwards College at Yale University, the place she had dreamed of being since she was old enough to know what a university was. She was a sophomore who was majoring in sociology. When she graduated, she was going to go to work for a congresswoman and learn how to get into politics.

Christie went back across the room to the door that led to the common room and opened it up. Tara and Michelle were sprawled on the floor out there, two happy, slightly chubby nineteen-year-olds with a bucket of buttered popcorn sitting between them. Christie used to be slightly chubby, too, but over the last few months she had gotten bone thin.

"Hi," Tara said, not looking up from what she had spread across the floor to read.

Michelle did look up. "You look sick," she said. "You've been looking sick all week. Maybe you ought to check into the infirmary."

"We're thinking of checking into a health club," Tara said. "Look at what we found in the mail today. 'A New Body for the New Year.' Don't you just love it?"

"I'd love to have a new body," Michelle said. "Six inches taller and twenty pounds thinner."

"The rumor's all over campus that Dr. Bandolucci got hold of one of these and now she's going to give a big lecture on the tyranny of slenderness. Can you imagine?"

"Well," Michelle said, "nobody could convict Martha Bandolucci of being oppressed by the tyranny of slenderness."

"Martha's always being oppressed by something," Tara said. "I keep waiting for her to start talking about how the shape of the banister rails in Woolsey Hall reflect the patriarchal obsession with reifying the female—"

"Oh, my God," Michelle said.

"All those dykes over at the Women's Revolutionary Caucus are going to be up in arms about it, too," Tara said. "They're probably going to picket. I've been telling Michelle we ought to sign up for this thing just to show the flag for real women."

"Don't call yourself a real woman," Michelle said. "You'll end up getting us both in trouble for saying unnice things about homosexuals."

"I want to say unnice things about everybody," Tara

said. "That's what I'm going to do as soon as I get out of here. I'm going to become the first female Howard Stern. I'm going to trash the world and get paid for it."

"Howard Stern makes a lot of money," Michelle said.

Christie sat down in the red beanbag chair and leaned over to pick up the brochure Tara had been reading. It was a full-color, first-rate professional production with the picture of a long-lined woman on the front flap that looked vaguely familiar. Christie tried to think of where she might have seen a picture of this woman before, but couldn't. *Magda Hale's Fountain of Youth Work-Out*, the smaller type said. That didn't ring a bell, either.

Christie dumped the brochure back on the floor. "Is that something that's going on in New Haven?" she asked them.

"The studio's up on Prospect Street," Michelle said. "I go by there every once in a while when I do tutoring at the Hispañola Center."

"She's got one of those half-hour shows on cable, too," Tara said. "I think she's kind of famous. She's supposed to be I don't know how ancient, except it never shows on her, if you know what I mean."

"It sounds more like California than New Haven," Christie said.

"According to the brochure, they've got studios in California." Tara stretched her legs and yawned. "It's just the usual thing, Christie. Eat right. Exercise right. Do what you're told to do and your life will be different. It's all a pile of crap."

Michelle giggled. "It's just that this pile of crap is getting a big push from an advertising agency, and they're having a kind of after-Christmas sale where you can get cut rates if you sign up now. I've been telling Tara that we ought to go. Really. We could use something to get us motivated. We could use something to help us lose a little weight. We aren't going to do it on our own."

"I don't want to do it," Tara said. "I don't want to succumb to the tyranny of slenderness."

Christie leaned over and picked up the brochure again. Magda Hale looked twenty-six, not ancient. The models on the inside were all tall and thin and blond, if they were women, and muscular and sexy, if they were men. *Diet and exercise are the keys to freedom,* the text on the inside read. *Freedom from fatigue. Freedom from aging. Freedom from disease and early death.*

Christie folded the brochure into its original thirds and smoothed it out on her knee. Someone had smeared popcorn butter on it.

"I might be interested in something like this," she said carefully.

You would have thought she had just expressed an interest in human sacrifice. Tara narrowed her eyes. Michelle got suddenly interested in stray threads on the carpet.

"What would you be interested in something like this for?" Tara asked. "You don't need to lose weight. You're too thin as it is."

"You've been losing a lot of weight lately," Michelle said. "And you haven't been eating the way you used to."

"I've been eating as much as I can," Christie said.

"So maybe you are sick," Michelle said. "Maybe you really should go talk to somebody at the infirmary."

"We were thinking maybe you'd gotten one of those eating disorders," Tara said bluntly. "I mean, okay, so you're not refusing to eat. We've seen you eat. But maybe you've started throwing it all up when you're finished."

"Have you ever seen me throw anything up?" Christie asked. "We head for the ladies room together half the time when we're out. Have you ever seen me throw up anything but too much beer?"

"That's what I told her," Michelle said.

"I've just been tired lately, that's all," Christie said. "And I've been a little depressed. Over things with David, and you know, that junk. And things with my father. Which haven't been going well. As usual."

"Oh," Michelle said.

"I wouldn't go home for Christmas if I could think of a way to get out of it." Christie suddenly realized that this was true. "I don't want to see my father. I don't want to see David. I keep trying to come up with an independent study project I'd have to do a lot of work on, but I haven't been able to talk anybody into anything. Didn't that thing say it was going on for the week between Christmas and New Year's?"

"That's what it said." Tara wasn't really buying this. Christie could tell. " 'A New You for the New Year.' I wouldn't want to be a new me. I like the old me."

"That's just advertising hype." Christie brushed it away.

"I wish it wasn't just advertising hype," Michelle said. "I'd love to be a new me. I'd love to have it all together for once. If you really want to go, Christie, I'll come back after Christmas and go with you. It might be fun."

"They wouldn't let you stay at the college," Tara said. "You wouldn't have any place to sleep."

"There are hotels in New Haven," Christie said.

Tara got up off the floor. "I think this is a terrible idea," she told them. "I can't believe either one of you is considering it. It costs five hundred dollars just to go up there, never mind what meals and room are going to run. And what for?"

"Maybe we just want to take some time out and bounce around for a while," Michelle said resentfully. "Why do you have to make an issue about everything? You make fun of the Women's Revolutionary Caucus, but you're just as bad."

"I'm not just as bad," Tara said. "I'm just talking common sense."

Christie got up off the beanbag chair and wandered over to the common room window. Like the window in her bedroom, this one looked out on the quad. The quad was deserted.

"It's just talk anyway," she said. "We haven't actually done anything yet. Don't get all worked up about it yet."

"If I don't get all worked up about it now," Tara said, "it will be too late to get all worked up about it later."

Christie put her hand up and rubbed it against her left breast. She couldn't feel the lump through her sweater and her other clothes. It was as if it had dissolved, which was just what ought to happen to it. Maybe, if she went into her room and lay down on her bed and felt herself against her bare skin, it would be gone.

"I think we ought to do it," she said firmly, and then she heard her voice slide into the mechanical singsong that had been the voice of her thoughts for a week. "I think we ought to take control of our lives and fight the good fight against fatigue, aging, disease, and early death."

Michelle giggled.

Tara blew a raspberry. "Oh, for God's sake," she said. "Give me a break."

— 7 —

Stella Mortimer had been working when Tim Bradbury brought the new instructor in, and she was still working half an hour later, when there were sounds in the hallway to tell her that the new instructor was not having an easy time settling in. Stella did not find this surprising. She had been working at Fountain of Youth, on and off, for fifteen years now. She always found it very uncomfortable when she had to spend the night at the Fountain of Youth house, instead of going home to her own small apartment near the cemetery and the Yale Co-op. Of course, the house was not uncomfortable in a physical sense. Magda had been born poor and only become rich in middle age. Like everyone else Stella had ever known with that kind of history, Magda liked her luxuries. Somewhere along the line, the house where Magda lived and did her work had been gutted and completely remodeled. The bathrooms were large and tiled and color coordinated in pastels. The bedrooms were large and color coordinated, too, but for those Magda preferred deeper, more soothing hues. Then there was the kitchen, a high-tech fantasy. It had two conventional ovens and two convection ovens and three microwave ovens and a whole countertop lined with different kinds of food processors in different sizes, so that anyone who wanted to could make anything they wanted to without being inconvenienced by inadequate appliances.

In Stella's own apartment out by the Co-op, the kitchen was a tiny galley space with only one conventional oven and no microwave at all. Her living room was smaller than the office she worked in at Fountain of Youth. Her bedroom was a loft space she was going to have to do something about soon, because now that she was in her sixties she was getting a touch of arthritis in her knees and having a hard time climbing the ladder. When the loft space went, she was going to mourn it. She had been sleeping there since she first decided to settle in New Haven, back in 1978. She'd had her first and only real love affair on the platform bed she had installed under the row of windows that looked out on her backyard. It wasn't until the love affair was over that she had realized that her backyard was a mass of weeds and broken concrete. Beyond it, there were vacant lots and the listing hulks of wood buildings left to rot. Like the rest of New Haven, like Stella herself, this view had been getting old in secret, wearing out, giving in to time. Stella Mortimer had no patience at all for the Fountain of Youth philosophy. She thought it was ridiculous to try to stay young when you weren't young anymore. She thought it was positively evil to punish yourself just because your skin had started to sag. Her skin was sagging and her hair was gray and her solid little body showed the thickening of menopause without complaint—but she thought she was better off than Magda, who was crazy.

The film that was running through her viewer was all wrong. It had shots of light in it and bursting air pockets on the edges. Half of it had been shot from the wrong angle. It was supposed to show a straight-on shot of Magda leading a class of instructors in a kick-jump dance. Instead, it showed feet and legs and seldom got much higher than that. When it did get higher, what tended to appear was Magda's face, bloated and blue looking. Stella reached around the side of the viewer and found her pack of Merit cigarettes. She was the only person at Fountain of Youth who was allowed to smoke on the premises, and she always felt guilty when she did it. That was another reason she would like to be home. In her own living room, she could smoke cigarettes and drink wine at her own pace. She wouldn't have to face a situation like this with nothing to take the edge off the frustration.

Stella bent over the viewer again. There were still shots of light. There were still air bubbles. There were still odd shots taken from odder angles, telling her that Robbie Boulter, their cameraman, had not been paying attention. Stella sat back again and said,

"Shit."

On the other side of the office, Faith Keller, Stella's assistant, looked up from the table where she was pasting up dummy mechanicals for a new brochure.

"What's the matter?" she asked. "Having a bad night?"

Like Stella, Faith was an older woman who had once led a more interesting life. You could read it in the lines on her face. Stella pushed herself away from the viewer and attacked her cigarette in earnest.

"I keep telling Magda she shouldn't hire young men," Stella said. "Not for camera work. Not if she's in a hurry. Their hormones get working and they forget about what they're doing."

"Did he make a mess of it?"

"Leg shots," Stella said darkly. "Ass shots. It's incredible."

"He'll be all right by the end of the week, though," Faith said. "It's like working in an ice cream store when you really like ice cream. I did that once."

Stella tried to imagine Faith working in an ice cream store. She couldn't. Faith was one of those tall, thin, wispy women who seemed to have been born to float.

"I know he'll get better," Stella said, "but in the meantime we're in a hurry, and this film is unusable, and we're going to have to shoot this dance all over again. I think Simon's being very shortsighted to put all the money around here into advertising. Advertising isn't going to help him any if he puts out a shoddy product."

"You're the one who's putting out the product around here," Faith said. "You and Magda. Neither one of you ever does anything shoddy."

"Neither one of us is getting any sleep lately, either," Stella said. "If you want to know what I really think is stupid, it's having Magda lead the dances on this tape and front the tour at all. She's over fifty, I don't care what kind of shape she's in. She's going to get out to Omaha or Kansas City and break an ankle, and then what are we going to do?"

"She won't break an ankle. She takes very good care of herself. And that's the point, isn't it? Bring your body to the Fountain of Youth. Eat right, do the right exercises, and you can stay young forever. Magda is certainly a great advertisement for it."

"If she's lit right," Stella said.

Faith turned back to her mechanicals. "You shouldn't spend so much of your time worrying about this kind of thing. Get your job done and go home. Try to relax a little. I can pick up the loose ends. I know how much you hate to get stuck here overnight."

"Well, I'm stuck here overnight now." Stella took a drag that burned her cigarette down to the filter. "It has to be after ten o'clock."

Faith kept her back to the viewer and to Stella, her shoulders rising and falling gently with her even, unhurried breath. Stella was struck for what felt like the millionth time by the fact that she really knew nothing at all about Faith Keller—not where she lived, not who her people were, not if she had a family. There was an address on the job application Faith had filled out when she first came to work here, stuck away in a file someplace in the main office. It wasn't a neighborhood Stella was familiar with or an address that brought up any associations, so it might as well have been nowhere at all. She knew Faith had been married and wasn't married anymore. That had come up once, at lunch, but Faith hadn't gone into details. Faith didn't mind staying late or sleeping over. That had made Stella assume that Faith must live alone. If Faith had been working at Fountain of Youth for only a few months, this would not have been extraordinary. Come just after the first of the year, though, Faith would have been working here for exactly three years.

"Faith?" Stella said.

Faith didn't seem to hear. Her head was bent over the mechanicals. Her shoulders were hunched under the red-and-white patterning of her holiday reindeer sweater. The sweater was cheap and a little frayed—bought at Sears, Stella thought, and kept forever.

"Faith," Stella repeated. "I'm going to go down the hall to the bathroom for a minute. All right?"

"Go right ahead." Faith sat up a little straighter, but she didn't turn around. "There won't be anything for you to do around here for a while. There won't be any crises I can't handle."

Stella was about to say something stupid about how there wasn't any crisis anywhere Faith couldn't handle—the kind if idiotic, condescending thing men said to their secretaries, that Stella didn't want to hear herself say at all—but she stood up instead and stretched a little to unkink her back.

"I'll only be a minute," she told Faith.

Faith didn't answer her. Stella took one long last look at the other woman's back and then left the office, leaving the door open just slightly to let the light spill into the hall. There were hall lights here, but almost nobody ever used them. The ceilings were high and the light fixtures were remote. The light bulbs Simon had the handymen put up there were too harsh, and cast the wrong kind of shadows.

The better of the two bathrooms up here was on the far end of the hall, near the back stairs. Stella always thought it must have been converted from an old-fashioned walk-in linen cupboard. She walked downstairs and let herself into the outer of the two small rooms without trouble, but when she tried the inner door it was locked. Stella leaned back against the counter with the two shell-shaped blue pastel sinks in it and called out: "Is somebody in there? If you want to take your time, I can go up the hall."

There was the sound of a toilet flushing, harsh and swift: Simon's infamous superplumbing. The inner door was unlocked and swung back. Stella found herself facing a tall young woman with blond hair wound into a chignon at the nape of her neck. The chignon had been braided first, the way it was done in sepia photographs from the days of the opening of the American West. Stella stood back and let the blond woman pass to the farther sink.

"I'm sorry," the blond woman said. "I was taking forever. I'm so tired, I guess I'm not thinking straight."

"You weren't holding me up," Stella said. "I just got here. I'm Stella Mortimer. I direct the videotapes and do the other film and production work that has to be done."

"I'm Frannie Jay."

"Step aerobics?"

"That's right."

"You don't know how frantic they've been about finding someone to teach step aerobics for the tour. I don't know why they didn't think of asking the studios in California if they had anybody who would suit, but they didn't. Simon's always saying that we don't think like an integrated corporation yet, and we're just going to have to learn. Was it a great sacrifice for you, coming out here like this?"

"Sacrifice?" Frannie Jay blinked. "No, it wasn't any sacrifice. I'm from New Haven originally. My mother lives out in West Haven with my aunt."

"Ah," Stella said. "You'll be home for Christmas, then."

"Christmas," Frannie repeated. She looked at her face in the long mirror that covered the wall over both the sinks. "Yes, I suppose I will be," she repeated. "I'm afraid I'm not very religious. I haven't put a lot of effort into celebrating Christmas up to now."

"Maybe it's harder to celebrate Christmas in a place like California, where there isn't any snow. Or were you in the north of California, where there is?"

"I was in Berkeley," Frannie Jay said.

Stella had no idea where Berkeley was. She had only been out to California once, and that had been to Los Angeles. She hadn't enjoyed the experience.

"Well," she said, "I hope you like it out here. I don't know much about this business, but I do know that it seems to be very difficult to find people who do what you do in the Northeast at this point, and I don't like seeing Magda upset. And this really is a very nice place to work, even if New Haven isn't a very exciting place to live in."

I sound like a recruiting agent, Stella thought—but Frannie Jay didn't seem to be paying much attention to her anyway. Frannie was bent over the sink, washing her face as well as her hands. Her skin was the dead white pale of someone who had just been very ill.

"Well," Frannie said very politely, drying her face on one of the sky blue hand towels that hung on the little rack near the door. "It was nice to meet you. I think I have to go lie down for a while now."

"You must be very tired," Stella agreed.

Frannie turned away and walked out of the bathroom, closing the door behind her. Stella stayed where she was.

I wonder, Stella thought, why that young woman has been crying.

— 8 —

It was an article of faith with all the people Greta Bellamy knew that spending your nights in bars was supposed to be fun. This was something Greta herself had believed all through high school and the two years she had spent at Southern Connecticut State College. She had at least been able to sit crammed into the corners of hardwood booths for hours without feeling either physically uncomfortable or terminally bored. Now Southern Connecticut State College had changed its name to Southern Connecticut State University, and Greta herself seemed to be going through a sea change. It's because I'm turning thirty, Greta told herself sometimes, although she knew this couldn't be true. Her best friend, Kathy Weddaby, was turning thirty, too, and Kathy was just as happy as she had always been to spend the hours after work investigating the relative merits of Molson Golden Ale and St. Pauli Girl light.

Tonight, they were all sitting together in a roadhouse called the Avalon—Greta, Kathy, Frank, and Chick. Frank was Kathy's husband. Chick was Greta's boyfriend, and had been, ever since they were all together in the class of '83 at Hamden High. Chick would have been Greta's husband, if she had let him, but every time Greta got started in that direction she pulled back at the last minute. She didn't know what she wanted out of her life, but she did know that it wasn't what Kathy had, or what Chick was able to give her, or what was on offer here at this roadhouse with its third-rate lounge acts bused in from the city and its fat old women in stockings and garters holding up the bar. The booth they were in tonight had a window looking out on the Housatonic River. If Greta craned her neck in just the right way, she could see a row of shuttered little shacks stretching out along the water and then the Stephenson Dam. Greta had a copy of *People* magazine open on the booth table in front of her. She couldn't read the words because of the dimness of the light. She had a bottle of Heineken light on the booth table in front of her too, and a glass to pour it in, but she had been ignoring it so long the beer had gone flat. Frank and Chick were smoking Marlboros and blowing the smoke into the circle of light cast by the side light next to the booth. The lounge act consisted of four guys in white dinner jackets and bad skin who had once cut a record for Columbia and appeared on *The Andy Williams Show*. Some of the women at the bar seemed to remember them, and sang along whenever they played. Greta looked down at her magazine and studied the big picture of the heavyset, Middle Eastern–looking man that took up the left-hand page. He reminded her of the men who had belonged to the Shriner's Club with her father, and he wouldn't have interested her at all if it hadn't been for the woman he was with. The woman was small and dark haired and very pretty, but what got to Greta was her attitude. Here is a woman who doesn't take shit from anyone, Greta thought. The headline on the right-hand page, in very large type but still unreadable in this dark, said:

AMERICA'S MOST ECCENTRIC MASTER DETECTIVE PULLS OFF ANOTHER ONE

Chick was tired of blowing smoke into the light. He turned back to the table, saw Greta's magazine, and snorted.

"Now she's reading in bars," he said. "Jesus Christ."

"It's just *People*," Greta said. "And I'm not reading. It's too dark in here. I'm just looking at pictures."

Kathy turned the magazine around so that it was right side up for her. "It's that murder story again. Don't you think that's morbid?"

"You're the one who bought everything there was to read about Amy Fisher," Greta said.

"She bought everything there was to read about Lorena Bobbit, too," Frank said. "Christ, I nearly took all the knives in the house and buried them in the backyard."

"I think Lorena Bobbit was stupid," Kathy said. "Saying her husband raped her and so she cut off his dick. If she wanted to cut off his dick, she should have just cut it off."

"Well, she did," Chick said. "That's the point."

"I liked the Amy Fisher thing much better," Kathy said. "You could understand what was behind that one. Although I don't think I'd do what Joey's wife did. Go back to him like that, I mean. I don't think I'd believe he had nothing to do with it."

"I would," Frank said. "I think that girl was just plain crazy."

Greta took her magazine back from Kathy and turned it around so that she could see it again. The man's name was Gregor Demarkian, but that wasn't important. The woman's name was Bennis Hannaford, and that was. Bennis Hannaford wrote novels about knights and ladies and dragons and magic trolls, and Greta had a copy of one of them—*The Chronicles of Zed and Zedalia*—hidden out of sight right now in her purse.

The lounge act started on a rendition of "Moon River," not a very good one. The piano they were using was flat. Greta took a sip of beer right out to the bottle, made a face at the sour flatness of it, and put the bottle down again. When she looked up, she found Chick staring at her, and blushed.

"I let it go too long." She felt slightly defensive.

Chick flicked his fingers at the beer bottle. "You're letting everything go too long these days. You haven't been paying any attention to business at all for months."

"Oh, she's been paying attention to business," Kathy said sharply. "That's how she got that promotion at work."

"It wasn't a promotion," Greta said quickly. "It was just an upgrade in title. And a little raise."

"Executive assistant." Kathy made a rabbity little face. "Aren't you important."

"I'm being a secretary to Mr. Wilder just the way I've always done," Greta said. "It's just that I did a lot of overtime, and some extra work when we had all that trouble just after Thanksgiving—"

Chick lit another cigarette. He let the match burn down until the flame touched his thumb, but didn't flinch. That was a macho thing all the boys had been into in high school. Chick had never given it up. He dumped the spent match in the ashtray in the center of the table. The ashtray was already overflowing with butts.

"I think that's our point here," he said seriously. "You aren't paying any attention to me. You aren't paying any attention to us."

"It's like you think you're an entirely different person," Kathy said, "It's like you think all of a sudden you've gotten better than us."

"Just because they're giving you a little extra money at work doesn't mean you're better than us," Chick said. "I mean, for Christ's sake, Greta. It's not like they made you president of the company. You're just working for chump change and playing the lottery like everybody else."

"She doesn't play the lottery anymore," Kathy said tightly. "She says she's saving her money for something else."

The lounge act had moved past "Moon River" and swung into a tinny version of "My Way." Greta looked at her flat beer and wished she had drunk it. It would really help right now to be a little numb. Chick was right. She hadn't been paying attention to him, to any of them. That was why she hadn't picked up on this hostility before. And yet it must have been there. The raise was new—it wouldn't even kick in until just before Christmas—but the other things, her preoccupation and, yes, that sense of difference, those had been here for months. Now the air was thick with anger turning slowly but inexorably toward hatred, and Greta felt a little sick. The four of them had been together for years now, ever since Greta and Chick had started going out in their high school freshman year. Greta didn't have any other friends, even at work. She didn't have any family left, either. Her parents had died in an accident on the Merritt Parkway more than five years ago. What would happen to her if Kathy and Chick and Frank stopped talking to her, and she was on her own?

She picked up her beer glass and put it down again. "I don't see why I have to buy lottery tickets on a week when I'm feeling short of cash," she said. "There's Christmas coming up."

"I use my Christmas bonus to pay for Christmas," Kathy said.

"She's saving up to pay her way into that health club." Chick smiled. "Five hundred dollars, can you believe that? For this spa. For a week. Fountain of Youth, it's called. Up in New Haven."

"I don't see what's wrong with my wanting to go to some

exercise classes for a week," Greta said. "You're the one who's always telling me I'm getting a fat ass."

"I have that week off from work," Chick said. "I wanted us to go to Atlantic City. I even said I'd pay for the whole thing."

"We can go to Atlantic City any week. This was a kind of sale price deal. It's going to happen and then it's going to be gone. I can't afford the prices they usually charge."

"You could have asked me to go with you," Kathy said. "You could at least have thought of the idea. If they charge more than five hundred dollars a week, they must get a lot of rich woman going there. I don't think you're going to fit in."

"I don't have to fit in," Greta said wearily. "I just have to do a lot of aerobics and some weight lifting and listen to some lectures on nutrition. I just thought I'd try to improve myself, that's all. I don't understand why it's turned into this big deal."

"I'm going to go up and get another beer," Chick said. "That fat-assed waitress is nowhere."

Fat-assed, Greta realized suddenly, was the way Chick described every woman he was angry with. Even if the woman was as thin as a rail and built like a toothpick, if Chick didn't like her he said she had a big butt. That must mean he doesn't like me anymore, Greta thought, but she didn't know what to do with that. He might not like her, but he still wanted her around. He was over at her house every night. He called her at work every lunch hour. He expected her to go out to bars with him as much as he ever had. Greta thought about all those articles in the women's magazines that Kathy bought—*Family Circle, Woman's Day*—about men who stalked women who didn't love them anymore. That doesn't apply to me, Greta told herself. I still love Chick. I love him more than he loves me. At least I like him.

Without realizing it, Greta had been staring down at her magazine again, at Gregor Demarkian and Bennis Hanna-ford, at a blurred vision in the background that looked like a very elegant room. Greta hadn't read the article yet, so she didn't know what it was about. Gregor Demarkian some-times investigated murders that took place in small towns or slums, which were boring. She hoped this murder had taken place among rich people. She put out her hand to touch the cloud of dark hair that floated around Bennis Hannaford's head. Then she took her hand away quickly and closed the magazine.

When Greta looked up again, Frank was gone as well as Chick, and Kathy was leaning far over the booth table, staring at her intently. Why didn't I ever notice how mean her eyes look? Greta wondered. Kathy really did have little piggy eyes in a round and overstuffed face. She had a line of pimples along her jaw and another one at the corner of her mouth. She looked worse than angry. She looked ready to tear somebody apart.

Greta took her magazine off the table and felt around on the booth seat for her pocketbook, so that she could put the magazine away. "I think I'll go to the ladies room," she said vaguely. "I think I need to run a brush through my hair."

"No," Kathy said.

"I think I can go to the bathroom when I want to, Kathy. I think you can't stop me from doing that."

"I got rid of the guys so I could talk to you," Kathy said, "and you know it. I'm not going to let you run away to the ladies room and act like I don't exist."

"I'm not acting like you don't exist. I just want to brush my hair."

Kathy turned sideways and propped her feet up on the bench. "I'm really sick of this. I'm really sick of the way you've been behaving for the past month. We're all sick of it."

"You've all made it clear."

"I wouldn't take anything for granted if I was you," Kathy said. "Just because Chick has been hanging around you forever doesn't mean he's going to go on hanging around you. You hurt his feelings when you said you wouldn't marry him."

"I wasn't ready to get married."

"Well, maybe Chick is ready to get married. Maybe he's ready to settle down. Maybe if he can't get you to go settle down with him, he'll get somebody else."

"Is this a particular somebody else you're talking about?" Greta asked. "Do you have an applicant for this position?"

"Chick has," Kathy said slowly. "You don't give Chick enough credit. It's not like it was back in high school. Chick has turned out to be a very hunky guy."

"That's nice. Who thinks he's so hunky?"

"Marsha Caventello." Kathy swung around so that she was facing Greta again. She was sitting back farther on the bench, in the shadows, so that Greta couldn't see what was going on in her eyes. "Marsha Caventello has been making up to Chick for the last two weeks. Coming into the plant when she doesn't have to. Dropping her clipboard on his feet and letting him pick it up for her. Telling him how wonderful he is. It's beginning to do the job."

"That's nice," Greta said stiffly.

"Frank told me that Chick told him that if you wouldn't go to Atlantic City, he was going to ask Marsha."

"That's nice," Greta said again.

Kathy leaned into the light. The expression on her face was feral. The smile that was spread across her mouth was as cruel as the smile of an executioner.

"Don't just say 'that's nice,' " she said with satisfaction. "Do something about it. Because if he goes away to Atlantic City with Marsha, Greta, he isn't going to come back to you."

— 9 —

Up at Fountain of Youth, at midnight, Frannie Jay was lying fully clothed on the hard mattress of her double bed, feeling that she really ought to make herself get undressed and take a shower and go to sleep. Tomorrow she had to learn two step dance routines and review the tour literature. She was supposed to be awake enough to participate in a staff meeting at nine o'clock. She had the lights in the bedroom turned off and the curtains on the windows opened. She was telling herself for the fifteenth time that she was only hurting herself by procrastinating like this, when she heard the noise outside in the drive.

Koo roo, the noise went. *Koo roo clank whoosh.*

Frannie got off her bed and went to the window. The se-

curity light on the front of the detached garage cast a wide
arc of brightness onto the gravel and the lawn. There was
nothing out there that Frannie could see.

Koo roo, the noise went again. *Koo roo clank whoosh
clank roo.*

Frannie undid the latch on her window and pushed it up.
Cold air streamed over her. She leaned out into it and looked
across the yard. Empty grass. Empty gravel. A three-car garage with its doors down, closed up tight. Frannie started to
back into her room again.

Koo roo, the noise started again, but then it stopped, and
Frannie stopped too. For just a moment there, she thought
she had seen something, close to the house, where there was
a small line of evergreen hedges near the back door. She
leaned out again, as far as she dared, and squinted into the
shadows. Then she backed all the way into the room and
went to sit down on the side of the bed.

A foot, Frannie thought, feeling the start of hysterical
giggles rising in her throat.

That's what I just saw out there.

A naked human foot.

Attached to a naked human leg.

Sticking out of the evergreen hedges next to the back
door.

Frannie Jay put her head between her knees and began to
heave.

Part 1

"New Year's resolutions are
what secular society has instead of
the confessional, and they don't work
half as well."
—Roman Catholic priest,
U.S. Catholic

ONE

— 1 —

For many years, Gregor Demarkian had thought of New Year's Eve as the celebration of the letdown that happened after Christmas. First there was the real holiday: tinseled trees, gold foil wrap and satin ribbons, carolers in the streets. Then there was the long slide into discontent and exasperation, with too many leftovers in the refrigerator and too much slush ice on the roads. Then there was the *pop*, the point when nobody could stand it anymore and nobody thought they ought to have to. It was that *pop* that caused so many fatalities on the roads and in otherwise stable marriages. Gregor had seen it through all his long twenty years with the Federal Bureau of Investigation. The Bureau didn't investigate local crimes, but it did rub up against them, especially in Washington and Virginia. It also had agents, who were just as susceptible to New Year's Eve explosions as anyone else. Maybe there was something about cheap champagne that was different from all other forms of ingestible alcohol. Men who had never before shouted at a football game gave their wives black eyes. Women who had never fantasized so much as a love scene from a Barbara Cartland romance left home with itinerant carpenters. Hundreds of loose and drifting people, without family, without friends, without ties of any kind, poured into the streets—and they were people with nothing to lose.

"Give me a guy with a job and a house and a mortgage," Gregor's favorite instructor out at Quantico was always saying. "Give him to me every time. That's a guy I can count on."

Outside the grimed window of the train, the small Connecticut towns were going by with syncopated regularity, each more or less like the one before it. There had been a couple of small cities on the way, but those had seemed oddly unreal, too clean, too firmly placed in a rural backdrop. Gregor tried to remember if Connecticut had ever been a serious manufacturing state but got only a vision of whaling ships and wooden nutmeg. The small towns all still had their Christmas decorations up. Tinsel and colored glass lights were wound in whorls from one streetlamp pole to another, across nearly empty streets. Big, fat cardboard Santa Clauses sat in store windows. Frantic elves and drunken reindeer were scattered across town parks. Every once in a while, Gregor saw a sign announcing a New Year's sale or a New Year's special or a "Get Ready for the New Year Extravaganza," but the signs lacked fire and conviction. Nobody in the shore towns of Connecticut was any more enthusiastic about ringing out the old and ringing in the new than Gregor Demarkian was.

Nobody on this train was in any hurry to get where he was going, either. Gregor was sitting up in his seat, at the back of the car, with his hands on his brand new black leather briefcase, but the other two passengers he could see were both asleep. One of them, a young white man in baggy clothes and blunt-cut hair that had been greased to stick straight up from his skull, had his feet up on the seat across from him. The other, an elderly woman with an oversize pocketbook, was sitting upright with her arms folded around a shopping bag. Gregor found himself wondering if either one of them would have qualified as someone who "could be counted on" by his old instructor at Quantico. He wondered if he himself would have qualified. All that time was so long ago and far away. A world where women were refused appointments as special agents of the FBI as a matter of policy. A world where there were no black people or African-

Americans but only Negroes—or something worse—and the Negroes were all serving drinks and carting baggage and going home on a different bus. A world where men like Gregor Demarkian didn't retire after twenty years' service, but got promoted into administration and were expected to stay put. Well, Gregor thought, I spent my time in administration, ten years in the formation and running of the Behavioral Sciences Department—and I didn't like it much.

The train began to slow down, surrounded by the debris of a cityscape again, tracks branching out in all directions and low brick buildings crammed too close together. Half the low brick buildings were empty. Half the empty buildings had their front windows smashed. Maybe the reason Gregor Demarkian didn't like New Year's Eve was that it was as much a nostalgia orgy as anything else it was supposed to be. Look back in befuddlement. Look forward in a haze of 150-proof courage. Gregor Demarkian did as much complaining as anybody else about what had happened to the world. The vandalism. The crime. The dirt. The violence. He knew better than most people how true it all was. He still didn't want to go back. His old instructor at Quantico might not have considered him a sterling character any longer. He didn't have a job. His wife was dead. He owned his floor-through condominium apartment free and clear. If push came to shove, he just might decide that he had nothing to lose he wasn't willing to lose. The statistics were terrible and they were probably getting worse. He really didn't care. He liked this world better than he had liked that one, in spite of how quiet that one had been. He liked himself better than he had liked the man who had gone to work one morning in his socks but without his shoes, because he had been too preoccupied with a case to notice what he wore. The only thing he wanted to bring back from that time was his wife, Elizabeth, and he only wanted her if he could have her without the cancer that had killed her. He wouldn't put Elizabeth, or anyone else he knew, through pain like that again.

The cityscape was becoming a jungle of tracks and wires and abstract shapes. The conductor came through from the back of the car, yelling, "New Haven. Last Stop. New Haven. Last Stop." Like all conductors, he was nearly unintelligible. The boy with the greased hair stood up. The elderly woman with the shopping bag shook herself awake and checked for her pocketbook. Gregor Demarkian put his briefcase on his lap.

The briefcase had come from Mark Cross and cost a mint. Gregor only owned it because it had been given to him by Bennis Hannaford as a Christmas present. Bennis Hannaford was the woman who owned the apartment just below his in the converted brownstone house on Cavanaugh Street in Philadelphia where Gregor had retired to be among people he knew. The scarf Gregor was wearing draped over the back of his neck under the collar of his Burberry topcoat was a Christmas present, too, but not an expensive one. It had been given to him by Father Tibor Kasparian, his closest friend and the priest of Cavanaugh Street's Holy Trinity Armenian Christian Church. It had probably been bought, like most of Tibor's presents were, at a charity shop in central Philadelphia run by five churches and a synagogue for the benefit of a homeless center west of Society Hill. When Gregor was still with the Bureau, he had not had the kinds of friends who gave him Christmas presents. He had had colleagues and family and the people that Elizabeth knew. In this way, now was better than then, too. Gregor sometimes surprised himself with how strange all that seemed to him now, living in isolation, living for work. He must have been out of his mind.

The train was gliding to a stop under a tangled web of lights and structural beams. Gregor stood up and shook out his coat and headed for the open space in front of the sliding doors. Of course, he thought, there was one small problem with the self-analysis he had been doing this morning, one little kink in the reasoning that just wouldn't go away and leave him alone. If he was so content on Cavanaugh Street and delighted not to be obsessed with work—why was it that it had taken only a single phone call to get him out of his living room and on a train to New Haven, Connecticut?

There was a big banner hanging over the platform next to which the train had stopped that said "HAPPY NEW YEAR AND WELCOME TO NEW HAVEN." It looked tattered and old, as if it had been dragged out of a trunk somewhere after several years' hard use and no trips to the dry cleaner. The train doors slid open; a blast of cold air rushed in. Gregor helped the elderly woman with the shopping bag across the little gap onto the platform.

"It gets wider and wider every time," the elderly woman told him. "People just don't think."

Gregor was thinking that Bennis Hannaford would have thought of the same question he just had, and that before he went back to Philadelphia and had to face her he ought to think up a fairly good answer. Of course, if he waited long enough to get back to Philadelphia, she would be gone, out to Los Angeles for a month to talk to the people who were turning her series of fantasy novels into a video game.

One of the things Gregor had found out in his retirement but didn't like to mention was that he loved video games. He especially loved really violent video games where the good guys did impossibly grotesque things to the bad guys, like tear out their hearts and turn their eyes into blood fountains.

"Law enforcement is frustrating," that same old instructor at Quantico used to say.

Gregor Demarkian could only suppose that it must have been.

— 2 —

Gregor Demarkian had never met Tony Bandero, or even seen a picture of him, but coming up into the main body of New Haven Station, he had no trouble picking him out of the crowd. There was, surprisingly, a fairly large crowd. Gregor's train had been so deserted, he had assumed that the New Haven Railroad had the same problem Amtrak did: not enough passengers to make it profitable. He had forgotten that the New Haven was a commuting line to and from New York City and that most of the people who lived down here, on what was called Connecticut's Gold Coast, worked in New York. New Haven did not look like it was possessed of much gold. The station was large because it had been built in the days when stations were built large. It was clean because the railroad was putting serious effort into keeping it that way. Otherwise, it was just like all the other large old stations Gregor had had the occasion to be in over the last few years. The waiting room was overrun with homeless people. The legitimate passengers were all crowded around the gates to the platforms or in lines at the ticket counters. The waste-baskets were full of crumpled newspapers and torn candy wrappers. The advertisements that hung as posters on the wall were faded, even though Gregor knew that some of them had to be new. If you moved quickly and in the wrong direction, you caught sight of a junkie before he had a chance to scuttle away. Gregor wondered what the laws of vagrancy were in this state. In New York, they had all been declared unconstitutional. If a man who belonged in a mental institution but couldn't get a place because there was no money to keep him there decided to take up residence on the stoop of your elegant East Side brownstone, you were stuck with him.

Gregor Demarkian recognized Tony Bandero because Tony Bandero looked like a cop, a good old-fashioned cop, a cop circa 1954. Bandero was tall and broad and potbellied, with a bald spot on the back of his head and a badly fitting brown wool suit. He had thick hairy hands and frayed shirt cuffs and a Timex watch that looked like it had taken some battering. Gregor was tall and broad, too—at six foot four, considerably taller than Tony Bandero—but a different physical type. Tony Bandero was heavyset. Gregor Demarkian was massive.

People were rushing into the gate, trying to get to a train whose arrival had been announced while Gregor was still waiting to get off his. There was a banner over the ticket counters in the station that said "HAPPY NEW YEAR" in glitter-stuck letters on a white background. Gregor had seen the same banner in a Hallmark store. He tucked his briefcase up under his arm to avoid hitting shorter people in the side with it. The shorter people were all in a massive hurry and not paying any attention to where they were going. Tony Bandero was surrounded by shorter people, all women, who seemed to be waiting for passengers from Gregor's train. The women all wore those short cloth coats with the rough sur-faces that came in such odd colors, like powder blue and copper-washed metallic green. Gregor made his way over to the little group and stuck out his hand.

"Tony Bandero?" he said. "I'm—"

Tony Bandero was carrying a copy of *The New Haven Register*. He shoved it under his left arm and stuck his right hand out to catch Gregor's own.

"Mr. Demarkian," he said. "Mr. Demarkian. I recognized you from your pictures."

"Gregor," Gregor said.

"The bishop said I should call you Mr. Demarkian," Tony Bandero said. "Not that I take the bishop's word as gospel in everything, you understand, but he called you for me. I figure I owe him a little courtesy."

"Actually," Gregor said, "your bishop called John Cardinal O'Bannion in Colchester. It was Cardinal O'Bannion who called me."

"Whatever. The church is the church. She's been taking a hell of a beating lately—deservedly, in some cases, if you ask me; who the hell can figure all those child abuse cases—but she still comes through when you need her. The bishop said I was to tell you there wasn't anything religious about this case."

"I know," Gregor said. "Health clubs. Diet gurus."

"It's more like exercise gurus." Tony Bandero shook his head. "The bishop said you might shy away from it if you thought it was a religious murder. He said you might have had enough of religious murders for a while. Three, he said you were involved in. You couldn't get me to touch a religious murder with a ten-foot pole. They don't think like us, you know, bishops don't. They get trained out at the Vatican and they don't think like Americans."

All the Roman Catholic bishops Gregor had ever known, and especially John Cardinal O'Bannion, had thought like hyper-Americans. O'Bannion practically snored "The Star Spangled Banner" in his sleep. There was a whole raft of beggars at the front doors to the station, standing in a row that reminded Gregor crazily of a debutante receiving line.

"I take it New Haven's having the same problems every place else is," Gregor said.

Tony Bandero examined the row of beggars and frowned. Then he turned away from them and hurried through the doors onto the sidewalk outside. His coat was a dirty trench that looked too light for the cold of the day. It flapped in the breeze as he walked.

"Yeah," he said finally. "We got the same problems as every place else. We got beggars. We got drugs. We got street gangs. Twice a month we pick up some high school kid who's just offed his best friend because they had an argument over the coolest color for a pair of sneakers. Does this kind of thing make any more sense to you than it does to me?"

"No," Gregor said.

They had reached a battered Ford Fairlane, its color the same brown as Tony Bandero's suit.

"The thing is," he said, "I used to like being a cop. It was dangerous, but it was fun. There were the good guys. There were the bad guys. The good guys chased the bad guys. Sometimes the good guys won. You know what I mean?"

"Sure."

Tony unlocked the passenger-side door of the Fairlane and motioned Gregor in. "Now I pick up these kids, thirteen, fourteen years old, sometimes twelve, they've just offed somebody, they've just raped some old lady and bashed her head in with a lead pipe, they're dealing six thousand dollars a week, and they want to pay me off, they just don't give a shit. Then I go up to the house, and what do I get? They've got this mother, she hasn't been straight since she was thirteen herself, she's turning tricks out of the back bedroom, she's got an eleven-year-old daughter turning tricks out of the hall closet, she's got a boyfriend who's pimping the both of them. Then we take the kid in and send him through medical, and it turns out his arm has been broken six times and the doctors know the breaks didn't happen the day before yesterday. Does this make any sense to you?"

"I don't think it's supposed to make sense," Gregor said. There was a little plastic statue of the Virgin Mary glued to the dashboard and a St. Christopher medal hanging from the back of the rearview mirror.

Tony Bandero went around the front of the car and got in the other side. He started the engine and the car immediately began to make a series of very odd noises. First it squeaked in a way that sounded like a bird mating. Then it clanked. Then it let out a long hiss, as if all its tires were losing air at once.

"The thing is," Tony Bandero said, "I don't hold with

these liberals who don't want to lock anybody up, but I can see some of the points they make. I mean, for God's sake, what can you expect?"

"I don't know."

"Half the time, I want to lock the mothers up along with the kids, only then it turns out the mothers had mothers and it was just as bad and you've got to go back to our generation practically before you find anybody who was making any sense, and then of course what you find is dope. I don't know what I'm supposed to do about it. Lock everybody up. Drop bombs on Colombia. Torch the Thailand poppy fields. Which is why I think I'm so hyped on this case I got you out here for."

"I didn't think this case had anything to do with dope."

"It doesn't." Tony Bandero was definite. "It doesn't have anything to do with dope. It doesn't have anything to do with prostitution. It doesn't have anything to do with battered child syndrome. It is not a mess."

"I thought you couldn't solve it," Gregor said.

"I can't. I haven't got the faintest idea in hell what's going on here. But, Mr. Gregor Demarkian, let me tell you this. In this case there are good guys and there are bad guys and the good guys are going to chase the bad guys and if the good guys catch the bad guys, I'm not going to spend a month lying awake nights wondering if I shouldn't quit the force and become a priest so I can do something about all this shit. I'm going to go out to a damned good steakhouse and celebrate."

The Ford Fairlane edged out onto the road. The cabs in the cab rank hooted their horns at it. Gregor restrained himself from pointing out the obvious. If it were true that Tony Bandero didn't know anything at all about how to solve this case, then this case could turn out any which way. It could be about dope. It could be about prostitution. It could be about battered child syndrome. When he got to the end of it, Tony Bandero might not like what he saw any better than he liked what he saw in the rest of his work.

Tony Bandero was easing himself into the traffic. The traffic was picking up in volume and noise. Tony was bouncing happily behind the steering wheel, singing something to himself that Gregor couldn't put a name to, but that he definitely connected to Frank Sinatra.

"Listen," Tony said. "This time, we've got it made."

— 3 —

Twenty minutes later, Gregor Demarkian got a look at why Tony Bandero thought they had it made. The Ford Fairlane was parked in the gravel driveway of a tall Victorian house on something called Prospect Street. All around them, the bare branches of tall trees bent in the wind and fat little evergreen bushes shuddered. The house was not only tall but elegant—Civil War vintage, Gregor thought, with a curving black mansard roof and elaborate wrought-iron grillwork balconies at all the windows. The glass at the windows, however, was new and thick and expensive looking—E glass, Gregor thought—and the rest of the house was expensive looking, too. Someone had done a first-class renovation here, careful and detailed. The place looked new, without looking newly built, and old, without looking decrepit. The lawn looked clipped and cared for even in the middle of winter.

They were parked well to the back, near the matching detached garage that might once have been a carriage house or could just as easily have been newly built at the time the renovation was done. The yard back here looked wide and blank, and to either side of the back door were thick collections of evergreen bushes, cut into gumdrop shapes. The arrangements looked like they had been copied from a landscaping magazine.

Tony Bandero climbed out of the car and looked around. The yard was deserted. The house looked deserted, too, but Gregor thought it probably wasn't. Tony had said something about a course of exercise workshops due to start inside today. It was only eight fifteen in the morning. Maybe the bouncing and stretching hadn't started yet. Gregor got out of the car himself and walked over to where Tony was standing, facing the back door.

"It was found over there," Tony said, pointing to the clump of evergreens to the left of the door. "Actually, it was seen before it was found. From one of the bedrooms on the third floor. A young woman named Frannie Jay—it was originally something Polish and she changed it—anyway, she looks out her window around midnight and sees what she's sure is a naked leg and foot sticking into the yard, so she goes to investigate."

"And found the body of Tim Bradbury?" Gregor asked.

"That's right. The naked body of Tim Bradbury, I may add, if that wasn't in the report I sent you—"

"It was."

"Anyway, it's lying in there under the bushes, sort of pushed back in there, and I have the word from forensics that it was naked when it was pushed. It wasn't shoved back in there and stripped."

"Why would anybody do that?"

Tony Bandero shrugged. "Why would anybody do anything? He was poisoned, by the way. With arsenic. But not here."

"Did you ever find out where?"

"Nope. No signs of vomiting down here. None in his room. None in any other part of the house. None in the garage."

"Are you sure he did vomit? I know it's usual with arsenic, but usual doesn't mean universal—"

"He vomited," Tony Bandero said. "I got that from forensics, too. Apparently, when you vomit you bring up a lot of acid and it strips the lining of your throat and does things to your tooth enamel. That's why bulimics have such bad teeth."

Gregor walked over to the bushes and poked at them. "The vomit could have been cleaned up," he pointed out. "Did anyone on the investigating team notice a strong smell of disinfectant anywhere in the house, or cleaning fluid, or lime—"

"Why lime?"

"It's a good cover for vomit in terms of the scent. It's a good cover for a lot of things. Lime and water is what people use when they want to get rid of the smell of cats in old houses."

Tony shrugged. "I asked about disinfectants," he said, "and everybody told me they smelled no such thing, but I

don't really know if they would have noticed when they
weren't notified in advance that they were supposed to notice. You can ask them yourself later. I've set up a time for
you to meet the whole team. As for the lime—even I didn't
know about the lime."

Gregor stepped back and looked up at the house. "Which
window did she look down from?"

"That one." Tony pointed to the third to the left from
the line of the back door.

"Why?" Gregor asked.

"She said she heard a noise," Tony told him. "That much
I know is in the report, but the noise was weird. It said *koo
koo* or something like that, like a bird noise, except she said
she could tell it wasn't a bird. So she opened her window
and leaned out to see if she could spot what it was."

Gregor nodded. The windows back here didn't have
wrought-iron grills or little balconies. "This was at midnight?" he asked Tony.

"That's right."

"But Tim Bradbury didn't die at midnight."

"That's right, too. Autopsy says no later than eleven
o'clock. There needed to be at least an hour for the abrading
to take place in the throat to the extent it had. You know
how that is. That's an estimate."

"I know. Bradbury was absolutely dead when she found
him?"

"He was dead by the time the ambulance got here. I
don't think he was twitching or anything by the time she
found him. She would have said."

"Did anybody else see him?"

"Sure." Tony jerked his head toward the house. "Half
the people in there saw him. She screamed."

"Right away?"

"She says."

"And when they came out, they all saw what they
thought was a dead body."

"Actually," Tony said, "you can ask them yourself, too.
I meant it when I said I wanted to bring you into this investigation as close to officially as possible. I've got you clear-
ance to talk to anybody you want. Of course, they don't

have to talk back, unless they work for us. Lawyers are lawyers."

"Right," Gregor said.

And that was true, of course, lawyers were lawyers—but Gregor didn't think they were going to have any trouble with lawyers this early in a case like this. In his experience, the stranger the cases were, the less intelligent the people involved in them were about keeping their mouths shut when they were talking to the police. This case was shaping up to be very strange indeed.

Suddenly, there was a high-pitched pulsing whine in the air. Tony Bandero reached into his inside jacket pocket and came out with a beeper. He shut the sound off and put the beeper back in his pocket.

"Don't you have to call in or something now that you've heard that?" Gregor asked him.

"Nah," Tony Bandero said. "I'll get around to it later."

TWO

— 1 —

Gregor had never been in a health club of any kind—not in a spa or an exercise studio or a hotel weight room. Most of the men he knew didn't exercise. Most of the women he knew didn't bother with health clubs when they did exercise. Donna Moradanyan, his upstairs neighbor back on Cavanaugh Street, had a few tapes she jumped around to from time to time. Gregor thought one of them had been put out by Jane Fonda. He remembered a background that had been made to look like a roof in a not-very-well-off part of a city. Television aerials, low-rising utility chimneys, security netting and arc lights: none of it went with Ms. Fonda herself, who was dressed from neck to ankle in black stretch lace. Some of the high school boys he knew worked out with weights to build themselves up for sports. Gregor didn't know if it did much good. The Armenian-American community hadn't produced a plethora of sports stars, except for Ara Parseghian, who coached instead of doing the grunt work. Coaching seemed to Gregor the best part of any sport. You got to sit down for most of the games, eat what you wanted when you wanted, and be boss of the whole enterprise. Gregor thought being head of the Olympic committee or commissioner of baseball would be even better.

The Fountain of Youth Work-Out didn't look like it would suit Jane Fonda any more than the roof had. Coming around to the front, Gregor saw that the deliberate Victorian reconstruction had been even more carefully executed here. The heavy brass knob and knocker on the front door were either antiques or were custom-made to mimic antiques. The curving trim around the windows had been cut to follow the curving scrollwork of the wrought-iron window guards. The two big concrete planters on either side of the front door had been molded with friezes of fruit around their bases, like the plaster fruit that adorned so many Victorian ceilings. A lot of money had gone into this, or a lot of debt. Did the women who came to Fountain of Youth for diet and exercise advice want to live in a Victorian fantasy? Weren't diet and exercise and the healthy foods movement much more modern than that? Wouldn't it have been a better use of funds to put the money into better equipment or bigger exercise rooms or a new advertising campaign? Of course, it was possible that money was no object. There was that. That would put a different complexion on things entirely.

Tony Bandero had marched up to the front door and rung the bell. "They've got one of those buzzer systems here, the same as everyplace else," he said. "Nobody lets anybody in the front door without seeing who they are first."

The buzzer system was well disguised. Gregor couldn't find the camera, which had to be hidden somewhere over his head. There was a long angry hum and the door popped open with a mechanical clack. Tony pushed it the rest of the way in.

"This is Traci." Tony motioned to the young girl behind the small desk. "Traci Cardinale. She's the receptionist here. This is Gregor Demarkian."

"Oh, yes," Traci Cardinale said. "The detective who was coming about Tim. Isn't it awful about Tim? I was working that night, too, right here until eleven o'clock. But I didn't see anything except the usual." She sounded sad.

"What's the usual?" Gregor asked her.

Traci shrugged. "Members coming in and out. Members losing half their stuff—we put up all these signs about how they ought to be careful and not leave their purses lying around on benches and things, but they do it anyway. I mean, they think that just because this place is expensive, nobody who comes here is going to steal. It's stupid. Oh, yes. The fat lady was here, too."

"The fat lady?" Gregor asked.

Traci Cardinale nodded. "I know I shouldn't call her the fat lady. It would hurt her feelings. But she is a fat lady, you know, really, really fat, not just overweight. Anyway, she came in around nine thirty that night to sign up for the course this week. She's upstairs right now with the beginners' class. She's really a very nice lady."

"She was on her way home from working the second shift at the Braxton Corporation," Tony said. "She lives in Derby with her father. He's got Alzheimer's."

"She really is a very nice lady," Traci said again. "She paid her deposit in cash and then she came in about a week later with the rest of the money in cash, too. I'd almost forgotten about her in all the fuss about Tim, but there she was. I'm glad she came to the course this week. A lot of them just put their money down and then never show up. You'd be amazed. We get five, six thousand dollars like that every time we run a course. People pay for it and then just disappear. They don't even ask for refunds. But Dessa Carter came. She really needs to do something about herself."

There was a long, thin window with frosted stained-glass panels in the wall to Traci Cardinale's right. Gregor went to it and tried to look out. He caught a glimpse of the drive and the wrought-iron fence that separated this property from the one just a little way down the hill. The glimpse wasn't much, and Gregor thought it would have been even less in the dark. Traci Cardinale was staring at him as if she thought he, too, needed to do something about himself. Gregor went back to her desk and tried to pretend she wasn't staring.

"You can't see very much from here," he told her. "You were here all that night?"

"Until eleven o'clock," Traci said. "Only, I was answering both doors."

She gestured toward the stained-glass window. Gregor saw that there was indeed another door back there, smaller and down a couple of steps to the side.

"That's the members' private entrance. People have keys to it. Not everybody, of course. People who sign up for the

Golden Circle memberships. They pay about three times as much as everybody else does and they can come and go as they want, twenty-four hours a day, seven days a week. Not that they do much of it, though. Nobody wants to be driving around in the dark on their own with all these car-jackings going on. Especially not Golden Circle members. They just come in at the regular times like everybody else."

"None of the Golden Circle members came in that night?"

Traci shook her head. "The only person who came to that door was Dessa Carter. I think she got confused about where she was supposed to go. We had advertisements on the radio and directions in these brochures we were giving out, but I don't think the directions were too clear. Dessa wasn't the only one who came to the wrong door or called the wrong phone number or got the dates mixed up."

"But she was the only one who came that night," Gregor said.

"The only one," Traci agreed.

"And you didn't see anything? Or hear anything? You didn't hear the strange sounds the other young woman reported?"

"Not a thing." Traci Cardinale sighed. "We all thought it was a mugging, you know, after it happened. With him lying out there in the bushes and all. And then there was all that stuff about him being naked and poisoned and all that, and we didn't know what was going on. We were all very upset—the staff here, I mean, all of us. And Tim was from around here, too, and that made it worse."

"Bramford," Tony Bandero said helpfully. "About twenty minutes away."

"We didn't any of us know him before he started working here," Traci said, "but I don't see that that should matter much. It wasn't like he was some stranger from Vermont. And nobody knows why it happened even now, so we're all walking around thinking it could have been anybody, it could have been *us*. If you see what I mean."

"Yes," Gregor said, because he did see what she meant. It was the most common reaction people had when they found out that someone they knew had been killed. What he didn't see was what good wandering around this foyer was going to do him. There were two tall, thin windows with plain glass in them on either side of the front door, but they looked out only on the front walk and on Prospect Street. There was that stained-glass window to Traci's right, but the limitations to looking through that had already been determined. Traci Cardinale could not have seen the Royal Welsh Fusiliers doing marching practice on the back lawn—and she might not have been able to hear them, either.

Gregor went back to Traci's desk. He seemed to be walking in circles. To Traci Cardinale's left, a curving staircase with a fluted rail swept to the balcony on the second floor. Three stories above his head, the stairwell ceiling was covered with those plaster fruits.

"What do we do next?" he asked Tony Bandero.

It was Traci Cardinale who answered. "You have an appointment with Simon Roveter," she said, picking up the receiver on her house phone and beginning to punch buttons. "Simon's the head of everything here. Magda's husband. You're supposed to see Magda one of these days, too, but not now because she's leading aerobic dance. Just a minute."

— 2 —

Gregor hadn't given much thought to what someone who did what Simon Roveter did would look like. He knew what Magda Hale looked like, because along with the cursory police report Tony Bandero had sent him after Gregor agreed to at least consider the possibility of looking into the death of Tim Bradbury, Tony had sent some Fountain of Youth brochures. Gregor remembered these now as Traci Cardinale led both him and Tony up the curving staircase to the second floor. On the balcony there, placed just far enough back so that it couldn't be seen from the foyer, was a life-size stand-up cardboard poster of Magda Hale holding a sign that said, "COME TO THE FOUNTAIN OF YOUTH. BE A NEW YOU FOR THE NEW YEAR." This was the same picture that appeared on one of the brochures. Magda Hale looked twenty-six and full of infinite energy. Traci Cardinale went past the stand-up poster and opened a set of double doors. The balcony was suddenly full of noise. There was fast, driving music with a heavy bass backbeat. There was the sound of something heavy being smashed against wood. Gregor was now sure that Traci Cardinale could not have heard anything that might have been going on in the backyard on the night Tim Bradbury died. Either the foyer was soundproof, or it was terminally well built.

"That's the beginner's class," Traci said, moving them along a hall carpeted in pearl gray pile. She stopped at the first door on the left and opened it up. The noise got louder. Added to the sounds Gregor had heard from the balcony was a woman's high, insistant voice commanding: "Leg up leg up leg up. Switch right."

"Come look," Traci Cardinale said.

Gregor expected to walk through the door and find himself in the middle of a lot of jumping women. Instead, he found himself in a little viewing area, installed several feet above the floor of the work-out studio itself, outfitted with half a dozen fixed plush chairs like a very tiny movie theater. In the studio, a dozen women stood in rows and moved in unison, following the lead of a woman standing alone at the front. The woman had her back to the class and was facing a long wall of mirrors. Gregor thought he had seen walls of mirrors like that in pictures of ballet practice studios. But there was nothing ballet-like about what these women were doing. They jumped. They turned. They marched. They loped from side to side. Most of them were heavyset and most of them were not graceful.

"That's Dessa Carter." Traci Cardinale pointed to a very fat woman in the last row of dancers.

Traci had not been exaggerating. Dessa Carter was enormous. She was not, however, silly. She was wearing a plain black leotard and plain black tights and black running shoes that looked less expensive than the ones worn by the women around her. Her body hung in folds and globes and shivered violently in the air every time she moved. She still had a great deal of plain old-fashioned human dignity. There were more normal-size women around her who did not hold up to scrutiny so well. Dessa Carter, Gregor thought, looked like a woman he might like to know.

"This is an aerobic dance class," Traci explained. "Most

of our members spend most of their time on aerobic dance, but we offer other things. Weight training and weight machines. Step aerobics. Yoga and stretch. Interval work."

Machines screeched. Music blared. Feet crashed into hardwood.

"Is it all this loud?" Gregor asked.

"Yoga is pretty quiet." Traci motioned them to follow her back into the hall. When they were all outside, she closed the doors to the studio viewing area again. In terms of noise, it didn't help much.

"We have everything we can soundproofed and protected," she said, "but it seems like there's no way to soundproof a door without spending the kind of money the Pentagon does, so the only soundproof doors we've got are the ones on the film room upstairs and the ones on the studio where we make the videotapes. Those have to be soundproof. You get used to the noise after a while, though. You'll see."

Gregor didn't think he would. Now that they were farther down the hall, he could hear other pounding and other music. He wondered how many studios Fountain of Youth ran. It was a big house, but there were more than studios in it. How many classes could Fountain of Youth fill at any one time? How many women were there in New Haven who were willing to put themselves through that kind of physical trauma at—Gregor checked his watch—twenty-five minutes to nine on a Monday morning?

Traci reached the door at the end of the hall and knocked. When nobody answered, she knocked again.

"Sometimes Simon puts his earphones on so he can't hear any of it," she explained. She turned the knob on the door and opened up. She stuck her head in and looked around. "He's not here," she said, in some confusion. "He's supposed to be here. He knew you were coming."

"Maybe we should go back downstairs and wait," Gregor suggested.

Traci shook her head and pushed the door open wider. "There's no need for you to do that. There are chairs for visitors to sit in. You should go in and take a seat and give me a minute while I go look for him. He's probably just gone down the hall to the bathroom."

Gregor looked over at Tony Bandero, to see if this setup was making him uncomfortable, too. Toward the end of Gregor's time with the Bureau, there had been new procedural guidelines issued for dealing with suspects and property belonging to suspects. One of those guidelines had stressed the necessity for any agent or group of agents entering a suspect's room or place of work or residence to have an invitation, a warrant, or a witness. It was too easy for defendants to claim illegal search in other circumstances. Surely, Gregor thought, Simon Roveter must be a suspect in this case. The dead man had worked for him. The dead man's body had been found on his own back lawn. Tony Bandero didn't seem to care. He had gone into Simon Roveter's office and begun to walk slowly around it, looking at the framed hunting prints that hung in clusters on the paneled walls. It was, Gregor had to admit, quite an office. Tall arched windows, set in the wall opposite the door overlooked a scene of bare tree branches and cloud-occluded sky. A desk with its back to this wall was six feet long and made of deeply polished oak. That, Gregor was convinced, was a replica. The desk had pigeon holes and odd-shaped little specialty drawers rising from the front of it. It had lots and lots of embossed fluted ornamentation. Like everything else self-consciously Victorian about this house, it must have cost a mint and a half and then some.

"Good," Traci Cardinale said when she saw that Tony Bandero was satisfied. "I'll be right back. Don't worry about a thing."

She went trotting off back down the hall, the thin heels of her high-heeled pumps catching in the carpet pile. Gregor turned his attention back to Tony Bandero.

"Well," he said. "This is an interesting place. Have you been in here before?"

"Yep," Tony Bandero said.

"And?" Gregor prodded.

Tony shrugged. "And I think these people throw around a lot of money," he said, "which is what you think, too. I also wonder where it all comes from, which you wonder, too. I also want to know if this business is really doing this well and if these people are in a lot of debt and if the late Tim Bradbury had anything to do with it. The questions are obvious. I've asked all the questions. It's the answers I don't have."

"You haven't been able to get hold of the financial records?"

Tony made a face. "This isn't the FBI. We can't just call up the IRS and demand to see a lot of tax returns. We have to have a whole lot of probable cause."

"You'd have to have a whole lot of probable cause even if you were the FBI. You've got a dead body."

"I've got a dead body, the one thing we know for sure about it was that it wasn't murdered on the premises. This is not the kind of thing that looks good when you ask the judge for access to private files."

"True," Gregor said, "but you could milk the rumors. You could talk to the people who do business with them. Suppliers, those kinds of people. Isn't there a local newspaper? *The New Haven Register?* You could talk to the financial reporter there."

"We tried. Maybe you could talk to her. Maybe she'd be more comfortable with a man in a suit than she was with a cop."

Gregor went over to look at one of the clusters of hunting prints. They were pen-and-ink reproductions, not originals. This Simon Roveter, whoever he is, hadn't let himself go that far. Still. These reproductions were good reproductions. They hadn't come cheap.

"I think one of the things we're going to have to do pretty soon," Gregor said, "before I start going off half-cocked myself and speculating about things I can't begin to understand, is to—what's that?"

That was the sound of something creaking, creaking and creaking, like a rusty hinge being pulled violently back and forth. Tony Bandero had heard it at the same time Gregor did. He had turned away from the scrollwork he had been examining at the front of the desk. He was frozen in the middle of Simon Roveter's office, his head up, listening.

"What the hell—" Tony began.

The creaking changed to a sound more like wood splintering. Then there was an enormous creak, the creak to end all creaks, a screaming whine like a vampire whose heart had just been staked. Then there was a crash, and a woman started screaming.

"Traci Cardinale," Tony said, just before he started moving.

Gregor started moving, too. He went out the door of Simon Roveter's office and into the hall. He went down the hall to the doors that led to the balcony. The doors were standing open. So were the doors that led to the viewing section of the exercise studio where Traci had shown them the beginners' class. Women were spilling out of that door and milling around in confusion.

"Somebody's screaming," one of the women kept saying—not Dessa Carter or the woman who had been leading the class. "Somebody's screaming. Why should somebody be screaming?"

Gregor pushed past her and then past Dessa Carter. He went through the doors to the balcony without looking where he was going. He nearly plowed into Tony Bandero's back. Tony was standing stock-still in the very middle of the balcony, his hands on his hips and his head thrown back.

"What the hell is going on around here?" he was demanding.

Gregor got around the side of him and saw what it was that was happening, as far as it was possible to see. A long low stretch of balcony railing was missing, gone from the center of the curved stretch that overlooked the foyer. When Gregor went forward a few steps, he could see what was left of it lying on the foyer floor below. A lot of the wood seemed to have been reduced to shards and splinters. There were raw nails sticking up out of the debris. Traci Cardinale stood with her back to the balcony wall. Her face was leached of color and the knuckles on both her hands were white. If she had been standing next to that balcony rail when it collapsed, Gregor thought, she would have been dead. At the very least, she would have been seriously hurt.

Traci Cardinale's skirt was torn. She was screaming.

"I'm going to call into the office and get a car out here," Tony Bandero announced to the assembled company.

Gregor thought that was a very good idea, although maybe not for the reasons Tony Bandero thought it was. Gregor walked to the raw open edge of the balcony rail and

back to the doors that led into the second floor and back to
the balcony rail again. It was a mess down there in the foyer.
There were pieces of wood scattered across Traci Cardinale's
receptionist's desk. There were more nails than Gregor had
realized would be necessary for a balcony of this kind.

In the background, Traci Cardinale was still screaming.
Tony had ceased hearing her because he was busy. Gregor
had ceased hearing her because he was thinking. She was going on and on and on, letting out a thin high wail that was
as even and unsubstantial as water from a lawn sprinkler.

Gregor went back to the gap on the balcony and looked
down. No one was hurt. No one was killed. No one was
even messed up, as far as Gregor could see.

It just didn't make any sense.

— 3 —

Gregor was still standing at the open place in the balcony
rail, thinking that nothing at all was making sense, when the
police finally showed up—but by that time Gregor wasn't
alone, and Tony Bandero had lost the fight to keep order in
the foyer. The police arrived with sirens wailing, as if there
were an armed robbery in progress. Their noise mingled with
all the other noise and became unintelligible.

"Get away from the wood," Tony Bandero was bellowing. "Get away from the wood."

There were now dozens of women in leotards in the foyer
and on the balcony. They had come streaming out of doors
and stairways all over the house, curious and tense, still
worked up from whatever exercise they had been doing
when the fuss started. The women who had come from the
third and fourth floors had their hair plastered to their heads
with sweat. Some of them were wearing clothing with Fountain of Youth advertising on it. Gregor saw one woman in a
pale green leotard with the words "A NEW YOU FOR THE NEW
YEAR" plastered across her chest in black. The letters made it
impossible to tell with any accuracy whether she was thick
or thin, in good shape or bad.

"Traci nearly got killed," women kept saying.

Traci was standing where she had been standing all along, with her back to the wall. She wasn't screaming anymore.

"Get away from the wood," Tony Bandero kept saying. "Get away from the wood and stay away from it."

Down in the foyer, the front door opened and two uniformed policemen stepped in. They were both young and jumpy. When they saw the crowds of women who awaited them, they both blanched. Gregor shook his head in exasperation and started down the stairs. That was all they were going to need now, two rookies put out of commission by sexual confusion. There were too many people around here who had been put out of commission by other kinds of confusion already.

Gregor gave Traci Cardinale one last look—she seemed on the verge of tears, but she wasn't crying—and then went all the way down into the foyer. He pushed his way through a crowd of older women in dark tights and brightly colored headbands and went up to Tony Bandero.

"Is everybody here you expect to be here? Simon Roveter? Magda Hale?"

"I don't know," Tony told Gregor. Beginning to redden, "I haven't had a chance to look. This is nuts."

"We need you ladies to step away from the wood," one of the young uniformed patrolmen was saying to five very young women in stretch bicycle shorts. "We need you to keep away from the wood." The women weren't listening to the patrolman any more than they had been listening to Tony Bandero.

Gregor stepped up to the wood himself and looked it over. There wasn't much more of to see close up than there had been from the balcony. The nails looked longer and newer. The splinters of wood looked bigger and more treacherous. Gregor rubbed his face.

"The important thing here," Tony Bandero said, coming up behind him, "is to find out whether this was deliberate or an accident."

"No," Gregor told him, still rubbing his face.

"No?"

"Well," Gregor said, "it couldn't have been an accident.

That's obvious. So the real question is not whether this was deliberate, but what kind of deliberate it was."

"I don't think I get your point here," Tony Bandero said.

Gregor walked away from Tony. There was wood everywhere in the foyer, so he couldn't walk all the way around it all. The nails gleamed. The shards flashed wickedly sharp points. The splinters looked like loose needles ready to prick and stab. Gregor wanted to kick something. It didn't make any sense.

"The important thing here," Gregor told Tony Bandero with an edge of anger in his voice, "is that nobody got killed, nobody got hurt, nobody got even scratched. And it just doesn't begin to add up."

THREE

— 1 —

When Greta Bellamy first heard that Gregor Demarkian was in the building, she was standing on the second-floor balcony just a few steps from the doors to the second floor proper in a cluster of other women, wondering what was going on. Ten minutes later, she was still wondering what was going on, but she had seen Gregor Demarkian in the flesh. He was less impressive than he had been in *People* magazine. That might have been because he was looking confused instead of wise. In *People*, he always looked a little like one of those ancient seers, a man with all the answers. It might also have been because he didn't have Bennis Hannaford with him, or didn't seem to. Greta was confused. She had thought, from what she had read, that Gregor Demarkian and Bennis Hannaford were always together, like Siamese twins. She looked around and around the foyer and through all the clusters of strange women that littered the stairway and the halls, but she didn't see anyone who looked like the dark-haired woman in *People* magazine. It made Greta feel a little let down. She had been tense and miserable all day, thinking about Chick and Marsha in Atlantic City, thinking about how ugly she must look in her leotard and how stupid she must seem trying to do aerobic dance steps when she had no sense of rhythm. She felt thick and awkward, the way she had when she first started going out with Chick. When Chick had asked her out for the first time, it had felt like a miracle.

Gregor Demarkian was a tall, broad shaggy man in an expensive winter coat. He had an air of authority, but he was much too old—much older than Greta had imagined a woman like Bennis Hannaford would be willing to put up with. Maybe they weren't lovers after all. Maybe they were just friends, and Bennis Hannaford had other lovers who weren't famous or didn't like publicity. Whatever was going on, she didn't seem to be with him, and Greta wasn't interested enough in Gregor Demarkian on his own to go on standing in a drafty hallway in a leotard and tights. There wasn't as much going on as there had seemed to be at first anyway. There had been some kind of accident, and part of the balcony railing had fallen over. The police had been called in, but no one was being arrested. The real reason the police were there had to do with a mugging that had taken place in the backyard almost a month ago. Greta found it very hard to straighten out.

The part of the railing that had fallen was a mass of splinters and nails. A tall black man with a dancer's way of moving came out onto the balcony and called for all the beginners' smorgasbord group to get back to their classroom. If he had come out ten minutes earlier, nobody would have listened to him, but by then everybody was bored. The women from the experts' class had already disappeared in the direction of their studio. Greta allowed herself to be herded back to work in the company of the very fat woman who stood next to her in the dance line and a smaller, older woman who was so well dressed and fierce she made Greta nervous. A lot of the women in the class made Greta nervous. Most of them looked like they had more money than she did. All of them looked like they'd had better educations.

Back in the studio, the pace suddenly seemed to be much faster and more demanding than it had been before. The black man introduced himself as Nick Bannerman, but unlike the woman who had run the first three dances the group had done, Nick Bannerman didn't talk on about his life and his feelings. He just got to work, and they got to work with him. Greta didn't think she had ever moved so much in her life, or come down so hard on her knees and ankles. By the end of the first dance Nick Bannerman led, her feet ached. By the end of the second one, her legs and hips felt stiff and frozen. By the end of the third, Greta wanted only to stop— and was surprised, when she looked up at the clock, to see that it was quarter to twelve. It didn't *feel* like quarter to twelve. There were windows at the back of the studio, over- looking the downward sweep of Prospect Street, showing hedges and houses and cars and spires. The sky was gray and thick with clouds. It looked darker now than it had when Greta had gotten up in the morning.

"We must have spent more time looking at the accident than I thought we did," Greta said to the very fat woman when Nick Bannerman had finished the third dance and gone off to drink some water from his plastic tube bottle.

The fat woman was panting and shaky. She had sweat so much, the top half of her leotard was soaked through. "Two and a half hours," she said, when she was finally able to catch her breath. "I kept checking the time."

Greta shook her head. "And we didn't even do anything. I mean we didn't accomplish anything. We just wandered around."

"I don't see that there was anything else we could do," the fat woman said.

The older, thinner woman turned around now and gave Greta and the fat woman a tight little smile.

"I'm Virginia Hanley," she said, in a mock-formal voice, like someone interviewing for a job she didn't really want. "You two are—?"

"Greta Bellamy," Greta said.

"Dessa Carter."

Virginia Hanley fussed with the top of her bright red Danskin leotard and the rhinestone stretch belt she was wearing at her waist. "That receptionist was a total little fool," she said, "screaming and screaming like that when nothing had even happened. If she'd kept her head, we wouldn't have lost any classroom time at all."

"I don't think we lost any dances," Dessa Carter said

drily. Sweat was making rivers down the sides of her face. "I think we just got them crammed into a very small space."

Virginia Hanley sniffed. "I couldn't believe the production they were making about it down there. I mean, for God's sake. Things like that happen in old houses like this all the time. Things get worn out."

"It didn't look like those nails were worn out," Dessa Carter said impassively. "It looked like they were brand new."

"They did look brand new, didn't they?" Greta said, startled. "You know, all the time I was looking at them, I kept feeling that something was wrong, and I couldn't put my finger on it."

"Oh, for God's sake," Virginia Hanley said.

The young girl standing next to Virginia Hanley turned around. "Excuse me. It's because of the murder. The fuss they made, I mean. I think they were worried that it might not be an accident, because somebody had already been murdered."

"He wasn't murdered," Virginia Hanley said. "He was mugged."

Dessa Carter was looking drier and more amused by the minute. "He died," she pointed out. "Someone killed him. That usually adds up to murder."

"It adds up to murder legally," Virginia Hanley said. "This girl was making it sound like Perry Mason or something."

"This girl" was very thin, thinner than Greta had ever seen anybody except in television documentaries about AIDS, and she looked extremely tired. There were dark circles under her eyes and deep hollows under her cheekbones. Her skin was far too white. Impulsively, Greta stuck out her hand again and said,

"Greta Bellamy."

"Christie Mulligan," the thin girl said. She pulled on the arm of the plump girl next to her and went on, "This is my friend, Michelle Dean. We came together."

"We came as a trio," Michelle said pleasantly. "The third one is Tara Corcoran. She went to the bathroom."

"Right before the last dance," Christie said. "I think she was fed up."

"I'm fed up," Michelle said. "I just don't have the guts to play hooky."

Christie Mulligan rubbed the top of her left breast reflexively. "It was because of the murder," she said. "It had to have been. I mean, we live not very far from here——"

"At Jonathan Edwards College. At Yale," Michelle put in.

"—and the story's been all over the place for weeks. I don't think the police are treating it like a normal mugging. For one thing, there are all these rumors. About how he died, I mean. What we heard was that he wasn't shot or strangled or anything, he was poisoned."

"That's why there was never anything about cause of death in the papers," Michelle said.

"And muggers don't poison people," Christie said. "But the other thing is, they're really going back and checking up on him, on the guy who died, I mean. He worked at Yale one summer at one of the cafeterias and they had police over there asking questions about him. He worked during one of the school years at one of the parking lots and they had police over there, too. I don't think they'd go back that far if they thought his death was nothing but your usual thing. I don't think they'd expend the energy."

"I'd heard they were checking up on him, too," Dessa said. "One of the women I work with has a brother who's a cop. She said he said they were really covering this guy's life, going back over everything he did and everybody who ever knew him."

"It will turn out to be about drugs, then," Virginia Hanley said dismissively. "It won't have anything to do with people like us."

Greta bent her knees a little, straightened up again, bent again. Her knees were stiff.

"I wish I knew what was going on," she said. "We're just standing around again. I wish I knew what was supposed to come next."

"We're supposed to go to lunch," Dessa Carter said. "At twelve-oh-five."

"Can you just imagine what lunch is going to be like in a place like this?" Michelle said. "Carrot sticks. Bean sprouts. Tofu. Gruesome."

Up at the front of the room, Nick Bannerman reappeared and surveyed the class.

"We're going downstairs to the first floor to the dining room now," he announced in a very loud voice, a kindergarten teacher roping in a class of tantrum-prone toddlers. "After we have lunch, you will all be given a free half hour to shower if you want to or just to rest. On your way downstairs, please be careful on the balcony. We've installed some safety board in the place where the railing collapsed, but I wouldn't want to count on it to keep me from falling. All right. Let's go."

"If I were Magda Hale," Virginia Hanley said, "I'd install a guard out there. I wouldn't put it past somebody to fall deliberately just to be able to file a lawsuit."

Virginia Hanley was walking out ahead, toward the door Nick Bannerman had already gone out of. Christie Mulligan caught Greta Bellamy's eye and winked elaborately. Greta bit her lip, hard, to keep herself from giggling.

"Oh, dear," she said, as Christie and Michelle came up beside her.

"Just wait till Tara gets a look at that one," Christie said, almost in a whisper. "Tara Corcoran is not the sort of person who sits still for phonies."

"Is that what she is?" Greta asked. "I thought she was just a bitch. You know. With money."

"Rhymes with rich," Michelle said, laughing out loud.

They were all walking toward the door together now, at the very back of the crowd.

"No matter what that silly old woman thinks," Christie Mulligan said, "I'm sure this murder isn't your ordinary kind of thing. I mean, your ordinary drug pusher doesn't kill his enemies with cyanide or whatever it was."

"Arsenic is what I heard," Michelle said.

"It doesn't matter. Have you seen the papers?" Christie turned to Greta. "They had pictures of him just after it happened, and there's going to be a story in *Connecticut* magazine. Tim Bradbury."

Greta Bellamy started. "Tim Bradbury?" she repeated. "Are you sure that was the name?"

"What's the matter?" Michelle asked eagerly. "Did you know him?"

Greta was at a loss. "I didn't exactly know him," she said, feeling unbelievably stupid, "and I'm sure it's not the same person anyway, I mean, it's not exactly an uncommon name—"

"It's not exactly a common one, either," Christie pointed out. "The only other Bradbury I know of is the science fiction writer."

Greta had never heard of a science fiction writer named Bradbury. They were on their way out the door into the hall again. The hall was darker than the studio had been. Greta ran a hand through her hair in exasperation.

"I'm sure it couldn't have been the same person," she murmured.

Christie Mulligan shook her head emphatically. "I don't think you ought to trust yourself about that. Not if you knew somebody named Tim Bradbury. I think you ought to find out the name of that police detective who was here and go tell him all about it."

"You know what happens in books when people keep information like that to themselves," Michelle said. "They get murdered, too."

Greta ran a hand through her hair again. A couple of college girls from Yale, she thought. What could they possibly know? They were so damned young. People in real life didn't get murdered for "knowing too much." They especially didn't get murdered for not knowing if they knew. Greta didn't even watch cop shows and murder mysteries on television, because she found them so unreal.

"I'm sure it couldn't have been the same person," Greta said for the third time—but she said it to herself.

Christie and Michelle had found their friend Tara, and gone off to collect her.

— 2 —

The first time Magda Hale had felt the pain in her hip, it was only halfway through the first dance of the morning. It was an awful pain, too—stabbing, sharp and undeniable.

Magda had been well into a high kick when it hit, and she had almost fallen over. High kicks were Magda's specialty. She had performed them on all three of the exercise videos she had made, and on local cable television, and at mall demonstrations from Connecticut to New Hampshire and out in California. She was scheduled to do a demonstration routine, with high kick intact, on Oprah Winfrey's show at the end of March. When the pain hit, the air in front of her changed colors. Her whole leg felt as if someone had doused it with gasoline and set it on fire. Her breath stopped and her heart seemed to stop with it. It took the most massive effort of will she had ever made in her life to get going again.

The second time Magda Hale felt the pain in her hip, it was right before lunch, after all that uproar with the broken railing on the balcony, and she was trying to get her advanced class through their last routine in time to pack them all off to the dining room. This time, the pain was not only sharp and stabbing it had staying power. It hit hard and spread quickly down her leg—but then it stayed, and stayed and stayed, no matter how she moved or what she put her weight on. There was one last cycle left in this routine: step, kick, step, kick, bend, turn, jump, repeat. After that, there was only the cooldown, which consisted of two and a half minutes of the kind of flowing waterbaby motions five-year-olds did in their first ballet recitals. Magda fully expected the pain to cease when she got to that part. There was nothing high impact about waterbaby motions. This time, though, they didn't help. Magda was sure she was imagining it, but sweeping hand movements and slow head rolls actually seemed to make the pain worse. By the time she got through the go-limp-and-relax phase, she was very close to throwing up. If she had had anything in her stomach, she would have thrown up. Her stomach was a rolling mass of cramps.

When the dance was over, Magda gave her usual speech about how wonderfully they had all done—a little breathlessly, but without abridgement—then told them they could go downstairs to eat. Usually, during promotional courses like this one, Magda made a point of eating lunch with each of the classes in turn, just as she made a point of teaching each of them in turn. Today, she couldn't have managed it.

She got herself out into the hall without trouble. After that, she couldn't keep herself from limping. She had let the class go on ahead of her. None of them saw how badly she was hurt, or how slowly she was moving. Magda went down to the opposite end of the hall from where the class was going and let herself into the service stairwell. She had to hold onto the railing with both hands to get down the stairs. The pain was getting worse. It had spread to both hips and both legs. It had begun to climb up her spine.

Magda's bedroom was on the third floor, at the back, near the service stairwell. Some things, at least, were working in her favor. When she got to the third-floor landing, she opened the door and looked into the hall. It was empty and quiet. The intermediate class must have already gone to lunch. Magda limped out into the hall, propping herself up against the wall with one hand. Now the pain was beginning to spread into her arms. Magda thought that if it went on like this much longer, she was going to pass out.

The bedroom was five baby steps from the stairwell door. Magda counted them as she took them. Then she braced herself on the door and contorted herself sideways and backward until she could reach the spare key she left on the top of the door frame. The movement made her heave again. She got the door open and stumbled inside queasily, sucking in great gulps of air.

The air didn't have enough oxygen in it. Magda was sure her lungs were collapsing. She got the bathroom door shut by kicking it shut. It should have hurt, but her legs had gone numb. Either that, or she was feeling as much pain as she was able to. Nothing she did could make her feel any more. She pressed her face down into the carpet and closed her eyes. *Count to ten*, she told herself. *Count to nine. Count to eight. Count to seven.* As an interior monologue, it didn't make much sense, but it didn't have to make much sense. It only had to work. That was what mantras were for.

Magda didn't know how long she spent lying on the floor. It felt like forever, but it could probably have been measured in seconds. Then the pain began to drain out of her, like water going down the pipes of a sink. The sharp stabbing changed to a dull ache. Give it a minute more, she told herself. Then make yourself stand up.

Carefully, Magda rolled over on her back. She counted from ten again. She made herself breathe. Then she got herself onto her side and made herself curl into a ball. That was the way she had been taught that injured people were supposed to get themselves up.

She got herself up. She had to hold onto the side of a chair to do it, but she ended up on her feet. The ache was really terrible. It made her dizzy. She was going to have to go on holding onto furniture just to get herself across the room to the master bath.

"Magda?" someone called from the other side of the door.

Magda stiffened. It was a mistake. The pain came back again for one horrible, stabbing second. Then the stabbing evaporated, she caught her breath.

"Who is it?" she called out. Evenly, with no sign of wrongness in her voice.

"It's Stella Mortimer. Can I come in?"

It was a million miles to the door of the master bath. Magda pushed herself in the direction of her bureau, gripped the edge of it, and let herself fall slightly. She caught herself at the last minute and made herself stand up again.

"Just a minute" she said.

The trick was to get into the bathroom quickly. The only way to do it was to go on her own two feet, and pretend that she didn't hurt. Magda pushed herself from the bureau to the bed, wincing. Then she took a deep breath and launched herself into the middle of the carpet.

"Magda?"

Magda made it into the bathroom and got the door closed halfway. She sat down at the vanity table and put her forehead on the cool glass top.

"All right," she said. "Stella? Come on in. I'm in the bathroom. I'll be out in a minute."

The master bedroom door opened and closed. Stella walked heavily across the carpet, moving without grace. Magda heard the bedsprings and knew that Stella had sat down on the side of the bed.

"Were you taking a shower?" Stella asked. "I forgot that you'd probably want to do that after a morning with the advanced class."

"I haven't actually gotten into the shower yet," Magda replied. "We ran a little late. Because of all the time we lost."

"God, yes," Stella said. "I've never been more tense in my life. I wasn't this tense when Tim died. What did you think of that man?"

"What man?"

"Gregor Demarkian. The detective. The *consultant*."

The vanity table was built into the wall, with a mirror above it. Just to the right of mirror was the medicine cabinet. Magda opened this up and looked inside. Asprin. Tylenol. Advil. Contac. She pushed all these aside and took down a little handful of prescription bottles.

"I don't think I like his attitude," Stella was saying. "And I looked him up at the library, you know, after we heard that Tony Bandero was going to call him in. I don't think he's the—right person for this kind of thing."

Penicillin. Erythromycin. Amoxidyl. Magda put the bottles down and reached for another handful. "Why is that?" she asked evenly.

Stella was swinging her legs on the carpet. The movement made little swooshing sounds.

"He does—complicated murders," Stella said. "Cases where there are all kinds of ramifications and mysteries. And I don't care what Tony Bandero thinks. I don't believe Tim was involved in some—plot."

Motrin. Vitamin D. Iron supplements. Magda reached for a third handful.

"It's hard to imagine Tim involved in a plot," she agreed.

Stella blew a raspberry. "It's *impossible* to imagine Tim involved in a plot. He wasn't that kind of person. And he was only, what, twenty-two? You know as well as I do that he couldn't have been taking serious drugs on a regular basis. He wouldn't have been able to do his work here if he had been."

"I think the implication was that he might have been selling drugs. People who sell drugs don't necessarily take them, do they?"

"Tim couldn't have been selling drugs. He didn't know enough arithmetic."

"Well, there has to be some reason he ended up full of arsenic and stark naked on our lawn. I can't see it as a likely suicide."

"Tim wouldn't have committed suicide, either," Stella said. "That's as silly as thinking of him as part of a plot. All he wanted out of life was a transfer to one of our places in California. I keep feeling terribly guilty that we never gave it to him."

"Don't."

"Maybe I'd feel better if we'd known more about him," Stella said. "I've been thinking about it for weeks now. Do you realize how odd it is, how little we all know about each other? I don't mean you and me. I mean most of us. I work with Faith every day. I don't even know if she lives in an apartment or a house."

"So ask."

"I don't ask, that's the point. None of us asks. Now Tim is dead and we don't know anything about him, and we aren't going to find out soon because nobody is going to tell us anything. Sometimes I wish this had made a bigger splash in the newspapers. Maybe some reporter somewhere would have found something out."

"This has been a big case," Magda said. "It has made a splash in the newspapers. They've had Tim's picture all over everything. What more do you want?"

"I don't know," Stella said. "Real information, maybe. Not just, well he went to high school here and his parents have left the area and he used to work as a parking lot attendant. Real information. Magda? About that thing with the railing this morning. Do you think it was an accident?"

This handful of prescription bottles was much more interesting than the previous ones. Valium. Lithium. Prozac. Percodan. Magda put these down on the glass top of the vanity and turned the last bottle over in her hands. Demerol. She remembered Demerol. Simon had been given it after his gallbladder operation last summer. It had knocked him right out.

"Magda?" Stella said one more time.

Magda shook a couple of white pills into her hands. "75 milligrams each. Take no more than one every six hours."

"I don't see what else it could have been," Magda said. "I can't see Traci pushing the thing over on purpose."

"Maybe she was just in the wrong place at the wrong time. Maybe someone cut the balcony railing apart, very carefully, and just left it there for someone to come along and get hurt by it."

"Why?"

"I don't know why, Magda, but people do that kind of thing. And you know, Magda, I think that Gregor Demarkian person had the same kind of idea. He kept walking around looking at all the junk on the foyer floor and saying it was interesting."

"That could mean anything, saying it was interesting."

"I know." Stella sounded out of patience. "I wish you'd take all this seriously, Magda. You've got a tour coming up. We're expanding. These kinds of things could end up causing us some seriously bad publicity."

What would really cause them some seriously bad publicity, Magda thought, was if she fell over in the middle of a dance routine in a mall in Eluria, Ohio. She looked at the white dosage strip on the bottle again. "75 milligrams each. Take no more than one every six hours." The words *no more than* had been underlined in blue ballpoint pen.

"I think you're making too much out of all this stuff," she said firmly. "Tim's death is tragic, but it has nothing to do with us. And that thing with the balcony rail is dramatic, but it's an accident. Things like this happen in old houses like this all the time."

"That balcony railing wasn't old, Magda. It was put in with the door moldings the year the major renovations were done. That was what—five years ago?"

"Six."

"Whatever. It still wasn't long enough ago to call that wood 'old.'"

Magda took two of the pills out of her palm and put them down on the glass vanity top. She ached. She was sure she would hurt like hell if she stood up. In less than half an hour, she had to go downstairs and lead another aerobic dance, complete with high kicks.

"If I were you, I'd let the police worry about all this," she told Stella decisively.

Then she picked the two pills up off the glass and swallowed them both.

Without water.

FOUR

— 1 —

Gregor Demarkian was not staying in his idea of a New Haven hotel. His idea of a New Haven hotel was the Taft, as it had existed in old movies about Broadway show lives and out-of-town openings. That was what New Haven had been famous for, besides being the home of Yale University, if it had ever been famous for anything. Producers took their new plays there to open them before they braved the critical climate in New York. Bad reviews could sink a play before it ever got to the city. Anne Baxter and George Sanders having it out in *All About Eve*. Judy Garland doubled up and tense before she had to go on with a big production number. Fred Astaire practicing tap routines in the hotel lobby. They didn't make those movies anymore. When Hollywood made movies about Hollywood now, they were all about bad sex and worse drugs and really sinister business deals. Gregor didn't like them. He didn't even like the fact that movies were no longer in black and white. The problem with color was that it made it too easy for directors to use what looked like real blood.

Gregor's New Haven hotel was not the Taft. It wasn't even in New Haven, if by that he meant within the urban landscape. It might have been within the New Haven city limits. Whatever its address, it stood on a large sloping patch of lawn that looked out over similar buildings in similar patches of lawn. From the concrete balcony outside his sliding glass doors, Gregor could see a Ramada Inn, a Holiday Inn, a Howard Johnson hotel, and a Quality Court. He was sure their rooms all had the same twin double beds his had, the same long closets, the same comfortingly antiseptic bathrooms. He had stayed in thousands of motels like this when he had been on kidnap detail in his first years at the Bureau. These days, they had better restaurants and sometimes even room service. The prints on the walls tended toward impressionism rather than Norman Rockwell. The towels came in pastels as well as hospital white. Gregor didn't mind the motel. He minded the location. Stuck out here without a car, with no idea at all of what direction to go in to get back to the action, he felt cut off and out of touch. The feeling was emblematic. Gregor knew what he had thought he'd done by accepting Tony Bandero's invitation to come out here and "look at" this case. Now that he was here, he was no longer sure what Bandero had invited him out here to do. It certainly wasn't to investigate in any way Gregor understood the term. Yesterday had been—

—what?

Gregor was lying on the double bed closest to the sliding glass doors, dressed in his pajamas and bathrobe, staring at the ceiling. It was very early morning, not even eight o'clock. The motel clock on the bedside table was glowing red. Through the double set of curtains, Gregor could see the faint patches of brightness that meant the day was not going to turn out to be completely miserable, at least as far as the weather went. Whether it was going to be completely miserable as far as Tony Bandero went was undetermined. Yesterday had been—

—frustrating, Gregor decided. Infuriating. Ridiculous. Something like that.

Gregor rolled over onto his side and sat up with his legs hanging over the edge of the bed, facing the other bed and the door to the hall. The other bed was covered with paper— computer printouts, typed reports, and lined notebook sheets Gregor had jotted points down on. There were even some books Gregor had brought up from Philadelphia, thinking he might need them, including his best physicians' drug reference and *Poisons and Toxicity*, the world's most authoritative volume on the ways in which people can kill each other with ingestible substances and chemicals of all kinds. *Poisons and Toxicity* was the size of an unabridged dictionary and weighed fifty-two pounds. Gregor sighed heavily in its direction and reached for the phone.

The phone was on a little night table that was bolted to the wall between the two beds. All the furniture in this motel room was bolted to the wall. Gregor wondered who on earth would try to steal a bed. Next to the phone there was a little cardboard notice, tented into an open-sided pyramid, that said:

Party All Night

in enormous red letters. The notice was advertising a sleepover New Year's Eve party being held in the motel. Gregor had read the notice the night before and decided that it sounded like a good idea. People who were staying over at a motel after drinking all night were at least not threatening sober drivers on the road. Gregor had been to only one New Year's Eve party in his life—unless you wanted to count the wine-and-old-movie sessions held every year in old George Tekemanian's apartment, which Gregor didn't—and he'd hated it. New Year's Eve was a nonholiday nonevent. It was a lot of people coming together in a desperate search for an excuse to get drunk, and not finding one.

Gregor's wallet was also on the table next to the phone. Gregor got his AT&T calling card out and began to punch numbers into the pad. He loved this new practice of making touch-pads standard on phones. His fingers had never fit comfortably into the old rotary dials. He got the bonging tone and the strange, lilting robot voice that inevitably startled him. "*Thank* you for calling . . . AT&T." He quashed the urge he always had to tell the robot voice that he was not calling AT&T. He was calling Philadelphia. The phone was ringing on the other end of the line. It was pulsing over and over again, unanswered. Gregor had a sinking feeling that he hadn't called early enough. Tibor was already down at the Ararat restaurant, having breakfast. It would be hours before Gregor would be able to get hold of him.

Out in Philadelphia, the phone was picked up. A low, distracted voice mumbled something Gregor suspected was Armenian, but that was too garbled for Gregor to be sure. With Tibor, it was hard to be sure. Tibor had been born and brought up in Soviet Armenia, so he spoke both Armenian and Russian with fluency. He also spoke Hebrew, French, Spanish, German, Italian, and modern Greek. He read Latin, ancient Greek, old English, Sanskrit, Arabic, and Welsh, too. When Tibor answered the phone still half asleep, he could be saying anything in any language at all.

Gregor turned the notice about the motel's New Year's Eve party to the wall, so that he didn't have to look at it. "Tibor? Did I wake you up?"

There was what sounded like a crashing pile of books on the Philadelphia end of the line—probable, since Tibor's small apartment behind Holy Trinity Armenian Christian Church was decorated almost entirely with enormous piles of books, ranging from Aristotle's *Poetics* (in the original Greek) to Mickey Spillane's *The Body Lovers* (in the most garish of its paperback covers). Gregor heard Tibor mutter under his breath and smiled slightly. It was a point of honor with Tibor that he did not swear, in any language, no matter what happened to him. Gregor always wondered what it was he said instead.

"Krekor," Tibor said finally. "Just a minute, please. The cookbooks."

Cookbooks? What cookbooks? Tibor couldn't cook. Tibor couldn't even make instant coffee.

"Take your time," Gregor told him. "I thought for a moment there that I'd missed you. I thought you'd gone down to the Ararat for breakfast."

"I'm not going to breakfast today, Krekor. I'm blessing a house. In Ardmore. It's Sheila Kashinian's cousin and Sheila asked me to come."

Gregor stretched out on the bed again, trying to prop himself up on a pile of pillows. People did this on television all the time, and looked really comfortable. When Gregor did it in real life, he always slid down to the point where his neck and shoulders started to ache and he had to sit up again. This time, he slid down almost immediately. He curled himself up and got his feet off the side of the bed again.

"I thought I'd call you for some advice," he said. 'I thought I'd find out how things were going back there. I'm in a motel room."

"Do you like it?"

"Yes," Gregor said seriously. "It reminds me of my early days with the Bureau. I didn't like my early days with the Bureau very much. And I don't think this should feel so natural. Being alone, I mean."

"It gets claustrophobic around here," Tibor said. "Everybody means well, but they press too close. It's not a terrible thing to want to get out on your own every once in a while. Even Lida does it."

"Is Lida going to California again?"

"The day after tomorrow. Bennis is going to California just after the New Year. Krekor, you should take a real vacation instead of doing the kind of thing you're doing."

"I don't think I've ever had a real vacation."

"I don't think you have, either. It's not healthy for you, Krekor. Now you're calling me at seven forty-five in the morning from a motel in Connecticut and your voice sounds tense."

"My voice is tense. I'm tense. I had a terrible day yesterday."

"Why?"

"Because," Gregor said, "I don't think Tony Bandero really wants any help with this investigation. I think what he wants is a body he can throw at the press. That's what he did yesterday. Throw me at the press."

Gregor explained the day before: the ride from the station, the conversation about Tim Bradbury, the cursory look around the backyard at Fountain of Youth, the falling balcony rail.

"Every time I tried to make him get really specific about times and dates and places and names and forensics reports, he got distracted," Gregor said. "And the way he handled the balcony rail incident—" Gregor traced gestures of exasperation in the air, that Tibor couldn't see.

"I thought you said he called the uniformed police in after the balcony rail incident," Tibor said. "Isn't that what he should have done?"

"It wasn't a bad idea," Gregor conceded, "but it also wasn't really necessary. And he wouldn't listen to reason. When we talked to WTNH last night, he made it sound like step two in a very sinister underground plot. It was right out of something by Sax Rohmer."

"Sax Rohmer," Tibor said. "I know. Fu Manchu. The Yellow Peril."

"Well, no Yellow Peril this time, Tibor. Just peril in general. The Forces of Evil out there. Generic."

"This was inaccurate, Krekor?"

Gregor shrugged, which Tibor also could not see. "In the long run, it may be accurate. You're the one who's always telling me you believe in the existence of the devil. In the short run, the whole thing is incredibly, almost deliberately, idiotic. The balcony rail incident isn't all that difficult to figure out, at least on a surface level. I knew how and I knew why within ten minutes of examining the debris. All I didn't know was who and the why of why."

"The why of why. That's wonderful, Krekor."

"I think it's the central point," Gregor said. "But the point I kept trying to make to Tony Bandero, and the one he wouldn't listen to, is that nobody got hurt and nobody got killed and *nobody was supposed to*. There might have been a corpse in the backyard at the beginning of December, that might mean that there's a killer in the vicinity who might be willing to kill again, but that business with the rail was definitely not attempted murder."

"Maybe it plays better in the newspapers if people think it was," Tibor said. "Maybe your Tony Bandero is just trying to get a little extra time or money from his superiors. Maybe it has nothing to do with you."

"If it had nothing to do with me, Tibor, either I wouldn't be here or he would be listening to me."

There were more muffled crashes and muttered exclamations on the Philadelphia end of the line. Gregor imagined Tibor in a falling rain of cookbooks, their pages opened to glossy photographs of crown roast of lamb with pearl onions and strawberry mousse surprise.

"Tibor?"

"Do you want to come home, Krekor? Is that what this is about? Do you want to wash your hands of this murder and come back to Philadelphia?"

Gregor leaned over and got his copy of *Poisons and Toxicity* from the other bed. Held in one hand like this, it threatened to break his wrist. He put it down in his lap.

"I think," he said, "that what I want to do for the moment is an end run around Tony Bandero. I want to cut him out of the loop. I want to investigate on my own."

"Is that possible?"

"It might be to an extent. For a while. Eventually, I'd be stopped cold, of course."

"You don't sound like you're in the mood to worry about eventually, Krekor."

"No, Gregor said. "I'm not."

"Then I think you should do it," Tibor told him. "You should make your end run. I know that normally you consider it unethical to work against the will of the local police—"

"Also just plain stupid," Gregor pointed out.

"True," Tibor said, "it's probably also just plain stupid. But in this case it sounds to me that the local police brought you in under false pretenses and are now attempting to prevent you from doing the job you agreed to do. And a boy is dead. Or a young man who was not much more than a boy. It doesn't sound to me as if the police are solving that case."

"The way they're approaching this, they haven't got a hope in hell."

"There then, Krekor. It's settled. This is your priest talking. You should do what you can do for as long as you can do it, and worry about eventually when it gets here."

"Right," Gregor said.

Gregor could have pointed out that for Tibor to consider himself Gregor's priest was worse than disingenuous, since Gregor was the only permanent resident of Cavanaugh Street who did not regularly attend church. He was also the only permanent resident of Cavanaugh who had doubts about the existence of God and was willing to say so. Why quibble, when Tibor was telling him what he wanted to hear?

Poisons and Toxicity was threatening to break his knee-caps. Gregor chucked it off to his side.

"Listen," he told Tibor, "I've got to make a couple of phone calls. I'll talk to you later."

"Not until tonight, Krekor. Because of going to Ardmore."

"Not until tonight, then. Maybe not until very late tonight. I have a lot of running around to do, and I'm going to have to do it all in cabs."

"Good luck," Tibor said.

Gregor hung up. He put the phone back on the side table. He stood and went over to the other bed. The forensics report was a clipped-together mass of photocopied forms that looked like it had been scribbled over by a gang of angry children. Gregor leafed through it until he found a page with the departmental letterhead showing through reasonably clearly. Then he checked the time again. It was exactly eight o'clock. If he'd been dealing with a doctor in private practice, he wouldn't have had a chance. Doctors employed by states and cities, though, worked on state and city schedules. He could only hope.

He punched in the number for the New Haven medical examiner's office. He got a phone that rang six times before it was picked up. He had expected to reach a receptionist or a switchboard operator. He got a man with a deep voice and a hacking cough.

"Medical examiner's office," the man said.

Gregor thought he might as well give it a try. "My name is Gregor Demarkian. I don't know if that will be familiar to anyone in the ME's office or not. I'm looking for Dr. Philip Brye."

The hacking cough went on and on. Either this man needed to stop smoking cigarettes, or he had the kind of cold that should have kept him home from work.

"Mr. Demarkian?" the man said. "This is Brye. Tony Bandero told me you might call."

"I didn't know if you'd be in this early in the morning," Gregor said.

Philip Brye chuckled. "I'm always in. Ask Tony. I'm here day and night. Since my divorce, I don't seem to have any place else to go. My wife said I wouldn't go any place else even when we were married. You have something you want to know?"

"I'd like to come in and talk to you in person, if you wouldn't mind," Gregor said.

"About Tim Bradbury?"

"About Tim Bradbury."

"I saw all that stuff on the news last night about the accident at Fountain of Youth and I wasn't sure. My, Tony was having himself a fine old time, wasn't he? Did you know that Tony Bandero had aspirations on the order of turning himself into a media star?"

"I'd begun to suspect it."

"Yeah, well, everybody does after about ten minutes. So come on in. I'll send out for coffee and Danish if you haven't had breakfast. We'll have a talk."

"I haven't had breakfast," Gregor said.

"Nobody really gets in around here until nine o'clock anymore anyway," Philip Brye said. "It's not like it was when I was starting out. We all got in early and stayed late. Now the only time this place is buzzing is on the holidays. New Year's Eve coming up. Do you find yourself giving lectures about how different everything was when you were young and feeling about three hundred years old?"

"Often," Gregor said, "but I don't think I really want the world to be like what it was when I was young."

"I guess I don't either, not in most ways. Look, if Tony's stuck you safely out of town without a car, call Bulldog Cabs. They're a bunch of college kids and they need the money. Also, they're reliable and they're cheap."

"Bulldog Cabs," Gregor agreed.

"See you in a while," Philip Brye said.

Gregor hung up again. That hadn't been too bad, he thought. Philip Brye hadn't hung up on him. He even sounded like he might turn into an ally.

Gregor got up and headed for the closet, where he had hung his three three-piece suits and his little collection of white button-down shirts: what Bennis always called his "determined to be unfashionable" wardrobe. He had taken a shower the night before, so he didn't have to worry about that. He had at least one tie—the lemon yellow and scarlet red rep tie Donna Moradanyan had given him for Christmas—that was in reasonably good shape. It wasn't in reasonably good taste, but Gregor tried not to ask too much of ties. It was enough that they shouldn't be fraying. Or actually in strips.

Gregor shed his robe and his pajamas and reached into his suitcase for a clean set of underwear. Bennis thought his underwear was "determined to be unfashionable" too, but the idea of fashionable underwear appalled him.

What made him happy was this feeling he had now that, finally, he was doing the right thing. He wasn't letting himself be pulled around by the nose by Tony Bandero. He wasn't drowning in theatrics and irrelevant details. He shoved his dirty underwear into his laundry bag, put on the clean set, and reached for one of those white button-down shirts.

Yes, he thought, he was finally doing the right thing. No matter what etiquette demanded in most times and most places, in this time and this place, he had every right in the world to do what he was doing.

If that meant that in the long run he put Tony Bandero's nose out of joint—so be it.

— 2 —

Gregor's mood lasted until he got down to the lobby to wait for his Bulldog Cab. It had lasted through a long and rambling phone call from Tony Bandero, in which it became obvious that Tony had no intention of rescuing Gregor from the boondocks until well after lunch. Gregor didn't bother to tell him about his imminent meeting with Philip Brye. Gregor's mood lasted through the discovery that he had somehow managed to rip the tie Donna had given him, even though he had only had it on for a few minutes, and that he didn't have another tie in good enough shape to replace it. Gregor's mood even lasted through his trip downstairs, which was a nightmare of helium balloons and shrieking posters. Sometime in the night some kind of invisible line had been crossed. New Year's Eve was suddenly an Event, a Matter of Urgent Importance, a Crisis. Signs were everywhere: advertising the motel sleepover party, wishing him

Happy New Year, asking him what HE intended to do about his New Year's resolutions. This last seemed to be some kind of public service announcement from a local rest home specializing in "substance abuse" problems. In small type at the bottom of the poster was a line that said, "If you won't get help from us, get help somewhere." Gregor wished he could. The elevator was full of red and white balloons, each of them imprinted with the number of the new year. Just enough of the helium had leaked out of them to make them float at a level with Gregor's face. He kept smashing his nose into them whenever he turned around.

When he got to the lobby, he walked past the check-in desk to the big wall of plate glass that looked out on the front drive. He saw no sign of a Bulldog Cab, so he walked back toward the elevators and stopped at the long line of white metal newspaper vending machines. There was another notice about the motel's New Year's sleepover party resting on top of these. There were more helium-filled balloons, too, tied to the pull handles of one of the machines. Gregor got some change out of his pocket and bought copies of the *New York Times* and *The New Haven Register*. He didn't think he'd have time, with everything he had to do, to get through *USA Today*.

The *Times* had a headline about the Middle East and another about Bosnia-Herzegovina. Gregor ignored this—he was tired of depressing himself with news about perennial and unresolvable wars—and maneuvered his copy of the *Register* to the top. Then he looked down into an enormous picture of his own face and blinked.

His own face.

On the cover of the *Register*.

With Tony Bandero's face hovering around in the background behind it.

Gregor got the paper all the way open and stared at it. The headline had been set in enormous type and said:

DEMARKIAN IN NEW HAVEN.

The subhead had been set in stylized italics and read:

Famed Detective To Aid Police In Bradbury Probe

The article had been set in ordinary type and started with a quote from Tony Bandero.

"Sometimes, you have no choice but to bring in the best talent you can find," Detective Tony Bandero said today in an exclusive interview with the Register . . .

Horseshit, Gregor thought angrily. Bandero hadn't given an exclusive interview to anybody. Bandero had talked to every single human being he could find who had a notebook or a microphone in his hand. Or hers. Now Gregor realized he must have been promising exclusives all over the lot.

Gregor Demarkian did not like publicity. Any tendency he might ever have had to like it had been bred out of him at Quantico. The Bureau liked its men gray, boring, and utterly anonymous. Even so, he was not a babe in the woods. He had worked on enough high-profile cases even while he was still with the Bureau to know how the press operated. He most surely knew enough not to cross them.

Cross the press was just what Tony Bandero had done—crossed them big time and in the stupidest possible way. Gregor himself had listened to the "exclusive interview" Tony had given to WTNH last night. Now here was another "exclusive interview." How many more were out there?

The automatic doors at the front of the motel's lobby sucked open. Gregor saw a young woman in blue slacks and a blue-and-white sweater with a bulldog appliquéd on it walk in. The young woman came directly over to where Gregor stood and thrust out her hand.

"Mr. Demarkian?" she asked. "I'm Connie Hazelwood. From Bulldog Cabs."

"Yes," Gregor said. Shortly. And ungraciously. He couldn't help himself.

Connie Hazelwood tilted her head sideways. "Are you all right, Mr. Demarkian? You look a little flushed."

"I'm fine," Gregor said.

"Well, good," Connie Hazelwood said. "Good. It's a big thrill for me to be driving somebody as famous as you are. Shall we go?"

"Yes," Gregor said again.

"Well, good," Connie Hazelwood said, also again. She had begun to look desperate.

Gregor felt sorry for her, he really did, but for the moment there was nothing he could do to help her. There wasn't even anything he could think of to do to calm himself down.

Connie Hazelwood walked back out the front doors, leading the way to her cab, and Gregor followed her.

He was still steaming.

FIVE

— 1 —

The New Haven medical examiner's office was in a long, low red brick building that looked like a small factory, set among more of the two- and three-story wood frame houses Gregor had come to think of as "typical" of New Haven. There was Yale. There was Prospect Street. There were a few blocks of churches and stores around the Green. Other than that, the entire city seemed to be made up of these double and triple deckers. Gregor let Connie Hazelwood jockey her cab into a tight parking space at the curb in front of the medical examiner's building's doors and considered the neighborhood. He knew his impression had to be wrong. Somewhere in New Haven there would be at least one rich neighborhood and probably several very poor ones. There would be a red-light district and a shopping strip. He just hadn't happened to run into them. The interesting thing about this neighborhood was that it was not as bad as Gregor had expected it to be. The houses were not noticeably dilapidated. One or two had sagging porches. Several had paint peeling off their sides. Everything looked a little sad and tired, but nothing looked desperate. There was something Gregor had noticed about official municipal buildings over the past few years—police stations, town halls, administration buildings, city hospitals.

Such buildings had become a magnet for the derelict and insane. Homeless old women slept on their steps. Drugged and violent men paced back and forth in the gutters in front of them. The houses and stores in the vicinity emptied out. Nobody wanted to live or work near people who could not be counted on to answer a smile with a smile and a good morning with a good morning. Nobody wanted to take the chance of getting knifed or shot because of some demon no one could see inside the head of a person no one could talk to.

Well, Gregor thought, it hadn't gotten that bad around here. Maybe the wanderers were spooked. The ME's offices were in the same building as the morgue. Down at the other end of the building, toward the middle of the block, Gregor could see the bays for the morgue ambulances and vans. They were closed. He got his wallet out of his back pocket and asked Connie Hazelwood what he owed her.

"Three dollars even," she replied.

Gregor assumed it was some kind of set rate. From this part of the city to that part of the city for three dollars even. It surprised him because New Haven was so urban, and set rates were such a small-town thing to do. He took out four dollar bills and passed them into the front seat.

"Thank you very much," he said, opening his door to get out.

Connie Hazelwood pocketed the money and took out a business card. "Ask for me if you call again," she said, slipping the card into the breast pocket of his suit jacket through his open coat. "I'm not always free, but I can always try."

Gregor got a sudden vision of Connie Hazelwood dumping an old lady shopper on an icy sidewalk to free herself up to take his call. He pushed it out of his head.

"Thank you," he said again. Then he stepped out onto the pavement and looked around.

No Christmas decorations. No holiday door wreaths. No sprightly red-and-white posters announcing commercial New Year's Eve parties. This neighborhood might not be dilapidated, but it was a little like a college student with a case of clinical depression. It wasn't engaged with the world, to put it the way Donna Moradanyan would. It wasn't even engaged with itself. Gregor wanted to throw a little tinsel on the nearest utility pole.

He went up to the building's front doors and let them slide open in front of him. He found himself in a wide, narrow front room with filthy vinyl on the floor and cork bulletin boards screwed into every wall. The cork bulletin boards were covered with signs that commanded: DON'T DRINK AND DRIVE—HAVE A *SAFE* NEW YEAR'S EVE. Opposite the front doors, there was a security desk with a guard at it. The guard was old and tired looking and very, very Irish. He was wearing an N.H.P.D. uniform, with the top button of the shirt undone.

Gregor walked up to the desk. "My name is Gregor Demarkian. I'm here to see Dr. Philip Brye."

Maybe the guard didn't read the newspapers. Or watch local television. He showed no flicker of recognition at all at the sound of Gregor's name.

"Phil Brye," he said, tapping numbers into his phone. Somebody must have picked up on the other end. The guard said, "Gregory Demark for Phil Brye," listened for a minute, and then said, "Okay."

Gregor thought about becoming Gregory Demark. It had its points.

"You can go on through," the guard told him. "Office is right there on this floor, all the way to the back, just keep walking till you run into a secretary. Secretary is a guy. We have guy secretaries in the department these days."

"Okay," Gregor said.

"We have girl patrolmen, too," the guard said. "I'm retiring at the end of the summer. Maybe they'll replace me with a girl guard."

"Maybe," Gregor said, edging toward the inner door.

"It's more than I can do to keep up with it," the guard said.

Gregor got through the door into the hallway. Like the front room, the walls were lined with cork bulletin boards. The posters here, though, were far more explicit than the ones at the front. HAPPY NEW YEAR, one of them announced in bold black letters—right under the picture of a dead man spilling out of a wrecked car with his leg severed. It was a real dead man and a real wrecked car and a real severed leg, too. Gregor checked. It made his stomach turn. Where would they have gotten a picture like that? And what the hell did they think they were doing, using it on a poster? What was a poster like that supposed to accomplish?

DON'T DRINK AND DRIVE, the next poster said.

Gregor walked past it without looking at its picture. Whatever the picture was of required the exhibition of a lot of very red blood. Gregor caught that much out of the corner of his eye.

The secretary turned out to be a clerk in a police officer's uniform. He was young and very efficient looking and obviously bored. Gregor wondered what he'd done to get stuck with duty like this. There was another bulletin board on the wall here. The poster on it said AULD LANG SYNE. It showed a young black man bleeding to death on a sidewalk with a knife in his back.

"Somehow," Gregor said, "you people around here don't have the same New Year's spirit as the rest of the country."

"That's because we pick up the pieces of the New Year's Eve spirit all through the hours of New Year's Day," the clerk said. "You know how many deaths we had in this town last New Year's Eve? Fifty-seven."

Gregor was startled. "Murders?"

"Nah," the clerk said. "Car accidents mostly. People are perfectly sane three hundred sixty-five days a year, gets to New Year's Eve and they down a couple of big bottles of champagne and go for a drive. We get other accidents, too. Glass."

"Glass?"

"Yeah. You wouldn't believe how many people go through windows. Second-story windows. Fifth-story windows. Plate-glass windows in stores they're trying to rob only they're too damned smashed to do it right. People get cut up and they bleed to death. Alcohol is worse than crack. It gets more people into more trouble. Believe me."

"I will."

"Doc Brye went down to the theater for a minute. Not to do an autopsy, you understand, just to check in on somebody. Come on down the hall, and I'll let you into his office."

The clerk got up and motioned Gregor down another hallway, limping a little as he went. Gregor followed him, staying a little behind. The limp explained a few things. The

clerk was either temporarily or permanently disabled. That
was why he was a clerk, in spite of being both competent
and young.

The clerk stopped at the door of the corner office at the
back, opened up and looked inside.

"Still not back yet," he said. "Why don't you go in and
sit down, and I'll get you a cup of coffee. Phil's always got
coffee hanging out somewhere. Also food. You want something like a cheese Danish? Or a chocolate doughnut?"

A chocolate doughnut? First thing in the morning? "A
cheese Danish will be fine," Gregor said.

"Back in a minute."

The clerk went out, and Gregor took the opportunity to
look over Philip Brye's office. It was a huge, square room
with a disintegrating accoustic ceiling and a vinyl floor that
looked like someone had gone at it with a fish scaler. Instead
of a desk, it had a long wood work table shoved into one
corner, entirely covered with papers and books and files.
There were cork bulletin boards in here, too, but they didn't
have posters on them. They had lists.

DUTY ROSTER NEW YEAR'S EVE, one said, and another,
CALL LIST NEW YEAR'S EVE. All the available display space
was taken up with lists of people who could be counted on
to come in on New Year's Eve.

It was, Gregor thought, less like a doctor's office than the
command post for an army under siege.

— 2 —

By the time Philip Brye got back from the theater, still wearing his white lab coat and one surgical glove, Gregor
Demarkian was established in the office's sole shabby club
chair, bolstered by a plastic foam cup full of instant coffee
and a cheese Danish the size of Detroit. He had finished
about half the Danish, but it still looked the size of Detroit.
He had no idea where Philip Brye bought his pastries, but he
wanted to learn.

Philip Brye turned out to be a short man with bad skin
and a very bad haircut. It was one of those haircuts that had

been cut too closely at the back of the neck, so that the skin there was red and raw and peeling. The skin on the knuckles of Philip Byre's one exposed hand was peeling, too. Coming into the office, Philip Brye stripped off his remaining surgical glove, opened the top of a bright red wastebasket, and held his other hand out to Gregor.

"I would have been more careful about washing up," he said blandly, "but I didn't actually touch anything in there except a clipboard. I take it you're Mr. Gregor Demarkian, America's greatest living detective."

"Well," Gregor said, "I'm Gregor Demarkian, anyway."

Philip Brye laughed and coughed and took a seat on the edge of his work table. "I've been checking out your publicity on and off since last night. You look like your photographs, oddly enough. People almost never do. I take it Tony's gotten you into a lot of trouble."

"It looks that way," Gregor agreed.

"He got the psychic into a lot of trouble, too. He probably didn't tell you about the psychic. That was last year, over a child murder we had—nasty piece of work and quite straightforward, really, except that Tony saw a way to grab himself some publicity, and he took it. And took it and took it and took it."

"Did the psychic do any good?"

"No. She put a good face on it, though, especially the way Tony got her played up on the six o'clock news. Murderer turned out to be the kid's stepfather, which is what we expected. It usually is."

"Stepfathers specifically?" Gregor asked curiously. "Not fathers or uncles or brothers?"

"Stepfathers and boyfriends," Philip Brye answered. "Especially with eleven- and twelve-year-old girls. It's practically a syndrome. I take it child murders were out of your field of expertise at the Bureau."

"Those kinds of child murders were. I worked on a couple of serial murder cases with child victims."

"Oh, lovely."

"I retired," Gregor said. "At the first possible opportunity."

Philip Brye coughed for a moment. "I keep telling myself I'm going to retire at the first possible opportunity, too," he said, "but I probably won't. I figure I'm addicted to this place. Did Tony tell you anything at all about what happened to Tim Bradbury?"

Gregor nodded. "He was poisoned. With arsenic. But not where he was found, because there were signs of a vomiting episode in his throat but none in the vicinity of his body, even taking the word *vicinity* loosely. No sign of a sickness episode on the grounds, in the garage, or in the house at the Fountain of Youth Work-Out Studio—"

"Do you know to take that with a grain of salt?" Philip Brye asked sharply. "Tony and his people aren't always exactly thorough. The evidence of an episode might have been cleaned up, and they might not have spotted the cleanup."

"That had occurred to me."

"Good."

Gregor went on. "The body was found in a small area of evergreen bushes next to the Fountain of Youth Work-Out's back door. It was naked, and there was no sign of the clothing Tim Bradbury might have been wearing at the time he died. He had been dead at least an hour when he was found. I think that's it."

Philip Brye considered this. "That's all? Nothing about Bradbury himself? Nothing about his people? Or his background?"

"No."

"Nothing about—the kind of speculation that's been going on since Tim showed up dead?"

"Tony sent me some newspaper clippings," Gregor said. "They contained a few theories."

"I'm sure they did. They weren't the theories I was thinking of." Philip Brye jumped off the edge of his work table, wheezed, then walked over to his single, overstuffed file cabinet. The cabinet was so overstuffed, none of the drawers would close. "I suppose it figures," he said. "Tony never tells anybody anything interesting if he can help it. Still, it's a little raw."

"Do you mean the forensic information wasn't complete?"

"Oh, the forensic information's complete enough. The forensic information isn't the point. Just a minute and I'll get you what I've got."

Dr. Brye began to search patiently and systematically through the second file drawer from the top. Files came out and were shoved onto the file cabinet's cluttered surface. Files went back in, crammed until they bent against other files that had already been crammed. Gregor Demarkian finished the rest of his cheese Danish and sipped at his coffee.

"Here we go," Philip Brye said after a while. "My personal file on the death of Tim Bradbury. Did you know he was a local boy?"

"I think it was in one of the newspaper clippings. Branford, I think it said. Or something like that."

"North Branford, yes, that's where he had his apartment before he moved in at Fountain of Youth, but that isn't the kind of local I meant," Philip Brye said. "He was born and brought up in the area, out in Derby. He started working in and around New Haven when he was a teenager. He took shit jobs at Yale. Dishwasher. Parking lot attendant. Road construction work when he could. We call that Connecticut's own state college scholarship plan. Every summer, the crews are full of kids working their way through college. Not that you really can work your way through college anymore. The prices are prohibitive. Anyway, my point here is that a lot of us knew him—not well, you understand, not as a friend, but enough to recognize him on the street and say hello to. New Haven isn't a small town anymore. Everybody doesn't know everybody. But some people do get around. Tim Bradbury was one of them."

"Did Tony Bandero know him?"

Philip Brye shook his head. "I don't think so. I don't think Tony's that much of a shit. However, the thing is, I knew Tim, maybe better than most people did. When I was still married, my wife and I had a house out in Hamden. Tim did our yard work and our snow plowing one year. Good kid. Very responsible. Came to work on time. Got down in good order. Gave value for money. Always polite. So, when all this happened, and I saw what Tony was turning it into, I decided to check it all out for myself."

"And?"

Philip Brye had a thick file folder in his hands. He walked back across the office and dumped it in Gregor's lap. "Take a look through that. That's the result of the first, and

God knows I hope the last, detective investigation I have ever conducted. It's probably a mess, but it's got to be a whole hell of a lot better than anything Tony Bandero has got."

As far as Gregor knew, Tony Bandero had nothing. On the other hand, Tony could have everything and just be keeping it to himself. Gregor positioned the file on his lap so that it wouldn't fall off and opened it up.

The first thing in the file was a glossy eight-by-eleven black-and-white photograph of what looked like a shack, boarded up and deserted. The second thing in the file was another eight-by-eleven photograph of the same shack. The third thing in the file was yet another photograph of the same shack—but here Gregor could see a difference. In this third photograph, there was very distinctly a lit kerosene lamp in the one gap in the boards that covered the windows of what Gregor thought was, or had been, a glassed-in porch. Gregor raised this picture in Philip Brye's direction and then raised his eyebrows, too.

"Well?" he asked.

"That," Philip Brye said, "is Tim Bradbury's mother's house. If you look closely at the last picture, you'll be able to see the Housatonic River in the background. The house was built originally—all the houses on that part of the river were built originally—as summer places. This would have been at the end of World War Two. The houses are small and they're not insulated. Most of them were built without heating systems on the assumption that they would only be used in the summer. But it didn't work out that way."

"Absentee landlords got hold of them."

"Yep. And people who were really too poor to afford to keep up a house got hold of them, too. I checked about Tim's mother. She owns her place. Such as it is."

"It looks boarded up," Gregor said.

Philip Brye shrugged. "It's cheaper to nail driftwood over a broken window than to replace the glass. The place is boarded up. It looks empty. But it isn't."

"Tim Bradbury's mother lives there alone?"

"She's got two cats. Otherwise she lives there alone. Tim moved out right after he graduated from high school."

Gregor looked over the last picture of the shack again. "I

don't suppose you can blame him for that," he said. "It isn't anyplace I'd want to live if I didn't have to."

"Me, either. What I find significant, though, is that Tim had apparently left that house emotionally long before he left it physically. I guess that's a polite way of saying he lied about his background. Consistently. To everyone."

"What did he say?"

"He said his parents had left the area," Philip Brye said. "Emphasis on parents, plural."

"I take it he didn't have parents, plural," Gregor said.

"I got hold of his birth certificate. On the line for 'father' all it says is 'unknown.' "

"That doesn't mean that the father was necessarily actually unknown. The mother must have known who he was. She may have been in contact with him for years. Was the family on welfare?"

"No. No welfare. No social security. No social workers."

"The mother had a job, then," Gregor said.

"Not as far as I could find out," Philip Brye said. "You're the detective and I'm the amateur. I've probably missed something obvious that you'll pick right up. It will turn out she was slinging hash in a diner someplace, and there's no mystery about it at all. But the thing is, what really got me going looking into this beyond the fact that Tim was somebody I knew, was that I had this talk with this woman who's now a staff assistant here in the department. Five years ago, she was a guidance counselor at the high school in Derby. That was Tim Bradbury's senior year."

Gregor scratched the side of his face. "I take it this has a punch line," he said. "She had some startling revelation that Tony Bandero wouldn't listen to."

"Bandero won't listen to anybody, but this isn't a startling revelation, no. But it is indicative. This woman was a guidance counselor, right, so she had access to Tim Bradbury's files. Father, unknown. Mother's occupation, housewife."

"I'm surprised she remembers all this. Even with the murder, it sounds like she can recall a lot of detail. Too much detail, maybe."

Philip Brye smiled wanly. "She's not an inaccurate witness, Mr. Demarkian. And she's not the sort of person who's prone to making things up. No, she remembers what she remembers because it was an issue at the time. Tim was an issue at the time. Tim's mother was an issue at the time. How strange she was."

"She came to teachers' conferences and that kind of thing?"

"Not on a regular basis, no, I don't think so. Mrs. Conyer—that's the ex-guidance counselor—says she came in once and looked just the way you'd expect her to. Acted just the way you'd expect her to, too. Very overweight. Very slovenly. Dressed in a big polyester tent and shoes run over at the heels. Not too recently bathed. White trash."

"Another good reason for Tim Bradbury to want to move out as soon as he could," Gregor pointed out. "Especially since, from everything you've told me about him, he wasn't the same type."

"Mrs. Conyer said the mother came as quite a shock to the teachers. Tim was always neat, polite, clean, very well behaved. He wasn't a world beater. He didn't make it into the top third of his class and sail out with a scholarship to an important college. He was just a stable, industrious kid. I know it's not fashionable to say so these days, but in my experience family counts for a lot. I get the children of mothers like the one Mrs. Conyer described in here all the time. Anyway, I get their bodies in here. Dope. Liquor. Knife fights. Not jobs teaching weight training for Fountain of Youth."

"Are you absolutely sure he was never on drugs?"

"No. I can be absolutely sure that I never saw him on drugs, and I saw him a fair amount. I can be absolutely sure he wasn't on drugs on the night he died."

"What about dealing drugs? Dealers don't often use. Not if they're smart."

"True," Philip Brye said, "and, of course, there would be know way to be positive that he wasn't dealing, because there isn't any way to prove a negative. But my take on this was that he just didn't have enough money. I don't know about checking accounts and savings accounts and that kind of thing. I don't think anyone has checked yet—"

Gregor snorted.

"However," Philip Brye said, "Tim didn't live like a drug dealer. He didn't even live like a part-time dealer. That job he had was no piece of cake. It required a great deal of physical effort. Why bother to do that if you've got five, six hundred dollars a week, minimum, coming in on the side?"

"He could have been trying to launder the money," Gregor suggested.

"He could have laundered the money by waiting tables or tending her or working in the library. Part time. Instead of that, he had a full time job at Fountain of Youth. There's also the evidence of what he didn't have. No seventy-five dollar designer jeans. No hundred-and-twenty-five-dollar Timberland boots. Just good old Levi's and Stride Rites."

"Let me try one more thing," Gregor said. "Let me try the possibility that he was just one very smart young man. Smart enough to know how to hide. Smart enough to know he had to bank his money because dealing drugs gets old fast and drug dealers don't stay alive if they try to stay too long in the business."

"No," Philip Brye said. "If Tim was the kind of smart that that kind of behavior would have made him, then he was the greatest actor since Laurence Olivier. He might have played a game like that and gotten away with it if he were the sort of kid nobody notices, but he wasn't. He was the sort of kid people like me tend to mentally adopt. Here's a good kid, we say. From a modest background. Really determined to make his way up. Let's give the kid a hand, we say. Let's at least take an interest in how he's doing. I think that's what happened at Fountain of Youth, don't you? They have some of their staff living in the house, but they don't have all of it. I think Tim got asked because he was—affecting."

"Possibly," Gregor said.

Actually, the secret ingredient in the lives of most successful psychopaths was precisely the fact that they were—affecting. Charming. Bashful. Boyish. Eager. Vulnerable. All on the surface, but all perfectly plausible. People want to believe in the struggling young man determined to make good. There were even some struggling young men out there worth believing in.

Most of the struggling young men Gregor had known, however—especially the boyish, affecting, vulnerable kind—had been struggling mostly to hide their rage. On the evidence of what was in this file folder, Tim Bradbury had had a lot to be legitimately enraged about. It bothered Gregor that nobody had ever picked up any such emotion in him.

Gregor leafed through a few more pages of the folder. Most of its bulk was made up of repetitions. Three pictures of the house. Four pictures of what looked like Tim Bradbury as a ten-year-old boy. Two copies of Tim Bradbury's page from the high school yearbook. Most of it would turn out not to mean anything.

Even so, Gregor thought, this was more than he had had when he got up this morning—a lot more. It was enough for him to move on with. It was a start.

Gregor hadn't realized it before this, but he had been desperately looking for a start ever since that piece of balcony rail had gone crashing to Fountain of Youth's polished hardwood foyer floor.

SIX

— 1 —

For Nick Bannerman, the idea of leaving Fountain of Youth for an hour in the afternoon to have lunch or go to the Co-op was appalling. Ever since the incident at the SuperHour Grocery, Nick had developed an odd kind of situation-specific agoraphobia. He had been at Yale for four years. There were still restaurants he knew and where he was known, stores whose owners he knew by sight and others whose owners he knew by name. There was also the strip out on Dixwell Avenue: the chain stores and the franchises, the malls whose managements had New York legal help and knew too much about liability and law suits to pull anything like what he'd been subjected to at the SuperHour. Not that that would necessarily do him any good. There was a black judge in Pennsylvania suing Bloomingdale's right now, because they'd had him arrested on suspicion of credit card fraud. Somebody in their security department had apparently decided that fraud was the only possible reason a black man could have a credit card. There were other things like that floating around in the air, too, in New York and Baltimore and Miami and San Francisco and Washington. Once Nick started thinking about it, he was shocked at how many incidents he could come up with. Incidents. It felt like the wrong word. An incident was the time you drank too much at dinner with your girlfriend's mother and threw up on your shoes, or the time you stopped paying attention in the K mart parking lot and dented your fender on a lamp pole. It wasn't this . . . creeping slime, that hid in the shadows and got you when you weren't looking. That was what frightened him. It was out there waiting for him. It would get him if he didn't watch out. He felt exactly the way he had when he was six years old and had first had to sleep in his bedroom in the new house in Larchmont, the one where the closet door would never entirely close.

The problem with me, Nick told himself, as he came out of his third dance of the morning—the intermediates, meaning he'd actually had to work up a little sweat—is that I've led a much too sheltered life. He wended his way through the women dressed in leotards in the corridor and headed for the stairway. He had grown up in Larchmont, not in Harlem. His father had been the first black man ever promoted into a vice presidency at IBM. He knew as little about the ghetto as any sorority president cheerleader at the University of Kansas. The only time he had ever seen a gun, except on a cop, was when he'd been mugged. Until the SuperHour, of course. The SuperHour had changed everything. Except that it probably hadn't changed anything at all. He'd been followed by store detectives, ignored by sales clerks, dismissed by bank tellers. He'd had teachers, even at prep school and Yale, who had behaved as if his vocabulary were restricted to words of one syllable. There had been a thousand and one little things and a hundred and one not so little ones, but nothing, ever, anywhere, anything like what had happened at the SuperHour.

If you went down the service stairs far enough, you got to a swinging wood door that led to the service hallway and what was still, after a hundred years and six renovations, the pantry. Nick pushed his way in there and looked around at the shelves. It was twelve o'clock and he was starving. He was also in no mood to sit down in the dining room again with all those women. Doing that yesterday it had given him a headache. It was incredible what some women could be like, when they wanted to be. There was the middle-aged one who had squeezed his thigh while they were waiting on line at the salad bar. There was the young one who had cornered him for an earnest conversation about the Problems of the Underclass and then been furious with him when she realized that he didn't actually know anybody in the underclass. She'd had her hand on his knee until she had gotten angry with him. Then, before getting up and stalking away, she had dug the tips of her very long nails right into the vulnerable place under his kneecap.

There was a can of tuna fish on the shelf and a bag of onions in the top bin of a stack of plastic bins. The bins underneath the onions all seemed to be full of beans. Nick took a can of tuna and an onion and a loaf of four-grain bread and looked around for some mayonnaise. He found six different kinds of vegetable oil and sixteen different kinds of vinegar. The vinegar surprised him so much, he had to count the bottles twice. Then he decided that Fountain of Youth must be out of mayonnaise, because the only glass jars of anything like it he could find were filled with tofu paste. Nick took the tuna fish and the bread and the onion out of the pantry and into the kitchen. The kitchen was one of those big empty places, built to be used by several people at one time, where all the appliances were too far apart.

Nick put his food down on the long wood picnic table that sat next to a row of windows overlooking the back lawn and went to the refrigerator. There was a second kitchen, a little smaller but much more efficient, where the group meals were prepared for the women who were taking the classes upstairs. That kitchen would be full of frantic people at this time of day. This kitchen was a haven. Nick didn't define to himself exactly a haven from what. He looked through the jars on the refrigerator shelves. More tofu paste. Eight different kinds of mustard. All-natural organic ketchup. The door to the hall swung open.

If Nick had been living at the house, he would have recognized her immediately. Since he was only there for the working day and she was not sociable, it took him a minute. His first reaction was simple surprise. She was so pretty, he almost dropped the jar he was holding. Tall. Thin. Blond. Perfect. The epitome of everything in the world of women that Nick Bannerman knew he should not want. He felt the stiffening in his pants and sidled hastily toward the refrigerator door, to make sure he was covered. God only knew, exercise clothes wouldn't cover him much. He looked at the jar he was holding and wondered why he had picked it up. It contained something called anise pickles.

"Ah," he said. "Hi. Well. Um. It's Frannie, isn't it?"

The blond woman had stopped dead as soon as she had seen him. She looked pale and frozen. When Nick spoke, she jumped a little. When he finished, she walked toward the middle of the room, slowly and deliberately, as if she were making herself do it.

"That's right. Frannie Jay. I'm sorry I bothered you."

"You didn't bother me," Nick told her. "I was looking for some mayonnaise."

"I won't bother you much longer," Frannie Jay said. "I just want to get a bottle of mineral water. As soon as I get a bottle of mineral water, I'll get right out of here."

Anise pickles. Nick put them back on the shelf, next to a jar of 100 percent all-natural carob sauce. It said it like that, in big jokey letters, as if it were a can of SpaghettiOs. The healthy foods movement meets American mass marketing. The palms of Nick's hands were wet with sweat. He wiped them off, as discreetly as he could, on the back of his T-shirt.

"You don't have to get out of here," he said. "Stick around and I'll make you some lunch. That's why I was looking for the mayonnaise. Tuna fish."

"I don't eat lunch," Frannie Jay said.

Frannie Jay didn't look like she ate much of anything at all. She wasn't anorexic, exactly. She had good muscle tone and rounded, strong calves. Still you could see every bone in her rib cage. Nick felt his erection wilt and then stiffen again.

He closed the refrigerator door. "If you don't want to spend the hour upstairs, you could stay here and keep me company," he suggested. "I could use a little company. I spend all my time either bouncing around or commuting."

Frannie looked toward the wall of windows next to the picnic table and blinked. "I don't really like this room. Those windows. I don't really like to look out there when I don't have to."

"That's right," Nick said. "You're the one who—ah—"

"Found the body."

"Exactly."

"I didn't really find the body. I only found the foot. It was sticking out of the bushes."

Maybe this was some kind of posttraumatic stress disorder. Nick had played a Vietnam veteran with posttraumatic stress disorder once. Frannie had moved farther into the kitchen and was staring out the window.

"Did you meet that man who was here yesterday?" she asked suddenly. "That Gregor Demarkian person, the detective?"

"Briefly." Nick was confused.

"It said in the paper that he was good at secrets. All the cases he's ever solved were full of secrets."

Nick had read this article. What it had actually said was that Gregor Demarkian was good at uncovering *guilty* secrets.

"I don't think the police brought him in here because he was good at secrets," Nick told her. "I think they were taking a lot of heat about not solving the case and not really doing anything to get themselves anywhere and Demarkian was a good bone to throw at public opinion. He's got a reputation."

Frannie walked all the way over to the picnic table, leaned against it, and looked out the windows.

"He drove me in from the bus stop, you know. Tim did. The night he was killed."

"I didn't realize that."

"He was a very nice boy. Man. Whatever. He seemed very young."

"Everybody says that about him, yeah. That he was sort of innocent."

"I think he had a secret," Frannie said. "That's why people get killed, isn't it? Grown-up people, anyway. Children get killed just for being children."

What was this about? It was like being in a room with a hypnotized person. No. It was worse. Nick wanted to go to the table to get his food, but all of a sudden he didn't want to get that close to Frannie Jay. His erection was a distant memory.

"I don't think you ought to worry too much about Tim Bradbury," he told Frannie. He isn't your responsibility. You didn't even know him."

"That's true."

"The police are supposed to worry about him. And Demarkian."

Frannie Jay swayed a little, and blinked.

"Oh," she said, in a much more normal voice. "I have to get out of here. I just came down for some—"

"Mineral water," Nick finished. He whirled around and opened the refrigerator door again. There were dozens of fat-bellied green bottles of Perrier on the bottom shelf. He took out two.

"Here you are," he said. "Perrier. Specialty of the house."

Frannie Jay looked at him as if he had gone crazy. Then she came back across the kitchen and took the bottles of Perrier out of his hands.

"Thanks," she said.

"You're welcome," he told her.

The bottles had the kind of caps you had to pry open with a can opener. Maybe Frannie kept an opener in her room for just that purpose.

"Well," she said. "I guess I'd better go. It was nice talking to you."

"It was nice talking to you, too."

"I have three more step classes this afternoon. I'm going to be a wet noodle by the time I'm done."

"I've got three more classes, too. I don't worry about watching my calories while I'm working at this place."

Frannie gave the last bit a smile as lame as the comment itself, said "Bye," and went out the kitchen door. Nick Bannerman leaned back against the refrigerator doors and closed his eyes.

Now that Frannie Jay wasn't acting crazy anymore, his erection was back. It was big and hard and solid, and any minute now he was certain it was going to hurt.

— 2 —

Dessa Carter knew something was wrong as soon as Mrs. O'Reilly picked up the phone in Derby. She could hear the sound of heavy thudding against wood and Mrs. O'Reilly's labored breathing. In spite of her heaviness, Mrs. O'Reilly was almost never short of breath. She was a rock of a woman, as she put it herself. Rocks did not have physical limitations. As soon as she heard the thudding, Dessa Carter stiffened. She had actually been feeling pretty good before that. It was step aerobics day on the smorgasbord. Dessa was surprised to find that she liked step aerobics. She was tired and achy and hot. She felt heavier than she really was. Yet she still felt better than she had a couple of days ago. There was something to this exercise stuff. It made her mentally light.

The thudding was rhythmic and strong, unyielding and brutal.

"I've got him locked in the bathroom," Mrs. O'Reilly was saying. "It was the best I could do. He broke the coffee table."

The pay phone was just off the foyer, in a little utility hall with a locker room in it and a cloakroom with a revolving coatrack but no attendant. At least, Dessa thought, I'll be private here. None of the women from her class was anywhere near this hall at all. The foyer was empty, too. If Dessa leaned back a little, she could see the place where the balcony railing had fallen apart. Someone had boarded it up with a piece of plywood.

"He doesn't sound like he's calming down," Dessa said.

"Oh, he's calming down," Mrs. O'Reilly told her. "It was a lot worse half an hour ago. I didn't have him locked up then. And he's stronger than you think."

"I know how strong he is."

"You're going to have to find a nursing home for him. You can't keep on with him the way he is. I can't keep on with him."

Dessa pressed her forehead against the shiny metal front of the phone. She had never been so hungry in her life. Never. She craved a grocery bag full of Mars bars, sticky sweet, sugar rush. She wanted to go down to Taco Bell and eat three ten-packs of tacos. She wanted to make herself a huge pot of mashed potatoes and smother them in butter. She wanted all the food on earth, right now, this minute, and then she wanted to lie on the floor of her own bedroom and feel the pain in her stomach until it got so bad she passed out.

"You can't leave now," she said, in a hoarse voice she barely recognized. "Not today."

"I'm not going to leave today."

Dessa relaxed a little. "I can't find him a nursing home this week," she said, forcing herself to sound reasonable. "It might take months."

"You can't hold onto people when they've changed," Mrs. O'Reilly insisted. "He isn't the father you knew when you were a girl. He's an addled old hulk with a disease. He needs twenty-four-hour-a-day nurses. You're not doing him any good keeping him here."

"I know."

"He's going to hurt somebody someday. Me or you."

"I know that, too."

"He's going to get out of this house when we've got our guards down and go wandering around the neighborhood and get murdered for his watch."

"I wouldn't mind putting him in a nursing home, Mrs. O'Reilly. It's not that I don't like the idea that's the problem."

"We all want to be loyal to the parents who brought us up," Mrs. O'Reilly interrupted. "When they have to go into nursing homes, we think we're abandoning them. You won't be abandoning him. He'll be better off."

Will he? Dessa asked herself, but she knew the answer to that. He wouldn't be, because she couldn't afford to put him any place that would be better off than he was at home. She couldn't afford to put him any place at all. She wanted to reach through the phone and grab Mrs. O'Reilly by the neck. She wanted to throttle the woman. Of course she had looked into nursing homes. Of course she had. The good private ones were out of the question, but as it turned out, the state facilities were out of the question, too. First, they'd told her, her father would have to "exhaust his assets," meaning sell the house and anything else he owned and use the money to pay nursing home bills. Then she would have to "sever any proprietary or custodial interest" she had in him, meaning declare him a ward of the state. Then, and only then, would a state facility have him. It would have him for good. She would have no legal standing to complain about his care, if it was bad—and from what Dessa had seen, it was likely to be bad. She would become a nonperson in the life of this man, this man—

"Miss Carter?" Mrs. O'Reilly was saying.

Dessa could see it, thrown up on her memory like a movie on a screen: the backyard in the days when the neighborhood had been a good one, the bright hard sunlight of an early afternoon, the thick greenness of the midsummer heat. Her mother, alive and whole and young, setting plastic knives and forks out on the red-and-white checkered plastic tablecloth spread across the round metal outdoor table. Her father—

But she couldn't see her father. It had been a long time, Dessa realized, since she had been able to remember her father clearly at all. She could remember things he had done, the wood swing set he had built her, the blue suit he had bought just to wear to her high school graduation, so that he wouldn't have to appear in work clothes and embarrass her. She couldn't remember *him*. Her mother, who had been dead for years, was still fresh in her mind. Dessa sometimes thought she could still smell her mother's lavender cachet in the big bedroom at home—although that was impossible; the smell of her father's illness blanketed everything. Her father blanketed everything. Her father, as he was now. What he had become had obliterated everything that he had been.

"Do you need me to come home?" Dessa asked Mrs. O'Reilly.

"I don't need you here. I can cope. I just don't know how much longer I can cope."

"What about tomorrow? Are you going to need me there tomorrow?"

"You take your time with your exercising," Mrs. O'Reilly said. "I know this is important to you. I was just talking about the long run. You have to think about the long run."

"Fine." Dessa was finding it easier to breathe now. She didn't have the faintest intention of thinking about the long run. Not here. Not today. "I'm going to go have my lunch now. You keep him locked up as long as you have to. I'll come right home at the end of the day."

"Take your time. Do what you have to do."

"We'll talk the whole thing through as soon as I see you. Is there anything he can hurt himself on in the bathroom?"

"We took the razors out months ago. We took the scissors out."

"Yes. Yes, I remember that. It ought to be all right, then. Just do the best you can."

"I always do the best I can."

"I know you do. You've been a godsend, Mrs. O'Reilly. I don't know what I would have done without you."

"You'd have managed. God always sends us the strength to do what we have to do."

God is in a nursing home, Dessa thought. God has Alzheimer's disease. God is dead.

"He's stopped pounding now," Mrs. O'Reilly said. "I'm going to go listen at the door. If he's fallen asleep, I'll open up."

"Good."

"It's not as bad as that time before. I don't think I'm going to have to tie him up."

"That's good, too."

"God only knows what those social workers would think, if they saw him all tied up. People don't understand what it's like anymore, caring for the old. People don't care for the old. They dump them in hospitals and walk away."

"Yes," Dessa said, even though this made absolutely no sense to her. Didn't Mrs. O'Reilly want her to dump her father in a hospital, or the next best thing to a hospital? Wasn't that what they had been talking about for the last five minutes? Dessa thought of her father tied to the bed that time, the harsh sound of his voice in the dark room, the stink of him as he soiled himself over and over again, the craziness.

"There was another one in the papers today," Mrs. O'Reilly continued. "Old lady left in the emergency room at Yale New Haven. Left in her wheelchair. Name unknown. Address unknown. Relatives unknown. People just take them out and drop them off and never look back again."

Oh, Dessa thought. That's what she's talking about. Granny dumping. "I've got to go now," she said. "We've only got an hour to eat lunch, and I'm starving."

"I'm sure you are. All that exercise. It works up an appetite."

It was really supposed to suppress your appetite, but Dessa didn't want to go into it, not with Mrs. O'Reilly on the phone, not with her father locked in the bathroom.

"I really have to go now," she said. "Do you want me to call you back? Maybe at three?"

"There's no need. If I have an emergency, I can call you."

"All right. All right then. I'll see you tonight."

Mrs. O'Reilly was making mewling polite little sounds, the kinds of sounds that could keep this phone call going forever. Dessa said a firm good-bye and hung up. Then she stood stock-still in the hall and stared at the phone she had been talking into. She felt weak. In the old days, pay phones were in booths with seats in them. Why weren't pay phones like that anymore? She knew the answer to that. Her father wasn't the only one who was crazy. Everyone was crazy all the time now. They fed on each other.

Dessa pushed away from the phone and went down the hall into the foyer. She was too aware of how her flesh jiggled and swayed against the stretchy fabric of her leotard. It made her feel as if she were wearing body armor. Oddly enough, she wasn't hungry anymore. The idea of going up to the dining room and facing a salad bar brought her close to despair. What she really felt was fear. I can't handle this. I can't stand this. I can't do this, she thought, but she was too close to paralysis to be hysterical. She could see it stretching out in front of her for years. Her father, who was only seventy-two. That house, sinking into the landscape of crack parlors and pimp hotels the neighborhood had become. Mrs. O'Reilly.

Dessa was crossing the foyer to the curving staircase when Traci Cardinale appeared on the balcony. Traci walked up to an unbroken piece of balcony rail, seemed to make a determined effort not to be afraid of it, saw Dessa, and waved.

"There you are," Traci said. "I was wondering where you'd got to. I went to the dining room, but you weren't there."

"I had to make a phone call."

"Well, it doesn't seem to have done you any good. Come

up and have lunch with me. You really have to keep your motivation in place around here, or the whole program falls apart."

"My motivation's all right, I think," Dessa said. "My body seems to be on the verge of collapse."

"That's just your muscle tissue breaking down so that it can build itself up again," Traci said earnestly. "That's a very good sign. Come on to lunch."

Dessa came on to lunch. She still wasn't hungry, but she liked to listen to Traci talk.

Traci was always so positive about everything.

— 3 —

Up on the second floor, Christie Mulligan wasn't at lunch yet either. She was standing on the closed top of the toilet seat in the last stall to the left of the vanity mirrors in the members' lavatory, trying to see her reflection in the polished glass of the small window near the ceiling. Tara and Michelle were out by the sinks, talking to each other. The small window was open, letting in streams of cold, raw air. Christie had her leotard pulled down around her waist and her bra off. She had her fingers on the wrong place in her left breast and she was kneading. It hasn't gotten any bigger, she kept telling herself. Doesn't that mean something? It means I must be right and the doctors must be wrong. The tests were false. The results were mistakes. Something went wrong at the laboratory and her medical card got mixed up with somebody elses's.

"I think the whole bunch of them are weird," Tara was saying to Michelle. "Especially that Virginia What's-her-name. I think she's psychotic."

"I like Dessa Carter," Michelle said. "And I like Greta Bellamy."

Christie let her fingers relax. It was no bigger than it had been, but it hadn't gone away, either. Maybe it was some kind of cyst. Maybe it was a strange form of bruise, an interior black eye, swollen and painful. Except that it didn't hurt.

"I like Gregor Demarkian," Tara was saying. "He's the only person I've met since I got here who is the least bit interesting. Everybody else thinks tofu paste is a food."

"Tofu paste is a food," Michelle said.

"They're like those kids at school who get so green, they're practically frogs. Brazilian tree frogs that live in the rain forest, specifically. When we get out of here tonight, I'm going to go down to Happy Jack's and buy myself a pepperoni pizza. Large."

"I like that police detective," Michelle said. "Tony Bandero. I think he's very reassuring."

"I think he's a jerk," Tara snorted. "He's less like a cop than he is like a con man. I mean, I can just see him, can't you, playing that walnut shell game down on the Green?"

"No," Michelle said. "He reminds me of our police chief back in Waterville. He's—avuncular. That's the word. Like he's got everybody's best interests at heart but he's a little embarrassed to show it."

"Tony Bandero wouldn't be embarrassed to show off his dick at high noon in front of the Congregational Church. Christie, are you all right?"

Christie felt the wrong place one more time. It should be getting smaller, she thought. When was it going to start getting smaller? When was it just going to go away? She grabbed her sports bra and started to struggle into it. When she had it pulled all the way up, it made her chest look flat. She gripped the top of her leotard and started to pull that up, too.

"I'm fine," she called out to Tara. "I'll be with you in a minute."

"Hurry up, or we'll be reduced to having nothing but Slim Jims for lunch. Instead of tofu paste and raw carrots."

Tara would prefer the Slim Jims. Obviously. Now that her leotard was pulled up, Christie found it easier to see herself in the window. She thought she looked very elegant, thin and ethereal, better than she ever had before in her life.

"Here I come," she said, stepping down off the top of the toilet seat. She opened the stall door and joined Tara and Michelle at the sinks. She looked at herself in the mirror and confirmed what she had thought when she had seen herself in the window glass. She did look thin and ethereal. She did look better than she ever had before in her life.

Tara didn't seem to agree.

"Jesus Christ, Christie," she said in disgust. "If I didn't see you eat, I'd swear you were starving yourself to death. What are we trying for here, the Siege of Sarajevo aesthetic?"

It will go away, Christie told herself.

She didn't say anything in answer to Tara at all.

SEVEN

— 1 —

There was one good things about the kind of publicity that made you out to be a sage and an oracle, the man who had the answers to everything: most people wanted to believe it. Gregor Demarkian thought of that as he sat eating a hot turkey sandwich in a little restaurant on Chapel Street that faced the Green. One of Philip Brye's clerks had dropped him off there, by request, when Gregor had finished at the medical examiner's office. Gregor hadn't wanted to go back to his motel. The idea of being stuck out there in the middle of nowhere, with no access to anything that was going on in town, made him shudder. On the other hand, he wasn't ready to do anything serious. He wanted to think—and the best place for that was his apartment back on Cavanaugh Street. Barring that, he thought anonymity would be a good idea. Tony Bandero wouldn't be able to find him sitting in this rickety chair at this rickety table next to this polished window. That is, if Tony Bandero was actually looking for him, which Gregor tended to doubt. The danger for Tony, as far as Gregor could figure out, was that now that Gregor was here, he might insist on doing something.

This restaurant still had its Christmas decorations up, such as they were. There were a few tinsel-fringed stars taped to the walls and a plastic bouquet of holly leaves and berries on every table. It had New Year's decorations up, too, although those weren't very much either. Gregor wondered why no one ever seemed to be able to come up with anything original as a decoration for New Year's Eve. Babies in diapers with beauty pageant banners across their chests. Balloons. Champagne bottles with their corks popped. The tables here had little cards on them with champagne glasses emitting bubbles the way Chernobyl had emitted radiation. They said "HAPPY NEW YEAR" across the top of them and gave the times the restaurant would be open on the holiday, on the bottom. The champagne glass wasn't a real champagne glass but the wide-brimmed martini glass most people thought of as a champagne glass. Real champagne glasses were tall and thin and narrow at the opening, to keep the carbonation in. This was the kind of thing Bennis Hannaford told him, late at night, when they went to Father Tibor's to play cards. It was the kind of thing Bennis Hannaford both knew and found important. Gregor wondered how Bennis was and what she was doing. If she had been here, she would have had no patience for this restaurant. She would have wanted to be up at Fountain of Youth, getting on with things.

Outside, a frail snow had started. It was coming down in salt grain flakes buffeted by the wind into streamers. Gregor looked down at the gravy congealing on his plate and decided it was time to go. For a hot turkey sandwich, it had actually been rather good. The problem was that by definition hot turkey sandwiches were starchy and thick and bland. Gregor checked the bill, put two dollars down on the table as a tip, and gathered his coat to take to the cash register. Like many men who had grown up poor and gotten successful only later in life, Gregor tipped too much. It would have embarrassed him, except that he knew waitresses didn't have any money. He put the bill down at the side of the cash register with ten dollars in cash on top of it. The old woman making change made change for him and stared right past his left shoulder while she was doing it. So much for fame. Gregor shoved the dollar forty-nine he had coming to him into the pocket of his coat and went outside. The wind had really picked up. The windows in the empty storefront next door were frosted at the edges.

Empty storefronts. Old men sitting on park benches with heavy fraying overcoats to protect them from the cold. Shreds of muddied paper lying in the gutters. Gregor crossed the New Haven Green feeling slightly depressed. It was the same everywhere, but he could never get used to it. They had cared about cities when he was young. Here there was a big stone courthouse looking out on the decay of everything. It was one of those massive gray edifices that had been built to be a Palace of Justice. It was so impressive, it demanded a better noun for itself than *building* could ever be. There was no way to tell if it was still in use. Near it, on the other end of the same block, a smaller, unimpressive, squat brick building was in use, but Gregor couldn't tell for what.

He reached a streetcorner on the other side of the Green from where the restaurant had been and pushed a button for the walk light. When it flashed, he crossed to the side of the street with three tall churches on it and nothing else. One of them was Congregational. He recognized the architecture. The other two were too far away for him to read their signs. He passed the lot of them and found himself, suddenly, in the middle of Yale.

The week between Christmas and New Year's is almost always a vacation week for American colleges and universities. Gregor had forgotten that. At first, the emptiness of the great stone and brick buildings spooked him. The deserted lawns and empty moats seemed futuristic: the scene the day after a clean bomb has destroyed all the people but left the buildings intact. Then he got into the spirit of things. There was something nice about there being no students around. Gregor didn't have to look at scruffy, bearded young men trying desperately to look like enemies of the Establishment they were working so hard to join. He didn't have to look at skeletal young women in tatters and lace. Gregor had never been fond of college Gothic, but Yale did it well. The arched entryways and low moat walls looked more real than the tired modest storefronts around the Green. Even the few more modern buildings had been designed to blend in. Every once in a while, Gregor saw an older man in a sweater or a middle-aged one in tweeds go in or out of one of the doors.

They looked so much like what professors ought to look like, he hoped they were. From everything he had read, professors didn't believe in what this seemed to represent any more: tradition, continuity, the weight and glory of shared history. Gregor didn't know if he believed in it either—especially the glory part; the history of Armenia was chock full of the less than glorious—but walking around in a place like this, it was nice to think he did. Fireplaces with fires in them. High ceilings with heavy beams. Leaded casement windows. Dickens read aloud. The spirit of a traditional English winter. Gregor had had Dickens read out loud to him once, by a young woman he had been dating before he began dating his wife. It had bored him stiff.

The land had gotten hillier and the sidewalks less well cared for. The sidewalks next to the buildings belonging to Yale were well repaired and clear of the slush and snow left over from whenever New Haven had had its last winter storm. Maybe it was just that the sidewalks of the *nice* buildings belonging to Yale were cared for that way. For all Gregor knew, all these buildings, even the really awful ones, were now part of the university. He went down one side street and then another, looking for a way to go that wouldn't plunge his feet into mud or water. He came out on Prospect Street near the steepest swell of the hill. It finally struck him why the name Prospect Street had sounded so familiar to him, even back in Philadelphia, when he thought he'd first heard it. Years ago, when he was still an agent-in-training, a friend of his had had a son with learning disabilities and taken him to the only place on the East Coast at the time that knew anything about them. It was called the Gesell Institute, and it had had an office on Prospect Street. Gregor looked around, but he couldn't see anything calling itself the Gesell Institute. He felt enormously frustrated. Here he was, stuck in this small city he knew nothing about, faced with a murder that seemed to require some knowledge of the area to solve. His police contact was less than no help. He knew nobody else in town. He didn't have the faintest idea how to go about finding out what he needed to know.

He walked farther uphill, slowly and deliberately, checking the names on the signs planted on the lawns in front of the buildings. There was a big modern high-rise thing that identified itself as a science building belonging to Yale; biology, Gregor thought, or some kind of biological research. At the crest of the hill, he passed a long, low white wall encircling a group of buildings a plaque identified as Albertus Magnus College. A Dominican nun in a short, snappy modern habit made up of a short white dress and a less-than-shoulder length black handkerchief veil was crossing the lawn at the front, coatless and gloveless, not visibly shivering. Gregor kept climbing upward until he got to Fountain of Youth. The snow was thicker up here, as if the elevation had caused more of it to fall—but that couldn't be right. The change in elevation wasn't that dramatic. Gregor looked down Fountain of Youth's gravel drive and saw the tail ends of five or six cars in the parking area at the back. The New Year's special program would be in full swing again today. It was easy to tell that New Year's was coming to Fountain of Youth's Victorian pile. Fountain of Youth appeared to be the only place on Prospect Street that was celebrating the event. On the stylized wrought-iron lamppost at the edge of its front walk, there was a clutch of helium-filled balloons in primary colors. Each and every one of them said: "GIVE YOURSELF A NEW YOU FOR THE NEW YEAR."

Well, Gregor told himself, as he went up the front walk to ring the bell. Maybe this will help. Maybe just being at Fountain of Youth without Tony Bandero around to get in my way will be enough to show me what I'm supposed to do next.

He doubted it, but it was worth a try.

— 2 —

Traci Cardinale answered the door, pert and thin and ridiculously cute in a short-skirted suit of scarlet and white. She was wearing a little plastic pin on the lapel of her jacket that said: "Bring Your Body to the Fountain of Youth." She saw Gregor through the security window and nodded vigorously. Then she opened the front door wide.

"Mr. Demarkian. I'm so glad to see you. And after all that fuss yesterday. You never got to talk to anybody."

This was not entirely true. Gregor hadn't had a chance to talk to Simon Roveter, who was the person Tony Bandero had said they were going to talk to. He had, however, talked to at least half a dozen reporters and a cameraman from WTNH News. He knew as much about how the local TV reporters went about getting the story *first* as any native of that region. He had a long talk about it with an extremely pleasant blond woman named Diane Smith, parts of which later showed up on television as an exclusive interview. Well, Gregor thought, it was an exclusive interview. Unlike Tony Bandero, he knew how to give one without getting himself into trouble, even if he gave it by accident.

He shrugged off his coat and let Traci take it from him. "I didn't get to talk to you," he said. "You looked like you were in shock and I had too much else to do."

"I was hysterical," Traci said, giggling. She hung Gregor's coat and came back to her desk. "I was crying and weeping and carrying on all afternoon. I got over it, of course. I mean, an accident is an accident."

"Even so, it must have been a shock. To put your hand against a rail for safety and then to have it collapse on you."

Traci Cardinale looked confused. "I didn't have my hand on the rail when it fell," she said. "I wasn't anywhere near it."

Gregor was confused, too. "But you screamed," he said. "It was your screaming that brought us running. And you were standing on the balcony with your back against the wall the first time I saw you after it happened."

"Oh, I was on the balcony when the whole thing fell over," Traci said, "but that was later. I screamed because a piece of the silly thing nearly fell on my head. Two pieces. The second one fell on my desk."

Gregor looked up at the railing. The gap in the railing was filled in with plywood. It was a nice wide gap. Traci was right. Some of it was almost directly over her desk.

"Pieces of it fell first," Gregor said.

"That's right. I thought at first that one of the two of you must have done it, because I'd just come from you, you know, I'd just left you in Simon's office. Not that I thought you were throwing pieces of the balcony at me or anything.

I just thought maybe Tony was tossing me a note or something."

"Why?"

"I don't know." Trace Cardinale flushed. "I wasn't really thinking about it. I was thinking about Simon and where he could have gone to. And then the pieces fell and then I freaked."

"And then you ran up the stairs," Gregor said, "to the balcony."

"Well, I thought somebody was up there, throwing things at me. It didn't occur to me that there might be something wrong with the railing. I mean, an old house like this, I should have guessed, but I just didn't. I thought someone was playing nasty games and I wanted to stop them."

Gregor looked at the plywood on the balcony rail again. "So when you got to the top, you put your hand on the rail—"

"I had my hand on the rail all along, Mr. Demarkian, but if you mean did I put it right there where the rotten part was, no I didn't. It fell all by itself."

"Without your touching it?"

"That's right. I mean, I suppose it was my fault, Mr. Demarkian. I probably shook it loose running up the stairs the way I did. But it just fell down by itself."

"And then you screamed again."

Traci winced. "It made a lot of noise. I guess I'm not too great to have around in a crisis, am I, Mr. Demarkian? I completely lost my head."

Gregor looked up at the plywood one more time. It was like the puffy scar you got after having a smallpox vaccination. It nagged at him.

"Is there somebody at the reception desk all the time?" he asked. "I don't suppose you work twenty-four hours a day—"

"I work almost that much. Sometimes I stay until ten or eleven o'clock."

"And it's always you? You don't have somebody to relieve you?"

"We have another girl who comes in weekends and when I need some time off or I'm sick, but mostly I work. I get time and a half after forty hours. I can use the money."

"Is this foyer ever left empty?"

"Sure. Late at night and early Sunday morning. Really late on Saturday nights, the place is practically deserted. Nobody wants to hang around if they don't have to. And if they do have to, they're in bed, upstairs."

"I would be, too," Gregor said. "When the place is deserted, as you put it, is it also locked?"

"It's always locked," Traci said. "It has to be. You know the kind of thing that goes on."

"Do the members of the staff have keys?"

"Some of them do. The ones that live in the house. The rest of them don't need keys, really, because there's always somebody to let them in. And you don't want to have too many keys floating around. It's bad enough with the Golden Circle Keyholders."

"What are Golden Circle Keyholders?"

"They're special members. You pay extra—a lot extra, Mr. Demarkian, about five times what a regular membership costs—and you get a key you can use twenty-four hours a day, seven days a week. Just in case you can only make time for exercise at three fifty on Wednesday mornings."

Gregor examined the foyer again: the front doors, the curved staircase, the side doors to the utility corridors. "Is that safe?" he asked. "There's nothing to say that one of your Golden Circle Keyholders couldn't be a thief. Or worse. Give him a key and he could get in whenever he wanted and do whatever he wanted. At the very least, you could get seriously robbed."

"It's not quite that bad," Traci Cardinale said. "All the Golden Circle Keyholders have a key to is the front door. We have a special work-out room down here, down that corridor to your left. That's what we leave open. The rest of the house can be sealed off. We seal it off."

"Every night?"

"You bet. If I'm working late, I do it myself."

"And these Golden Circle Keyholders do have access to this foyer?"

"Of course."

"How many Golden Circle Keyholders have you got?"

Traci Cardinale produced an elaborate, deliberately ironic shrug. "We've got about a dozen, but if you're really worried about one of them skulking around here in the middle of the night, I wouldn't bother. I've been here for ages now, and I've never known a single one of them to use their keys in the off-hours. Most of them don't even exercise much. It's just a status thing, like those Louis Vuitton handbags. We got a new one with this batch, you know. Virginia Hanley. She's just the type. Look-at-how-wonderful-I-am-that-I-have-all-this-money-to-spend."

"Mmm," Gregor said. "But you wouldn't necessarily know, would you, if someone came in late at night? You wouldn't be here. From what you've said, neither would anybody else."

"Well," Traci said, "I could say that we'd know by the way things had been moved around and the way the exercise equipment had been left, because you absolutely wouldn't believe the mess people leave in around here, Keyholders or not. Maybe especially Keyholders. Anyway, we've got video cameras." She pointed toward the front door.

Gregor turned around and saw it, just. It had been very artfully disguised by what looked like just another cluster of plaster fruit. He turned to the entrance to the corridor Traci had indicated was the one with the special work-out room on it and saw that there was another camera there, also disguised by fruit.

"Is the system comprehensive?" he asked her. "No blind spots?"

"I'm sure there could be some blind spots, Mr. Demarkian, but I can't see that somebody could get in and go clomping all over the place around here without getting caught by the cameras at some point. Do you?"

"No," Gregor said.

"I like the security system at this place," Traci said. "I'm the one who has to work alone in this foyer most nights, and I feel really safe. And Tony said it was a good system, too. He checked it out for me."

A buzzer went off on the phone on the little desk and Traci Cardinale picked up the receiver and listened. When she put the phone down again, she said, "That was the nutritional lecture getting out. Simon gives it. They all go in there together, no matter what class they're in. Simon will go down to the kitchen now and have a cup of coffee. He'll be on his own for at least half an hour. I'm sure he wouldn't mind talking to you. This thing with Tim has been on Simon's mind a lot." Traci got up and beckoned him along. "This way. You don't even have to go up any stairs to get there. There aren't any balcony railings to fall down. Isn't that a relief?"

— 3 —

The kitchen, Gregor thought as soon as he saw it, was a much better place to talk to a man about a murder than that office upstairs had been. It was an unpretentious space with a picnic table and windows looking out on the yard where the body had been found. There were no self-consciously tasteful prints or pretentious pieces of furniture to skew the atmosphere. Unfortunately, Simon Roveter looked capable of skewing the atmosphere all on his own. Gregor didn't think he had ever seen a man who looked more like an actor trying to play himself. Graham Greene, that's who Simon Roveter reminded Gregor of—not the writer but the writer's characters. He was even wearing a tan linen suit. It should have looked out of place at this time of the year in this part of the country. But it suited Simon Roveter so well, it didn't. He was an arresting presence, thinning hair, slack jawline, and all. So arresting, it took Gregor a moment to realize that Roveter was not alone. Standing at the far end of the picnic table, positioned a little sideways so that she could see both the kitchen door and out into the yard at the same time, was a woman in well-preserved middle-age: Magda Hale. She wore a bright green spangled leotard and bright green tights with bright green fairy boots to match. She needed to gain at least thirty pounds, just to look normal.

Simon Roveter looked confused when Traci ushered Gregor in, but as soon as he got an introduction, he brightened.

"Excellent," he said. "Excellent. You don't know how glad I am that you came back to talk to us. After all that mess yesterday—"

"I don't think I've ever seen so much confusion," Magda Hale said. "I still don't think it was really necessary to have the police here with their sirens and everything, and I don't know who notified the reporters. It was a circus."

"They made us sound like the Fountain of Death on the news," Simon Roveter said. "This is a bad time for bad publicity, in case you didn't know. We're going national in a week. We've got a forty-city tour lined up. We're opening studios in sixteen new cities across the Midwest and South. We're starting a line of exercise wear. From a business point of view, Tim's death was bad enough. But this—"

"It's not that we look at Tim's death mainly from a business point of view," Magda Hale put in quickly. "We were all very fond of Tim. And, of course, we saw a lot of him."

"He was living in the house," Simon Roveter explained. "Temporarily."

"We often have members of our staff living in the house," Magda Hale put in. "Especially high-level members we really need to keep. We can't always pay a lot in absolute cash terms, but this is a lovely place to live. In a good neighborhood. It's a great incentive."

"Tim wasn't here on that basis, though," Simon Roveter said. "He was just temporarily between apartments."

"He had to get out of his last one because they tore the building down," Magda Hale said. "I think it might have been condemned."

If the staff had to live in buildings that were about to be condemned, Fountain of Youth must need an incentive like rooms in the house to keep good people. Gregor wondered how much this pair kept for themselves. He didn't have the expertise to judge the relative costs of exercise clothes, but those would surely be considered a business expense in this case. The tan linen suit was off the rack, but not cheap.

Gregor walked over to the picnic table and looked out the window into the backyard. "I've just been talking to Miss Cardinale about your security systems. The cameras. The Golden Circle Keyholders. If you'd ever asked me about it, I would have told you it wasn't a very good idea."

Simon Roveter nodded. "The Golden Circle Keyholders, you mean. I agree with you. I'm afraid we just got stuck with it. It started with our studio out in California, which is just a regular studio without a house attached to it, and then one of our members from out there moved out here." He shrugged.

"People are really very, very picky," Magda Hale said. "I tried to explain that to the detective, that Mr. Bandero, but I just couldn't seem to get across. I don't think he's a man who listens very well, do you?"

"He's a policeman," Simon Roveter said. "He has a job to do. He isn't supposed to listen to us complain about our clients."

"I'm not complaining about our clients." Magda spoke sharply. "I'm just explaining something. I don't feel we've been served very well by the police in this matter."

She's older than she looks, Gregor thought. She's at least as old as I am. He stood awkwardly at the table, wondering what he was supposed to do next. That was the trouble with not having been brought fully into the police case. He didn't know what these people had been asked. He didn't know what blind alleys Tony Bandero had already stumbled into. He wished these two people didn't make him so uncomfortable.

Gregor moved away from the table and walked around the room. It was a nice but perfectly ordinary kitchen. Refrigerator. Cook top. Oven. Microwave. Sink. He stopped at a door at the back of the room.

"Where does this go?" he said. "To the backyard?"

"No, no," Simon Roveter told him. "The door to the backyard is down the hall you came through to get here. That's the door to the pantry."

"It's a wonderful walk-in pantry," Magda Hale said. "You should take a look at it. This house has been gutted and renovated at least six times before we did it, but nobody's ever renovated the pantry. I don't know why they don't design them into houses these days. I'm sure the women of America could use them."

Gregor opened the pantry door and stuck his head inside. It was too dark to see, but he could smell a sharp sourness that he imagined must be rotting vegetables. It was strong enough to make him queasy.

"There's a light switch right there on the wall next to the

door to your right," Magda Hale said. "You'll never see anything in the dark."

Gregor reached around and found the switch. The smell was really awful, thick and wet and sharp. A triple row of track lights embedded in the ceiling sprang on. The room was full of muted pinks and greens directed at bins of vegetables and shelves of other vegetables in cans. Nothing was directed at the body on the floor, but the body was there, crumpled into a heap, and there was no doubt at all that it was dead.

"Oh, my God," Magda Hale said, coming up beside Gregor. "It's Stella Mortimer."

Gregor must have stepped back when he saw what was in there on the floor. He didn't remember doing it, but he was now out of the way of the door, giving everyone in the kitchen a clear look at what he had found.

He had forgotten that Traci Cardinale was still in the room. Now she rushed up to the door, took one look at the corpse lying on the floor, and started screaming again.

Dear Jesus Christ, Gregor thought. Doesn't this woman ever do anything else?

Part 2

"Nobody really wants to turn over a new leaf and start a whole new life. They'd only make just as much of a mess of it as they've made of the one they have."

—ALTERNATIVE PSYCHOTHERAPIST,
Psychology Today

ONE

— 1 —

Tony Bandero was in the house. He had been in the house for hours. The enormity of this—that Tony had gotten him all the way out from Philadelphia and then cut him out of the loop; that Tony had made him look like a cross between Sherlock Holmes and Nero Wolfe in the newspapers and then done everything possible to ensure that he could not perform even as well as he normally did—did not strike Gregor at first. There was too much to do. Gregor had never been in on a scene of the crime when he was an agent with the Bureau. The Bureau didn't work that way. Even when Gregor was chasing serial killers, all he ever really did was to sit at a computer, or at the head of a table full of people who knew more about computers than he did, and talk about things that had happened miles away in Seattle and Salt Lake. Every once in a while, he had gone out to the places where crimes had happened months, or even years, before. He had stood at the edge of a ditch where a soft-spoken young man who worked for the phone company and collected Mickey Mouse cartoons on videotape had buried sixteen five-year-old boys. He had walked around the edges of dense thicket of brush where a drifter with a record as long as the *Oxford Unabridged Dictionary* had murdered the college sorority girl he had kidnapped three states away. The scenes were always sanitized and past usefulness, spiritual journeys instead of professional ones. Gregor hadn't seen an actual murder scene, with the body on the floor and the tech men trying to measure the distances between ruts in the carpet, until he was retired and living on Cavanaugh Street. That was his first extracurricular murder and the case that had introduced him to Bennis Hannaford. That was also the case that had started *The Philadelphia Inquirer* calling him "The Armenian-American Hercule Poirot." By now, everybody had picked up on "The Armenian-American Hercule Poirot," a circumstance that made Gregor a little crazy. He wasn't anything like Hercule Poirot. He wasn't small. He wasn't short. He wasn't fussy. He didn't go around telling everybody what a wonderful brain he had, because he often wasn't sure that his brain was that wonderful. He couldn't think of a fictional detective he was anything like. They were all much too sure of themselves. He knew which fictional detective he would like to be. Nero Wolfe got to sit in a chair and eat all day. He was never present at the scenes of crimes where middle-aged women seemed to have strangled on their own vomit.

Stella Mortimer hadn't strangled on her own vomit. Gregor knew enough about how people died from arsenic poisoning to know that. She would have been sick, yes. She would have had cramps. She would have been violently and painfully ill for at least half an hour. She wouldn't have fallen flat over until the very end, and then it would have been too late for her to strangle on anything. She would have been dead. This was different from cyanide, where the victim died right away, and from taxine, where the effect was so slow that strangling would have been eminently possible. Stella Mortimer hadn't died from either cyanide or taxine. She wasn't blue along her jawline. Her face hadn't turned that odd color, like ecru dough. He couldn't really know for sure until the lab tests had been done, and the medical examiner had made his pronouncements: but under the circumstances, he thought he had a right to make a guess. Tim Bradbury had died of arsenic poisoning. It was going to turn out that Stella Mortimer had died of it, too.

Tony Bandero came in while Gregor was on the kitchen

phone, trying to arrange for the right New Haven cops to arrive at this scene—looking, in fact, for Tony himself. The door to the pantry was closed tight. So was a door to the pantry that came in on the other side, from some kind of servants' staircase. Gregor had gone around the long way and shut it. Of course, the scene wasn't secure. Gregor didn't know enough about these people to have any sense of who he might be able to trust. It was better than nothing. He had even been careful to use a handkerchief when closing the pantry's back door, just in case there were useful fingerprints on the doorknob.

By the time Tony Bandero came in, Gregor was talking to Philip Brye, asking for instructions.

"I'll make the call myself," the medical examiner was saying. "It's not that complicated if you know what you're doing."

Obviously, Gregor wanted to say, I don't know what I'm doing. Why should I?

Then Tony Bandero was there, swaying in the kitchen doorway, his thick flabby bulk rippling the surface of his brown wool suit. His suit, if anything, was more wrinkled and creased than it had been the day before. It was like he was pretending to be Colombo and making a bad job of it. Gregor gave Philip Brye the news of Tony's arrival and hung up. Then he turned to Tony and demanded, "Just where did you come from?"

It was Magda Hale, not Tony Bandero, who answered. She sounded puzzled. "He's been here since quarter to nine this morning," she said, "interviewing people. We were all so disappointed that you couldn't come, too."

"Couldn't?" Gregor asked.

Tony Bandero pushed his way across the room to where Gregor was standing and then beyond him. Traci Cardinale was still screaming, but he didn't even look at her.

"What's going on here?" he demanded.

It was Magda Hale who answered, again. "It's Stella Mortimer. She's in the pantry."

"Dead," Gregor added.

Tony looked from Gregor to Magda Hale to Simon Roveter to Traci Cardinale, whose screaming had become background noise, unheard and unimportant. Then he went to the pantry door and opened it up.

"Jesus Christ," he said.

"I've been trying to call you," Gregor said.

Tony closed the pantry door. "I'll call myself," he said. "Even if she just got sick and died—"

"She was poisoned," Gregor said firmly.

"You can't possibly know that," Tony shot back.

"I know it as well as I know anything," Gregor told him. "I'm the one who's good at poison, do you remember? That was supposedly one of the reasons you wanted me to come out here."

"You can't tell if somebody's been poisoned unless you see them die." Tony was stubborn. "And even then, you're making a guess."

"She was poisoned. I'll bet my life on it. She was poisoned with arsenic. I'll bet my left leg on it. You should call your cops in, Tony. We need the tech men."

"I didn't say we weren't going to call the tech men," Tony said. "Under the circumstances, I'd call the tech men if a butterfly farted around here. I'm only saying—"

"Oh, stop arguing," Magda Hale said desperately. "Please stop arguing. I don't think I can stand it anymore."

Traci Cardinale had stopped screaming. Gregor didn't know when. She had backed up until she was flat against the wall next to the windows looking out on the backyard, sat down on the floor, and rolled into a ball. Magda Hale was crying.

"All right," Tony said. "I'm going to make a call."

Gregor got away from the phone. "Go right ahead."

Tony picked up, turned his back to the rest of them, and started dialing.

"Good God," Simon Roveter said.

Gregor sat down on the bench at the picnic table. "Who was she?" he asked Magda and Simon. It would have been useless to ask Traci Cardinale anything. "A guest? A member? One of the staff?"

"Stella was our videotape director," Simon Roveter said. "We make exercise tapes here that you can buy to bring home with you. So you can work out even if you can't get into the club."

"She's been with us absolutely forever," Magda Hale said. "Since about the fifth year we were in operation, and we've been open for nearly twenty. Of course, it wasn't videotapes back then. It was commercials for the local stations. Stella made them for us."

"She had a background in film?" Gregor asked.

"She made a couple of highly acclaimed documentaries when she was younger," Simon Roveter replied. "One on what she called the Bubba drug culture. Rednecks with long hair who smoke dope. That was back in '68 or '70. One on welfare mothers. That was a couple of years later."

"You can't make any money on documentaries," Magda explained. "Unless you're doing really sensationalistic ones on murder trials or executions or something. I think by the time she came to us, she was tired of scrambling around for cash."

"Did she live here, in the house?"

Magda Hale shook her head. "Oh, no. Stella wouldn't have liked that. She was a very reclusive person. She had an apartment out near the Co-Op someplace."

"Alone? With a husband? With a lover?"

"Alone," Magda said definitely. "I know she was never married. She always said she didn't approve of it. And I know she wasn't living with a lover, because I don't think—" Magda stopped.

"What is it?" Gregor asked her.

Magda waved her hands helplessly in the air. "It's just odd," she said. "I was just going to say that I didn't think Stella believed in lovers any more than she believed in husbands, and then I realized that I didn't really know that. I've known the woman for fifteen years, and I didn't really know that. I'm not even sure, if Stella ever had a lover, I'm not even sure what sex the lover would be."

"Oh, God," Simon Roveter groaned.

Magda turned to him. "But Simon, it's true. It's really true. I never asked and she never said, never once in all those years. And it's even odder, because yesterday we were talking about that, about how we all work here but we don't really know very much about each other, about what goes on on the outside. Stella said our relationship with each other was different, but now I'm not so sure it was."

"What got you started talking about that kind of thing?" Simon looked bewildered.

Magda made another of her helpless gestures. "It was Tim, of course. Stella was all upset because we knew so little about him. I think she thought there was something disrespectful in that, disrespectful to the dead, or maybe just that it was a wrong way to be about somebody you knew who had died. She kept saying that she wished the papers would be better about it, so that we could find out what his life had been like."

"We know what his life was like," Simon said. "He lived right here in the house."

"She meant what his life was like outside."

"There wasn't anything to know about Tim Bradbury's life outside. He was a local kid who wanted to go to California."

Magda Hale sighed. "You always make it sound so easy and uncomplicated, Simon, but it isn't. People have histories. Even people like Tim. Stella only wanted . . . to feel like she'd been more of a friend, I think."

"She wasn't a friend. She barely knew him. None of us knew him. He taught weight-training sessions." Simon sounded impatient. "—The kind of knowing you're talking about is the kind that only happens between confidants. Or lovers."

"Oh, Simon. You don't have to be a confidant, or a lover, to know if somebody's parents are alive or if they tried out for their high school basketball team or if they dated women or men. Casual acquaintances know that much about each other sometimes."

"My casual acquaintances don't."

"Simon is a very private man," Magda said to Gregor. "If he were a Catholic, he would only go to confession to a priest who had been struck dumb."

Tony Bandero thumped the phone receiver down. "It's all set up," he announced. "The tech men are on their way. Some uniforms are on their way. An ambulance is on its way. Does that satisfy everybody?"

"It's a start," Gregor said.

Tony Bandero's face reddened. "At this point the procedures are routine," he said. I'm sorry I don't share your sense of emergency, Demarkian, but there's no emergency here. We don't have a bunch of terrorists holding hostages on the roof. We've got a dead body that isn't going to be going any place soon."

Traci Cardinale hadn't moved in minutes. Now she did, slowly at first, then faster and faster, unfolding herself and standing straight up at the same time. She was shaking and her face was streaked with tears, but she didn't looked anguished as much as she looked angry. In fact, she looked furious.

"You," she spat out in the direction of Tony Bandero. "I can't believe you. How can you be so callous? How can you be such a—such a son of a bitch?"

It might have been interesting to find out what Tony Bandero had to say to all that, but nobody got the chance. Because Traci Cardinale walked up to him, reared back her right arm, and slapped him resoundingly across the face. Then she whirled on her heel and marched out of the kitchen.

— 2 —

Tony Bandero must have called the press at the same time he called the tech men. The press arrived first, in the form of a WTNH mobile news van that pulled up the drive and parked right in front of the front door. Then the reporter for *The New Haven Register* arrived and parked his ancient Volkswagen Beetle behind the mobile news van, blocking any chance it had of being able to turn around and get out on the street again. Then the van for the CBS affiliate showed up and parked behind the Volkswagen Beetle. Nobody went to the back, where there was a sizable parking lot filled with the cars of people who would not be allowed to be in a hurry. When the tech men arrived, they had to go back there. The ambulance had to park on the street.

"It's one of Phil Brye's ambulances," Bandero told Gregor. "Don't worry about that. I'm not having the body sent to Yale New Haven."

Gregor hadn't been worried about it. What he was worried about was getting the tech men and the other official people into the house without letting in a lot of reporters and letting out half the attendees at the Fountain of Youth's New Year's special exercise week. The attendees were getting particularly frantic. The seeds of the panic mentality had been planted. Ever since the murder of Stella Mortimer had become generally known—which had taken no time at all, really; Gregor could never believe how fast these things spread—rumors had been jumping from one class to the next. There was a serial killer loose in the house. There was poison in the food. The house was being used as a center for drug gangs. It didn't matter how preposterous the theories were. They all sounded real enough to a crowd of women who had been exercised into exhaustion and half starved to death all day. Gregor watched the ripples of fear and worry spread through the classes like fault lines. Give any one of them a push in the wrong direction, and the plates would start moving, whatever weak bulwark of calmness and control was left would come tumbling down.

The head of the mobile crime unit was not a tech man, but a tech woman. Gregor let her in through the back door, both because it was the door closest to where the van had parked and because the reporters were waiting around the front. The women in the classes were around at the front, too, spread out across the foyer and up the stairs to the second-floor balcony, just as they had been after the railing fell the morning before. Philip Brye himself pulled in behind the mobile crime unit van. He drove a Volvo so battered it looked like it ought to have been awarded battle medals. When he got out of the car, he was wearing a large enameled pin on his coat that said: "DON'T DRINK AND DRIVE. BE ALIVE TO SEE IN THE NEW YEAR." Gregor stood at the back door, holding it open as the doctor ran the last few steps. Tony Bandero stood behind him in the first-floor hallway, snorting.

"Phil," Tony Bandero said, as the medical examiner stepped inside. "I'm surprised. Didn't think you made house calls anymore."

Philip Brye unbuttoned his coat. "I'm taking an interest in this case," he replied. Then he held his hand out to

Gregor. "Hello, Mr. Demarkian. I didn't expect to see you again so soon."

"Again," Tony Bandero said.

"Mr. Demarkian came to see me at the morgue this morning. You did tell me I was supposed to answer any questions he put to me, Tony. You told everyone in the department."

"I didn't know Demarkian had been out this morning, that's all. I thought he was sleeping in this morning."

"I never told you I was sleeping in," Gregor said.

Two ambulance men appeared around the back of the house, carrying a colapsed stretcher between them. Gregor opened the back door for them, too.

"The thing is," Tony Bandero said, "stuff around here seems to be getting out of control. We're not coordinated, that's the problem. We've got to let each other know what we're doing or we're going to be stepping on each other's toes."

"I take it that the scene of the crime is this way." Philip Brye pointed in the direction the tech woman had gone in.

Actually, Gregor thought, the scene of the crime could have been anywhere on this floor. Men and women in white coats seemed to be everywhere he looked, taking fingerprints, photographing floorboards, measuring the distances between nails in the walls. Gregor knew that all the things they did were important. Cases had failed because of inadequate or incompetent tech work. He just didn't understand exactly what it was the tech people did.

He went back into the kitchen. Magda Hale and Simon Roveter had been ordered out. They had probably gone to sit in the foyer with their work-out students. Tech people were attacking the kitchen, too, and the pantry door was open. As Gregor watched, Philip Brye backed out of there, shaking his head. The stench was worse than awful now. It had soured and spread.

"Well?" Gregor asked Philip Brye.

"Poisoned," Philip Brye said. "That's virtually certain. Arsenic would be a good guess."

"That's what I told Tony Bandero."

"And?"

"He told me I couldn't possibly know that until the lab reports came in."

"Well, that's true enough. That doesn't mean you have to act like you never saw a dead body before. And there's one relief here, at least. It's not like Tim. We don't have to wonder where this woman died or how her body got here. And she is, thank God, fully clothed."

"I wonder what she took the arsenic in," Gregor said. "And when. And where."

"Assuming it was a good strong dose, she took it half an hour ago or so, that's when. As to where, I wouldn't know. As to in what—well, the lab reports will probably tell us. We'll do a stomach content analysis."

"What had Tim Bradbury taken the arsenic in?"

"Hot chocolate. Very sweet hot chocolate."

Gregor considered this. "Do you know what's always bothered me about poisoners?" he asked. "Poison is not like a gun, or a knife. You can't aim it at somebody and let it go from there. A poisoner has two choices. Either he can put the poison in something in his victim's possession. Or he can feed the poison to his victim himself. Those are the only two things he can do. "But they both have drawbacks," Gregor continued. "If the poisoner puts the poison in something his victim already owns, then the first thing that happens is that he loses control of the time schedule. Some are on regular medication or take vitamin capsules at a scheduled time every day, but most people don't. And some people who do do one or the other take pills instead of capsules, and it's damned hard to put poison in a pill." He sighed. "Then you have the innocent bystander factor. Unless the poisoner is dealing with prescription medication, there's always the chance that somebody else will end up dead instead of the intended victim. The victim's girlfriend decides to take one of his time-release cold capsules and gets the wrong one. The victim's mother decides she needs a little herb tea this morning and opens the wrong box. It gets messy. I think that's why, in all the years I've been working, I've only known of one case where the poisoner operated that way."

"In your experience, most murderers like to watch their victims die," Philip Brye said.

Gregor was startled, but not completely surprised. "You

know," he said, "I think that's true. Not only of the poisoners I've known in my career, but of all the other murderers, no matter what kind of murderer they were. I knew someone once who poisoned a man with lye and stood right there and watched him drink it."

"Ouch. How did he get conned into drinking it?"

"That's the problem the direct poisoner has," Gregor said. "He makes coffee for himself and his victim. He puts the poison in his victim's coffee. Now what he's got to do is get his victim to drink it. Which means, in the first place, that the victim can't suspect that the murderer would go so far as to kill him."

"Most people wouldn't suspect that," Philip Brye pointed out.

"True," Gregor said, "but most people who end up murdered in complicated and deliberate ways such as this do know that their murderers hate them, or have a reason to fear them, or want something out of them. They're not entirely without a clue. And what if we're not talking about the first victim?"

"Do you think victims always suspect?"

"Well," Gregor said. "Let's look at what we have here. First, Tim Bradbury is poisoned and his nude body is dumped in the yard. Then, yesterday, a piece of the balcony railing falls down and causes havoc, on the premises and in the media. These are both high-profile events."

"True."

"So," Gregor went on, "what we have here is, we have a house in a crisis atmosphere, part of something that probably looks to the people who are living here to be creepy and maybe nearly supernatural. You can see the mood people are in."

"Now."

"Now it's worse, yes, but it was bad when I was here yesterday. Especially after that railing fell."

"I don't see what you're getting at." Phil Brye was coughing again.

"What I'm getting at is, either this woman died because she ate or drank something arsenic had been placed in or she was fed arsenic by someone who did not make her think that she might be at risk. If she ate or drank something poison had been placed in, we have a very serious situation here, because that would mean we have a poisoner who just doesn't care."

"But that isn't what you think," Philip Brye said.

"No," Gregor admitted, "it isn't. I think she took something from somebody, something she was deliberately handed. I wish I knew more of what she was like, if she was a suspicious person or a pragmatic one, if she was optimistic or pessimistic. I wish I knew whether the chances were good or poor that she would have felt it necessary, in the present circumstances, to look out for herself."

"My guess is that the chances are nil," Tony Bandero put in.

Gregor and Philip Brye turned to him in surprise. He must have been standing there for quite some time, Gregor realized, and he must have been very interested in hearing what Gregor had to say. When Tony Bandero wasn't interested, he interrupted. Now he was rocking back and forth on his feet with his hands stuck into the pockets of his pants, his red face getting redder with every moment.

"The chances are nil," he repeated, even more positively this time. "In my experience, nobody ever expects to get murdered except the professionals. The professionals are always watching out for it. But everybody else—" Tony gave a massive shrug. "Some woman starts nagging at her husband, putting him down, screaming and yelling at him, one day he takes out a forty-five and shoots her dead, and you can see it in her face, she was *surprised*."

In Gregor's experience, this was not the usual scenario when husbands killed wives. He let it go.

"It's really useless to speculate about this anyway," he said. "We don't know anything about her yet. Dr. Brye hasn't even gotten confirmation that this was an arsenic poisoning."

"I haven't even asked for one."

"Maybe it'll turn out to be a stroke or something," Tony said. "If it doesn't, I think we've got to go with the idea that what we've got here is a nut. That's what you're really the expert in, Mr. Demarkian, isn't it? Nuts?"

Gregor was expert enough on the subject of what Tony Bandero called "nuts" to know that these two deaths didn't have the shape or feel of the start of a serial murder case. He let this go, too.

"Why don't we just let your technical people do their work," he told Tony Bandero. "We can talk this all out later, when we finally have something to say."

TWO

— 1 —

There were police in the house again, and Frannie Jay was in a state of paralysis. Again. That was what she couldn't help thinking about, sitting on the stairs in the foyer, listening to the sounds of them at the back of the first floor. This was happening to her *again*. How many times was it going to happen to her before she just lost it, before she went so rigid at the terror of it that she couldn't move anymore? She thought of herself answering questions at the table after Tim Bradbury died: *When did you meet him? How long had you known him? What were you doing looking out the window that made it possible for you to see his foot?* There were all those gleaming copper molds hanging from the beams in the kitchen. There were all those stainless-steel bowls sitting on the kitchen counters. She thought of herself sitting on the back steps of the house in California, the steps that led to the beach: *Where were you? What were you doing? What happened next?* The policeman in California had been young and grim and very angry. He had made it clear to her from the beginning that he thought it was all her fault. Frannie remembered only the little silk flower he had worn through one of the buttonholes on his blue shirt, a poppy in honor of Veteran's Day. The smell coming in from the ocean was high and rank. The air was wet and cold. Out here it was always cold. Frannie had been freezing since the moment she stepped off her bus. How long was it going to take them to think of the obvious? Before she came, everything was fine. Since she came, two people had been murdered. She might even have murdered them.

It was late now, after five. The work-out students had had their names and addresses taken by the police and had been sent home. Half a dozen of them or so would not be back, but most of them would. Frannie knew how it worked. Most people didn't really believe it could happen to them. Most people were not smart enough to be afraid. They were excited. They imagined telling the story to friends and acquaintances, when it was over. *Do you remember those murders at the Fountain of Youth Work-Out Studio? Well, I was taking a class there at the time ...*

The foyer was empty, except for the occassional policeman or lab technician passing through to one of the vehicles outside. Most of the press vans had been forced out of the driveway into the road. There were still reporters and cameramen out there, but they were on foot. WTNH had a delay-remote setup out on Prospect Street. When the local news came on this evening, the pretty black woman who had already stopped her three times (*Can you tell us what the feelings of the staff are at this moment?*) would be standing in front of the house, holding a microphone to her lips and pretending that she wasn't being chilled to pneumonia by the wind. Frannie wondered where the rest of the staff had gone. Magda and Simon were holed up in their bedroom. That was to be expected. Nick Bannerman and Traci Cardinale and Cici Mahoney and Susan Dietz and all those people seemed just to have disappeared. Maybe they had gone out for pizza without asking her to come along. Maybe it would be here like it was in California, after it was all over. Maybe she would functionally cease to exist.

A young patrolman carrying a white paper bag came through from the back, glanced without interest at Frannie sitting at the bottom of the stairs, and went out the front door. He was walking very fast and looking very distracted. Frannie stood up and flexed her knees. She couldn't really tell if she was stiff from fear or from too much exercise. If everyone else had gone out without her, there was nothing she could do about it. If she confronted them with it, they would only deny it. They would say that they hadn't been able to find her or that they hadn't thought she would be interested. In California, after her picture had been in the paper, there were people who hadn't been able to find her when she was sitting next to them on the bus.

Frannie went up the steps and onto the landing. From there she could see through the fan window over the front door and out onto the lawn that sloped to Prospect Street. That police detective, Tony Bandero, was standing in the middle of a crowd of people, apparently giving an interview. He always seemed to be giving interviews. Frannie went through the doors onto the second floor proper. She passed the exercise studio where the beginners' class worked out and went to the door to the back staircase. Somebody, probably Simon, had gotten ambitious between yesterday and today. The walls on this floor were now decorated with life-size cardboard cutout posters of Magda Hale, the new ones where she was standing on a double-decker pyramid of words that read; "THE BEST NEW YEAR'S RESOLUTION YOU'LL EVER MAKE."

Frannie climbed up past the third floor, where Magda and Simon were, to the landing that led to her own bedroom. The hallway was dark. The window at the other end of it was heavily curtained and the curtains were closed. Frannie shook her head. What difference did it make if the curtains were closed? It was evening and January. The hallway would be dark even if the curtains were wide open and the sashes were all the way up. She found a light switch and used it. Little globe lights made to look like nineteenth-century gas lamps sprang on in two long lines on either side of the hall. They didn't do much good, but at least they showed the path to Frannie's bedroom door. After this, I'll have to lock it when I leave it, she thought. It wasn't locked now. She went down to it, opened up, and turned on her overhead light.

"Frannie?" somebody said from behind her.

Frannie jumped nearly a half foot in the air—and then instantly felt guilty about it. She realized that she was trembling in every part of her body, and had been for quite some time. She forced herself to turn slowly in the direction of the voice and to keep her face perfectly blank. Nick Bannerman was coming down the hall to her from the direction of the main staircase.

"Oh," Frannie said.

"I frightened you." Nick was already out of his exercise clothes. He was wearing black jeans and a black turtleneck and a big oversize black cotton sweater. With his dark skin, set in a shadowed room or on an unlit street corner, he would just have disappeared.

"You didn't frighten me," Frannie told him. "I'm jumpy."

"Everybody's jumpy." Nick stopped at the door. "I just got finished talking to the world's greatest detective and I'm absolutely wrung out. I thought if you hadn't eaten yet, you might want to come out with me for some food."

"I haven't eaten yet." Frannie thought of the way she had talked to this man just hours ago at the beginning of the day and blushed a little. She had been having one of her moods. She had been behaving as strangely as hell. She looked into her room and was glad to see she had made the bed this morning. "By the world's greatest detective, did you mean Gregor Demarkian?"

"No, I didn't mean Demarkian. I meant our own personal cop, Tony frigging Bandero. Excuse me. He talked to me for forty-five minutes and then he marched straight out onto the front lawn and told a crowd of reporters that he had a serious suspect in the case, but he couldn't name him before he had more evidence. Meaning *me*. Which is, quite frankly, bullshit. I'm just the one Tony Bandero *wants* to be guilty."

"Why?" Frannie was totally bewildered.

"Well," Nick said drily, "I am the only African-American male in the group. And we all know how violent African-American males can be."

"Oh. Does he say it like that? Does he say African-American like that, I mean."

"He just says it. I don't think the switch in nomenclature is working out too well. Jesse made a mistake with this one."

"Jesse?"

"Jackson."

"Oh," Frannie said again. This was hopeless. She had heard of Jesse Jackson, sort of, but she couldn't really pin him down. Some kind of Afri—black politician, she thought. Or maybe Negro? What was the right thing to say these days? Frannie didn't know any black people really well. The ones she knew casually—the head teller at her bank in California; the preschool teacher who had the house next to hers on the beach—she wasn't in a position to talk about race with. Or "nomenclature." Frannie's mother didn't know any black people either, but she talked about them enough. "Those people" was how she put it. Frannie *knew* that was the wrong thing to say.

She looked back over her shoulder into her room. "Well," she said. "I'd love to get something to eat. I just need to get changed."

"Wear black and wrap your hair up in a hat," Nick told her. "We'll sneak out the back way."

"Is that necessary, sneaking out the back way?"

"It is if you don't want to end up on Channel eight."

Frannie desperately didn't want to end up on Channel 8. "Well," she said. "I—um—I have to take a quick shower and then, well, I can't ask you in while I'm getting dressed because—um—"

"Oh, no. I understand."

"Well, I'll only be a few minutes. If you could just, uh—"

"I'll wait down on the second-floor balcony," Nick said quickly. "I've got some reading I have to do anyway."

"I'll be about twenty minutes."

"Good."

"Good," Frannie repeated. Then she blushed again.

Good heavens, she thought. How many years have I been dating? How many times have I said yes to an offer to go out? Doesn't it ever get any easier?

The answer, as far as Frannie could tell, was no.

— 2 —

When Virginia Hanley walked into the New Temple Bar, the television in the back was turned to *WTNH Action News* and Detective Tony Bandero was talking about the important suspect he had and how close he was to closing the case. Virginia took this with a grain of salt. It was all dope and *them*, that's what it was. "Them" was Virginia's currently favored term for Hispanics from South America. That was where all the dope came from, South America, but Virginia didn't really blame the South Americans. The South Americans were just trying to get rich. It was the North Americans Virginia had absolutely no respect for. There was no way to tell what the North Americans were getting out of their part in the drug trade, except poorer by the minute and dead too soon. Or maybe not soon enough. Virginia hadn't really thought this through. It was not on her agenda. She was just tired of listening to the sound of Detective Tony Bandero's voice, and she didn't believe him when he said he knew what he was doing. Virginia didn't believe any man when he said he knew what he was doing.

The New Temple Bar had streamers wrapped around the decorative wood posts that were supposed to look like they were holding up the ceiling. It was one of those places that had been heavily antiqued when it was built, to make it fit what the owners thought Yale had been like back in the 1920s and 1930s. Virginia didn't believe the vision was accurate. She wasn't old enough to have known Yale in the 1920s and 1930s, but she had known it in the 1950s, when it was still supposed to have had its cachet intact—all-male senior societies; no multiculturalism; no gay and lesbian studies or shanty-town protests in the quads. Yale in the 1950s had been nothing at all like the New Temple Bar.

Virginia sat down at the bar and ordered a martini with an olive. Steve and Linda Bonnard were sitting with their knees together at a little round table all the way back in the corner near the rest rooms. Steve had a martini with an olive, too, but Linda had only a glass of white wine. Linda Bonnard did things like that. She bought ecologically sensitive notepaper. She knew which cosmetic products had and which had not been tested on animals. She put her savings in an investment fund that promised not to do business with South Africa. Next to her on the table now, she had a thick paperback book that Virginia knew—because Virginia knew that Steve had loaned it to her—was *Culture and Imperial-*

ism by Edward Said. Virginia's martini came and she took a sip of it, swinging her legs above the floor as she did. Bar stools were always too tall for her.

Steve was hunched over the table, far forward in his chair, talking earnestly. Linda had her legs crossed at the ankles and her hands in her lap. They looked—sweet, Virginia decided. Like a hyperintellectual college couple trying to convince each other that the only thing that mattered in a love affair was a lover's mind.

Virginia hopped off her stool, picked up her martini, and walked across the room to the back. She put her glass down on the small round table Steve and Linda were sharing and pulled a chair away from the empty table next to it. She was very, very aware of looking very, very good. Linda was wearing a dull-colored jersey thing that made her legs look heavy and shapeless. Virginia was wearing her best green silk dress and full makeup. Besides, Linda's legs *were* heavy and shapeless. Virginia's had always been very, very good.

"Oh, Christ," Steve said, watching Virginia sit down.

Linda sat up a little straighter in her chair. "Hello, Virginia," she said carefully. "I didn't know the New Temple was one of the places you customarily came to."

"It has been lately," Virginia said.

Steve finished the rest of his martini in a gulp. "Let's get out of here," he said. "Let's go eat somewhere. Let's go back to your place."

"I don't think we have to go to extremes," Linda said.

Linda never went to extremes. Virginia took her olive out of her drink and ate it.

"I was just trying to tell you something important," she said dreamily, "something I thought you'd really want to know."

"What I want to know from you, I can hear from your lawyers," Steve said.

"But there wasn't time to go through the lawyers. There's a certain element of time involved. And I didn't want you to be embarrassed."

"I'm embarrassed by your being here," Steve said. "I'm embarrassed now."

"Shh," Linda said. "She could have gotten some mail for

you. There could have been a phone call to the Orange house. You don't know what's going on here."

"All your credit cards have been canceled," Virginia said.

Steve Hanley was usually a very expressive man. His eyebrows twitched. His mouth twisted into grimaces and grins. The creases on his forehead rose and fell. Now, Virginia was tickled to see, he was completely blank. It was as if a magic genie had popped up in the middle of the table and turned him into a doll. Virginia nearly laughed out loud.

"What do you mean, all my credit cards have been canceled? Why would they have been canceled?"

"Because I canceled them."

"You couldn't have canceled them. They don't let anyone cancel credit cards. They insist on talking to the cardholder."

"They would talk to Sharon Abruzzi about your credit cards. They do it all the time."

"Sharon Abruzzi is my secretary."

"Well," Virginia said, "they don't have a voice print on her, do they? Any woman could call up and say she was Sharon Abruzzi, if she knew enough about Sharon Abruzzi."

"I don't understand this," Linda said. "Why would you want to do this? What are you going to get out of this?"

"I told them that your wallet had been stolen and all your cards were in it. That was really all they needed to hear."

"Virginia, for God's sake," Linda said. "What good does it do to try to hold onto a man who doesn't want you?"

"I don't think wanting has anything to do with it," Virginia said. "I don't care a fart in hell for what he wants."

"What good does it do to try to get revenge?" Linda asked. "What do you get out of that except more miserable?"

"I'm not more miserable," Virginia said. "It's this son of a bitch who's more miserable."

"I've got to check this out." Steve stood up abruptly and pulled his wallet out of his back pocket. "I'll be right back."

Virginia had only half her martini left, so she decided to nurse it. She had deliberately not taken a tranquilizer before she came out here—tranquilizers took too much of the edge off—so she had nothing but the liquor to keep her steady in the face of all this pressure. Linda was steady without anything at all, but that was Linda. Steady. Reliable. Even-tempered. Calm. Virginia wondered if she managed to work up the energy to get excited during sex. Or to fake it.

"I can't believe you're doing this," Linda said. "I really can't believe it."

Steve was coming back from the phone booths in the vestibule. His face was white.

"You really did it," he said, as soon as he was within earshot of the table. "You really did."

"You can't have checked all those cards that fast," Linda said.

"I didn't. I checked my Visa card. I wasn't going to stand out there all night arguing with clerks in South Dakota about whether my cards had been stolen or not."

"But maybe she just got one of them canceled," Linda said. "Maybe she just got lucky and you picked the only one."

"I got all of them canceled," Virginia said.

"I've got an automatic debit on my Visa card," Steve said. "My car insurance goes on my Visa card."

"It won't," Virginia said.

"I'm going to sue you," Steve said. "I'm going to get a court order to get rid of you. Like hell I'm going to let you have the house."

"I don't want the house."

"Steve," Linda said.

Virginia stood up. She hadn't noticed it before, but the New Temple Bar was heavily decorated in anticipation of New Year's Eve. They didn't call it New Year's Eve, though. They called it Auld Lang Syne and left little business card–size pieces of cardboard on all the tables inviting their patrons to "Drink the Wassail Bowl in Good Company." There was multiculturalism for you, Virginia thought. The people who owned this bar had studied so many cultures, they didn't know the difference between Scotland and Scandinavia.

"Well," Virginia said, "I think I'll be going along. I have a lot to do tonight."

She started to move away from the table and caught her high heel in a crack in the floorboards. She fell heavily into

Steve's side and felt him push her away from him, onto the floor. She got up and dusted herself off.

"If you're going to try to cripple me, you're going to have to do better than that," she said.

"Of course Steve isn't trying to cripple you," Linda said.

Of course he *is*, Virginia thought. Steve is a lot more like me than he is like *her*.

"Bye, bye," she said.

She walked back up to the bar and stopped to look at the television set one more time. There was a new news program on, but it was still WTNH and it was still all about the new murder at Fountain of Youth. Right now there was a picture of Tim Bradbury up on the screen behind Diane Smith's left shoulder. Virginia made a face at it. That police detective was just trying to make himself famous. He had to be. There were no deep dark murder plots in real life and especially not when the victim was someone like Tim Bradbury. Virginia had run into Tim once or twice. She'd recognized him as soon as she'd seen his picture in the paper right after he died. The Hollingfields next door had used him as their yard boy. Virginia thought at the time that he was some kind of mental defective.

Now she left a dollar tip on the bar and went back outside. She walked to the corner of the block, turned left, walked to the corner of the block again and turned left again. She was on a street lined with small stores, all of them open and all of them heavily protected by security equipment. There were liquor stores and convenience stores and newsstands that also sold Connecticut State lottery tickets. Every one of them had hinged metal gates across their plate-glass windows and doors that opened only when somebody buzzed the lock from inside. Virginia was glad she didn't actually want to buy anything.

The street was mostly deserted except for the people already in the stores. Virginia stood under one of the streetlamps and turned just a little sideways, so that she couldn't be seen inside the SuperHour Grocery. Then she reached into the pocket of her dress and pulled out Steve's wallet.

Very nice, Virginia thought. Clumsily done, but adequate for a first try.

She opened the wallet and looked through it. Credit

cards—useless now. Business cards. Driver's license. Picture of Linda. Cash. She counted the cash and came up with three hundred and thirty-six dollars. She looked through the business cards and decided they were much too innocuous for her purposes. A dry cleaner. A dentist. A carpentry service. A plumbing supply house. A Chinese restaurant. She shoved the cards back into the wallet and pocketed the cash. Then, at the last moment, she decided to keep the picture of Linda.

Well, why not? Virginia asked herself, going on up the street, throwing the wallet into the next reasonably full garbage can she passed. Why not? She had at least as much use for it as Steve did. She could stick pins in it. She could burn it in effigy. And Steve could always get another one from Linda.

Virginia reached the corner and turned left yet again. She walked up the street for half a block until she saw a cruising cab. She stepped out past the parked cars and raised her hand.

Steve was upset now, but he'd be more upset later. She just knew it.

After all, when it came to doing what she had to do to get things going her way, she hadn't even started yet.

— 3 —

Ever since Greta Bellamy had started going to classes at Fountain of Youth, she had been going home alone, and watching television alone, and waking up alone, so that it felt as if her entire life was lived in leotards. The part of her life that was not lived in leotards was not real, because it was so silent. It had gotten to the point that she hated the sound of her own breathing. When she woke up in the night and heard her legs rubbing against the rough surface of her new polyester sheets, she wanted to cry. It was ridiculous, really. It had only been two days. Had she always been this dependent on other people? Greta thought back over her life and was surprised to realize that she had never spent any significant amount of time alone. Even after she moved out of her parents' house to "be independent" and "be by herself," she had spent most of her time with Chick. It was worse than that. When she was not with Chick and not at work and not with company of any kind—she had the television on. Always. She lived her life in a sea of white noise, the incessant, demanding chatter of other people's ideas driving any ideas of her own she might have had right out of her head. She didn't think, ever. She didn't read, except for romance novels and magazines. She didn't go out to theaters or museums or lectures or any of the other things that were available in New Haven. She didn't do *anything*. It was a shock to admit it, but nice job or not, promotion or not, her life could have served as an illustration in *The White Trash Cook Book*.

Still, it was because of the silence she knew she would find at home that Greta decided to stop at the library. It was one thing to decide that your life needed changing. It was another to go ahead and change it. The parking lot of the little branch library was mostly deserted. Greta parked directly under a security lamp directly in front of the glass main doors and got out into the cold air. The library was brightly lit inside as well as out, but almost as deserted as its parking lot. Greta went inside and unbuttoned her coat. The heat was on full blast in here. She was roasting.

All the other times Greta had been to this library, she had gone straight to the fiction shelves and found what she was looking for without help. Now she went the other way, to the reference librarian's desk, and waited while the young woman there helped a very frail old man find where copies of *The Armchair Detective* were kept. It took forever, but the young woman was infinitely patient. The very frail old man seemed to have forgotten how to tell his right from his left.

"Sorry I took so long," the young woman said to Greta when she was done. "That's what it is mostly these days. Old people. Nobody else seems to want to use the library any more. What can I help you with?"

"I want to find a copy of *The New Haven Register*. I'm not sure which copy exactly, but it would have been somewhere in February 1988."

"Eighty-eight." That would be on microfilm, then."

"Microfilm?"

"We put all our newspapers on microfilm at the end of

the year. We have to, or we couldn't keep them. We don't have the space."

"Do you microfilm the pictures, or only the words? It's a picture I'm looking for, you see."

"We microfilm everything. Pictures. Words. Cartoons. Dust motes. You name it."

"But will I be able to really see the picture? Or will it be really small or fuzzy or something?"

"You'll be able to see the picture better than you could have in the paper if you want to. You can adjust the viewer. Come on with me and I'll get you set up."

"All right."

The young woman led Greta across the blue carpet of the reference section to three little carrels that had been installed in front of a blank wall. Then she disappeared and came back in a moment with a box the size of a card catalog file drawer.

"Here we are," she said, putting the box down in the carrel next to the machine. "This is all of 1988. First you find February." She found February. "Then you do this."

She leaned over Greta's shoulder and showed her how to work the viewer. Do this to make the picture bigger. Do that to make it smaller. Do this other thing to move the microfilm around. It was really very easy, Greta thought in relief, more like a typewriter than a computer. She thought she would be all right using it.

"Thank you very much," she told the young woman.

"No problem at all," the young woman said. "It's nice to see somebody in here who isn't geriatric. Holler if you need help."

Greta looked through the viewer at the banner headline on the front page of the February 1, 1988 issue. When she looked up again, the young woman was back at her desk. Greta got her handbag onto her lap and felt carefully in the outside pocket for the piece of paper she had left there. It was a torn-away section of yesterday's *New Haven Register* with the standard picture of Tim Bradbury on it, captioned TIMOTHY JOHN BRADBURY: MURDER VICTIM.

It's probably nothing, Greta told herself, as she smoothed the picture out on the desk surface. It probably has nothing to do with anything. Still, she would feel a lot better when she knew for sure.

Besides, why shouldn't she check it out? It wasn't like she had anybody to go home to, or anything to do. There was nobody to care if she was out until midnight. And she would feel so much *safer* being sure.

Greta bent her head over the viewer, flicked past the front page, and went searching for the "Lifestyles" section.

THREE

—1—

The most sensible thing to do would have been to rent a car. That was what most people would have done if they found themselves in a town they didn't know with a lot of traveling to do and inadequate public transportation. But Gregor couldn't take that option. Although he had a driver's license, he was a legendarily bad driver. He hadn't even tried to drive for over ten years, except once on a vacation in Cape Cod with Bennis and Tibor, when Tibor needed to go to the hospital with a cut foot. The results had not been gratifying. Bennis said afterward that she hadn't known it was possible to strip gears like that on an automatic transmission. The cop who stopped them on the little road in Orleans where they got lost for the last time said he thought that all of them must be drunk. Why else would they be weaving back and forth across the lanes that way? It was a good thing Tibor's cut turned out not to be serious. It was a good hour and a half by the time the cop stopped them. By then, they didn't even know where they were.

Gregor got up the morning after the death of Stella Mortimer and called Bulldog Cabs. Philip Brye had promised to messenger over copies of the forensics reports as soon as they came in. That meant that Gregor could do an end run around Tony Bandero's obstructiveness when he wanted to. He very much wanted to. Tony had been all over the television set again last night, giving interviews, making broad hints, suggesting the threatening and the sinister for the benefit of the viewing audience. If Madonna ever became a detective, she would be the kind of detective Tony Bandero was.

Gregor asked for Connie Hazelwood specifically, and it was Connie Hazelwood who showed up in the lobby, wearing another blue-and-white Bulldog sweater and sporting a big enameled button that read: "YOU DRINK—WE DRIVE—EVERYBODY HAS A HAPPY NEW YEAR." Gregor decided not to buy a copy of *The New Haven Register* with Tony's picture on the cover. He bought a copy of *The New York Times* instead, and then realized he'd stuck himself with one more series of stories of one more round of Middle Eastern peace talks. Maybe if they talk peace long enough, they'll get around to doing some of it. Gregor threw the *Times* in the nearest wastebasket and told Connie Hazelwood where he wanted to go.

Connie Hazelwood considered the proposition seriously. "Do you have any idea what kind of place this is you want to go to?"

"Shabby," Gregor said, remembering the photograph of Tim Bradbury's mother's house. "Poor. Very rundown."

"It's a rural slum," Connie Hazelwood said bluntly. "And don't think it's not dangerous just because it's got a lot of trees and grass around the buildings. Alcohol. Drugs. Rifles."

"I thought the problem in urban slums was handguns."

Connie Hazelwood shrugged. "Handguns are nice when you only want to aim and shoot short distances, but you need a rifle to really drive off the revenuers. If you know what I mean. They had one of those stills out there blow up last summer; it burned for four days."

"The person I'm going to see is an old woman. From the way she's been described to me, she couldn't hit the side of a moving van from two feet away with an elephant gun."

"She may not be the one you have to worry about. There are people out there who have been known to shoot at passing cars when they got tanked enough. You're going to show up over there in that coat, and six guys are going to decide you're from the government."

"What's wrong with my coat?"

"It costs six hundred dollars and it looks it."

Actually, Gregor thought, it cost seven hundred fifty. He wasn't an extravagant man, but he liked good coats.

"I really do have to go out there," he told Connie Hazelwood. "I can't see any substitute for talking to this woman and she isn't going to come to me."

"You should just have warned me in advance," Connie Hazelwood said. "I could have brought us both body armor."

Body armor only keeps you from getting shot in the body, Gregor wanted to say. You could still get shot in the leg. You could still get shot in the head. Even the old-fashioned head-to-toe tin-can armor of the Middle Ages hadn't worked. Plenty of knights had died in battle.

"Come on," Gregor said. "The sooner we do it, the sooner we have it over with."

Out on the sidewalk in front of the porte cochere, someone had put up two tall sandwich signs announcing the motel's New Year's Eve party, complete with a list of the musical acts slated to appear. Connie looked over the names and said,

"Oh. Old people's stuff: '60s music."

Okay, Gregor thought. Connie was talking about Bennis Hannaford's generation, not his, and Bennis was twenty years younger than he was. Gregor wondered if Connie had ever heard of Guy Lombardo or Lester Lanin or Peter Duchin or even Benny Goodman. There was a reference to Benny Goodman on a Joni Mitchell album Bennis had, but maybe Connie hadn't even heard of Joni Mitchell. Maybe this was what was wrong with the world. Maybe we needed to go back to the days of folk songs and ritual traditions, when all the generations shared the same music. It would be just fine, Gregor decided, as long as he got to pick the music.

Gregor climbed into the back of Connie's cab and crossed his legs. Connie got into the front and went through the collection of cassette tapes she kept under the seat.

"Let's do some Meat Loaf," she said. "It sort of fits this expedition."

— 2 —

Meat Loaf didn't fit any expedition Gregor had ever heard of, except maybe a gang war sequence in a Mad Max movie, but by the time they got to the Housatonic River, Connie had changed her mind about the music anyway. By then, she was playing very hokey-sounding hayseed stuff. "Elvira" was the name of one of the songs. "Wallflower" was another. Gregor did not think this was fair. First there was New Haven, which was definitely a city. Then there was a tangle of access roads and semiurban strips lined with gas stations and car dealerships and fast-food restaurants. Then there was a short stretch of four-lane bliss with a grass median and thickly wooded patches next to each of the outside lanes. Then there was Derby. There were a lot of words that could be used to describe Derby, Connecticut, but "rural" was not one of them. The place seemed to have survived, intact and untouched, from the Great Depression. Rickety two- and three-story frame houses were crammed onto postage-stamp lots in thick profusion up and down the steep hills. Schools and churches were massive edifices in faded red brick. Banks were imposing and heavy, temples of commerce, with their hours stenciled onto their first-floor windows in metallic gold paint. There were some signs of the times. Stopped at a red light on Main Street, Gregor found himself just across the street from a tattoo parlor and the Adult World bookstore. The bookstore promised "videos, videos, and more videos," but didn't have any of the video covers on display. It wouldn't have had anyplace to put a display if it had wanted to. The only window on the Adult World bookstore's storefront was in the door. On the other side of the street, there was a bar with a blinking neon martini glass in its window. The martini glass was blue and pink and had an electric green olive inside.

"Depressing place," Gregor told Connie Hazelwood.

"Oh, yeah," Connie said. "My mom said it used to be a national joke. Because of Yale, you know."

"No."

"Well, look at it this way. New Haven wasn't always a pit, but Derby was. My mom says that it used to be the rich

people who lived in New Haven, mostly, and the middle
class, and what you had in Derby was the Polish immigrants
who worked in the factories and those kinds of people. It
was always a low-rent sort of place."

"It still looks like a low-rent sort of place."

"Yeah, it is. Only there used to be this thing called Derby
Day, where the kids from Yale would come over and cause a
lot of trouble and trash the place. And everybody laughed
about it, you know, except the people who lived in Derby."

"I can see that."

"Yeah, well, there are still some rich people who live in
New Haven. On Edge Hill Road and Prospect Street and
places like that. There still aren't any rich people who live in
Derby." My mother says that the surest way you have to
drop off the face of the earth as far as all your New Haven
friends are concerned is to move to Derby. It's like living in
Levittown or Beverly Hills. It brands you."

They were out of the center of Derby and into a dilapidated maze of concrete abutments, closed factories and sagging overhead wires. The closed factories all had most of
their windows broken. Then Connie took the car around a
sharp bend in the road and the factories fell away. To the
right of them there was a steep hill going up to nowhere,
dotted here and there by 1930s-style shingle-sided bunga-
lows. To the left of them there was another steep hill, going
down to the river. Gregor stopped straining to see through
the grime on his window and rolled it down. He saw a long
line of little shacks marching along the water toward a high
dam. The dam looked like one of those big 1930s public
works projects that were supposed to solve the unemployment problem. Right now, no water was spilling through it.
The riverbed on this side of it was nearly dry.

"What's the number of this place you're looking for?"
Connie asked.

"Forty-seven."

Connie slowed down and peered through the windshield.
There was no other traffic on the road. There were no signs
of people anywhere.

"Fifty-two," she muttered under her breath. She pulled
up a few more feet and stopped. "Forty-seven."

The shack was even smaller and shabbier than it had

looked like it was going to be in the picture. The boards that had been used to cover the windows were warped and split by the weather. The screened-in porch was sagging so badly, a bad patch of wind would have sent it into collapse. The shacks on either side of this one were not in such bad shape. The one to the left had a new set of steps leading up to its front door. The one to the right had clean windows with blue-and-white curtains in them. Gregor got out of the car and walked to the edge of the dropping slope.

"Well?" Connie Hazelwood asked, getting out to stand beside him.

"I was thinking that it isn't entirely hopeless here," Gregor said. "Look at the steps. Look at the curtains."

"I didn't say the people who lived here weren't human, Mr. Demarkian. I said that a lot of them were nuts."

Closer to the dam, one or two of the shacks had packed dirt driveways. Up here, there was nothing but dirt and mud and grass.

"There isn't a path I could use to get down there?"

"Not that I know of," Connie Hazelwood said. "But don't trust me. I've never been down there."

Gregor looked down at his shiny black wing-tip shoes and sighed. A modern fictional detective in a modern detective novel would not have had this problem. He would have been dressed in jeans and Timberland boots to show his independence from Establishment authority and his friendliness toward the earth. Gregor was from a generation of men who wore their ties from the moment they got up in the morning to the moment they went to bed, even on Saturdays.

Gregor picked a place where the grass seemed thicker and the mud seemed thinner than it did anywhere else—an optical illusion, he was sure—and let himself slide a little as he went down the bank. He stumbled against a pile of rotting twigs and uprooted rocks. When he reached a place where he could safely stand without being pitched forward by the incline and gravity, he turned around. Connie Hazelwood was still standing on the road, leaning against the car, her hands in her pockets.

"I'm going to skip it if it's all right with you," she called down to him.

It was all right with Gregor Demarkian. He walked from

one corner of the shack to the other along the length of the
roadside. Then he began to circle the building. Here and
there, he could see flecks of green paint. Otherwise, the walls
were bare and as warped as the boards over the windows.
Some of the boards had fallen off the windows that faced the
river. Torn and rusted screen showed through, along with
broken glass. The only door was the door to the screen
porch. It stood at the top of a short flight of decaying steps,
only nominally boarded up. There was a single board ham-
mered across the top half of it, loose and easy to pry off.

Gregor didn't try to pry the board off. He stood to the
side of the steps—if he'd stood on them, they would have
crumbled into splinters—and knocked instead. Nobody came
to answer it.

"I don't think anybody lives in that place," Connie Hazelwood called down to him.

Gregor waved to acknowledge that he'd heard what she
said and went on walking around the shack. He looked
through the cracks in the boards that covered the windows.
He went back to the door and tried the handle, only to find
that it was locked. Of course, it wasn't too securely locked.
Whoever had built this place hadn't been able to afford to
put in a really strong lock. Gregor could have broken in in
a minute. He wasn't ready to do that yet.

He was still standing near the door, trying to get a look
in through the small window next to it, when the door to the
shack next door opened and a woman came out. She was an
enormous woman, three or four hundred pounds at least,
wearing a flower-print polyester tent dress that came down
to the middle of her calves. She had white ankle socks on her
feet and thick brown men's boots she had left unlaced. she
would have looked slatternly, except that she had taken a
great deal of trouble with her hair. It was long and straight,
freshly washed and freshly combed, held back in a blue plastic flower barrette.

The woman stood at the top of her brand new steps, staring at him in suspicion. The flesh of her neck hung down in
folds. The flesh of her upper arms wiggled and swung every
time she moved. Gregor finally realized what it was about
her face that had drawn his attention. Under all the fat, this
woman exhibited all the signs of Down's syndrome.

The woman crossed her arms over her chest.

"Whatchoo doin'?" she demanded.

Gregor stepped a little ways away from the door. "I'm looking for the woman who lives here," he said. "For—" he checked the piece of paper he had shoved into his coat pocket. "For Alissa Bradbury."

The woman didn't believe him. "Ali don't live there no more. She's gone."

"You mean she moved away?"

"I mean she's gone. Gone. She's not there no more."

"I understand that. Do you know if she went to another house to live in?"

"She didn't say good-bye to nobody around here," the woman said.

"Do you know when she left? Was it yesterday or last week or last month or—"

"A long time. Years. I know about years. Every Christmas is a new year."

Gregor remembered the kerosene lamp shining through the boards on the screen porch in the picture Philip Brye had shown him. He thought of this way of telling time: every Christmas is a new year. Somewhere, sometime, somebody had considered this woman worth enough to teach that to.

"I had Christmas by myself this year," the woman said suddenly. "I put up a tree. I took it right off a bush next to the river. It wasn't a bush what belonged to anybody."

"I'm glad you had a tree."

"It wasn't nothing I could get in trouble for. It wasn't a bush what belonged to anybody."

"Even if it was, I don't think they'd mind."

"You can get in trouble, taking what isn't yours. I don't do it no more."

"Good for you."

"Only thing is, I had to have a fish. For my dinner. I caught it in the river. You can't get a turkey from the store without you have money."

"That's true."

"I don't have no money. And I don't know how to cook a turkey, neither, because it's hard and you have to use the oven. I know how to cook a fish."

"I'm sure you cook a very good fish."

"I would've liked to've had company, though. That wasn't right. Being all by myself on Christmas."

"Maybe next Christmas will be better."

The woman reared back and pointed at the boarded-up shack. "Ali's not there any more, but her husband comes. He comes and makes fires."

Kerosene lamps, Gregor thought. Father: unknown.

"You mean a man comes to this house and stays in it?"

"He comes and makes fires," the woman said definitely. "He's going to burn the place down and he's going to burn me with it. I been telling him and telling him."

"Has he been here recently? Last week? Last year?"

"He comes all the time. He was here before Christmas. I was trying to be nice to him. I asked him to come and spend Christmas with me."

"But he wouldn't do it."

"He wasn't nice to me," the woman said. "He just comes and makes fires."

"Do you know what this man looked like? How tall he was? What color hair he had?"

But the woman seemed to have had enough. She turned around in a little circle on her brand new porch steps—who cared enough about her to build those steps for her, but not to keep her company on Christmas?—and ended by keeping her back to him.

"I don't want to talk to you anymore," she said. "I want to watch television."

"That's fine," Gregor said.

"I got a little television I got for a present. I didn't steal it from nobody."

"I'm sure you didn't."

"I'm going to go in the house now."

The woman opened the screen door at the top of her steps and went inside. The last Gregor saw of her was the massive expanse of her back, covered with sprigged flowers and teased by wisps of hair. Then the inner door slammed shut, and she was gone.

Gregor slowly and very deliberately made first one and then another circle of the house. He checked every inch of the surface he could see. Then he walked around the two spindly trees that bordered the place on the road side and checked them. There was nothing. No paper notice. No board notice. No warning sign. Nothing.

Gregor climbed back up the hill to where Connie Hazelwood waited for him.

"I want to find the Derby town hall," he told her. "Either that, or the Derby tax assessor's office. Can you do that for me?"

"Sure. Why?"

Gregor motioned back over his shoulder. "That's a house. Taxes have to be paid on a house. No matter how awful a house is."

Connie Hazelwood blew a raspberry. "If taxes have to be paid on that house, Derby is ripe for violent revolution. The Derby town hall, huh?"

"The Derby town hall."

Connie climbed back into the car and fired the engine. "I just hope this isn't in one of those neighborhoods Derby's got. Drive-by shootings. Hookers shooting up in broad daylight. Of course, we've got those neighborhoods in New Haven now, too, but we don't like to talk about them. You got your seat belt on?"

Gregor had his seat belt on.

"Go," he told her.

— 3 —

It took longer than Gregor expected it would. Property tax records are defined as information available to the public, like filed wills. The problem was not in getting someone to let him see the records on number forty-seven, but in figuring out where those records were kept and how to locate them in the computer. The days when property tax records were kept in large ledgers on a corner of the tax assessor's desk were long gone. Gregor found the Derby records in a squat modern building that looked a little like an elementary school and a little like a highway rest stop. The woman in the records office was enormously cheerful and enormously accommodating, but she wasn't really much help. She had moved to Derby only four years ago, from California, because her husband had been hired as an administrator down at Electric Boat.

"We got this absolutely huge house for practically no money, especially by California standards, and it wasn't until six months later that we realized we couldn't have chosen a worse location. It's like living directly above the San Andreas fault with a big gaping hole in your backyard."

"Try D for 'Derby Road,' " Connie Hazelwood suggested. "That's what it used to be called when I was growing up."

"Oh, people call the roads all sorts of things in Connecticut," the woman in Records said. "Only mostly, the names aren't official. And have you ever noticed how there are practically no street signs outside the center cities? We try to tell people how to get to where we are and we can't say 'Turn right at Hoolihan Road' or 'Turn left at Mortlake Place,' because there aren't any signs to tell you which road is Hoolihan and which is Mortlake Place."

"That's to foil robberies," Connie Hazelwood said. "If the burglars don't have any signs to go by, they can't find their way around."

"The burglars in this state can find their way around much better than I can," the woman in records snapped. "They were born and raised here."

She tapped a couple of route numbers into the computer, came up blank, and tapped in a couple of more. Then she tapped in "Stephenson" and sat back.

"Oh," she said. "There it is. Stephenson Road. That's the town name for it. Did you say number forty-seven?"

"Yes," Gregor said.

She tapped a few more things into her computer. "Oh, this is very nice. Very nice indeed. Taxes all paid up and current. And they have been for absolutely years."

"What's the name of the deedholder on the house?" Gregor asked.

The woman in records squinted at her screen. "Alissa Bradbury."

"Who do the tax bills get sent to?" Gregor asked. "And where do they get sent to?"

"They get sent to Alissa Bradbury at number forty-seven, Stephenson Road."

"When was the last one paid?"

"Three days before Christmas."

"Cash? Check? Money order?"

"Check."

"Do you photograph the checks?" Gregor asked her.

The woman shook her head. "Oh, no. I know some places do it, but it would be much too expensive for Derby."

Gregor ran a hand through his hair. He had assumed, when he was talking to the mentally retarded woman, that the "husband" she kept talking about was actually Alissa Bradbury's son, Tim Bradbury, come back to help his mother out off and on. But Tim Bradbury had died the first week of December. Who had paid Alissa Bradbury's taxes three days before Christmas? And if Alissa Bradbury had paid them herself, then where was she? Gregor knew he couldn't count on the testimony of the woman he had talked to. She was confused, and her sense of time lacked precision. But he could count on the evidence he had seen with his own eyes. Kerosene lamps burning on the screened-in porch in Philip Brye's photograph notwithstanding, nobody could be living in that shack. Not on a day-to-day basis. Not with the shape it was in.

"Was that everything you needed to know?" the woman in records asked brightly.

It didn't begin to be everything Gregor Demarkian needed to know, but he didn't want to say that.

FOUR

— 1 —

One of the problems with working outside of official police sanction is that you can never know when you are covering old ground or when the ground you are covering is already known to be—because of factors you have no knowledge of—a dead end. In the detective novels Bennis Hannaford and Father Tibor were always pressing on Gregor Demarkian, the detective was always operating outside official police sanction, and he always knew more than the cops did. Even Miss Marple, Bennis Hannaford's favorite and, in Gregor's opinion, the most ludicrously unbelievable character in the history of detective fiction, figured out more about a case while she was knitting baby booties than the forces of Scotland Yard did while running all over the English countryside. In real life it was not like that. Tony Bandero might be a jerk—a *world-class* jerk, as Bennis would say—but he would also have access to vital information Gregor needed but had no way of getting on his own. Philip Brye would be able to get him some of it, and that was a comfort, but there was no way around the time-delay factor. If Gregor wanted to waste the day, he could call Dr. Brye, tell him what was needed, and wait until Dr. Brye both got hold of it and was able to deliver it. Gregor didn't want to waste the day. There was something about this situation that made him very nervous. It wasn't just the obvious. Of course it was nerve-wracking to have a poisoner running around loose. It was nerve-wracking to have any kind of a murderer running around loose. It was statistically correct that most homicides were not committed by psychopaths. It was also statistically correct that any unexplained homicide could have been committed by a psychopath. It was the randomness factor that was terrifying. A murderer with a known motive was a calculable risk, to an extent. If you knew someone was killing the heirs to the Hipplewhooper fortune and you were one of those heirs, you could take steps to protect yourself. It wasn't so easy when there was only pattern, because you could never be sure that you had the pattern right. A serial killer who has been described as preying on young women with long brown hair parted in the middle might actually be preying on young women wearing sea green sweatshirts. Practically every young college woman in the country had long brown hair parted in the middle. A serial killer who is said to favor little old ladies in tennis shoes may actually favor little old ladies in horn-rimmed glasses. There could be no real answers until the killer was caught, and sometimes he (or she) wasn't.

Of course, Gregor thought, gathering his coat together as Connie Hazelwood pulled up in front of Fountain of Youth's big Victorian house, there was no question of a serial killer here. The signs were all wrong, and getting even wronger the more Gregor looked into them. That wasn't what was making him so nervous. He wasn't entirely sure what was. It was all just—off, that was the problem. Off. That balcony. The first body, naked in the bushes, appearing out of nowhere. It was an article of faith with Gregor Demarkian that, the conventions of the murder mystery notwithstanding, real killers in real life did not hatch elaborate plots with bizarre twists in them unless there was absolutely no other way to get what they wanted to have. That meant there had to be a reason for Tim Bradbury's body to have been found the way it was, a perfectly logical and straightforward reason. It was like looking for a perfectly logical and straightforward reason for crows to start painting themselves red.

Gregor got out of the car and looked around. There was

no sign of Tony Bandero. There was no sign of the gentle-
men and women of the press, either. Gregor thought this was
sensible, since Tony and the press seemed to be joined at the
hip. Yesterday, the doorway at Fountain of Youth had
sported a tired-looking Christmas wreath. Now the wreath
was gone, and nothing had been put in its place. Gregor
missed Donna Moradanyan, his upstairs neighbor, who had
once decorated their brownstone for Valentine's Day by
wrapping the entire five-story facade of the building in shiny
pink foil and big red aluminum hearts.

"You sure you don't want me to stick around?" Connie
Hazelwood asked. "Just in case you need to make a quick
getaway?"

Gregor could easily imagine himself wanting to make a
quick getaway, especially if Tony showed up. He noted that
there were no cars parked under the porte cochere. There
were several in the parking lot out back, but there ought to
be. It was ten o'clock in the morning and classes were in full
swing.

"Go have lunch or do your homework," Gregor told her.
"Come back to get me at two."

"It's too early for lunch," Connie Hazelwood said, "and
I'm too old to have homework."

"Go," Gregor said.

Connie Hazelwood sighed heavily and revved the engine.
Gregor went up the walk to the front door and rang the bell.
Deep in the foyer, Traci Cardinale must have checked him
out in the security camera. The intercom next to the door
crackled on. Traci said, "Hello, Mr. Demarkian" in what
sounded like a garbled and slightly nasal way. The door
clicked open. Gregor went inside and closed it again.

"Goodness," Traci Cardinale said. "I didn't expect to see
you here this morning, Mr. Demarkian. I didn't think we
were going to have anybody here from the police until later
this afternoon.

Gregor was not exactly "from the police," in spite of
Tony Bandero's invitation, but he wasn't going to point that
out to Traci Cardinale.

"Is that the official word?" he asked her. "Later this afternoon?"

"That's what that policeman told me. That detective who

was here at the end last night. The one in the uniform. Mr. McKay."

"He wasn't a detective. He was a patrolman."

"Oh. I thought all policemen were detectives. Anyway, I wasn't expecting you. Is there something I can do to help?"

The balcony railing had still not been repaired. Gregor wondered how long it would take.

"I wanted to talk to three of your students, if they're here," he said. He fished around in his coat pockets for the note he had written to himself. He had to stop writing notes to himself and putting them in his pockets. He lost half of them. He always ended up reminding himself of Columbo. He really *hated* Columbo. It was bad enough that so many cops were stupid. It was worse that there was one who was supposed to want to look stupid. It was nonsense that looking stupid would get you more information than looking smart. He had to start getting more sleep. He was going off on tangents again.

He found the note he had written to himself. "Dessa Carter," he read off. "Christie Mulligan. Virginia Hanley. Are they here today?"

"Oh," Traci said. "Well. None of them has canceled. They're all in the beginners' class."

Gregor had thought they might be all in the same class. The best way for three people to witness more or less the same thing was to be in more or less the same place at more or less the same time.

"Why don't you tell me where the beginners' class is meeting," Gregor said, "and I'll just go up there and wait until they've finished with whatever it is they're doing."

"Oh, I couldn't do that," Traci said quickly. "Not everybody in a class likes to be observed. And the instructor may object to it, too. Are you—I mean, are these women suspects or something? Do you think one of them killed Stella?"

"No. It's just something I overheard during the questioning yesterday afternoon that I would like to clarify."

"Oh." Traci Cardinale looked uncomfortable. "Well. The thing is, Mr. Demarkian, I mean, I'm not really authorized to make a decision like this and, well, everybody is in class right now—"

"I'm not in class right now," Magda Hale said.

Gregor and Traci looked up. Magda Hale was leaning over the balcony a little to the side of the plywood barrier. She looked tired and—Gregor was sure of this—a little high.

"That's Mr. Demarkian, isn't it? Do you want to take an exercise class?"

"He wants to talk to some of the women," Traci said. "Miss Carter and Miss Mulligan and Ms. Hanley. I've told him I didn't really think he ought to do that—"

"Why not?" Magda Hale interrupted.

"Oh," Traci said. "Well, I don't know. It didn't seem right. And I didn't even know if they were all here today."

Magda Hale brushed this off. "They're all here today. They're in the beginners' class, aren't they? That's step aerobics this morning. It's not the students I'd worry about if I were you, Traci. It's Frannie Jay. For someone who spends her life jumping up and down in front of dozens of stranger in a leotard, she's awfully touchy about her privacy. Are the beginners' still in the second-floor studio today?"

"Yes," Traci said. "Yes, they are."

"Then come on up, Mr. Demarkian. You can witness your first step aerobics class."

Gregor shoved himself out of his coat, handed it to Traci Cardinale, and climbed the stairs to the second-floor balcony.

— 2 —

"What you have to remember about an operation like this," Magda Hale said as she led him down the second-floor hall to the studio he had been in on his first day at Fountain of Youth, "is that no matter what else you're offering women, you *have* to offer them a method of losing weight. That's the bottom line. You can talk all you want to about staying young and staying fit and staying healthy. The staying young part might even be a draw for some of the older women. Most of your clients, though, are going to want one thing and one thing only, and that is to get thinner fast. It doesn't matter how much they weigh, either. Twenty pounds over-weight or twenty pounds underweight, they all want to get thinner fast."

They stopped at the door to the studio and Magda Hale opened up and poked her head inside. Music rolled out.

"That's 'Shake Your Body,' and it's just started," she said. "This version takes about twelve minutes. Come in and sit down, Mr. Demarkian."

Gregor let Magda Hale lead him to one of the theater chairs on the platform overlooking the studio floor. On the studio floor itself, the same rows of women he had observed the first time were now moving back and forth in front of lit-tle black plastic platforms, led by a young woman with long blond hair who was facing the mirror at the front of the room. Gregor assumed the mirror must be for the benefit of the instructor. He couldn't see that it was doing the students any good. If he was a woman who thought she needed to lose weight, he would have hated looking at himself in it.

"To the right. To the middle. To the left. To the middle. And *step*," the blond instructor said.

The women stepped. Gregor wondered how they man-aged to stay in sync like that. He recognized Dessa Carter in the back row, because she was unmistakeable. The fat one.

"This is called step aerobics," Magda said, leaning against the low rail that separated the viewing area from the studio proper. "It's this year's miracle discovery. There's al-ways a miracle discovery. A couple of years ago, it was the ultra-low-fat diet. We were all supposed to keep our fat in-take down to ten or fifteen percent of our total calories. Then we could eat as much as we wanted without ever gain-ing weight."

"I take it it didn't work," Gregor said.

"Oh, it worked just fine," Magda told him. "The prob-lem is, nobody could stand to stay on the diet for long. No butter. No cheese. No oils except in very minimal amounts. No yogurt. No milk except skim. No ham or dark meats, ever. No chicken skin."

"What was left?"

"Rice and beans. Potatoes eaten plain. Raw green vegeta-bles and steamed vegetables. Oh, and pure sugar sweets.

Cakes and cookies have too much fat in them, but if you wanted to you could sit down with a jar of orange marmalade and eat it with a spoon. People did."

"And they still lost weight?"

"Sure. Ultra low fat was basically just another calorie restriction diet, another variation on a theme. There isn't anyone on earth who can eat enough rice and beans in combination to exceed, say, two thousand calories a day. Even if you're adding marmalade to that, you won't go much above twenty-five hundred. Since most women with serious weight-loss needs are doing at least thirty-five hundred, you get—"

"Weight loss," Gregor said.

"Exactly. Then there's the Puritan factor. The women who go on a diet like that who don't really need to lose weight tend to be obsessives. They won't eat the marmalade even though the diet says they can. They won't eat until they're full, either. They'll sit there with a little plate of rice and beans all calculated to USDA portion sizes, when everybody knows that USDA portion sizes aren't big enough to satisfy a hamster. So you see, one way or another, everybody lost weight while it lasted, but it didn't last. Life isn't much fun if you can never have butter on your mashed potatoes."

Gregor cocked his head toward the women on the studio floor. "This isn't a diet."

"No, it isn't," Magda agreed. "For the last ten years or so, we've been very big on exercise. There's nothing really wrong with that, of course. We could all use more exercise, except maybe for exercise instructors, who could probably use less. But the theory is, of course, that exercise can help you keep weight off and probably even help you take it off. And, if you're in reasonably good shape when you start, you can dress up for it."

The women in this class didn't seem to be dressed up for exercise. Most of them were wearing plain black leotards and plain black tights. The instructor, however, was wearing a silver and silver-blue lamé striped leotard, silver-blue tights, and a silver-blue Greek fisherman's cap. Gregor could see what Magda Hale meant.

"I suppose I didn't expect you to be so cynical about it," he said finally. "From your advertisements and the other ma-

terial I've seen around here, I thought you'd be a true believer."

"Oh, but I am." Magda Hale shook her head. "I believe
in diet and exercise, especially for keeping yourself young
and healthy. But most of the women who come to these
courses don't give a damn if they're healthy. They only care
if they're thin. And that, you see, is the dirty little secret of
the whole diet industry."

"What is?"

"That some people can't be thin. Not on a long-term basis. No matter what they do. I'm not saying they have to be
as fat as Miss Carter." Magda and Gregor looked across the
room at Dessa Carter. "Most women aren't that heavy and
won't get to be that heavy no matter what they do. I'm saying that there are a lot of perfectly normal women who are
twenty pounds heavier than the charts say they should be—
the old charts, that is—and nothing they ever do is going to
change that."

"Are there new charts?"

"Oh, yes," Magda said. "And we don't have any of them
out here. In fact, I don't know a single diet or exercise business that does have the new charts anywhere where the clients can see them. According to the new charts, it's just fine
for a forty-year-old woman who's five four to weigh as much
as a hundred and fifty pounds. According to the old charts,
the outside limit is about one hundred thirty, and the recom-
mended weight is more like one twenty or one fifteen. That
means that eighty-five percent of American women over
forty are too heavy. That means means that they're also un-
healthy, and getting unhealthier every year. Never mind minor little facts like the one that says American women are
living longer every year."

"You do sound cynical."

Magda shrugged. "You don't tell potential clients about
the new charts. You don't tell them they're wrong to want to
lose weight, even if they're anorexic as hell and ready for a
hospital. You don't tell them they've simply got a body type
that doesn't fit the present fashions and is never going to.
You always hold out hope of salvation through fasting and
discipline. And if you don't do that, if you try to be honest
about what you can do for people, you go out of business."

"I take it you're not in any danger of going out of business."

"No, I'm not," Magda Hale said, "but at least I haven't gone as far as some people go. I'd probably have been ready to expand a long time ago if I had."

"How far do people go?"

"Well," Magda Hale said, "a couple of the diet companies used to dress their salespeople up in white coats and not quite say they were doctors and not quite say they weren't, if you see what I mean. So that people thought they'd had a medical consultation or a session with a nutritionist. Congress held an investigation and had a fit. Did you hear about it?"

"No."

Magda Hale smiled. "Of course you didn't. Practically nobody did. The regular press didn't cover it. The women's magazines didn't cover it either, because they get huge amounts of advertising money from the diet centers and the fitness clubs. And most people just didn't want to know. Tell the average American woman these days that she's never going to lose the extra twenty pounds, and she's going to think you just sentenced her to death. Hell, most of the people we get here would rather be sentenced to death. They'd rather hear that they had cancer than that they were always going to be what they call fat."

"Step *up*," the blond woman at the front of the group insisted. "Step up. Step up. Step *right*. Step middle. Step *left*. Step *up*."

Magda Hale checked her watch. "One more sequence and then the cooldown. You wouldn't believe how hard we work to make this sound all New Age and professional, nothing at all like those futile exercise programs your mother went on when you were a kid. God, I don't understand people sometimes. Especially women."

"Step up. Step *up*. Step right. Step middle. Step left. Step middle. And *breathe*," the blond woman said.

— 3 —

Dessa Carter was the fat one. Christie Mulligan was the extremely thin one. Virginia Hanley was the fortyish woman who looked like she ought to be presiding over the latest meeting of the local Junior League. When the class had finished their step routine to "Shake Your Body," Magda Hale called a time-out and separated these three from the rest and called them over to talk to Gregor. Christie Mulligan's friends didn't like it. The one called Tara even threatened to call a lawyer, on the assumption that Christie was about to be questioned by a hostile government force who might suspect her of a crime and, therefore, needed the protection of official representation. When Christie herself turned this suggestion down, Tara moved as close as she could to the platform, so that she could listen to everything that was said. Gregor didn't care if the entire class listened to everything that was said. He was, in fact, a little put off by the way Magda Hale had arranged things. It was all too organized. He didn't want to come off as the school principal, ferreting out miscreants in the girls' rooms.

Dessa Carter and Virginia Hanley sat on chairs. Christie Mulligan sat on the floor, her legs folded under her in a quasilotus position. All three women looked solemn, as if they were invited guests at a funeral. Virginia Hanley looked bored, too.

Now there's somebody who wouldn't surprise me if she turned out to be a serial killer, Gregor thought. Aside from looking bored and solemn, Virginia Hanley also looked smug. Serial killers were always smug.

Gregor leaned forward and put his hands on his knees. "What I wanted to talk to you about," he said, "was something each of you said to the detectives doing the questioning yesterday afternoon. You may remember that I sat in on some of those interviews."

"You sat in on mine," Virginia Hanley said. "I didn't like it. I almost registered a protest."

Of course you did, Gregor thought. He said, "Yes. Well. What I want to do now is get more specific about just a single point. Each of you were talking about the period of time just around lunch, and you said you were on your way to the dining room—"

"We were late," Christie Mulligan said crisply. "At least, I was. Tara and Michelle and I were in the bathroom so long, we missed the line."

"I was late, too," Dessa Carter said, looking tired. "I had to call home."

Gregor looked at Virginia Hanley and Virginia shrugged. "I was probably late, too," she said. "I stopped to look at the brochures about the new line of exercise clothes."

"Fine," Gregor said. "Fine. Did the three of you see each other when you were going upstairs?"

"We saw Dessa," Christie Mulligan said. "She was on the landing ahead of us."

"I heard them coming up behind me," Dessa said.

"I didn't see anybody," Virginia said.

"All right," Gregor told them, "now. From what I remember, Miss Carter, when you were asked if you heard or saw anything out of the ordinary, you said that the only thing you could fix on was a bird—"

"Oh," Christie Mulligan said. "Did you hear that, too? Wasn't that odd?"

"I didn't hear a bird," Virginia Hanley said.

Dessa Carter shifted her bulk around in her chair. She was almost fat enough to need two chairs. Gregor thought she would be much more comfortable in something without arms.

"It went *koo roo*," Dessa said. "Like that. And then there was this odd metallic sound—"

"A *clank*," Christie Mulligan put in.

"Right. A *clank*. And then this other sound that went *whoosh*. Like air being let out of a chamber."

"That stuff didn't sound like a bird," Christie Mulligan said, "and that was what was so odd, because every time you got the bird noises, you got the *clank* and the *whoosh*. As if they were connected somehow."

"That's right," Dessa Carter said.

"Excuse me," someone else said.

They all looked up—Dessa Carter, Virginia Hanley, Christie Mulligan, Magda Hale, and Gregor—to find the tall blond step aerobics instructor leaning across the rail to them. She looked pale.

"Excuse me," the instructor said again. "My name is Frannie Jay?" She made the statement a question. We talked yesterday. I don't know if you remember?"

"I remember. Did you hear this bird or whatever it was yesterday afternoon, too?"

"Not yesterday, no. It was the night Tim Bradbury died, the night I came here. I was the one who found Tim Bradbury's body."

"I remember that, too," Gregor told her. What he didn't remember was anything about a *koo roo* or a *clank* or a *whoosh* in any of the reports Tony Bandero had given him. Tony was either keeping information from him again, or engaging in sloppy police work. Unless Frannie Jay hadn't mentioned the sound at the time.

Gregor asked. "Did you tell the police about this the night Tim Bradbury died?"

"Oh, yes," Frannie Jay replied. "Such an odd noise. *Koo roo, clank, whoosh.* Over and over again. Just like that. I thought it was some kind of bird, too."

"Except for the *clank whoosh* part," Christie Mulligan interjected.

"After a while, I just got spooked," Frannie Jay said. "I—it just sounded so odd. So eerie. In the dark like that. So I went over to my window to look out and see if I could spot it, and I saw—I saw—well, the leg. Tim Bradbury's leg. Instead."

"Oh," Christie Mulligan said. "Maybe it's a sound a corpse makes, and when we were going upstairs we were hearing that Stella Mortimer woman. Hearing her dead body, I mean."

"I don't know when you went upstairs," Virginia Hanley said decisively, "but I went upstairs nearly an hour before they found the body. Maybe more."

"Maybe she'd been dead for an hour by the time they found the body," Christie Mulligan suggested.

"I don't think dead bodies say *koo roo*," Dessa Carter objected. "I don't think they say anything."

"What time was it when you came upstairs?" Gregor asked them, trying to keep to the point.

"Just about twelve o'clock exactly," Dessa Carter told him. "I saw the clock on Traci Cardinale's desk before I started up."

"I was going to say I didn't know," Christie Mulligan said, frowning, "but we were just behind Dessa, so it must have been around the same time. Somehow, wearing a watch doesn't seem to go with wearing exercise clothes," she explained.

"Wearing a watch goes with wearing my exercise clothes," Virginia Hanley said. She held her right arm in the air, displaying an intricately worked gold band. It was the kind of watch that went with full formal evening dress, not thirty minutes of step aerobics.

Gregor turned his attention to Virginia Hanley. "You reported hearing a noise yourself. I remember hearing you do it. Was it this same noise?"

"It went *koo roo*," Virginia Hanley said. "It went *clank* and *whoosh*, too, but it wasn't a bird, for God's sake. It wasn't a corpse talking, either. That was just ridiculous."

"Everything anybody says around here that she doesn't agree with is just ridiculous," Christie Mulligan told Gregor. "You should hear her on the subject of the vegetarian menu. And she doesn't even have to eat it."

"You should hear her on the subject of my weight," Dessa Carter contributed. "If I wasn't used to that kind of thing, I would have decked her by now."

"You should deck her the next time you feel she deserves it," Christie Mulligan said. "It will be very good for your self-esteem."

"I don't think I have a problem with my self-esteem," Dessa Carter told her icily.

Gregor didn't want to get caught in the trap of discussing everybody's self-esteem. "Mrs. Hanley," he said. "Please. You were where when you heard this noise?"

"Halfway up the stairs between the first and second floors, on the half-landing."

"And this noise was coming from the first floor, from the direction of the kitchen or the pantry?"

Virginia Hanley looked surprised. "Of course not. How could it possibly have been coming from there?"

"That's where I thought it was coming from," Christie Mulligan said.

"That's where I thought it was coming from, too," Dessa Carter said. "You know, Virginia, it's just possible, just remotely possible, that every once in a while, you might be wrong."

"Well, I'm not wrong about this," Virginia Hanley said. "I can't see how it would have gotten into the kitchen, never mind the pantry. And I can't see that no one would have noticed."

"That no one would have noticed what?" Gregor asked, slightly bewildered.

"Why, the car, of course," Virginia Hanley said. "That's what it was. A car with an exhaust system problem. I forget what it's called, but it's very common. It happened to me just last year. And really, after all the trouble it cost me, I'd know that sound anywhere."

FIVE

— 1 —

The worst thing, Magda Hale decided as she eased her bright
red Toyota Corolla more or less into a parking space in the
empty back corner of the lot at the Fleck Medical Group in
Orange, wasn't her reaction times, but caring about her reaction times. She could make the stops at red lights and respond to other drivers wanting to change lanes, but the
whole procedure seemed infinitely silly, useless, utterly unimportant. She longed to put her head down on the steering
wheel and go to sleep. She longed to think about floating.
She longed to go back to her bedroom and take another one
of these pills, because the ones she had taken at ten o'clock
this morning were beginning to wear off.

It was now three thirty in the afternoon, and every part
of Magda Hale's body ached. She had spent the entire morning with her advanced aerobics class. To be here now, she
had to hand that same class over to Cici Mahoney for the afternoon. She didn't like to do it. Cici had begun to notice
how many corners she was cutting, how much time she was
spending slacking off. All the young instructors had. If
Magda wasn't careful, Simon would start to notice, too.
Magda didn't know what she would do then. Fountain of
Youth was Simon's entire life. It belonged to him more than

it did to Magda, no matter what the legal papers said, because it had been his idea at the beginning and his idea to incorporate and his idea to expand. Fountain of Youth was certainly Simon's entire life with Magda. Magda didn't think they had talked about anything else for years. What would they say to each other if Magda couldn't be part of the business anymore? What would the clients say if they found out Magda was getting old?

Getting old.

I'm not getting old, Magda told herself now, pulling the keys from the ignition and climbing out onto the asphalt. There was a wind blowing in swiftly from the east. It was very cold. All of Magda's joints ached. She hadn't wanted to take more pills when she was coming down here. How would she be able to tell the doctor where it hurt? She was just so afraid of the pain. If Jimmy Fleck wouldn't give her more Demerol, she wasn't sure what she would do. High-impact aerobics was the most important part of her day. Leaping and bouncing, stomping and twirling: there were people who said they got high from that alone; the more vigorous the workout, the better it sold. She couldn't go out on the road and do only the geriatric stuff, or the yoga, or the lectures on how to stay young forever. Nobody would listen to her.

I'm not getting old, Magda told herself again, and then, because the Demerol hadn't completely worn off, she hurried across the parking lot to the medical center's front doors, forcing her legs to move swiftly in the chill. She had two more Demerol in her purse, just in case she needed them. There were six more in the little brown plastic prescription bottle back home. Already, her legs were beginning to send out warning signs of sharp shooting pains waiting under the dull ache.

Jimmy Fleck's office was on the first floor: a good thing, because Magda wasn't sure she wanted to climb stairs. Magda gave her name to the receptionist. The receptionist was new in the last six months and not somebody who knew her. Jimmy Fleck always had new receptionists. He couldn't seem to keep women working for him. Magda wondered why that was.

The waiting room was empty. There was a small artificial Christmas tree on a table in one corner, covered with tinsel and glowing with tiny white lights. There was a pile of magazines on the coffee table that could not have belonged to anyone intimately connected to Jimmy Fleck's life: *Woman's Day Christmas Crochet Patterns* and *Family Circle's 1001 Things to Make for the Holidays*. Magda started to sit down, and Jimmy Fleck himself appeared in the doorway to the offices, looking concerned.

"Magda?"

Magda forced herself to stand up straighter. Jimmy Fleck was at least fifteen years younger than she was. He didn't look forty. Magda always felt slightly anxious around him, as if he were judging her, as if the judgments of young men were somehow what really mattered. In all likelihood, Fleck only judged the swiftness with which her bills were paid.

Magda held out her hand to shake and winced. Her hip was acting up again.

Jimmy cocked his head. "What's wrong?" he asked. "Is that the leg you were telling me about?"

"Leg, hip, back, everything," Magda said, catching her breath. "I think I must have strained something. And I have the introductory seminar this week. And a tour that starts next week."

"You've been working?"

"Of course I've been working. I have to work. Working with me personally is what people pay for when they come to these seminars."

"Have you been taking some kind of painkiller?"

The dull ache was definitely giving way now to sharp shooting pains. The pains were starting in her hips and snaking up her back.

"I found some Demerol in the medicine cabinet. I've been taking those when I needed them."

"Do you need them often?"

"I need them when I work. The last few days, when I work, I'm in pain."

Jimmy Fleck stepped back, contemplated her from one end to the other, and shook his head. He was a tall man with a slight stoop and too much thick black hair. He wore wire-rimmed glasses like the prep school boys at Yale.

"All right," he said. "Come on back with me."

"Yes."

"We're going to take some x-rays. We're going to take quite a lot of x-rays."

"I thought you would."

"Then I'm going to pull at you a little, to see what I can find. Have you taken any of that Demerol recently?"

"Not since ten o'clock."

"Good."

He led her thought the rabbit-warren maze of cubicles that all doctor's offices seemed to be these days. The more Magda walked, the harder she found it to go on moving. The walls of the cubicles were covered with posters exhorting her to quit smoking, lose weight, do a monthly breast exam, count her cholesterol. The x-ray room was at the very back, in one of the only two rooms in the warren with real walls instead of just partitions. The other one was Jimmy Fleck's own office. Why was it, when doctors made so much money they wouldn't spend it on decent renovations?

"Marie?" Jimmy Fleck called out.

Marie was Jimmy Fleck's nurse, the one woman he had been able to keep in his employ. Magda thought she must have been with the practice forever. She was an older woman who believed in older things. Marie still wore a white dress and white stockings and white shoes and the fancy winged white cap she had been given at her hospital nursing school. Now she appeared out of nowhere, impassive but ready.

"Oh, Marie," Jimmy Fleck said. "Magda here needs a set of x-rays done. Both legs. All angles. Both hips. All angles. Her back—Magda, does this pain ever start in your back?"

"No."

"Do a set anyway," Jimmy Fleck told Marie. "We might as well be sure. When you're done, send her down to my office. Use a wheelchair, if necessary."

"I won't need a wheelchair," Magda snapped. "Don't be ridiculous."

"I only said 'if necessary,' " Jimmy Fleck told her. "You forget. I've seen a lot of sports injuries."

"I haven't forgotten. That's why I'm here."

"I've especially seen a lot of aerobics injuries. Especially in older women. And you are an older woman, Magda. No matter what your publicity says."

"I know I'm over fifty. You don't have to rub it in. But I'm in very good shape, Jimmy."

"I know you are."

"And I'm not going to stop working. Not this week. I can't. I only came in because I thought you could prescribe some more painkillers. To get me through."

"More Demerol."

"More whatever. The Demerol works well enough."

"The Demerol is dangerous," Jimmy Fleck said grimly. "Especially taken on a regular basis. We give Demerol to terminal cancer patients on a regular basis."

"I said it didn't have to be Demerol, Jimmy."

"We'll see. If you're badly injured and you go on working, Demerol won't help you much. You'll end up hospitalized."

"I won't let myself be hospitalized," Magda said, and meant it.

"Why don't you come in here and lie down on the examining table," Marie said. "We might as well get these x-rays over and done with."

Magda let herself be let into the x-ray room, away from Jimmy, away from the bright lights of the corridor. Her legs hurt terribly now. Jimmy disappeared down the corridor and Marie closed the x-ray room door.

"Here we go." Marie handed Magda the heavy lead-filled chest protector she would have to wear while her legs were being photographed.

Magda lay down on the examining table and put the chest protector on. If Jimmy wouldn't give her any more painkillers, she would just have to make other arrangements. The one thing she couldn't do was stop working. Not this week. Not this month. Not this year. Not ever. If Jimmy didn't understand that, she would just have to find somebody who did.

Magda stretched out her legs the way Marie wanted her to and winced. The ache was now almost all gone. The shooting pains were excruciating. She wanted to take the Demerol she had brought with her out of her purse and swallow them right now.

"Here we go," Marie said. "I'll just step out of the room for a minute. Don't move that leg while I'm gone."

Magda couldn't have moved that leg if she had wanted to. It felt like it was burning up.

— 2 —

Dessa Carter knew that something was wrong as soon as Mrs. O'Reilly picked up the phone. She could hear all the danger signs in Mrs. O'Reilly's voice, including the oddly grammatical stiltedness that crept into it when Dessa's father was not only very bad, but listening. It was a shame. Dessa had only called home out of a sense of duty. When she had called at lunchtime, everything had been all right. Now she had been invited out "for Perrier and a salad or beer and pizza" by Traci Cardinale, and she wanted to go. It had been years since she'd had dinner out with a friend. It had been years since she'd had a friend to have dinner out with. Until Traci Cardinale asked her to go out, Dessa hadn't even realized how completely her life had been eaten up by what had happened to her father. She had been fat in high school, but not this fat. She'd had only a few friends, but she'd had those few. Now she had nothing but her job (which she hated) and her food (which she wasn't all that fond of anymore either) and her father, who was something worse than dead.

Once Dessa heard Mrs. O'Reilly on the phone, she had no choice. She had to tell Traci that she wouldn't be able to go along. She had to get into her car and point it in the direction of Derby. She had to do the right thing, take the responsibility, lead the cavalry to the rescue. There was no one else. She spent the entire drive home wishing she had never made that phone call in the first place. She hadn't been obligated to make it. Her agreement with Mrs. O'Reilly was clear. One phone call at lunch. That was it. If Mrs. O'Reilly had an emergency, she could call Fountain of Youth.

When Dessa pulled into the driveway of the house in Derby, everything seemed to be quiet. All the lights were on on the first floor, but Mrs. O'Reilly sometimes did that when she was alone with Dessa's father. Dessa sometimes did it, too. When her father got really spooky, it helped not to have to talk to him in the dark. Dessa got out of the car and half ran to the back door. She got her keys and let herself into the kitchen. One of the things she had been afraid of, when she talked to Mrs. O'Reilly, was that the problem here would not be with her father but with the kids in the neighborhood. Too many of the kids around here knew that Dessa's father had Alzheimer's disease. Too many of them were wild. Every once in a while, the kids would come tapping at the windows and rattling at the doors, trying to make the old man scream and shout.

The old man was not screaming and shouting now. There was no sound in the house at all. Dessa walked out of the kitchen and down the hall to the living room. She could see Mrs. O'Reilly standing next to her father's chair. Mrs. O'Reilly saw her too and nodded.

"Shitfire," the old man said suddenly.

Dessa Carter stopped in her tracks. Oh, no, she thought. Not this. Not now. The bottom dropped out of her stomach. All the muscles in her back curled into painful knots. Mrs. O'Reilly walked around the old man's chair and came out into the hallway.

"I've got the rope out," Mrs. O'Reilly said briskly. "Maybe we're not too late."

"You should have called the ambulance," Dessa said. "You should have forced them to come."

"Nothing forces an ambulance to come to this neighborhood on anything less than an hour's notice," Mrs. O'Reilly said. "People bleeding in the street, that doesn't force them to come. I didn't want to try it on my own. I didn't think I could imagine it."

"*Shit*fire," the old man repeated.

Mrs. O'Reilly ducked into the bathroom and came out with a long length of rope.

"We've got to come at him from behind," she said. "If he sees us on the way, he'll really start screaming."

He would really start screaming anyway, Dessa knew that. The only way they could stop him was to gag him, and they had never done that. They had tied him up. They had even tied him up and left him in the bathtub, where it was safest. They had never gagged him.

"Take this end and try not to let him see you," Mrs. O'Reilly said.

Dessa Carter didn't need instructions in this from Mrs. O'Reilly. She took one end of the rope and began to move, slowly, into the living room. Her father was sitting in his chair, his hands gripping the arms, his back to the hallway. Dessa could see the veins in his hands, blue-black and popping out.

Move slowly. Move carefully. Don't panic. The rope felt slippery and prickly in Desse's hands, like wet nettles.

"Shit*fire*," the old man said.

He was so loud and so unexpected, Dessa jumped. In the moment that she jumped, he seemed to see her. He seemed to see *something*. It was hard to know what he saw anymore. It was impossible to know who he thought she was.

"Shit*fire*," the old man screamed at the top of his lungs. Then he leapt to his feet and spun around, picking up the flimsy occasional table beside the chair as he came. It was incredible, how fast it happened. One minute he was sitting with his back to them, more or less calm. The next minute he was on his feet, crouched and wild. He held the table over his head and then brought it crashing to the floor. It was made of plywood and spit and splintered on contact.

"Shitfire and hellfire and fire up your ass you little cunt you big fat cunt you little whore."

The occasional table broke in two and the old man flung it away. Mrs. O'Reilly began to back up along the hallway. Dessa stayed where she was. The old man pushed his chair out of the way and went for the coffee table. He lifted it without difficulty and heaved it in the direction of the front window. The glass shattered. Shards went everywhere.

"Shitfire and hellfire and cuntfire and I'm gonna go home you goddamned suckers I'm gonna go home—"

"I'm going to call the police," Mrs. Reilly announced.

The old man picked up the coffee table again and threw it at the other front widow. The glass broke there, too, and scattered. Dessa could see great piles of sharp-edged pieces glittering in the light of the overhead fixture. The old man was wearing only slippers on his feet, the kind of slippers that have no backs. As he walked through the glass, he got cut. His heels and ankles were bleeding. He picked up the coffee table again and smashed it into the floor, smashed it once, smashed it twice, smashed it three times, gutting the carpet and the wood floor underneath it, making shards of coffee table wood to go with the shards of glass.

"Shitfire shitfire shitfire shitfire shitfire," he screamed.

Mrs. O'Reilly grabbed Dessa by the arm. "Get out of the way," she hissed, pulling Dessa along. "Get out of the way before he sees you."

Dessa couldn't get out of the way. She couldn't move. He was so strong. That was what she could never get over. His mind was as weak as marshmallow fluff, but his body was as strong as it had ever been, stronger maybe, getting stronger by the day. She remembered him at the Danbury State Fair when she was young, lifting the big hammer to ring the bell and get her a Teddy bear from the booth. She remembered him the day the floor rotted out from the upstairs bathroom and the bathtub fell halfway through. He'd stood in the downstairs hall and kept it up there until the emergency plumber came. He had always been strong. His strength was all he had ever had. Now it was all he had left except for his jumble of dreams about a war only he was left to fight.

"Shitfire hellfire cuntfire shitfire *home* I'm gonna go *home* I'm gonna go right through you suckers and I'm gonna go *home*."

"Get out of here," Mrs. O'Reilly said.

It was too late. He had seen her. Dessa knew that look in his eyes. He hadn't really seen her at all, of course. He had seen some German soldier on a ridge in eastern France, or some Italian tank commander in the Alps, or a sniper on a ridge in Alsace-Lorraine. Dessa didn't know enough about the war her father had lived through to pinpoint it. She only knew that he had met the enemy and engaged them, and now he was meeting that same enemy again. He threw away the coffee table and picked up the big brass floor lamp that stood next to the fireplace that was never lit. He ripped the lampshade off the top of it and pulled the plug out of the wall. The coffee table crashed against the sofa and cracked in two. Somewhere far away, police sirens were blasting into the air, whooping and screaming.

The old man put his hands around the lightbulb now exposed in the lamp and crushed it. His hands ran with blood, but he was smiling.

"I'm gonna go *right through* you suckers," he said.

And then he started coming, the heavy lamp held out in front of him like a sword, his free hand clawing at the air. He was more than halfway across the room to her. His eyes were lit up and eager and blank. Dessa felt a thick hot acid wash of vomit rising into her throat.

"Suckers," the old man said.

Dessa spun around and ran into the bathroom. She slammed the door shut and leaned against it. There was no way to lock this door from the inside. There was nothing to do but to lean against it and hope she was too heavy for him, or that Mrs. Reilly could hold him off, or that the police would come soon. She heard him stop on the other side of the door and begin to bellow again. Then what must have been the base of the lamp began to smash against the wood next to her ear.

"Let the police come now let the police come now let the police come right this second," Dessa prayed, out loud, into the air, into the sound of his screaming.

The base of the lamp slammed down against the bathroom door again and again and again, until the door began to crack just like the coffee table had.

Dessa buried her face in the side of her arm and started to cry.

— 3 —

For Christie Mulligan, the pain started during the very last step aerobics routine of the day, almost at the very end, during the part where the music got slower. Pain was a bad sign, she knew that. Pain meant the bubble was getting bigger and the problem had spread. For the routine, she was supposed to hold her hands up over her head and wave them in the air. This was called "making like a palm tree" and supposed to be fun. Christie put one hand on her breast and felt for the bubble instead. It hadn't gotten any bigger, as far as she could tell. It hadn't gotten any smaller, either. It was just there, there there there, and—

What was it, exactly, that she thought she was doing?

When the last step aerobics routine was over, Christie took a shower in the locker room, dried her hair, got dressed in jeans. In the shower she felt for the bubble half a dozen times. Getting dressed, she felt for it half a dozen times more. That was when she started to be afraid.

It wasn't a bubble. It was a tumor. And it had been there for weeks now. Weeks.

There was a window stuck open somewhere and the locker room was cold, but Christie had sweat running down her back. The skin on her scalp itched, even though she had just washed her hair. Christie put on her turtleneck and her sweater and sat down on the bench. Tara and Michelle were all dressed and ready to go. She was taking too much time. She had taken so much time already, the three of them were the only ones left in the locker room.

What did she think she was doing? she asked herself. She hadn't talked to David since the beginning of December. She hadn't gone home for Christmas. She hadn't kept the appointments Dr. Hornig had made for her. She hadn't even answered her own phone, just in case it was Dr. Hornig herself on the other end of the line.

"Hey," Tara said now. "Are you ready? I want a Big Mac."

Christie's L.L. Bean Marine Hunting Boots were sitting on the floor with their laces pulled loose. All she had to do was put her feet into them.

"Come here," she told Tara. "I want to show you something."

"Show me what?"

"I want you to feel something."

When Tara came close, Christie pulled up first her sweater and then her turtleneck and began to pull down her bra. Tara looked embarrassed.

"Hey," she said. "Christie. I mean—"

"Don't be stupid," Christie said. She grabbed Tara's right hand by the palm and pulled it close to her. "Feel that," she ordered. "Right there."

"Should I go somewhere else?" Michelle asked.

"No," Christie said.

Tara's fingers touched the spot where Christie pointed. She had a puzzled look on her face.

"But what is that?" she asked, taking her hand away. "Is that some kind of cyst?"

"It's a tumor."

"But you can't know that, can you?" Tara said. "Not without a biopsy."

"Tara, I had a biopsy. Right after Thanksgiving."

"And they found out it was a tumor?"

"Yes."

"A malignant tumor?"

"Yes."

"But I don't understand," Tara said. "Why is it still there? Why haven't they done something about it? Are you on chemotherapy or radiation treatments or something?"

"I was supposed to have it out."

"When?"

"About four weeks ago."

"Oh, Jesus," Michelle murmured.

Tara sat down hard on the bench. "But. But—" And then she exploded.

"Jesus *Christ*!" she shouted. "Four *weeks* ago? Why didn't you get it done? Why didn't you tell anybody about it, for God's sake, what do you think you're doing here, did they want to take the whole breast, is that what you were afraid of, well, they've got implants and things now and for Jesus Christ's sake—"

"Don't scream at her," Michelle said, close to tears. "Why are you screaming at her?"

"I'm not screaming at her," Tara screamed.

"Listen," Christie said, and almost laughed, because all of a sudden she was the calmest person in the room. "Listen, the two of you, you've got to help me out with this."

SIX

— 1 —

There were real detectives in the real world who specialized in finding missing persons and filling in the backgrounds of people whose histories were suspect or sketchy. Gregor Demarkian had never been one of those detectives. Toward the end of his career in the FBI he had been very good at backgrounding, but then he'd had the resources of the Bureau behind him, and the resources of the Behavioral Sciences Department particularly. It was one of the truisms of work with serial killers, in the criminal justice system as well as in psychotherapy, that background was everything. The courts read a lot of details into the no-unreasonable-search and no-self-incrimination clauses of the U.S. Constitution, but the bottom line was that it didn't matter what you did to get the information you needed, as long as you didn't need to use that information in court. Gregor had never been part of the McCarthyite school of federal law enforcement. He didn't use wire taps the way high school cheerleaders used dental floss or hidden cameras like Allen Funt. He wasn't above petitioning phone and credit and bank records when he had to. He tried to keep it to cases where urgency was necessary. Urgency was necessary here, but he didn't have the resources of the Bureau behind him anymore. Even if he had

had them, he wouldn't have had time to interpret them. What he really needed was an aunt or a mother or a sister or a husband—but like half the other people involved in this case, the late Stella Mortimer didn't seem to have had them. Maybe it was Fountain of Youth that was to blame. Maybe, if you became a new you with a new body for every new year, you couldn't have relatives, because they wouldn't be able to recognize you from one change to the next.

Magda Hale had had to go out, and Traci Cardinale had had to leave a little early, but Magda handed Gregor over to a woman named Faith Keller and told Faith Keller to get Gregor what he wanted.

"It's not that I ever really knew anything about Stella," Faith Keller said as she led Gregor to the small room on the west side of the first floor where the records were kept. "I came here as her assistant about three years ago, but we weren't close. Stella was never very close to anyone."

Of course not, Gregor thought. It would be against the will of God if anybody involved in any way with the murder of Tim Bradbury was close enough to anyone else to actually tell them anything. The room where Faith Keller was leading him was small and crowded and chaotic. Papers were lined up in stacks on the desk and spilled out of the overstuffed metal files. Faith cleared a stack of papers off a chair and pushed it toward Gregor.

"You sit in that and I'll sit on the desk." I know it looks like a terrible mess, but it really isn't too bad. You can always find what you need if you need it. And it's all pro forma anyway."

"Why pro forma?"

Faith Keller smiled wanly. "Because Magda Hale doesn't hire on credentials, or records, or training. She hires the instructors after seeing them instruct a class. She either likes what they do or she doesn't. She hires the rest of us on sight. When I came in to interview, she said I was wearing a lovely dress. And then I had the job."

"You were Stella Mortimer's assistant but Magda Hale hired you?"

"Oh, I talked to Stella first. I was only sent to Magda to be cleared. It was obvious what she wanted, nonetheless.

When Traci Cardinale was first hired, she couldn't even type."

"When Stella Mortimer was first hired, could she direct videotapes?"

Faith Keller shrugged. "I think so. She used to make documentaries, you know, out in Califor— she was a student at the University of California film school in Los Angeles when she was younger. And she worked in New York for a while."

"Do you know what she was doing in New Haven?"

"Oh, she was from around here, Mr. Demarkian," Faith Keller said. "That's the usual reason people— places like L.A. or Ne— pened the day before yesterday, been with Fountain of Youth for fifteen years."

Magda Hale had said something about this. Gregor thought she might even have said something about it to Tony Bandero on the afternoon that Stella died. "Did Stella Mortimer and Magda Hale know each other before Stella came to work at Fountain of Youth?" he asked.

"You'd have to ask Magda Hale, I'm sure," Faith Keller said. "But if you want my impression, I'd have to say no. Oh, they might have met informally before Magda offered Stella the job or Stella asked for it, however that worked, but they were always saying how they had known each other *for twenty years*. That doesn't sound like they knew each other before, does it?"

"No," Gregor said, "it doesn't."

Faith Keller rearranged the broad lace collar on her gray-and-white flower-patterned dress. "It's funny the way you're asking all these questions now," she said, "because they're just the kind of thing Stella was talking about ever since Tim died. Personal questions, I mean, about how we none of us knew much about each other even when we'd been working side by side for years. It was disturbing, in a way. I do value my privacy. In my position, I am forced to."

"What's your position?" Gregor asked.

Up until then, Faith Keller had come across as a fluffy, wispy, ethereal woman, the sort who goes into retirement to tend flowers and take up theosophy. Now the look in her eyes sharpened into acid. Gregor thought she was going to tell him to mind his own business.

"My friend and I have been together for the past twenty-..." she said tartly, "My friend is not a man."

"Ah," Gregor said. "You know, I don't think most people are as conventional on that subject as they used to be."

"Some are and some aren't. My daughter is twenty-six, two years, and she's extremely conventional on that subject. I have a very nice job here, Mr. Demarkian. I work with very nice ... With Stella gone, I'm going to be moved in here to you like me to ...cords. That will be nice, too. I'd like every-put it?"

Faith Keller looked amused. "You can come right out and call me a dyke if you want to, Mr. Demarkian. I don't know any more about the etiquette of these things than you do. But no. Stella didn't know. I didn't tell her."

"Did she ask?"

"As a matter of fact, she didn't. I thought she was going to, with all the talk about how we had to connect better with each other and what a terrible thing it was that Tim had died without us knowing anything about him. But Tim seemed to be the only one she was really interested in. Stella even had his personnel file on her desk for a few days. Not that there was anything in it. We only keep personal files to stay in compliance with federal and state employee law. Social security numbers. Yearly medical checkup if relevant to the job. With Tim it would have been relevant, because he gave weight training and that's strenuous work. Anyway, some companies dredge up extraordinary details on their employees, but Magda and Simon don't bother. If they like your performance, they think that's enough."

Gregor didn't think this was a bad way to operate. It was the way most of the small businesses on Cavanaugh Street back home operated. "You said Stella had Tim's file on her desk for a few days," he asked, "does that mean she didn't have it on the day she died?"

"Oh, no. She didn't have it then. I brought it down here myself about a week ago. Like I said. There isn't really much of anything in it."

"Can I see it?"

"Of course." Faith Keller got down off the desk and went to the file cabinet. She went through the second file drawer from the top until she found what she was looking for. She handed the file over to Gregor. It wasn't much of a file. It couldn't have had more than three or four pieces of paper in it. Gregor took it out of Faith Keller's hand and opened it up on his lap.

Workmen's compensation insurance registration. Social security number. Federal and state income tax withholding information. Salary schedule. Weight trainers, Gregor learned, did not make much more than minimum wage. He pushed past all the official information and went for the piece of paper at the bottom, the official Fountain of Youth employment application. There wasn't much on that, either. Name, address, phone number. Known medical conditions. Known physical disabilities. Next of kin.

"This really isn't very much," Gregor said.

"I warned you. Stella was interested in it anyway. Because of the next-of-kin business."

Gregor looked down at the next-of-kin business: "Next of kin: Alissa Bradbury. Address: 47 Stephenson Road, Derby, Connecticut. Phone number: (203) 297-7162."

"It looks fairly straightforward to me," he said.

"Oh, it was," Faith said. "But Tim used to tell everybody that his parents had moved out of the area. Stella was quite upset when she found an address in Derby in the file. She thought she'd forgotten to change it, you see, when his parents had retired to Florida or wherever, and now we wouldn't be able to notify them that he was dead. She even tried calling the phone number to see if they had one of those this-number-has-been-changed-to tapes running on it."

"I take it you thought there was a different explanation," Gregor said.

Faith Keller nodded. "Oh, yes. I don't know what you know about this area, but Stephenson Road—"

"I've been to Stephenson Road," Gregor said quickly.

"Well, then. You see what I mean. I think Tim just lied, Mr. Demarkian. I think he told the truth on the application because he thought he had to, but when he was talking to other people he just lied. Not out of malice. Out of embarrassment. Stephenson Road is an embarrassing place to be from."

"I can see it would be."

"Stella couldn't see it. She was all worked up about it. I told her to go talk to Magda about it, but she said she'd tried and she just couldn't get Magda interested. If I know Stella, she probably went about it backward—indirectly, you know, so that Magda had no idea what she was worried about or how worried she really was. Stella could get like that."

There was a red cardboard pencil holder on the desk near the tallest stack of papers. Gregor got a Bic medium point out of it and picked up a piece of blank notepaper from the floor. Then he wrote down all of the information on Alissa Bradbury and stuck the piece of paper in his wallet.

"What about Stella Mortimer's personnel file?" he asked. "Can I see that?"

Faith Keller took back the file on Tim Bradbury and shoved it into the second drawer from the top of the cabinet without paying attention to just where she was putting it. If this was the way she handled files when she went to work in the records room, Fountain of Youth was going to be in even more of a paper mess than it was already. Faith opened the third drawer from the top of the cabinet, rummaged through it, and came up with another file. This one was thicker than Tim Bradbury's, but not by much.

"Here you go," she said.

Gregor opened the file. Workmen's compensation insurance registration. Social security number. Federal and state income tax withholding information. Salary schedule. Health insurance information for Fountain of Youth corporate plan. Gregor turned to the employment application. It was so old, the paper was brittle and yellowing. The only interesting thing on it was the fact that the next-of-kin information had been left blank. Even fifteen years ago, when Stella Mortimer had only just heard of Fountain of Youth, she had been an isolated woman.

Gregor handed the file back. "I think I understand what Miss Mortimer was so upset about. You people really don't seem to have any contact with each other."

"Some of us like it that way."

There was a time when Gregor had thought he might like it that way. He had changed his mind. It was a crazy way to live.

"That's all I'm going to need this for," he told Faith Keller. "Do you mind if I use the phone?"

"Why should I mind? I'm not paying for it."

Right, Gregor thought. He picked up the receiver of the instrument she pushed across the desk to him, and called Philip Brye.

— 2 —

The neighborhood surrounding the New Haven morgue and the New Haven medical examiner's office was much more threatening in the dark than it had been in the daylight—so much more threatening, Connie Hazelwood tried to talk Gregor out of going there and taking her with him. It was only six thirty-two, but it might as well have been midnight. The streets were no longer deserted and the double- and triple-decker houses no longer looked respectable. In Gregor's younger days, people who were breaking the law used to try to stay out of the way of the police. Now there were prostitutes working not fifteen feet from a building patrolmen went in and out of all night, and junkies shooting up on porches just across the street from the place where their bodies would eventually end up. Maybe the junkies were all smoking these days. Gregor hadn't kept up with the fashions in street drugs. Except for a few self-appointed holy knights of the drug war, Gregor didn't know a cop of any variety, federal, state, or local, who wanted to have anything to do with drugs. Drugs were a black hole that ate time and energy. It was depressing as hell to be confronted daily with the job of protecting the lives of people who were determined to end up dead. Gregor told Connie Hazelwood to go cruise a safer neighborhood for an hour and got out onto the curb. Right here, right next to the morgue building itself, the sidewalk was empty. On the other side of the street, very young girls in very short skirts and very high heels were parading back and forth, trying to keep warm. All of them were under eighteen, and all of them had their hair dyed one shade or another of violently yellow blond.

Gregor went into the relative warmth of the morgue foyer, gave his name to the guard at the desk, and let himself be checked out and buzzed through. This time, though, when he got back to the clerk's desk, Philip Brye was ready and waiting for him. The clerk was a short, roundish young woman with dark hair and plump hands. She wrote his name in her book and otherwise ignored him. Philip Brye was holding two gigantic Danish pastries. He handed the cheese one over to Gregor.

"It is cheese, isn't it?" he asked. "You can have the strawberry one if you want instead."

Gregor couldn't imagine eating a strawberry Danish. He took the cheese one and began to follow Philip Brye back to his office.

"I take it you put some kind of rush on the lab reports for Stella Mortimer," he said. "Either that, or you've been doing them personally."

"I can't do lab reports." Philip Brye kicked open his office door and gestured Gregor inside. "I get the vapors every time I see a test tube. I did the autopsy myself."

"And?"

"And what did you expect? Death consistent with poisoning by arsenic, which, by the way, is what the lab people found when they analyzed the contents of her stomach. That and traces of what was probably an English muffin, with butter. Also coffee. Stella Mortimer wasn't much of a health food nut."

The lab reports were lying in the middle of Philip Brye's desk, enclosed in a file clearly marked AUTOP: SM in red felt-tipped pen. Gregor picked them up and took them over to a chair where he could sit down and examine them. He took a large bite of Danish and flipped the file open.

"She didn't have to be," he said in answer to Philip Brye's comment about the health food. "She wasn't hired to be a role model, like the instructors. She was hired to take the pictures. Are all these numbers down this side supposed to mean something to me?"

"Not really. They're for administration. Take the next page."

Gregor turned to the next page. This was the stomach analysis, and he understood all of it. He couldn't count the number of stomach analyses he read while he was heading up the Behavioral Sciences Department. Eventually, he had gotten an agent trainee to read them for him. They always made him a little ill. Gregor ran through the technical language that added up to an English muffin with butter and a cup of coffee—gluten simplex, sucrose, dextrose, paraphalymides—and looked up.

"She took a lot of sugar in her coffee."

"She did this time, yes."

"Do you think somebody made the coffee for her? The sugar would do something to hide the taste of arsenic." Gregor sighed. "You know, I've investigated maybe half a dozen arsenic poisonings in my life, and you know what always bothers me?"

"No," Philip Brye said. "What?"

"Arsenic tastes awful," Gregor told him. "Arsenic tastes really, really awful. I know. I've tasted it. In the interests of research, if you get me. And yet people eat the stuff all the time. They eat massive quantities of it. That's why they die."

"Be reasonable, Gregor. Stella Mortimer didn't eat massive quantities of arsenic. She ate, or more probably drank, just enough to kill her. And the taste was disguised in the food she ate with it."

"Arsenic isn't cyanide," Gregor pointed out. "You need more than a drop or two."

"True. But arsenic is a hell of a lot easier to come by and it does the job. You wouldn't believe how much of the stuff we have sitting around here in the evidence room. You're not supposed to be able to buy straight arsenic without signing for it, but people do. They most certainly do. Then they go out and poison other people's dogs with it."

"Is that what most of the arsenic you collect has been used for?"

"Oh, yeah. Dogs and cats. People are incredibly nasty about other people's pets. Dogs are as fussy as humans are about the tastes of the foods they eat. At least some dogs are.

If you can disguise the taste for dogs, why couldn't you disguise the taste for people?"

"Maybe it's the politeness factor. Maybe if somebody gives you something to eat, or makes it for you, maybe you feel obligated to eat it even if it tastes awful."

"Remind me never to do that again," Philip Brye muttered.

Gregor flipped through to the next page in the file. This file was much thicker than the file at Fountain of Youth, but Gregor didn't think it was much more revealing. Height. Weight. Eye color. Hair color. He couldn't find anything unusual. At the time she died, Stella Mortimer hadn't been on any of the common recreational drugs. She hadn't been on the pill. She had gone through menopause. She had had her gallbladder removed. Gregor could have said the same things about a Park Avenue Chihuahua. He flipped another page in the file and came to the detailed physical descriptions of internal body parts. He flipped the file closed and handed it back to Philip Brye.

"She hadn't been dead very long when we found her," he said. "None of the vomit was dry."

"None of the smell had cleared off, either," Philip Brye said. "Now that's something else about arsenic. It takes time. With cyanide, you hand the poison over, and seconds later, your victim is belly-up. And there you are, right on the scene. With arsenic, you have time to arrange an alibi. Or at least a getaway."

"Did anybody get away from Fountain of Youth yesterday?" Gregor asked.

"You'd know more about that than me," Philip Brye replied. "Tony Bandero is supposed to be trying to find out where she was when she ate last, but he doesn't seem to be making much progress with it. The general assumption, from what I heard, was that people who work at Fountain of Youth eat at Fountain of Youth, because the nearest restaurant is a hefty walk away. I didn't see anything like English muffins or butter in that kitchen, though."

"I didn't either," Gregor said, "but she could have brought all that with her. Did she have a refrigerator in her office, or anything like that?"

"I don't know. We could ask. The uniforms will be talking to you, even if Tony Bandero isn't. In fact, from what I hear, the uniforms are real interested in you."

"Tony is real interested in me too," Gregor said, "it's just the wrong kind of interest. I keep wondering what it is he isn't telling me. In spite of all the hotdogging, my guess is that he's a better than competent cop. He's got to know more about what's going on here than he's letting on."

"So that he can pull it out of his hat at the last minute and look like a genius? Yeah, that would be about Tony's speed. What is it you think he might know?"

Gregor had been considering this question for some time now. If he was looking to make a media splash and stage a public coup, a clear win over the most overhyped murder investigator of the second half of the twentieth century (which was what Gregor considered himself to be; *way* overhyped), what information would he hold back? What information was it that this case could not be solved without?

"I think," Gregor told Philip Brye, "that there may be more information than he's been letting on about where Tim Bradbury's body was before it showed up on the lawn at Fountain of Youth. That naked body is the single most troublesome factor in this entire case. It's the one thing that makes this case odd."

"I can get you the original lab reports," Philip Brye offered. "I can probably get you the investigating officers' reports, too. It may not be legal, but Tony could hardly complain after all the time he's spent talking to the television reporters about how he's made you a full-fledged part of his team and how he's given you complete access to all the relevant information."

"Could you get me transcriptions of the interviews, too? I want to know if anybody else heard this bird or car or whatever it was—have you heard about that?"

"*Koo roo. Clang. Whoosh.*"

"That, yes. I've got three people who say it was a bird, and one who swears it was a car. Maybe if I can find more people who heard it, they would describe it to me as other things."

"I suppose a car is more likely. I can't think of any night-singing winter birds in this part of Connecticut. The car could have belonged to the killer, I suppose."

"If it was a car, I'd say it almost certainly did. Virginia Hanley told me that the sound she heard was the result of an exhaust system problem that is relatively common. Do you know anything about that?"

"All I know about cars is that you put gas in them and they go," Philip Brye said. "I've never had one make a *koo roo* sound at me."

"If it were a car and the problem is common, the *koo roo* sound doesn't matter," Gregor said. "It wouldn't prove anything. We couldn't use it. If the problem is uncommon—"

"Is Virginia Hanley the middle-aged one who looks like she's heading the ball committee for the American Cancer Society benefit?"

"That's the one, yes."

"She doesn't look like someone who would know all that much about cars to me. I mean, if it's a problem with cars and she's heard about it, then I'd think the problem would have to be fairly common because—" The phone started ringing. "Just a minute."

Gregor relaxed and let Philip Brye pick up. He could see what Philip was getting at about Virginia Hanley, although you never could tell. People knew the oddest things. Philip Brye had picked up a pencil and started writing a note on his memo pad.

"Ward six," he was saying. "All right. All right. The emergency room first. I'll tell him."

Philip Brye hung up.

"Start of a bad night?" Gregor asked him sympathetically.

"I don't know." Brye looked pensive. "That was one of my ambulance men. He was passing on what he thought was some interesting information. He's at the emergency room over at Yale–New Haven."

"What's happened?"

"What happened is that one of the regular ambulances brought in an apparent attempted suicide about twenty minutes ago, a young woman in her twenties, vomiting all over the place, they went right to the stomach pump. There wouldn't be anything strange about that, except that this young woman had identification in her purse saying that she worked at the Fountain of Youth Work-Out Studio."

Gregor sat up very straight in his chair. "Did you get a name?" he asked.

"Yeah," Philip Brye said. "Traci Cardinale."

Part 3

"The problem with days of auld lang syne is that they always make you look like a jerk."

—TIMES SQUARE REVELER,
LIVE ON WCBS, CHANNEL 2,
NEW YORK

ONE

— 1 —

As soon as Gregor and Philip Brye entered the hospital, Gregor could smell the smoke. One corner of the waiting room was taken over by six large young men in sleeveless vests and toxic orange hats. The backs of the vests were stenciled in white paint: "BLOOD BROTHERS." Most of the young men had tattoos on their arms, coiling snakes being a favorite. Most of them were smoking cigarettes. Philip Brye passed them without notice. Gregor thought only that it was the better option, given the several that might have presented themselves, for the staff to ignore the cigarettes. Somewhere in this building, one of the Blood Brothers was probably bleeding and might be dead. The last thing the Yale–New Haven, or any other hospital, needed was a gang war in its emergency room waiting room.

Up at the nurse's window, there was a stand-up cardboard sign that said: "KEEP THE NEW YEAR HAPPY. APPOINT A DESIGNATED DRIVER." Two cops were standing next to it, looking tired. The nurse behind the window was wearing a white tunic top with a name pin over the pocket identifying her as S. Caloverdi, LPN. Also behind the window was a plump young woman with short-cropped hair in civilian dress, operating a computer. The emergency room waiting room was not too crammed, which was a kind of miracle for this time of year. Aside from the Blood Brothers there was what looked like a mother and her three young children. None of the four was visibly hurt. There was an old man with a cane. There was a young couple looking sullen. It was still early yet, too early for major gang fights or that perennial problem of American emergency medicine, drug overdoses. Why was it that so many addicts overdosed at night? Too many things happened at night, as if the division was not between rich and poor or young and old or black and white, but between daylight and darkness.

Philip Brye stuck his head through the nurse's window and said, "Susan? I got a call about a Traci Cardinale?"

The LPN looked up. She was younger than Gregor had thought she was when he first saw her. Her skin was very pale and pasty looking. A line of angry red pimples ran along her jaw. Her nose was too big and too crooked to be attractive. Still, there wasn't a single crow's foot line at the sides of her eyes. Gregor guessed that she wasn't more than twenty-five. If that.

As soon as Susan Caloverdi recognized Philip Brye, she got even paler. "Oh, Dr. Brye," she said. "Traci Cardinale? Do you mean she's—"

"Not as far as I know," Philip Brye said quickly.

Susan was relieved. "Oh, good. We really worked hard over that one. We didn't know what was going on. But the last I heard, she was stable."

"I'm glad to hear it," Philip Brye said.

The two officers standing by the sign shifted on their feet. "Dr. Brye?" the taller of them asked.

"That's right," Philip Brye said.

"I'm Officer Tom Mordeck. This is Officer Ray Haraldsen. Dr. Lindner asked us to meet you here."

"Pete Lindner is the man I called just before we left the office," Philip Brye told Gregor.

Philip Brye had called several people just before he and Gregor left the office, including a take-out Chinese restaurant. Gregor put his hand out to Officer Tom Mordeck and said, "How do you do. My name is Gregor Demarkian."

"Oh, hell," Officer Haraldsen said. "So that's what all this is about."

"We're not sure," Philip Brye said.

"It's interesting seeing you in person," Mordeck said, speaking to Gregor. "You look a lot bigger in person than you do on television."

"On television, he was standing behind Tony Bandero," Haraldsen pointed out.

"On television, everybody stands behind Tony Bandero," Philip Brye said.

"We're the ones brought the Cardinale woman in here," Mordeck said. "Next door neighbor heard her vomiting and called us. Don't ask me why she didn't call an ambulance."

"She told us why she didn't call an ambulance," Haraldsen said. "She wanted to be sure somebody had the authority to break down the door."

"We called the ambulance and then we waited," Mordeck said, "and then we came right in behind them."

"I think they got there faster because it was us who called," Haraldsen added.

"Anyway, we've been hanging around here ever since." Tom Mordeck looked a little guilty. "Don't ask me why. The whole thing just felt wrong, if you know what I mean. She wasn't having the right kind of fits. I mean—"

"Jesus," Haraldsen said.

"There's a way they have fits when they've taken too many tranquilizers and there's a way they have fits when they've taken too much dope, and this wasn't either of them," Mordeck said stubbornly. "I mean, for Christ's sake. I've picked up enough of these guys. I know what I'm looking at when I see it."

"Why don't we just go see Pete Lindner," Philip Brye suggested. "Have either of you two notified anybody official about this?"

The two officers looked confused. "Who's to notify?" Haraldsen asked. "Do you mean, have we filed a report?"

Philip Brye shot his eyebrows up his forehead, looking at Gregor. "I hate to do this to you, but under the circumstances, I think it might be a good idea if they called Tony."

"I know," Gregor said sadly.

Tom Mordeck seemed stunned. "You want us to call in Bandero? He'll turn the place into a circus. He'll bring five television reporters with him. He'll make everybody nuts."

"It's his case," Philip Brye said.

"The only case that ever matters to Bandero is the case he's got on himself," Mordeck said. "Why don't you two guys just wrap this one up and save his appearance for the press conference?"

Gregor Demarkian could see the elegance of this course of action. It was the course he would have taken himself if he could have thought of any way to justify it. There was no way to justify it. Jurisdiction mattered, even when it was held by a publicity-seeking jerk who only wanted in so that he could get his name in the papers.

Gregor Demarkian had known a lot of publicity-seeking jerks in his career, the most notable of them being J. Edgar Hoover himself. Before Tony Bandero, however, he had never known one who took such unhampered glee in the whole process. Even good old J. Edgar had at least pretended to be "a very private person." Tony might be that rarity of rarities, a budding celebrity who would come out and say what everybody knew about him anyway: that he loved the hell out of publicity and wanted to live as public a life as possible.

Tom Mordeck and Ray Haraldsen were leading the way down a gleaming polished hallway into the bowels of the emergency room, their guns bumping against their hips as they went.

— 2 —

Dr. Peter Lindner was not the doctor who had actually taken care of Traci Cardinale, and pumped her stomach, and assigned a nurse to monitor her vital signs. Dr. Lindner was the head of emergency medicine for the entire Yale–New Haven complex, which made him much too important to do any of that. He sat in a large office with charts hanging from hooks on the walls and books piled every which way on the built-in shelves, but his own desk was scrupulously clean. He was, Gregor thought, like one of those executives from the largest corporations, who proved how well they delegated responsibility by showing how little paperwork they had on their desks to do. Dr. Peter Lindner himself did not look like the head of a large corporation. In spite of the Nordic sound of his name, he was small and dark and more Italian looking than Tony Bandero. The tops of his hands were covered with dark black hairs. His eyebrows met together over the bridge of his nose. His body was short-legged and long-trunked, the standard Mediterranean peasant's. Gregor wondered where the "Lindner" had come from.

"It was Rama Kadhi who took care of her," Lindner told Gregor and Philip Brye when he had gotten them both settled. He was passing out cups of coffee. Gregor didn't know what it was, but all the police and emergency room people he ever met had near-obsessions with making sure their guests had coffee. "Kadhi's a very good man in emergency, very competent and very calm, but I think he's a little confused. He's only been over from India for about two years, and then it took a while to transfer his accreditations. In fact, accreditations are the only reason I have him now. He has to complete the equivalent of an internship and residency to satisfy the board. After that, I suppose he'll move out to the suburbs and start charging by the hour."

"Are you having the contents of her stomach analyzed?" Philip Brye asked.

"We always do."

"We'd like you to check for a few things you don't usually check for," Gregor said. "Starting with arsenic."

Pete Lindner's mouth quirked into a smile. "I already did. As soon as Phil here told me that you were coming, Mr. Demarkian. I do read the papers."

"You wouldn't have had to bother," Philip Brye said. "The way the press has been on this case, the only way you could have missed any of it was to have been blind, deaf, and dumb."

"True," Pete Lindner said. "If I'd realized at the start that all this was connected with that, I would have handled the case myself. Fortunately, as I said, Kadhi is a very good man. Did the officers tell you how she was found?"

"They said something about a neighbor calling," Gregor said. "A neighbor heard her vomiting and called the police."

"She wasn't just vomiting, she was pounding," Pete Lindner said. "After I talked to Phil here, I went down and talked to the ambulance men. They said she was lying in her bathtub, absolutely dry and fully clothed, vomiting all over the floor and hitting the heel of her hand against the bathroom wall. That's the wall that connects with the bathroom wall in her neighbor's apartment. The heel of her hand was bruised black."

"She was still vomiting when the ambulance men got there?" Gregor asked.

"Oh, yes," Pete Lindner said. "She slipped into unconsciousness just a few minutes after they arrived. You can talk to them a little later, if you want. I've got them filling out forms to waste time. She didn't say anything to anybody. She wasn't capable."

"Do you know if she said anything to the police officers?" Gregor asked. "Weren't they there first?"

"They were definitely there first," Pete Lindner said, "and, again, you can ask them yourself. But I don't think she did. Once I knew that Phil was bringing you in here, Mr. Demarkian, I called in everyone I could find who was even remotely connected with this thing and told them we had a probable attempted murder on our hands. We did all try to work out what we knew so we'd be able to present it to you when you got here. Not that I told anybody it was you who was coming. The way news spreads around a hospital, information like that would have been damned near lethal."

Gregor agreed. He got out of his chair and walked around Pete Lindner's office. Through the barred E-glass windows, he could see the first signs of a light snow in the lights from the line of streetlamps that marched down the sidewalk outside. This was another terrible neighborhood. The sidewalks were deserted. The paint on the streetlamps was blistered and peeling. Only the streets themselves were in good repair. Probably because they didn't want the ambulances getting flat tires in potholes.

"She left work early," Gregor said, stopping near Pete Lindner's empty desk. "I needed something over there today that she usually would have been the one to get me, and Magda Hale told me that. Traci left work at four o'clock to go to a dentist's appointment."

"That can be checked out," Philip Brye said.

"We can check her teeth to see if anything's been done to

them," Lindner said. "Of course, the dentist's appointment may just have been for x-rays."

"I don't think we have to go so far as to check her teeth," Gregor said. "Is she still unconscious?"

"Yes," Pete Lindner said. "She'll probably be unconscious for most of the rest of tonight. She'd had a very bad time."

"But you do expect her to survive?"

"Oh, yes. Unless something very unusual happens, she should survive quite nicely."

"And she'll be whole?" Gregor persisted. "She won't have brain damage or affected speech or anything like that?"

"There's no reason why she should have. This isn't lye we're talking about here, or even strychnine. Being poisoned with arsenic shouldn't have any long-term consequences much different from being poisoned with sleeping pills."

"People are in comas for years after taking overdoses of sleeping pills," Gregor said.

"I know, Mr. Demarkian. But Traci Cardinale isn't in a coma now, and there's no reason to think she's going to be in one. Would you like to go down and see her? I was having her kept on the ward until the two of you arrived."

"It would probably be a good idea to keep her on the ward until Tony Bandero arrives." Gregor sighed.

Pete Lindner laughed. "Oh, *Tony*," he said. "He'll bring an entourage."

— 3 —

Gregor Demarkian would have been hard-pressed to explain why he wanted to see Traci Cardinale in her hospital bed. She was wan. She was sick. She was asleep. The little information this provided him with was of no use to him whatsoever. The hospital wasn't interesting, either. It was more or less standard, as hospitals went—maybe a little more high-tech than average, because this was a teaching and research hospital connected with Yale, instead of just a health care facility. There were too many machines with too many gauges. There was too much white and operating room green. Right outside Traci's room, there was another of those New Year's Eve signs, this time written in letters that were supposed to look like dripping blood. "NEW YEAR'S DEAD," the blood letters said. Gregor thought he would spend this New Year's Eve locked safely in his own bedroom with a television set and a cup of hot chocolate.

The nurse sitting beside Traci's bed stood up when Gregor and Philip Brye entered the room. Then there was a movement in the shadows and a small man appeared, dark and diffident and very serious. Dr. Rama Kadhi, Gregor realized. The doctor wore a stethoscope around his neck that had been polished so well it shone. He bowed his head first to Philip Brye and then to Gregor. Then he stepped over to the bed and pointed at the young woman lying in it. Traci Cardinale had an IV drip in her arm.

"Dr. Lindner has told us that this woman may be the victim of a homicide attempt," Rama Kadhi said very formally. "This is what you are thinking?"

Rama Kadhi was looking at Philip Brye, but Gregor Demarkian answered. "This woman is connected to a case in which two homicides have already occurred," he said. "We feel we have to be cautious."

"Ah," Rama Kadhi said. "I feel I have to be cautious, too. We did start work on her in time to save her. She will be all right."

"Good," Philip Brye said.

"In the meantime, there are difficulties," Rama Kadhi continued. "We are having a difficult time keeping her calm and quiet. It is necessary now that she stay calm and quiet. Do you understand?"

"Yes." Traci seemed calm and quiet enough to Gregor Demarkian. She seemed inert.

"In a different kind of case, we would give her sleeping pills now to help her rest," Rama Kadhi was going on, "but in this case it is not possible. She is unconscious. It is not indicated to give sleeping pills to a woman who is unconscious."

"If she's unconscious, why does she need help to relax?" Gregor asked. "Isn't that relaxed enough?"

The nurse next to Traci Cardinale's bed stirred. "She's

having dreams," she said. "She's having terrible dreams. She keeps calling out in her sleep."

Dr. Khadi shot the nurse a disapproving look. "It is not possible to have dreams while unconscious. This I was taught in India. She is quite restless, however. She does cry out."

"Wood," Traci Cardinale said, quite distinctly, as if to prove the nurse's and doctor's point.

The upright people stared steadily at the bed, but Traci Cardinale didn't cry out again. She didn't move. Her face looked as if it had been sculpted from wax.

"Well," Pete Lindner said. "I told you she wasn't in a coma."

"Of course she is not in a coma." Rama Kadhi said, surprised. "If she were in a coma, we would have put her in the Intensive Care Unit. Right away. The police do not come first here."

Gregor moved closer to the bed.

"Wood," Traci Cardinale said again.

Her lips barely moved. Gregor didn't understand why this was enough "restlessness" to worry about. She wasn't about to pull the IV drip out of her arm with this.

"Is *wood* all she ever says?" Gregor asked the doctor and the nurse.

"*Wood* is all I've ever heard her say," the nurse said. "I've been assuming she means wood as in trees. Maybe she's saying *would* with a *you el*. As in she would or wouldn't do something."

Rama Kadhi looked disapproving again. "This is very foolish," he said stiffly. "Why would she said *would* with a *you el*? This would not make sense."

"I don't think the woman has to make sense while she's unconscious," Philip Brye said.

Gregor looked around the room. There was no locked cupboard or personal closet. This was the emergency ward. There was no sign of what he was looking for.

"What happened to her things?" Gregor asked. "What was she wearing when she came in here?"

"She was wearing a little suit," the nurse said. "I've sent it upstairs already, to Ward six. There wasn't any place to keep it down here. I don't know if she's ever going to be able to use it again, though. It's covered with vomit and it's ripped in places, too. We had to rip it just to get it off her."

"This was a navy blue suit with a sort of boxy jacket that came down long over her hips?" Gregor asked.

"That's right," the nurse said. "It was a beautiful suit. Expensive."

"Was that what she was wearing when you saw her at work?" Philip Brye asked.

Gregor nodded. "What about shoes?" he asked the nurse. "And stockings. Was she wearing those?"

"She was not wearing shoes," Rama Kadhi said. "I thought they had been lost in the ambulance."

"She wasn't wearing stockings, either," the nurse said. "Stockings are always the worst to get off in cases like this. We take scissors and just rip them up. It's the only efficient way. But we didn't have to."

"Wood," Traci Cardinale said again. This time she did move, side to side, making the IV drip jiggle in its frame. The nurse bent forward quickly to steady it.

Rama Kadhi sighed. "This woman is no longer unconscious in the medical sense. She is only in a very heavy sleep. This is the problem."

"In the long run, it's not a problem," Philip Brye said. "In the long run it means she's going to recover. What about it, Gregor? Is there anything else you need here? We should let these people get on with what they're doing."

Gregor was thinking. There wasn't anything else he needed here. He'd picked up more than he'd expected to.

"I'd like to go see that suit she was found in," he said. "You might consider sending it for laboratory analysis."

"Good idea." Philip Brye nodded vigorously. "I know where Ward six is. I can take you up."

"Point me in the direction of a bathroom first," Gregor said. "I'll be with you in a minute."

Philip Brye took him out into the hall, handed him a key, and pointed him toward where he wanted to go.

"I have hospital privileges here," he explained, "and those are to the staff toilets. You don't want to use the ones available to the general public."

Gregor would have asked why not, but he didn't have the heart.

— 4 —

It was nearly three minutes later, when Gregor had just shut the water faucet off and started to put his coat back on, that he first heard the *koo roo*. He didn't realize, right away, that that was what it was. He was simply aware of a sound that was distantly and vaguely familiar, and that for some reason filled him with sharp anxiety. Then he heard it again, and the sequence became brilliantly and undeniably clear.

Koo roo, *clank*, *whoosh*, it went. *Koo roo*, *clank*, *whoosh*, *clank*, *whoosh*, *clank*, *koo roo*.

I know what that is, Gregor thought suddenly. I've heard something make that noise.

The staff toilet suddenly felt very claustrophobic. He went to the window above the sink and tried to force it down. It wouldn't go. He put his ear to the glass to see if he could hear better, but he wasn't even completely sure the sound he was hearing was coming from outside.

Koo roo, *clank*, *whoosh*, it went. *Koo roo*, *clank*, *whoosh*, *clank*, *whoosh*, *koo roo*, *koo roo*.

It was definitely coming from the outside.

Gregor had his coat half on. He shrugged himself the rest of the way into it, unlocked the staff toilet door, and charged into the hallway. Philip Brye was waiting for him there, looking idly at the notices on a bulletin board while he did. Gregor grabbed him by the shoulders and spun him around.

"What's on the other side of that wall?" he demanded, pointing into the staff toilet.

"A street," Philip Brye said, bewildered. "Gregor, what—"

"Come on."

Gregor grabbed Philip Brye by the arm and pulled him a few steps before taking off on his own. All he could think of was that he had to get to that street fast, wherever it was. He still wasn't sure what it was that made that noise, but for some reason he was convinced that if he didn't hurry, it would disappear. He flew up the corridor, moving faster than he could remember himself doing since they had mustered him out of the army. He passed the Blood Brothers talking to a nurse and the woman and her children in an open examining room. He slammed through the swinging double doors into the waiting room—

—and got stopped, dead in his tracks, by Tony Bandero.

To say, as the uniformed officers had, that Tony Bandero was bringing a "circus" with him would have been putting it mildly. Tony Bandero had brought what looked like every piece of camera equipment in the Western world with him. The camera equipment and the people who operated it were blocking the doors to the emergency room. A nurse was running frantically around the lot of them, telling them in a shrill voice they had to get out of the way. Tony Bandero was holding court, like Muhammed Ali giving a press conference after a successful fight.

"The Fountain of Youth Work-Out Studio," he was saying, "is becoming a Fountain of Death for the people who work there."

Gregor started to wince, but he felt his own arm grabbed and he was dragged, stumbling, to Tony Bandero's side. Tony threw an arm around his shoulders—a good trick, since Gregor was half a foot taller than he was—and grinned for the cameras.

"And here's Mr. Gregor Demarkian, our expert consultant on this case, to give you a few of the details."

At any other time, Gregor would have bitten Tony Bandero's hand for pulling something like that on him. Now, he almost didn't care. For it had suddenly come to him.

He knew where he had heard that sound before. He knew what had made it. He knew who had killed Tim Bradbury and Stella Mortimer and tried to kill Traci Cardinale. He even knew why somebody thought Tim and Stella and Traci had to die.

Now all he had to do was prove it.

TWO

— 1 —

Greta Bellamy had to wait until after ten o'clock to find Gregor Demarkian, and by then she was frantic. It didn't help that Christie Mulligan and her two friends hadn't shown up for class. More and more people were dropping out, disappearing, not even saying good-bye. It made Greta feel immeasurably sad. This had been, in spite of the murder, one of the best weeks she could remember in her life. Everybody here was exactly the way she had expected them to be, and it was true what they said in all those lectures about self-esteem. If you really went to work on yourself, you could change the way you looked in the mirror. Lately, Greta had been looking a lot taller, and stronger, and smarter to herself than she had before. Once or twice, she had even looked like somebody who might have a master's degree. It was an interesting thought. It wiped whatever nostalgic feeling she had left for Chick right out of her brain. Greta didn't think she was ever going to see the inside of a roadhouse again. What she wanted now was a full-time membership to the Fountain of Youth Work-Out Studio, so that she could come up here every other night or so on her way home from work. Chick could marry Marsha Caventello if he wanted to. Kathy could adopt Marsha as her best friend. There were at least three women in this class Greta liked better than Kathy. One of them, Dessa Carter, was even trying to stay on at Fountain of Youth after the end of the week, just like Greta herself.

Greta and Dessa and a tall, pale woman named Cindi were sitting together during the break, working out the ways in which Dessa could find the money for a Fountain of Youth membership, when Greta saw Gregor Demarkian come in with a man she didn't know.

"What you've got to do," Cindi was saying, "is go to a doctor and get him to say that you have to have the membership for health reasons. It's got to be a prescription, like medicine."

"They're going to take a health club membership for a medicine?" Dessa asked.

"Or a treatment, yes," Cindi said. "For your weight. There's not a health insurance claims adjuster alive who knows the difference between correlation and causality, they all operate on voodoo, so what you do is—"

Greta and Dessa and Cindi were sitting on the second-floor balcony overlooking the foyer. Gregor Demarkian came in with his coat already open and his face red with cold. Greta stood up and leaned over the balcony railing. She wished they would get it fixed. It was the one wrong note in the Fountain of Youth symphony. It was even worse than the murder, because it was out in front, calling attention to itself all the time. Greta took her terry cloth sweatband off her forehead and bit her lip. Maybe it was just as well that Bennis Hannaford wasn't with Demarkian. What would a woman like Bennis Hannaford think of someone like Greta, in a leotard?

"Mr. Demarkian?" Greta called.

Dessa and Cindi were bent over together, going through the ways in which Dessa might convince her *company* to pay for Fountain of Youth. Greta had never before known how many different ways there were to get something like this paid for.

Gregor Demarkian stopped in the middle of the foyer and looked up. The man he was with stopped with him. Greta Bellamy blushed.

"Oh," she said. "Mr. Demarkian. Um. Could I come down and talk to you a minute?"

"Of course."

Greta's blush seemed to be getting worse, if that was possible. Dessa and Cindi were looking up at her curiously. So were Gregor Demarkian and his friend. Greta rubbed her palms on the sides of her leotard and took a deep breath.

"Just a minute," she said.

Dessa and Cindi seemed to lose interest. Greta ran down the curving balcony stair and arrived panting at the bottom, feeling foolish.

"Oh," she said. "Excuse me. It probably isn't even important."

I'd do better if the man didn't seem so damned amused, Grace told herself—but it wasn't Gregor Demarkian who seemed amused. It was his friend. Gregor Demarkian looked polite.

Greta rubbed the palms of her hands on the sides of her leotard again. "Well," she said. "The thing is. It's that boy. The one who used to work here and he died?"

"Yes?" Gregor Demarkian said.

This was not the way Greta had imagined this working out. She bit her lip and twisted her right leg behind her left. She wished she could stop fidgeting. It was better than just as well that Bennis Hannaford wasn't here. Bennis Hannaford would think she was some kind of silly little hick.

"Well," Greta said again. "The thing is, I knew him. Sort of. I mean, it probably isn't anything, of course, you know, but I thought I ought to tell you because he is dead and that woman is dead too and I thought—I thought—"

"You thought you'd better tell me, just in case," Gregor Demarkian said.

"I didn't really know him know him," Greta blurted out. "He was too young. And the time I'm talking about, it was in February of 1988. He must have been in high school."

"He must have been in high school when what?" This was Gregor Demarkian's friend, whom Greta had already decided she didn't like. Greta tried to pretend he wasn't there.

"I got the picture from *The New Haven Register*," she said. "I went to the library and had it copied off the microfilm. We were in a singing group together, you see. The New Haven County All-Country Choir. We were all in church groups."

"What church group was Tim Bradbury in?" Gregor Demarkian asked.

"Baptist," Greta said. "I wouldn't have remembered on my own, but it was in the caption. To the picture I looked up. I made a copy of the caption, too. Anyway, I remembered because his mother used to come to all our performances, and it was really sad. She was this huge woman who wore tent dresses all the time and cut her own hair, you know the kind of woman I mean. And Tim was so embarrassed."

"Nineteen eighty-eight, Gregor Demarkian said. "That's interesting."

"I don't think he was just being snobbish," Greta said. "I mean, it wasn't just the way she looked. She was drunk nearly all the time. And then she'd come to these things and fall asleep in her chair, and everybody could hear her snore."

"Nineteen eighty-eight, Gregor Demarkian said again. "You said you had a copy of this picture. Where is it?"

"In my purse. In my locker."

"Where's your locker?"

Greta pointed down the corridor at the side. "It's not very far. I could go get it for you right now if you wanted me to."

"Do you have time?"

"Oh, yes," Greta said.

Greta didn't know if she had time. The breaks were ten minutes long. She had no idea when the class had been dismissed for this one. She had no idea how long they had all been sitting around on the balcony. She ran down the corridor to the locker room. It was a very elegant locker room, not like the one off the gym in high school. The lockers had combination locks, but they were built in.

Greta went thirty-four right, twenty two left, nineteen right and opened the locker door. Her purse was right where she had left it. She felt in the outside pocket and came up with both the copy of the choir photograph and the newspaper picture of Tim Bradbury she had used to make sure it was the same person. She put the more recent picture of Tim back and locked up again. Then she ran back out to the foyer.

"Here you are," she said, handing the photograph over.

"I tried to tell that other detective about it, the one from the New Haven police department—"

"Tony Bandero?" Gregor Demarkian's friend asked.

"That's right," Greta said. "Detective Bandero. I did try to tell him, but he wasn't very interested. He said it was all so long ago it couldn't have anything to do with what happened now. And that's probably true. But I thought about it, you know, and it didn't feel right. On television things like this matter all the time. So I thought I'd give it to you and let you decide what to do with it. You're the one who's supposed to be the expert."

Gregor Demarkian looked long and hard at the choir photograph. Then he folded it carefully into quarters and put it into the pocket of his coat.

"Thank you," he said. "I don't think this is necessarily unimportant."

"You don't?" Greta was thrilled. "Oh. Well. I'm glad I stopped you. I'd tell you more, you know, but that's all I really remember. And I don't suppose Tim's mother has anything to do with it."

"What's your name?" Gregor Demarkian asked.

"Greta Bellamy."

"Thank you again, Miss Bellamy," Gregor Demarkian said.

The gong sounded upstairs. The break was over. Greta hesitated for just another moment—she had done something right; she had done something right for the great Mr. Gregor Demarkian—and then raced back up the stairs, back to the balcony where Dessa and Cindi were waiting for her. Of course, that other detective had probably been right. It probably hadn't been really important. Gregor Demarkian had probably just been polite. It felt good anyway.

In fact, Greta thought, sailing down the hallway to the studio, it felt great. She hadn't spent a lot of time feeling great in her life.

She was going to have to find out how to turn this into a habit.

— 2 —

Nick Bannerman had had a headache all morning. By lunchtime—sitting at the picnic table in the kitchen with a glass of Perrier and a brown paper bag from Goldman's Deli sitting in front of him; waiting for Frannie Jay—his skull felt like the diamond mine for Snow White's seven dwarves. Maybe it was the workshop for Santa's elves. Something was pounding and pounding in there. Even two double-strength Advils hadn't helped. In half an hour, Nick had to go back upstairs and lead another aerobic dance. What was in the bag from Goldman's Deli was a corned beef sandwich on rye with mustard, a bag of potato chips, and a garlic pickle. He'd been feeling a lot better when he came into work this morning.

They were inching up on the New Year, and there were starting to be signs. Someone had tied little blue banner ribbons to all the cabinet handles. The little blue banner ribbons were the preprinted kind from Hallmark with "HAPPY NEW YEAR" written across them in tiny letters made of glitter. Someone had put a big cardboard magnet-backed card on the door of the refrigerator, too. The card showed a bleary-eyed drunk collapsed on the floor under a pile of champagne bottles under the words IS IT NEW YEAR'S YET? The card was supposed to be funny. There was going to be a New Year's Eve party for all the women who had attended this seminar week, although it was going to be held too early in the day for anybody to see the New Year in. Nick didn't imagine the party would include alcohol. Too fattening.

The weather outside was getting worse. It had been blustery and gray and cold all week. Now the sky was thick with clouds and the air was heavy with snow. Sometime soon, they were going to have an ice storm.

The kitchen door swung open and Frannie Jay came in. Nick took a long pull on his Perrier and watched her move across the room to him in her leotard. He had been aware of that from the beginning: what Frannie looked like in her leotard. Then she had begun to seem strange to him, and he had been put off. Now he knew her better, and she didn't seem strange anymore—just tense.

Very, very tense.

Right now, Frannie was as tense as he had ever seen her.

Maybe we should stop meeting in this kitchen, Nick thought. Maybe it's just looking out on the lawn where she saw Tim Bradbury's body that makes her get this way.

Frannie came over to the table and sat down. Usually she got something to eat first, alfalfa sprouts or raw spinach or yogurt mixed with raisins, but this time she didn't even glance at the refrigerator. Nick felt himself getting tense, too, in reaction. It was impossible not to. Whatever Frannie had was catching.

Frannie put her palms flat on the table and spread her fingers out. She had very long fingers, but her nails were short and bitten off.

"Listen, I've got something I've got to tell you. In view of last night."

What had happened last night was that Nick and Frannie had gone to bed. They had gone to bed here, in Frannie's room at Fountain of Youth, because Nick was still staying with his friend Tom and there wasn't any privacy in that apartment. There wasn't a whole lot of privacy at Fountain of Youth, either, but there was enough. They had had what Nick considered to be a very good night.

Now what? Nick wondered. She's married. She has herpes. She has AIDS. She can't go on seeing me because her family would never accept anyone black. *His* family would never accept anyone white, but he figured he'd worry about that when he had to.

"All right," he said, as calmly as he could. "Tell me something. In view of last night."

"In view of the fact that I think you might want it to be more than just last night."

"I do."

"I thought so. I hoped so. It's about something that happened in California."

Nick's brain immediately switched gears. This was going to be a victim story, then. He could see it coming. She would tell him the intimate details of the time she was raped or the time she was stalked or the time she was beaten up by two black guys who wanted her wallet, and if he was sensitive enough, he would have passed the test.

"All right," he said. "What happened in California?"

Frannie looked up at him quickly, and then looked just as quickly away. At the backyard. At nothing.

"In California," she said evenly, "I was arrested for a murder."

"What?"

"I was convicted of negligent homicide. I went to jail for six months and a day."

Nick was desperately trying to switch gears again, but for some reason it wasn't working. Frannie was still staring out the window. Her face was impassive.

"What are you talking about?" he asked finally. "Do you mean you had some kind of accident? Isn't negligent homicide what people get convicted of when they've been drunk driving?"

"I wasn't drunk driving."

"Then what happened? And when was this? Last week? Last year?"

Frannie was flexing her long fingers, first her right hand, then her left, over and over again.

"It happened six and a half years ago," she said, very distinctly. "In the summer. When I was living at the beach. That's what I remember most of all about it, sick as it is. The beach."

"Who did you kill?"

"My daughter. She was seven months old at the time."

The air was as thick as mayonnaise. That was the problem. The air was as thick as mayonnaise, and Nick couldn't breathe it in. His headache was suddenly a volcano, bellowing and hot.

"Jesus Christ," he said.

Frannie was rubbing her hands together, top to bottom, back to back. There were thick salt tears welling in her eyes.

"I'd like to tell you I remember just what I did or what she was like or even what she looked like, but I can't. I can't. I don't even have a picture of her. I never had one taken. Her name was Marilee. I remember that."

The air was something worse than mayonnaise. It was poison gas.

"I don't understand," Nick said. "Seven months. What

did you do? Were you careless with fire? Did you leave her too long in the car?"

"As far as anyone could tell, I drowned her."

Whoosh, Nick thought.

Frannie took a ragged breath. "I was doing about sixteen vials of crack a day at the time," she said, still evenly, still calmly. Everything else about her was agitated, but her voice was eerily calm. "I was doing enough to kill myself, if you want to know the truth, and I wasn't conscious most of the time, and one day, the way it looked afterward, one day I decided to give her a bath and I lost interest in the middle."

"Oh," Nick said.

"Anyway," Frannie said, "later that day I ran out, and I started to need it again, you know, so I was going around the house, looking for some cash, and when I went into the bathroom there she was, just floating in the water. So I got scared, you know, and I picked her up and tried to give her mouth-to-mouth resuscitation, except it was too late, she'd been dead for hours, and I didn't know resuscitation anyway. And then I started screaming, screaming, and screaming, and someone heard me and called the cops. My lawyer said later that it was a good thing it happened that way, because if I'd done anything to try to cover it up, I probably couldn't have gotten off with negligent homicide. I would just have gone to jail for murder."

"Were you thinking of covering it up?"

Frannie shuddered. "I wasn't thinking at all. I was just screaming and screaming. And I was coming off, you know. The police came and I just went and sat on the steps and looked out at the ocean, and I was shaking and crying the whole time, and they thought I was for real. They thought I was a real grief-stricken mother. They knew better later, of course."

"So you went to jail," Nick said—which was stupid, because he already knew that. His brain was on hold. He couldn't work out what was important here.

"I just got off probation about two months ago," Frannie said. "If I hadn't, I wouldn't have been able to take the job here. I thought I'd come back home, you know, and it would be like I'd never been to California at all, it would be like it never happened. And I could start over again."

"Have you? Started over again?"

"I don't think it's possible." Frannie stood up. "I don't feel much like eating lunch, Nick. I think I'm going to go work the machines for a while."

"All right. Good idea."

"That's why I don't do dope anymore. I can't do dope and work the machines."

"Yeah," Nick said. "I can see that."

Frannie wrapped her arms around her body and rocked a little. "Well," she said finally. "See you around."

The drunk on the magnetic refrigerator card had bubbles rising over his head. The bubbles were supposed to make him look as drunk as he could possibly be. Nick looked around and saw that Frannie was gone. He couldn't remember her leaving.

"Jesus Christ," he said, out loud, into the mayonnaise. His lungs must have collapsed by now. He must be living on his own carbon dioxide.

"Jesus Christ," he said again.

Once, hours ago, he had thought he was falling in love with a WASP American princess.

— 3 —

When Virginia Hanley had first imagined doing what she was about to do, she had seen herself doing it in the dark. She saw herself doing everything in the dark. She was a natural night person. Then she thought it through and realized that doing it at night would be impossible. Unless she wanted to wait for Steve and Linda to go on vacation—or stake out the house for months until they decided to eat at a restaurant and she knew for sure they would be gone for hours—she would have to do what she wanted to do in the daytime, when they were both at work. She had no trouble at all buying the gun. She had gone about it just the way they said you could on those news stories that ran during sweeps week on Channel 11 in New York, and the method had turned out to be applicable to New Haven with no variations at all. Capitalism was a wonderful thing. It would get you anything you wanted, with no trouble whatsoever, as long as you had the money.

Virginia had chosen to come out to the Litchfield house because the Litchfield house was where Steve and Linda were mostly living, and where they intended to go on living after the first of the year, when Linda left her job to go back to the land. Or whatever Linda thought she was doing. The Milford house was part of an old life. It didn't count anymore. The Litchfield house was what Steve had fallen in love with, more than he had fallen in love with Linda.

Virginia pulled her car up the long drive and parked it next to the barn, out by the back porch. The house wasn't much, but there was lots of land around it, acres and acres. There were lots of trees around it, too, hiding it from the road and its nearest neighbor, who was three miles away anyway. If you wanted to be isolated, this was the place to be.

Virginia got her shiny new Colt .45 and her brown paper bag from The Card Store off the front seat and climbed out of the car onto the drive. The air was frigid and wet. The stones in the gravel drive had begun to slick up. Virginia walked over to the back door, tried the knob, and found it locked. She raised the Colt and fired four times into the door, separating the lock from the wood.

"That's very nice," she said to nobody at all. She had a whole box of ammunition in the brown paper bag. She wasn't worried about running out. She was even feeling pleasantly proud of herself. The Card Store didn't sell ammunition. It sold cards and "party materials." The ammunition was in The Card Store's paper bag in case the police stopped her. Although why they would, Virginia couldn't imagine.

Steve has probably got a restraining order out on you by now, Virginia told herself. Coming through the back door led you directly into the kitchen. There wasn't a vestibule or a pantry to go through first. Virginia looked around at the old-fashioned refrigerator and the antiquated stove. Everything was so out of date and shabby. She put the brown paper bag down on the kitchen table and took the Happy New Year streamers out of it. She hung one of the streamers from the light over the kitchen table. She hung another from the door handle of the microwave oven. She put the rest of the streamers back into the paper bag. Then she took the Colt, aimed it at a shelf of decorative plates, and blew two of those plates into shards of glass.

Time to reload, Virginia told herself. She got her ammunition out and fussed with the gun. It hadn't been hard to learn to operate it. It hadn't been hard to learn to shoot straight, either. She just spread her legs apart and held onto the Colt with both hands, just like on *Hill Street Blues*.

Virginia took the gun and the paper bag into the living room. She took out three more of the New Year's Eve streamers and draped them over the fireplace mantel, catching them on the heads of exposed nails. Everything here needed to be repaired. Everything needed to be renovated. The couch was worn in dozens of places and the springs in the chair were showing through underneath. Steve was insane if he thought he could really live like this. He would absolutely hate it.

Virginia aimed at the coffee table in front of the fireplace and made three skidding holes in its already splintered surface. She aimed at the five bottles of Scotch lined up on a bookshelf that was supposed to substitute for a bar and got three of them. The room was full of the smell of liquor.

Time to reload again, Virginia told herself. She had started to hum, the "Off to Work We Go" song from the Disney version of *Snow White*. Someone had been talking about *Snow White* just the other day—the black man who worked as an instructor at Fountain of Youth. How odd.

Virginia went into the bedroom. It was a terrible bedroom. The mattress and the box spring looked firm and new, but the rest of the room was a disaster. The four-poster bed was splintered. The canopy frame was bare without a canopy. Virginia hung the rest of the Happy New Year streamers from the canopy frame. Then she blasted the hell out of the vanity table mirror. It was a good thing there weren't any neighbors close by. If there had been, they would have called the police by now.

Virginia put the gun down on the night table next to the bed and took off her shoes, and her stockings, and her dress. Then she took off her bra and her panties, too. Then she got in under the covers and picked up the gun again.

When they came back home tonight, she would be waiting for them.

She would be lying right here, where they couldn't miss her.

She would take care of the both of them, once and for all.

Virginia put the barrel of the gun into her mouth and pulled the trigger.

THREE

— 1 —

One of the advantages of never having gotten a private detective's license was that you were able to bend the rules when you needed to. The problem was to decide how far to bend the rules. The courts were strict. Information obtained outside of normal channels was not information at trial. Information obtained in a way that could be considered illegal could get half a dozen people fired. Gregor could hardly plead ignorance in the event of a mess. His name was sitting in the *amicus curiae* briefs filed in a half a dozen cases heard by the U.S. Supreme Court. Then there was the question of just what evidence would be deemed inadmissible, once the court discovered that the rules had been bent. If it was just the details, Gregor could live with it. If it was the fact that anything had been found at all—.

"The problem," Gregor told Philip Brye and Connie Hazelwood, sitting over cups of coffee just before noon in that little restaurant he had found on the Green, "is to get into that house to search it without alerting the present owner of that house that we're going to search it."

Philip Brye frowned. "But you have to present a search warrant. Who are you going to present the search warrant to, if not the owner of the house?"

"I need to be more clear," Gregor said. "There is, in this case, an owner of record and a real owner. I don't care one way or the other about alerting the owner of record—"

"Who is who?" Connie Hazelwood asked.

"Who is Alissa Bradbury," Gregor said. "Alissa Bradbury's the name on the deed. She's the name on the tax polls. She pays the tax bills. And all the other bills, too, I'd imagine. At least, she does in theory."

"I take it that means you don't think she does in reality." Philip Brye signaled the waitress for another cup of coffee.

"I don't see how she could. And since she is the owner of record, I'm sure a court would issue a search warrant in her name. What I'm not so sure is that the court would issue a search warrant for one of us—say, for Dr. Brye here—without also insisting that we inform Detective Bandero. And if we inform Detective Bandero—"

"It will be a media event," Connie Hazelwood said. "Everybody in the state of Connecticut will know."

"Exactly," Gregor said.

Philip Brye shook his head. I don't understand the need for all the secrecy. What difference does it make if the owner of this house does know what you're doing? He's going to have to know eventually. Or she is. Do you mean you think someone's going to go into the house and remove the evidence you're looking for?"

"No. At this late date, that wouldn't be possible. It's not a marble we're going for here. It couldn't be carried out of there in a pocket. If we want to make sure nothing gets taken out of that house that we don't want out, all we have to do is post a guard. It's the element of surprise I'm worried about. Just finding what I'm looking for isn't going to be enough."

"I keep hoping that Traci Cardinale will wake up tomorrow and just tell us who gave her that poison," Philip Brye said. "That would solve the whole thing."

"It would," Gregor said, "assuming she does in fact know, and also assuming she could prove it. 'I had dinner with so-and-so and the next thing I knew I was falling over' won't quite do it. First, I want to search that house. Then I want to dig through a few of the public records. Marriage and divorce certificates. Real estate transactions. Hospital admissions. I'm not expecting to find anything. Everything's been done very carefully up to now. We may have some luck just because all this has been going on for so long. There's nothing to say everybody involved in it was careful all the time."

"If we're not likely to find any of these records," Connie Hazelwood objected, "then you're back to saying what Dr. Brye thought you were saying in the first place. That this whatever-it-is you're looking for is the only thing you need. Because if it isn't the only thing you need and all these records you're talking about aren't going to do any good, then it isn't going to matter how you get into that house, you aren't going to be able to catch the murderer. Not catch him to arrest him, anyway. And what's the point of catching him if you can't arrest him?"

"I can't arrest anybody," Gregor pointed out. "But I do have at least one other piece of evidence to use in this case, and given the element of surprise—I'm back to surprise again—I can use it to good advantage. But it's not going to be of use to anybody at all if the murderer knows it's coming."

"So what do you intend to do?" Philip Brye said. "Hide in this guy's closet and then leap out at him while he's getting into his pajamas with your evidence at the ready?"

Gregor had finished his coffee. He looked up and signaled the waitress, an older woman in a white polyester uniform and white orthopedic shoes. The come-celebrate-New-Year's-Eve card in the sugar holder looked like someone had bitten it. There were unmistakable teeth marks in the upper right hand corner. The waitress came to the table with her Pyrex pitcher full of coffee and filled all their cups, even Connie Hazelwood's, whose cup wasn't half empty. Gregor took a long sip of coffee and nearly scalded his mouth.

"What I'm going to try to do," he said, "is what everybody always expects me to do. I'm going to set up a confrontation scene."

Connie Hazelwood brightened. "You mean like in Agatha Christie murder mysteries?" Where you get all the suspects into one room and tell the story of the murder and then name the murderer?"

"Exactly."

"Don't be an ass," Philip Brye said. "You'll get shot."

"Where are we supposed to have this confrontation?" Connie Hazelwood looked eager.

Gregor had thought this over on their way to the restaurant. "The Fountain of Youth living room, the one on the first floor next to the foyer. It could be the foyer itself, but there aren't enough places to sit. We'll have to ask Magda Hale's permission. Then we'll have to invite the people who need to be there."

"You've got a list?" Philip Brye asked skeptically.

Gregor took the pen out of his jacket pocket and a napkin out of the napkin holder. The restaurant was full up for lunch. They should probably order some instead of taking up a table having nothing but coffee. The owner probably didn't want to bother two men in good suits. All the rest of the customers were dressed rough. There were a lot of dark-colored workmen's uniforms. There were a lot of jeans and sweaters, too, but not designer jeans and J. Crew cotton sweaters. Too many of the men had grease caked into their fingers and streaked through their hair. This was not a hangout for history professors from Yale.

Or maybe it was.

Gregor wrote on the top of the napkin:

Magda Hale

"The more people, the better I like it," he explained, "so Magda can bring Simon Roveter if she wants. Actually, we couldn't keep him out. He owns half the house. Then I want to get invitations to, let's see."

Gregor wrote down the napkin in a list:

Dessa Carter
Frannie Jay
Nicholas Bannerman
Christie Mulligan
Greta Bellamy

He hesitated. "I want to write Virginia Hanley down here, because of that remark about the car, but I'm not sure. She's not strictly necessary, and she's an annoying woman."

"Leave her out, then," Philip Brye said. None of this was making him happy. "What are you going to do when you finally get all these people into a single room?"

"Ah, well," Gregor said. "Then we're going to need the cooperation of Detective Bandero. He's certainly going to have to be there. And we don't have to tell him what I'm up to in advance. That may head off the media blitz to a certain extent. I just wish there was some way to get in touch with him at the last minute."

"You can get in touch with him any time you want," Philip Brye said. "He's got one of those beeper things. You call his work number and the beeper goes off and he finds a phone and calls in for your message. All the detectives have them these days, in case of emergencies."

Gregor thought about it. He had seen Tony Bandero with a beeper, that first day he had come to Fountain of Youth. The beeper had gone off and Tony had said something about dealing with it later. That did not bode well for getting in touch with the man on short notice. Maybe they would just have to give it up and invite Tony well in advance, just like everybody else. Maybe that was one of the risks Gregor was going to have to take.

Gregor folded the napkin and put it into the pocket of his jacket along with his pen.

"None of this," he said, "is getting us into that house, and if we don't get into that house, we might as well give up on the rest of it. I wish Tony hadn't made such a big public deal out of hiring me as a consultant. If I were a little less official, I could just go over there and break in. I might even get away with it."

"You'd lose your element of surprise if you didn't get away with it," Connie Hazelwood pointed out. "You'd get arrested and be in all the papers."

Philip Brye drained the coffee from his cup and put the cup very precisely back into its saucer.

"I think," he said carefully, "that I may know of a way to get into that house. Perfectly legally. And without letting Tony Bandero know about it."

— 2 —

If the drug war were a real war, it would have command centers as well as armies, bunkers as well as ordnance. Of course, the drug war was supposed to have all those things. Presidents kept appointing drug czars. Drug czars kept setting up offices. Policy kept switching between "punishment and detention" and "prevention and treatment" with no known effect whatsoever. Nobody seemed to notice that "punishment and detention" got more and more people arrested and more and more people in jail without shrinking the addict population one iota. Nobody seemed to notice that students who graduated from the most popular high school drug prevention program had a rate of drug use higher than students who didn't or that there wasn't a single drug rehabilitation program with a recidivism rate under 96 percent. Gregor Demarkian had spent his life as a federal cop, not a politician, so he knew numbers most people never saw. That was how he had ended up chasing serial killers. He would have allowed himself to end up pushing paper in an office in Salt Lake City if it had protected him from having to work on drug cases. Almost every agent he had known in the Bureau had felt the same way. Somebody had to like chasing drug dealers and picking up addicts. There were drugs squads in police departments across the country. There was a Drug Enforcement Agency. As far as Gregor knew, these projects had no trouble attracting personnel. But he couldn't imagine doing the work himself. He didn't think it really had anything to do with criminal justice, in the classic sense, or with fighting crime. In 1800, cocaine had been both legal and widely available in the United States, and almost nobody had wanted it. Now it was not only illegal but dangerous to acquire, too often involving guns and gangs and bad neighborhoods, and the tide of addicts seemed to get higher every year.

The drug war in New Haven, Connecticut, was represented by a short, slight, bookish-looking man named Roger Dornan. There were also police officers on the regular force who investigated drug cases and a group of social workers who provided "drug education" in the public schools, but

Roger Dornan was New Haven's official liaison with the federal drug enforcement programs, and that had made him somehow "official." When the papers needed a quote for a story having anything to do with drugs in the New Haven area, they went to Roger Dornan. When the television news people had to identify Roger Dornan to the public, they said he was "head of drug enforcement operations for the city of New Haven." This was inaccurate, but it suited everybody involved. There was no one else in town who wanted to be "head of drug operations for the city of New Haven."

"It's a dismal job to have," Philip Brye had explained to Gregor, unnecessarily, on their way over to Roger Dornan's office, "because you never do anything but lose."

Roger Dornan didn't look like the head of anything. His office was a cubbyhole in an administrative building otherwise filled with women who worked for social services departments. He had a desk and one chair and a lot of bookshelves crammed with papers. Gregor and Philip Brye had left Connie Hazelwood circling the block in her taxi searching for a parking space. Gregor thought the state of Roger Dornan's office was indicative of what was wrong with the drug war. It was cramped. It was dark. It was overworked. And nobody else in the building wanted to go near it.

Roger Dornan had listened to Gregor and Philip Brye explain their problem and ask their favor, fiddling all the time with a five-by-five inch stand-up cardboard sign that said: "MAKE IT TO THE NEW YEAR. DON'T DRINK AND DRIVE." Gregor had gotten so used to these signs, he had almost stopped seeing them. This was the way city and state officials celebrated New Year's Eve. They got ready to deal with the carnage.

Roger Dornan said, "Forty-seven Stephenson," and stood up. He took a big blue plastic spiral notebook off the shelf behind him and opened it on the desk.

"Forty-seven Stephenson," he said again, paging through a stack of plastic-coated maps. "That's Derby, I think. Just inside the Derby town line. We'll have to ask the Derby police. It might be Oxford. That's the next town over."

"Would that be a problem?" Gregor asked. "If it was in Oxford instead of Derby?"

"No, no," Roger Dornan said. "It's just a question of

who we ask the favor of, that's all. I like Derby a little better than I like Oxford because I know Hank Balderak fairly well. I don't have to be too polite about what I want from him. It helps that you're looking for something in that particular neighborhood."

"You've been having drug problems in that neighborhood?" Gregor asked.

Roger Dornan smiled wanly. "I don't have any problems with that neighborhood. It's not in my jurisdiction. The town police forces have a problem with it, though. All kinds of problems. Have you been out there, Mr. Demarkian?"

"Once."

"Once might not have been enough to do it. To get the full flavor of it, you'd have to go out there on a Saturday night. Or on New Year's Eve. Now, that would be an experience. You do understand, though, that this particular house, number forty-seven, hasn't been involved in any drug investigations so far."

"Can you be sure?" Gregor asked.

Roger Dornan turned the map book around so that Gregor could see it. The maps were in black and white, with little red crosses dotted over them. Roger Dornan pointed to a spot on the middle of the left-hand page. Looking closer, Gregor could see a snaking black line that was meant to represent the Housatonic River.

"No red," Roger Dornan said. "Every time we go into any place in the area on a drugs call, we mark the location on these maps with a red *ex*. And we keep each other informed. Derby. Oxford. Stepney. Branford. We're not exactly computer literate and technologically coordinated, but we do try."

"Would you have any other information on that house?" Gregor asked curiously. "Do you keep records on fires and arrest calls and that sort of thing?"

"Not on a house that hasn't had a drug connection, we don't," Roger Dornan said. "And we wouldn't keep that kind of soft information on a place in Derby or Oxford anyway. You could ask the local police forces there, if you really wanted to know."

"What is it you want to know?" Philip Brye asked

Gregor. "I thought this thing you were looking for was singular."

"It is," Gregor said. "It is. I was just curious, that's all. It might be interesting to see what the record is like. Domestic disputes. Disturbing the peace. Child abuse reports— although there might not be any of those, that far back. I don't know how the law operated in Connecticut when Tim Bradbury was a child."

"It operated the way the law operated everywhere in those days," Philip Brye said. "Meaning it didn't. You can have all this information for the asking if this plan of yours works, you know, Gregor. Once the police actually arrest somebody, you can get anything you want."

"Maybe I will," Gregor said softly.

Roger Dornan looked down at his book of maps and scowled. "I just want to get one thing straight. What you two want me to do here—what my friend Phil wants me to do here, which is why I've been listening to this request at all—is to ask for a warrant to search the house at forty-seven Stephenson in connection with an ongoing investigation. And then I'm supposed to take the two of you with me."

"Right," Philip Brye said. "To be specific, you're supposed to take him with you," he jerked his head in the direction of Gregor Demarkian, "because he's the one who knows what we're interested in."

"You won't be lying, you know," Gregor said. "This is a search in connection with an ongoing investigation."

"If you talk to old Judge Varley, you won't have to say much of anything at all," Philip Brye said. "That's what I was hoping you'd do, Roger, because it's the only way I can think of to get around telling Tony Bandero."

"I know." Roger Dornan was still scowling. "You two are absolutely sure this is absolutely necessary?"

"Positive," Gregor Demarkian said.

"There's no other way to get this done."

"I've been through this problem in my head a dozen times, Roger," Philip Brye said. "I can't think of one."

"Let's try this," Roger Dornan said. "You're both sure that there's no other way to successfully complete the investigation you're working on without getting this done, this way."

"No," Gregor Demarkian said. "But there's no way to be absolutely sure that we can get this murderer arrested and tried unless we go about this this way. We can go about this in the ordinary manner, Mr. Dornan. We can inform Tony Bandero of what we want to do and let him turn it into a media circus. But if we do that, I don't think we will see an arrest, and I'm sure we won't see a conviction."

Roger Dornan rubbed his face with his hands. "Shit," he said. "All right, Mr. Demarkian. I'll take your word for it. You'll have to give me a couple of hours to make a few phone calls and fill in the paperwork. You both ought to be very grateful that I don't like Tony Bandero any more than you do."

"We are," Gregor Demarkian said.

"It's not like you've never done this before," Philip Brye said. "I really didn't invent this idea out of a fervid imagination. I heard about that case of Carol Dillerby's—"

Roger Dornan shot Philip Brye an absolutely poisonous look. "I'm not saying I haven't done it before," he barked. "I'm not saying I'm the only one who's ever done it, either. I'd just like to make sure it was worth it in case I get caught."

— 3 —

Nobody got caught. Not then, anyway. The process seemed to take forever, but it was a process, and by four o'clock that afternoon, Gregor and Philip Brye and Roger Dornan were standing by the side of the road in front of the little collection of shacks that lined the Housatonic River on the Derby side. Connie Hazelwood was still in her taxi. A pair of police officers in the uniforms of the Derby Police Department had parked their cruiser half onto the slick cold grass. The cruiser was tilted slightly downward, like a car that had not quite gone off the side of a cliff.

Four o'clock in the afternoon in December is dark. The lights in the house on the hill behind them were lit. The shacks in front of them were showing light, too, although in some places that was only the light of a flickering television screen. There was a flickering light on in the house of the retarded woman who lived next door to number 47. It seemed to be a candle or a kerosene lamp. The two uniformed patrolmen were making a circuit of Alissa's Bradbury's shack. When they came back to the roadside, they climbed the hill again and joined Gregor Demarkian and Philip Brye and Roger Dornan.

"The place is completely boarded up," one of them said. "The only way in is to break in."

"You've got permission to break in if you have to," Roger Dornan said.

"Let's make sure we've all got flashlights," Gregor said. "I don't think there's any electricity on in that house."

They all had flashlights except Philip Brye, who said it never would have occurred to him. Connie Hazelwood gave him the one she kept in her glove compartment. It was small and inadequate, but it would keep him from tripping over himself in the dark.

"The only door's over on this side," one of the patrolmen said, leading the group to the river side of the house. Gregor had stood on the steps to it while he talked to the woman with Down's syndrome next door. Now one of the patrolmen climbed the steps and tugged at the board nailed across the screen.

"Watch out," the other patrolman said. "Those steps are rotted right through."

The first patrolman got out a claw hammer he had hanging from his utility belt and tried that on one of the nails holding up the board. It didn't work and he cursed softly and put the hammer back and took up the crowbar instead. The crowbar bit into the soft wood and came up with splinters and a soft substance like wood putty. The patrolman put the crowbar back in his belt and used his hands instead. He got a grip on the middle of the board and pulled. The board came away like paper.

"Bad plywood and rotten on top of it," he said, clearing away the remaining wood with his hands. He pulled at the screen door and it came open without complaint. He pushed at the door inside that and it came open, too. "No locks," he said, stepping into the shack.

Gregor followed the patrolman inside and looked

around. Coming in the door, you walked right into a tiny room meant to be a combination living room–dining room–kitchen. The kitchen consisted of a single wall of cabinets and small appliances. The dining room consisted of a small round table and two chairs. The living room consisted of a couch and an ancient television set. Even in the bad light given off by the flashlights, Gregor could see that there were thick layers of dust over everything. Some of the dust would have been disturbed, of course, but they could come back for that. They could pull the boards off the windows and do it in the daylight later.

"Find the bathroom," Gregor said.

One of the patrolmen made a comment about how a place like this ought to have an outhouse. Gregor ignored him and went through the only other door beside the outside one that he could see. He found himself in a small square space with two other doors opening onto it. Gregor shone his flashlight into the closest of these doorways and found the bedroom. He shone his flashlight into the other and found the bathroom. It wasn't much of a bathroom. Half the floor appeared to be rotted out.

"It's cold as hell in here and it still smells bad," Philip Brye said.

Gregor shone his flashlight in the direction of the toilet, and then into the toilet and then onto the walls next to the toilet.

"There," he said finally. "In that corner."

"What's in that corner?"

"Vomit," Gregor said. "Considerably dried, of course. There should be more on his clothes."

"On what clothes?" Roger Dornan sounded confused.

"Tim Bradbury's," Gregor said. He backed out of the bathroom. "They'll be in here, I expect," he said, meaning in the bedroom. "Left in a heap, probably, unless our murderer was smart enough to get rid of them right away. I don't see that there would have been any need to bother, though. It wasn't like there was any danger of anyone coming out here any time soon."

"I would think there would be," Philip Brye said. "If I were a cop, I'd come here practically right away. After all, it was his mother's house."

Gregor played his flashlight from one corner of the room to another. The room was small, but it was crammed with stuff. There were discarded clothes everywhere. Gregor turned his attention to the floor. The floors in the living room and the hall were carpeted. The floor in the bathroom was covered with linoleum. This floor wasn't covered at all. It was made of wood, but not wood planks. It was composed of cheap sheets of plywood. The whole house was made of plywood, Gregor thought. If somebody put up a shack just like it today, it would be made of pressboard.

The plywood floor was dirty and warped, but otherwise untouched,

"Do you think the two of you could move the bed?" Gregor asked the patrolman nearest him. "I want to see what's underneath it."

"Probably rat droppings," the patrolman said, but he got to work.

The bed wasn't hard to move, in spite of all the clothes and bottles piled on top of it. When it was out of the way, Gregor got down on his knees and shone the flashlight on what had been uncovered. The plywood was dirty and warped here, too.

"We're going to have to go through all the clothes in this room until we find Tim Bradbury's," he said absently, looking at the seams between the boards. "We aren't going to absolutely need them, but they wouldn't be bad to have. Wait a minute. There it is."

"There what is?" Philip Brye asked.

"The difference," Gregor said. He stood up and pointed his flashlight at the floor. "Right there," he said. "If these two officers would be kind enough to pull up the floor starting right there—"

By now the two Derby patrolmen were no longer interested in asking questions. They got right down on their knees and went at the relevant place on the floor with hammers and crowbars. This wood didn't splinter as easily as the wood that had covered the door had. It was newer. One of the patrolmen got up a corner of the board and tugged at it. It bent in his hand, but it didn't break.

"It's the river," he said apologetically. "Everything this close to the water gets wet."

"I've got it," the other patrolman said.

The board was made of very good plywood indeed. It came off in a piece, barely splintered where the nails had been driven into it. Gregor was willing to bet that the nails were of a better quality than the ones used in the rest of the shack, too.

"What the hell is that?" the patrolman asked, peering into the hole left by the discarded plywood board. Then he blanched. "Oh, Christ," he said.

Gregor Demarkian bent closer. What "that" was was a now fleshless skeleton, curled into the fetal position and still wearing a locket necklace—turned green with age—around its neck.

What "that" was was all that remained of the body of Alissa Bradbury.

A single bullet was lodged in the bone in the center of its chest.

FOUR

— 1 —

The envelope from Jimmy Fleck did not contain a prescription for Demerol. It contained copies of her x-rays, with little notes written on them in green felt-tipped pen. "Hairline fracture," several of the notes read. Others were more complicated, containing words Magda only vaguely knew the meanings of, the names of bones, the designations of injuries. If I had injured a muscle, I would have understood it better, Magda told herself when the package came. Then she put the package away in the long center drawer of the antique desk in her bedroom.

"You haven't just injured yourself once," Jimmy Fleck explained to her that morning. "You've injured yourself over and over again and you've never done anything about it. Your legs are about to disintegrate. This must have been going on for months, for God's sake. Didn't you ever notice you were hurt?"

Well, yes, Magda thought now, looking at herself in the mirror as she dressed for her last class of the day. She had noticed that she was hurt, if by "hurt" Jimmy Fleck meant to say "in pain." She had noticed the pain quite frequently. She had simply assumed that it was, well—

(getting old)

something unthinkable, something she didn't want to deal with. It seemed impossible to her, after all the work she had put into this, that she would end up just like everybody else. That wasn't the way it was supposed to work. You were supposed to work hard. You were supposed to give it everything you had. You were supposed to get what you'd worked for. There was no room in Magda Hale's life for inevitability.

The pills were lined up on the vanity counter around the sink, thirteen of them, too many to take all at once. Magda had gotten them the easy but expensive way. When Jimmy Fleck had refused to give her a prescription for more than ten ("people get addicted to this stuff, Magda") she had simply gone down to the Green and said in a rather idle voice that she wished she had some. The whole transaction had taken less than five minutes. She had gotten real pills, too, not substitutes or placebos. She had brought one of her own pills along for comparison. Of course, she wouldn't be able to go on getting them this way. She would be in too much danger of being caught. She would have to find a doctor who didn't mind handing them out.

Magda picked up two of the pills, put them in her mouth, and swallowed them straight, without water. She swooped the rest of the pills into her cupped left hand and put them into the bottle the prescription Jimmy had written for her had come in. She felt a little dizzy. These were not the first pills she had taken this morning. She was taking too many of them, and not just because when she didn't take them she was in pain. She liked the feeling they gave her, the flying floating feeling, and the way she was never worried *(getting old old old old old)* about anything. It was even better than falling in love, because it didn't make you pick at yourself all the time, wondering if the other person was going to love you back.

"You're going to have to give up the high-impact aerobics," Jimmy Fleck had told her. "That's the only solution to this. You're going to have to give them up for at least six months and maybe forever. If you don't, you're going to cripple yourself."

Someone had come in through the bedroom door: Simon. Magda put the pills away in the medicine cabinet and checked herself out one more time in the mirror. She had her hair pinned up in the way most likely to come down in a tangle of wisps and sweat halfway through the dance. The customers liked to see their Fearless Leader really getting knocked out by her own workout. It made them feel that they were getting what they paid for.

Magda adjusted the top of her leotard and the legholes, too, so that they didn't bind. Then she got up and went into the bedroom.

Simon was standing at the window with the curtains drawn back, looking at the backyard.

"I talked to that Gregor Demarkian person a while ago," he said.

"Did he want something in particular?" The pills were beginning to work. Magda felt positively lightheaded. She sat down on the side of the bed and began to put on her workout shoes.

"He wants to have a meeting here tomorrow morning at ten o'clock," Simon said. "A big meeting with a whole bunch of people in it, including some of the students in the beginners' class."

"The students? But the students couldn't have been involved in Tim's murder. They didn't even know him."

"You can't be sure of that, Magda. Tim was local. The students are local. Maybe they all knew him."

"I suppose."

"Maybe it's not Tim he's thinking about now. Maybe it's Stella. They were all in the house when Stella died."

"I keep forgetting that Stella is dead," Magda said. "Maybe it's because I didn't watch it all on the news the way I did with Tim. I think I must have been depressed. I slept through he whole thing."

"You haven't even lived through the whole thing yet, Magda. Maybe Mr. Demarkian will have some answers tomorrow morning. I'm a little nervous about the effect of all this on the tour."

"You said before it wouldn't have an effect," Magda said. "You said there would be a mention or two about a tragic mugging and that would be it."

"That was before Stella died."

Magda undid the knot on her work-out shoe. It was a

Gordian mess. She had no idea how it had gotten that way. Her fingers felt like elastic. She started to tie up again.

"I think we should just go on tour and get it over with," she said. "The police haven't told us not to leave town, have they?"

"No, Magda. I don't think they do that in real life."

"Then we should go, and get on with it, and get it over with, and come back. Then I think I'm going to take a nice long vacation, a month or six weeks. It'll all blow over, you'll see. It'll just disappear into thin air."

"What if they don't catch anyone? What if that Detective Bandero decides to make a public issue out of it?"

"He's already making a public issue out of it. He'll stop when he realizes it isn't going anywhere. He won't want to be embarrassed. And besides—"

"What?"

The left shoe was tied. Magda went to work on the right, more slowly this time. Was she imagining it? She thought she was getting shooting pains in her hands.

"Well," she said. "I've been thinking about it. And you know, it seems to me that people who get murdered—not people who get mugged, but people who get murdered on purpose—have usually done something to cause it."

"Are you trying to say Stella was asking for it?"

The right shoe was laced. No mistakes. She did have a shooting pain in her hands. She sat up.

"I'm saying that we really didn't know anything much about Tim Bradbury," she said firmly, "not anything important. He could have been up to anything. That's probably why Tony Bandero called this Gregor Demarkian in. I've been reading up on Mr. Gregor Demarkian over the last few days."

Simon was giving her a very odd look. "That's funny," he said.

"What is?"

"This attitude of yours. Ever since Tim died, really. And I always thought you liked Tim."

"I liked him as well as any of the other people we employ here. Cici Mahoney. Juliet Nash."

"What about Traci Cardinale, Magda? Do you think she did something to cause it, too? What about Stella?"

"I don't know about Stella. I don't know about Traci, either, I haven't been paying much attention. I've had work to do, Simon."

"Yes, I know."

Magda got up and flexed her knees. They hurt, but the pain was very far away. "Are you going to let Mr. Demarkian use the house?"

"Of course. He's asked us to be in attendance. I think we both should be. If only so we don't show up on the news later as a couple of uncooperative shits."

"All right."

"You don't seem to be very interested in having this solved, Magda. Two of the people who worked for us are dead. A third very nearly died. I'd think you'd be very anxious to make sure that whoever is doing this is safely put out of the way. If only to make sure that whoever it is doesn't decide to do *you* in next."

Magda flexed her arms, and then her fingers, and then her toes.

"I'm not going to be next," she said with perfect conviction, "and neither are you."

"Famous last words," Simon said.

"Oh, no," Magda told him. "Inside knowledge."

— 2 —

Usually, when the police came, after her father had had one of his outbursts, Dessa Carter refused to let them do anything at all about calling an ambulance or putting him in the hospital. It seemed obvious to her that the old man didn't need an ambulance and didn't belong in a hospital. Or at least not in an ordinary kind of hospital. Aside from the Alzheimer's, the old man was as healthy as a horse. He was healthier than she was. He was stronger than she was, too, which was the terrifying thing.

This time, when the police had insisted on calling Yale–New Haven Hospital, Dessa Carter had given in. She hadn't even made much of a protest. The idea of spending the night in that house, with the old man crazy on the inside and the gangs and addicts rocketing through the streets on the outside, was suddenly horrifying to her. Why it would be that now, when it had never been before, she didn't know. The gangs had been there for years. Her father had been crazy for years. What was different?

"It's not like this is anything new," she told Greta Bellamy as she got ready to leave Fountain of Youth that night. "It's not like I haven't been through it before. It's just that I don't seem to be able to see my way to living with it anymore."

"It's probably self-esteem," Greta said solemnly, and then broke into giggles. "Oh, Lord. I don't know how I kept a straight face in that lecture. I'm sorry. I didn't mean to change the subject."

"Maybe you didn't change the subject," Dessa said. "Maybe it is all about self-esteem. I keep thinking about trying to sell the house, to have the money to put him in a nursing home, and then I think it wouldn't be enough and what would I do with myself anyway?"

"You'd come and live with me," Greta said. "We talked about that."

Dessa dropped her work-out shoes on top of her pile of dirty exercise clothes and pulled the string closure of her gym bag shut. It was a terrible gym bag, cheap and shoddy, and she was suddenly ashamed of it.

"Well," she said, "I've got to go talk to the social worker, and after I do that I'll probably realize that there isn't anything to do but wait for him to die. Sometimes I wish I was a different person from the one I am. One of those people who could just dump him in the hospital emergency ward and disappear."

"No, you don't want to be that," Greta said.

"I don't want to be who this social worker is going to think I am, Greta. The fat lady. Fat ladies have nothing else to do with their lives than take care of their senile parents until they're old enough to be senile themselves. Thin people have goals and aspirations that have to be respected."

"Do people really do that to you?"

"All the time."

"Go talk to the social worker," Greta said. "Then come

over and spend the night with me. We'll sit down and think
the whole thing through and try to work it out."

"I don't think there's anything to work out."

"Then come and we'll talk about the big important
meeting tomorrow. Gregor Demarkian unmasks the killer.
I'm sure that's what he's going to do. Won't it be exciting?"

Dessa parked her car in the parking garage right under a
security lamp and got out. She always parked under security
lamps, just in case, in spite of the fact that nobody had ever
bothered her. There was one good thing about being this fat.
You didn' worry about getting raped, even if you ought to.

Dessa let herself into the core well and then into the elevator. As far as she could tell, the garage was absolutely deserted. She pressed the button for the first floor and tapped
her foot while the elevator was getting ready to move. She
thought about going over to Greta's after all this was over
and not seeing the house in Derby at all. Greta's place
sounded nice—not big, but nice, and away from the worst
things. No gangs. No addicts. No crazy old men smashing
up the furniture. Was it such a terrible thing, under the circumstances, that she wanted so desperately for her father to
die?

The elevator stopped on the first floor and opened. Dessa
got out. Nobody in the lobby looked like a doctor or a
nurse. Nobody was wearing a uniform. Dessa thought something wonderful had gone out of the world when nurses
stopped wearing their graduation caps.

Dessa went up to the visitors' desk and gave her name. "I
have an appointment with Claudia Dubroff," she told the
woman.

The woman turned away from her computer and pointed
down the hall. "Down there. Follow the signs. Up one flight.
All the social workers' offices are together."

"All right," Dessa said, and thought: "all" the social
workers' offices? How many social workers does a place like
this need?

There were not only signs on the walls but colored lines
on the floor. To get to Social Work, all she had to do was follow the blue line. Dessa went past a row of offices with only
names in them and letters following the names. Except for
"M.D.," she didn't know what any of the letters meant. She

went past little clusters of Christmas and Hannukah decorations, too, and in once place a display that seemed to have something to do with the Hindu festival of Dewali. Then she went around a corner, up a short flight of stairs, and around another corner. There was a pair of swinging metal fire doors with a round safety window in each one. She lumbered through the doors and came out on a hall with a big black-and-white sign on the wall of it: SOCIAL WORK.

I should have gone up and seen my father first, Dessa told herself, but she couldn't make herself feel guilty about it. She didn't want to see her father. Not now. Not for a couple of days. She would have him back soon enough. She went down the hall, reading the names on the signs outside the doors. Thomas Fitzpatrick. Annemarie Gonzalez. Tammy Wu. When she got to the one that said Claudia Dubroff, the door was open.

"Miss Dubroff?" Dessa asked, sticking her head through the doorway. The office was empty. It was also incredibly tiny. Dessa was going to choke to death if she had to sit in there. She backed out into the hall.

"It's Ms. Carter, isn't it?" a voice behind her said. "I'm sorry I'm late. I've been running late all day."

Dessa Carter turned around, prepared to find One Of Those Women, the kind of woman she called in her mind a Career Woman Barbie. Perfect hair. Perfect clothes. Perfect makeup. Perfect body. All of that accompanied by the unshakable conviction that any woman on earth could be a Career Woman Barbie, too, if she only really worked at it.

The woman at the other end of the hall was not a Career Woman Barbie. Her hair was in pretty good shape. Her makeup was flawless. Her clothes were nothing spectacular. It was her body that disqualified her. Claudia Dubroff, Dessa Carter realized, was a good fifty pounds heavier than Dessa had ever managed to get herself.

She was also shorter.

Dessa Carter turned to look at the other woman full face. Claudia Dubroff stopped in her tracks and stared. Dessa felt herself start to smile. Then she felt herself start to laugh. Claudia Dubroff started to laugh, too.

"Oh, dear," Dessa Carter said.

"Oh, I know," Claudia Dubroff said. "Were you worried about what I'd think of you?"

"Petrified," Dessa Carter said.

"I was worried about what you'd think of me, too. You wouldn't believe the kind of reactions I get."

"I bet you get lectured once a week on how you shouldn't try to solve other people's problems until you've solved the ones you've got yourself," Dessa said.

"Oh, yes," Claudia Dubroff said. "I also get offered diets. By strangers on the street. People just walk up and hand me some diet book they've been reading."

"People just walk up and tell me I've got to do something about myself," Dessa said. "Or else they won't talk to me at all. Saleswomen in stores are the worst."

"I always have a problem with waitresses in restaurants. They act like I'm not there. It's as if anybody who's as fat as this shouldn't actually allow herself to eat anything."

"As if you should go on rations of bread and water until you got thin," Dessa agreed.

"As if there must be something *really* wrong with you if you aren't ashamed of yourself," Claudia Dubroff said. "That's the worst of it. They're always expecting you to be ashamed of yourself. I belong to a fat liberation support group, by the way. Do you think you'd be interested?"

"I don't know," Dessa said. "I've just started going to the Fountain of Youth Work-Out. I like it there."

"Isn't it terribly expensive?"

"I'm trying to figure out a way for my insurance to pay for it."

"Oh, that shouldn't be any problem," Claudia Dubroff said. "That's just the kind of thing insurance companies like to pay for."

"Don't you find it incredibly claustrophobic in this office?" Dessa Carter said.

The two women turned and looked into Claudia Dubroff's tiny office. To Dessa, it looked even smaller now than it had when she had first seen it. It looked more crowded, too. It was a very neat office. The books were in their proper places on the shelves. The file cabinet drawers were neatly closed. Except for a single file lying in the middle of it, the desk was clear of papers. The furniture looked too small. How did Claudia Dubroff sit on these chairs without half-falling off?

"Well," Claudia Dubroff said, "I suppose we could go down to the lounge. It's supposed to be for staff only, but at this time of the evening there won't be anyone there to notice. And the chairs are bigger there."

"All right," Dessa said.

Claudia hurried into the office and picked up the file in the middle of the desk. Then she hurried out again, file in hand.

"I've researched all these alternatives for long-term nursing home care for your father," she said. "I don't know if you're going to like any of them, but you might as well know what's available. Isn't Fountain of Youth the place where they've had all those poisoning murders?"

"Only two," Dessa told her. "Or maybe three, if you count Traci Cardinale. Except that she isn't dead."

"Oh, I know," Claudia said. "She's right here. Upstairs in Ward six. Do you know her?"

"Yes," Dessa replied. "Yes, I do."

"You ought to go up and see her, then. She's been more or less conscious all day from what I hear, though I wouldn't think she'd be doing much talking yet. I hear she's very depressed. You ought to go and try to cheer her up."

"Maybe I will," Dessa Carter said.

Claudia Dubroff opened a door with no name sign on it at all and stepped through it.

"Here we are," she announced. "The staff lounge. It's even got a coffee machine that makes hot chocolate."

— 3 —

If it hadn't been for the request from Gregor Demarkian to stick around for the meeting tomorrow morning at ten, Frannie Jay would have already been gone. She wanted to be gone even before the meeting. She hadn't murdered Tim Bradbury. She hadn't even known Tim Bradbury. It was bad enough to have to deal with the police when you had actually done something wrong. Then she thought that she had an obligation—to Fountain of Youth, because they had hired her in spite of knowing everything there was to know about her background; to Magda Hale—and she knew she had to stay. All this publicity about the murders couldn't be doing Magda's business any good, especially right before the nationwide tour. Frannie would stay long enough to give Gregor Demarkian the help he needed tomorrow. Maybe that would be enough.

It was ten o'clock at night now, and Frannie had her clothes lined up in piles across her bed. There weren't a lot of them. Seven complete leotard-and-tights work-out combinations. Seven pairs of white athletic socks. Two pairs of white work-out shoes. Then there were only a few things: turtlenecks, jeans, button-down blouses in pastel colors, one dress, one pair of loafers, one pair of heels. Frannie found it hard to look at these things, harder, even, than she found it to look at the one thing she had left of Marilee: a small pink cap, knitted out of stretchy yarn, that they had given her in the hospital.

Frannie picked up the cap and put it in the duffel bag. She had taken it everywhere with her since Marilee died. She had even taken it with her to jail. Was there ever going to be a time when this didn't matter to her anymore?

There was only one thing Frannie was sure of: It was time to leave New Haven. She should never have come back here in the first place. She shouldn't stay now that she knew it was wrong. Tomorrow was not only the day of Mr. Gregor Demarkian's important meeting. It was also the last day of the special seminar week. Once she finished her classes, they wouldn't be counting on her for anything. They would have time to find someone else to lead step aerobics on a regular basis.

Frannie took two pairs of underwear out of the stack: one for tomorrow morning and one for tomorrow afternoon after her classes. She put the rest of her underwear in the duffel bag. She took out a shirt and a clean pair of jeans. She put those aside, too. She could get away with the sweater she was wearing as long as she didn't spill anything on it. She put the rest of her things in the duffel bag and pulled the string at the top of it closed, tight. The string was a fashion statement. The real closure on the duffel bag was a short, heavy-duty zipper. Frannie pulled that closed and fastened it to the body of the bag with the tiny padlock that had come with it.

Maybe I'll go to Montana, Frannie thought. Or Vermont. Or Oklahoma. Somewhere I've never been before.

There was a knock on the door. "Frannie?" Nick Bannerman said.

Frannie froze. She hadn't seen Nick Bannerman for hours. She hadn't even run across him in the halls. It was as if he had been hiding from her.

"Frannie?"

Frannie went to the door and stood right in front of it. It was such a big, heavy door. It had a good bolt lock on it. If she locked herself in, Nick would never be able to break the door down.

Nick would never want to.

"Frannie," Nick said again. "For God's sake. Open up, will you please?"

The door isn't locked, Frannie thought irrationally. He can come right in. Why doesn't he come right in? She reached forward and pulled the door open abruptly, making a breeze.

Nick was standing in the hall in his dark outdoor jacket. He looked like an African-American version of Lou Reed in that television commercial from a couple of years ago.

"Can I come in?" he asked.

Frannie stepped back away from the door. Nick came in. Frannie shut the door again.

"Well," Nick said. His eyes were on the duffel bag.

"I was packing," Frannie said. "I thought that, after tomorrow, you know, I'd move on."

"I thought you had family here."

"I do. I don't talk to them much."

"Do you have any idea where you want to move on to?"

Montana, Frannie thought. Vermont. Oklahoma. She went over and sat down on the bed.

"I'm surprised you came," she said. "I thought you'd taken off for somewhere."

"I'm not the one who wants to take off. I was out walking around. I was thinking."

"About what I told you?"

"Yeah. About what I told you."

"I don't think there's much to think about," Frannie said.

"Yeah. Well. One of the things I was thinking about was what the issue was. I mean, what is it exactly you were trying to tell me?"

"I was trying to tell you what happened," Frannie said.

There were a chair and a desk next to the window Frannie had looked out of that first night. Nick took the chair and straddled it, backward.

"So you told me. But what was it all supposed to mean, Frannie? What did you want me to get out of it?"

Frannie was confused. "I wanted you to know what kind of person I am."

"If that were the point, you left a few things out. Like everything that's happened since."

"Nothing has happened since."

"A lot has happened since. You've gotten off drugs. You've been to jail. You've gotten a job. Entire universes have been born and died since."

"Nothing important has happened since."

Nick closed his eyes and put his head down on his arms. "Nothing important from your point of view, maybe. Did you every think of going into therapy?"

"I had therapy coming out of my ears when I was in jail. They were real big on it."

Nick opened his eyes. "Do you know why I came here?"

"No."

"I thought that since both of us were supposed to be at that meeting tomorrow morning, and since neither of us is leading any classes tomorrow, you might, you just might, want to go out for a drink."

"I don't—"

"Drink," Nick interrupted. "I should have guessed. You can have a cup of tea. I can have a drink. I'm beginning to think I need one."

"Do you really think Gregor Demarkian is going to unmask the killer tomorrow morning?" Frannie asked. "Do you think it's going to be just like Hercule Poirot where the killer leaps up out of the crowd and tells the whole story?"

"I doubt it. That son-of-a-bitch is going to be there, you know. Detective Bandero. He's probably going to give a little lecture on why it is that African-Americans are more likely to commit murder than white people are. Then he's going to arrest me on the spot."

"Oh," Frannie said.

Nick reached across the space between them and touched her lightly on the knee. "Frannie? Do you want to go out?"

"Yes," Frannie said softly. "I think I do."

"Good. Go get your coat and we'll get out of here."

"All right."

"It will be just like the last time, you know. Three guys will ask you why you're wasting your time on the homeboy. Never mind the fact that I wouldn't know a homeboy from a hero sandwich?"

"I didn't mind that. They were just stupid."

Nick got off of his chair.

"We'll talk about the other stuff later," he said, "when I've got a glass of Scotch in front of me. Maybe once we both calm down, we can figure out where to go from here."

Frannie hadn't known there was anywhere to go from here, except out, or further on, or gone.

She got her coat.

FIVE

— 1 —

Gregor Demarkian didn't really believe in confrontation scenes. He liked them—in the books Bennis gave him to read, the confrontation scenes always seemd to be the least confusing part—but his thinking ran along the lines Philip Brye's did: it was a wonder one of these fictional "detectives" hadn't been shot. Especially Nero Wolfe. Gregor's personal favorite among fictional detectives was Nero Wolfe, who sat in his favorite chair all day and ate perfect food and solved impossibly complicated crimes without ever leaving his house. If Gregor had been able to choose a method of detection for himself, that would have been it. The problem with it was the problem with all the other methods of detection in all the other books Bennis gave him. Eventually, it required the Great Detective to meet the murderer face to face and make an accusation. Philip Brye was right. In real life, the Great Detective would have been shot, time and again, and stabbed, too, and pushed out of high windows. Murderers in real life didn't kill people just because they "knew too much"—or, at least, amateur murderers didn't. Murdering somebody was messy and dangerous. Still, having someone jump up in front of your face and declare that he had the evidence to convict you of murder was something else. Your first impulse could easily be to take care of the problem in the next split second. Your next impulse might be to laugh. Gregor had had that happen to him a couple of times. Everybody watched the cop and court shows on television these days. Everybody knew it had become almost impossible to convict anybody of anything in the United States of America.

The Fountain of Youth Work-Out Studio didn't look like a place where anybody would get murdered, or arrested, or even confronted with a violent crime. Sitting in the pale sunlight of this cold mid-morning, it looked like the setting for an English children's book, all fancy grillwork and gingerbread details. Gregor got out of Connie Hazelwood's taxi and looked it over. Connie intended to park out of sight somewhere and come in for what she called "the festivities." Gregor wanted to tell her that there was nothing festive about playing a nasty trick on someone, even someone you didn't like. When you played one on someone you did like, it could leave a bad taste in your mouth for weeks.

Gregor went around to the side, to see the place where Tim Bradbury's corpse had been found. Then he went to ring the bell on the front door. As he did, Tony Bandero's Ford pulled up, squeaking and whirring and clanking and complaining all the way.

"Hey," Tony shouted through the window. "Right on time. What's the big production about, anyway?"

Gregor waved him along—park in back; come ahead and talk to me—and rang the bell. The door was opened almost immediately by an excited-looking Greta Bellamy in a sky blue leotard and sky blue tights. Over the leotard and tights she had a fuzzy sky blue mohair sweater, and on the sweater she was wearing a pin that said: "I GOT A NEW BODY FOR THE NEW YEAR." Cold air blew in on her and she swiped hair out of her face with the side of her hand.

"Everybody's in the living room," she said in a rushed whisper. "Nobody can sit still. We're all so glad you're finally here."

"Everybody's here?" Gregor asked her. "Dr. Brye, too?"

"Oh, no," Greta said, her face falling. "He isn't. Does this mean we can't start until he gets here?"

"He'll be along in a minute," Gregor promised her.

"What about the phone? I asked Simon Roveter and he said there was a jack in the living room, and he would—"

"Put a phone in," Greta interrupted. "This is the first time I've been in the living room, but there's a phone in there now. You should see it. All white and gold and a fancy receiver with brass flutes. It's gorgeous."

"As long as it works."

"Magda Hale already made a phone call on it. It's got a rotary dial. I haven't seen a rotary dial in years."

A car pulled up to the curb outside and Philip Brye got out. Connie Hazelwood started to walk up the drive. Gregor waved to them both and went the rest of the way into the foyer. Up on the second-floor balcony, the railing was still not repaired—but, like the rest of the foyer, it had been decorated. Indeed, everything Gregor could see had been decorated. Long streamers of red, white, and blue crepe paper had been wound around the railing posts and hung from the high ceiling and twisted to fall like animated water from the chandelier. Why red, white, and blue, Gregor didn't know. Silver and gold crepe paper had been fashioned into a sculpture of a woman's naked body, with high breasts and long legs and flowing silver paper hair. The plywood safety board in the gap in the balcony railing was obscured by a large sign, painted in glitter on white cardboard and festooned with glitter shooting stars, that said: "NEW YEAR. NEW BODY. NEW LIFE. WELCOME TO THE FOUNTAIN OF YOUTH." It made Gregor think of that movie Bennis Hannaford and Donna Moradanyan were so fond of: *Night of the Living Dead*. He could see the zombies rising up from their graves this minute, dressed in leotards and tights.

As Gregor stood in the foyer, the doors to the living room opened and Magda Hale stuck her head out. Even at this distance, Gregor could tell that she was high as a kite. Higher. The door to the street opened behind him again and Philip Brye and Connie Hazelwood came in.

"What are you all waiting for?" Magda Hale demanded. "Don't you want to get started? Do you want to keep us here all day?"

"We're waiting for Detective Bandero," Gregor said.

Magda Hale made a face. "I think that's too damned

bad," she said. Then she disappeared back into the living room.

Philip Brye and Connie Hazelwood were standing together, shifting uneasily on their feet and confused about what to do next. Gregor was about to tell them both to go into the living room when he heard Tony Bandero humming somewhere in the back of the first floor. He must have parked in the lot and come in through the back door. His big feet pounded against the hardwood floor in the side corridor. He came into the foyer wearing his perennial rumpled brown suit and one of those MAKE-IT-TO-THE-NEW-YEAR—DON'T-DRINK-AND-DRIVE buttons Gregor had seen all over the morgue. Gregor wondered what it was about New Year's that made people feel they needed to put up signs and sport buttons, to declare themselves on one side of an issue or another. Not that there was another side to this issue. Gregor hadn't seen anyone wearing a SMASH-UP-YOUR-CAR-AND-GET-IT-OVER-WITH button yet.

"So what's all this?" Bandero said. "What's going on?"

"Everybody else is waiting in the living room," Gregor said. "We were just about to go in there."

Bandero's eyebrows twitched. He went to the doorway to the living room and looked in. He came back to where Gregor was standing in the foyer and shook his head.

"I can't believe this," he said. "I really can't believe this. You're going to stage some kind of confrontation scene."

"Something like that, yes," Gregor admitted.

"You should have notified me in advance," Tony Bandero said. He was getting red. "We could have got the people from Channel eight out here. Nobody stages confrontation scenes in real life. It could be great TV."

Gregor devotely hoped it wouldn't be. "Let's just go in and get it over with," he said. "I've acquired a burning ambition to be home in Philadelphia for the holiday."

Tony Bandero went back to the living room doors again, looked in again, and came back to Gregor in the foyer again.

"Quite a collection. I would never have suspected any of them. Not for real."

"I thought you suspected Nick Bannerman," Philip Byre said.

"That was just for the newspapers. You have to give the newspapers something or they turn you into hamburger."

Gregor was hot. He shrugged his coat off his shoulders and folded it over one arm. He wasn't wearing any buttons or signs at all. It made him feel a little out of step. Even Connie Hazelwood was wearing a message sweatshirt: "THE DEAD ARE ONLY GRATEFUL WHEN THEY DIDN'T HAVE ANYTHING TO LIVE FOR IN THE FIRST PLACE."

"Why don't we all go inside and get started," he said. "Magda Hale wants everything back to normal around here as soon as possible, and I don't blame her."

"Nothing is going to be normal around here for hours if you've really got something to tell us," Tony Bandero said. "I'll have to make an arrest. I'll have to call in some blues. The news will be all over the police band. Reporters are going to descend on us like locusts." He sounded gleeful.

"We've already got some blues," Philip Brye said coldly. "We've got two of the officers assigned to my office. Maybe you could let them make an arrest. Then the reporters wouldn't descend on us like locusts."

Tony Bandero's face reconfigured itself into a mask of sadness. "Phil, Phil," he said. "You just don't get it. Police work is at least sixty percent public relations these days. If you don't blow your own horn, the civilians start to think you aren't doing anything, and the next thing you know, your appropriation has been slashed."

Gregor couldn't imagine that Detective Bandero's department's appropriation amounted to that much. New Haven wasn't New York. He didn't want to go on with this conversation. If it continued long enough, Tony might get the idea of calling in the press right away. Gregor was a little surprised that he hadn't suggested it already.

"Let's go," Gregor said. "You can call Channel eight when it's over if you want to. I'm just going to get this finished and go home."

Tony Bandero sniffed. "I don't have to go to Channel eight," he said. "*They* come to *me*."

— 2 —

Everybody but Tony Bandero had been informed that this was a confrontation scene. Gregor found them sitting in a jagged semicircle near the massive stone fireplace, artfully arranged as an audience. The patrolmen from Philip Brye's office were standing on either side of the doors to the foyer, their hands clasped behind their backs. They looked like guards—an impression Gregor thought was unfortunate. He didn't want anyone to think he was jailed in here. Gregor watched as Greta Bellamy scooted across the room to sit in the empty space on the couch next to Dessa Carter. Dessa looked more tired than Gregor could remember seeing her before, but also calmer. In fact, most of the people here looked calmer than Gregor could remember them being in all the short partial week he had known them. Frannie Jay and Nick Bannerman were sitting side by side in a chair that was really too small to hold both of them. They seemed to be collapsed in on each other, as if they were melting together. Christie Mulligan looked worse than tired, worse even than exhausted, with great black crescents under her eyes and deep hollows under her cheekbones. What she did not look was frantic, which was the way Gregor remembered her from the couple of times he had spoken to her. Her two friends looked as if an electric charge had drained out of her and into them. It was only Magda Hale who seemed tenser than she had been before—and that, Gregor thought, might be the result of whatever drugs she was taking. Her tenseness seemed to have infected Simon Roveter. His Graham Greene–character charm came off as being a thin film over the surface of a personality soon to be out of control.

Dessa Carter and Greta Bellamy were sitting together trying to make themselves inconspicuous. Philip Brye and Tony Bandero moved in behind Gregor, facing the Fountain of Youth staff and students like the members of a chorus line review. Gregor put his coat over a table near one of the officers at the door and cleared his throat.

"So," he said. "Here we are. I have to thank you all for coming here just because I asked you. You didn't have to."

"We all want to know who the murderer is," Christie

Mulligan's friend Tara said. "That's what we're doing here. You are going to tell us, aren't you?"

"I am going to tell you," Gregor promised, "but before I do, I want to tell you a few other things."

"About Tim Bradbury?" Frannie Jay asked. She was very pale.

"Yes," Gregor said. "About Tim Bradbury, and also about his mother, because this is mostly a story about Tim Bradbury's mother. Which is ironic in a way, because Alissa Bradbury—that was her name, Alissa Bradbury—was not the kind of woman who usually has stories told about her. She was, in fact, what is commonly referred to as white trash. By the time she died, she was a big, fat, slovenly, alcoholic mess. The only two things she'd ever had in her life were her son and her house. Her house was falling apart and her son was barely speaking to her—for good reason. Alissa Bradbury was not a woman who cared for other people, even for her own child. She did what she had to do to get what she needed to have. Then she locked herself up and refused to talk to anybody about anything until she needed something again. The few times she did try to get out of herself and do the normal things she was expected to do as a mother, she created disasters. When she came to see Tim perform in a choir, she was loud and abusive and embarrassing. When she showed up for teachers' conferences, she was a disgrace. Tim got to the point where he pretended she didn't exist. He told people that his 'parents' had moved away from the area—that's 'parents' plural, in spite of the fact that his father was legally listed as 'unknown' on his birth certificate and nobody had ever seen him with a man who could have been his father. There are people who had seen Alissa with a man they presumed to be her husband, but these people aren't exactly reliable. Most of them are neighbors. One is a woman who quite definitely has Down's syndrome. She isn't too clear or too convincing about much of anything."

"Poor Tim," Magda Hale murmured. "What a mess."

"It was a mess," Gregor agreed. "And on the surface, the most remarkable thing about it was that Tim turned out so well. He didn't turn to drink or drugs or gangs or crime. He just went on his way, working as hard as he had to, and he ended up with a good job and a lot of people who liked him very much and were rooting for him even harder. Under the surface, though, there was a lot more that was strange about the circumstances of Tim Bradbury's—and especially his mother's—life. There was, for one thing, the money."

"It doesn't sound like Alissa Bradbury had any money," Dessa Carter said. Her hands were clenched tightly in her lap.

"Well, she didn't, in the way we usually mean that phrase," Gregor said. "What she did have was more money than she ought to have had. There was, for instance, the house at forty-seven Stephenson Road."

"Stephenson Road?" Frannie Jay asked sharply. "People who live on Stephenson Road don't have money. That's a slum."

"It most certainly is a slum," Gregor agreed. "But the fact remains that it costs money to own property even in a slum. And Alissa Bradbury did own the property she lived on at forty-seven Stephenson Road. She bought it free and clear, for eight thousand five hundred dollars, the year her son Tim was born. Tim, by the way, was born at the old St. Mary's Hospital in Derby as the son of a charity patient. The medical fees were picked up by the Community Health Project of the Diocese of Bridgeport."

"My, my," Tony Bandero said. "You have been busy. This must have taken you days."

"No, Tony, it didn't take me days. It just took me most of last night and some help from some people at the Diocesan offices and the Derby police. And I knew what I was looking for, of course, because I had already run across one or two strange items in Alissa Bradbury's financial affairs. There was the fact, for instance, that she was not on welfare. Not when Tim was a child. Not even later, in the late 1970s and early 1980s when, according to my contacts in the Derby police, the eligibility rules were relaxed in this state and it was easier to get on the rolls. No welfare. No food stamps. No Medicaid. Not ever."

Greta Bellamy was frowning furiously. "But I don't understand. Did she have a job? I saw her myself a few times. I can't think who would have hired her?"

"Nobody hired her as far as I can tell," Gregor said. "No welfare and no job."

"Maybe she was engaging in prostitution," Simon Roveter said.

"Maybe she was," Gregor agreed. "Whores don't have to be good looking to get business, but they do have to be decent looking to make serious money. Alissa may have been decent looking when Tim was first born. I haven't seen a picture of her from that time and I wouldn't know. What you have to take into account, however, is that by the time Alissa begins to be seen by other people in her role as Tim's mother, she is already everything I have described her to be. Not only enormous but slovenly, ill-groomed, unkempt, and alcoholic. But she still wasn't on welfare or food stamps or Medicaid. And her bills were getting paid. I wasn't able to check on her electricity or her heat. I didn't have time. Up until about three years ago, the taxes were paid every six months at the Derby tax collector's office, on time and in cash and in person."

"What happened three years ago?" Nick Bannerman asked.

"The taxes started to be paid by check," Gregor said, "and mailed in. But they were still paid and they were still paid on time."

"Maybe she was the one who was dealing drugs," Magda Hale said.

"If she was, she was very, very good at it," Gregor said. "Nobody in any drug squad anywhere in this part of Connecticut has ever connected that house to drugs. I was able to check. I'll tell you something else I was able to check on. At ten o'clock last night, I got court permission—actually, a man named Roger Dornan got court permission—to do a global search of the bank records in this state for any sign of a bank account under Alissa Bradbury's social security number. If we had found such a bank account, we would have had to get court permission to pull the records of it, but it didn't matter. There was no such bank account. Not in the state of Connecticut. My guess is that there isn't any such bank account in any state, anywhere."

"Roger Dornan," Tony Bandero said incredulously. "Roger Dornan went behind my back?"

"Nobody went behind your back," Philip Brye said in exasperation. "You're the one who went on television and said that everybody in every department connected with the New Haven police should give Mr. Demarkian whatever helped he asked for."

"I know I said that," Tony Bandero said sharply, "but I expected to be kept informed, for Christ's sake. Of course I expected to be kept informed."

"Wait a minute," Nick Bannerman said. "If there isn't any bank account, where are the real estate tax checks coming from?"

"Ah," Gregor said, "very good question. And the answer is that right now, we can't be absolutely sure, because the town of Derby does not photocopy the tax checks it receives. My assumption, however, is that the tax checks are coming from the same place the cash was coming from, from the man who was Tim Bradbury's father, and who kept Alissa Bradbury just well enough to ensure that she would not file a paternity suit against him or otherwise annoy him in public, all the time Tim was growing up."

Simon Roveter shifted in his seat, uneasy. "If that's really true," he said slowly, "then why the sudden switch from cash to checks? Wouldn't that be a very stupid thing to do? Even if Derby doesn't photocopy its tax checks, the checks can be traced, can't they? Especially if the police know exactly what it is they're looking for and who they want to investigate?"

"Checks can be traced," Gregor said, "but about three years ago, something happened that left our murderer with no choice. Alissa Bradbury died. To be precise, she was murdered. There's no way for us to know now, unless the murderer tells us himself, why that happened. It might have been that our man was tired of keeping Alissa Bradbury. He had a woman of his own by then. He was probably tired of being tethered to the past and not sure that he could walk out on her even after all those years without being exposed. There might have been some kind of violent argument. It doesn't matter. What does matter is that Tim Bradbury either saw this murder happen or found out about it soon afterward."

"But why would he cover it up?" Dessa Carter asked. "This is his mother you're talking about."

"It's his mother, yes, but he wasn't close to her, and remember it was his father who killed her. I think that in spite of that 'unknown' designation on his birth certificate, Tim

Bradbury knew who his father was—after the murder, if not before. I think his loyalties were divided and his reactions were confused. At any rate, Alissa's body was stashed under the floorboards in the bedroom in the house at forty-seven Stephenson Road, the utilities were shut off and the house was boarded up. And that's where everything sat, for three long years, until Tim was no longer able to rationalize what he knew about the death of his mother."

"I want to know how you got into that house and dug up a body without it at least appearing on the police band," Tony Bandero demanded angrily. "What the hell is is going on here?"

"Forty-seven Stephenson is in Derby," Philip Brye said. "It was on the Derby police band."

"Let's go back to Tim Bradbury," Gregor said. "Sometime recently, I would guess at November of this year, Tim decided he had to do something about what he knew. He contacted his father and demanded a meeting. He got a meeting, in the house at forty-seven Stephenson. During that meeting he was fed something, possibly very sweet coffee, possibly something else, that was full of arsenic. He would have died between thirty and sixty minutes later. Yesterday afternoon, we found vomit in the bathroom and vomit-stained clothes in the bedroom. Once he was dead, our murderer stripped the body, made sure it was clear of external vomit, and put it in the trunk of his car. Then he brought it here, and deposited it in the yard. At that point, the most important thing was that there be nothing on or near the body to connect it to forty-seven Stephenson Road. Stripping the body actually helped with that in more ways than the obvious one. Aside from removing most forensic connections with forty-seven Stephenson and the arsenic that poisoned Tim, it also sensationalized the case in a way that brought the spotlight firmly to Fountain of Youth. It looked like whatever had happened to Tim Bradbury, even if it hadn't happened to him here, had to be connected to here."

"Of course it was connected to here," Magda Hale said sharply. "There has been a murder and an attempted murder since Tim died, and both have been visited on our people."

"Wait," Frannie Jay said. "Tim Bradbury died the night I came to Fountain of Youth. He picked me up just about

nine o'clock. I think we got up here around nine fifteen.
Would there have been time, after that, for Tim to have gotten all the way out to Derby and been killed and gotten all
the way back again, stark naked?"

"Sure," Philip Brye said. "If traffic was light and the
meeting was set in advance. It isn't all that far out to the
Stephenson Road."

"Let's stipulate at this point that there was enough arsenic in what Tim Bradbury ate or drank that night to kill
him quickly," Gregor said.

Magda Hale was gesticulating angrily. "It *has* to be connected to here," she insisted again. "How else can you
explain what happened to Stella? And Traci Cardinale?"

"Traci Cardinale is the easy part," Gregor said. "The attempt to murder her was entirely practical. Traci was, you
see, the person who staged the incident with the collapsing
balcony rail. She staged it quite deliberately, at the request of
the murderer, although she didn't know he was the murderer.
It wasn't until Stella Mortimer died that she put two and two
together. At the time of the balcony rail incident, she thought
she was doing a favor for the man she loved, for a man who
loved her. She thought she was directing my attention away
from him by setting up a situation he could not possibly have
caused and making it look like it must have some connection
to Tim Bradbury's death."

Simon Roveter was rubbing his hands together, over and
over again. There was a sheen of sweat across his forehead.
"That still doesn't tell us what happened to Stella. Are you
trying to tell us that she knew something about Tim Bradbury's mother? Why would she?"

"She didn't," Gregor said. "What Stella Mortimer knew
was something about Tim Bradbury's father." Gregor
reached into the inside pocket of his suit jacket and pulled
out a folded piece of paper. "After Tim Bradbury died, Stella
Mortimer was concerned about the fact that she had known
so very little about him. She expressed this concern to several
people, but she also did something about it. She went to the
records here. She got Tim Bradbury's employment application."

"Our employment application couldn't have helped Stella

find out about Tim's father," Magda Hale said crisply. "There's practically nothing on it."

"I know. This is a copy of that application, and it certainly is short. It does, however, have one interesting feature. In the section on next of kin, Tim put down the name and address of Alissa Bradbury, and he also put down her phone number: two-oh-three, two-nine-seven, seven-one-six-two."

"Two-nine-seven?" Greta Bellamy asked. "But that's not a Derby exchange. That's a New Haven exchange."

"Do you mean Tim put down his father's phone number?" Frannie asked.

Nick Bannerman stirred. "Do you mean Stella Mortimer just called this number and got the murderer on the other end of the line?"

"Something like that. Yes. And that, you see, was unacceptable." Gregor turned to look at the officers standing near the door. "Would one of you two, please—?"

"Sure," the one to the right of the doors said, coming forward to take the copy of the employment application out of Gregor's hand. He went to the ersatz antique phone and started dialing.

"None of it had anything to do with Fountain of Youth, you see," Gregor continued, "not really. This was just a convenient place to shunt suspicion, and every development made it even more convenient. That was luck, but luck counts. Luck always counts."

"Okay," the officer at the phone said. "She's ringing."

At just that moment, Tony Bandero's beeper began to go off.

It took a while for the obvious to sink in. The beeper's tone was high and strident. It bounced around the room like a rogue germ, leaving everyone blank. Then Nick Bannerman stood straight up and said, "Jesus *Christ*."

Gregor Demarkian turned to Tony Bandero, who seemed to be frozen in place.

"Traci Cardinale is awake," he said gently. "She seems to think she has a lot to say."

"Does she?" Tony Bandero said.

The cop on the phone had put the receiver on the table, stunned. The phone was still making the beeper beep. The shrill high note seemed destined to go on forever.

"You should get that car of yours fixed," Gregor told Tony Bandero. "It makes a very distinctive sound. I heard it when you picked me up at the train station. Frannie Jay heard it on the night Tim Bradbury died. At least four people now in this room heard it the day Stella Mortimer died. And, of course, I heard it last night, at the hospital. If I had been able to connect the sound to the descriptions I had been given of it, I would have been on to you before I was."

"I'm not going to get the car fixed now," Tony Bandero said. "I'm not going to have time."

Epilogue

*"Here we come awassailing, among
the leaves so green"*
— *"The Wassail Song,"*
traditional

The story of Virginia Hanley's suicide made the six o'clock news on the CBS affiliate in Philadelphia on New Year's Eve, serving as a sterling example of what Gregor had always thought of as the "bizarre footnote" school of journalism.

"In a bizarre footnote to the tragic events at the Fountain of Youth Work-Out Studio in New Haven," the reporter started.

Gregor ducked under the gigantic crepe paper sculpture of Janus that hung from the ceiling just past the archway between the living room and the dining room in Father Tibor Kasparian's apartment and wondered what the news was doing on. Tibor didn't watch the news on a regular basis. He gave himself enough trouble reading the newspapers, which he defined as anything being sold at a newsstand and printed on newsprint. Tibor's apartment was full of copies of the *National Enquirer* and the *Weekly World News* stuck into copies of Plato's *Republic* in the original Greek. Right now, Tibor's apartment was also full of crepe paper, because Donna Moradanyan and her friend Russell Donahue had just gotten finished decorating it. Aside from the two-faced Janus hanging from the ceiling, there was a crepe paper sculpture of a grinning New Year's baby on the dining room table, a glitter-and-papier-mâché display of shooting stars on the living room wall over the fireplace, and a trick Fountain of Youth made of mirrors and water on the pantry cabinet in the kitchen. There were also balloons, but they were not Donna Moradanyan's fault. It had been Bennis Hannaford's idea to fill one hundred and one of them with helium and let them float unanchored through the copies of Heidegger and St. Thomas Aquinas and Mickey Spillane.

"It isn't a bizarre footnote to anything," Gregor said to the television set. "That woman hardly noticed anything at all was going on at Fountain of Youth."

Bennis Hannaford came out of the kitchen with a big bowl of onion dip in one hand and a bigger bowl of potato chips in the other. She was followed closely by little Tommy Moradanyan, who had onion dip all over his face and right hand.

"What are you talking about?" Bennis asked, putting the bowls down on the coffee table. Then she saw the television set and made a face at it. "That's not supposed to be on until Russ gets the new VCR hooked up. Why are you watching the news?"

"I wasn't watching the news," Gregor said. "I was ambushed by the news. It was blasting away when I got here."

But Bennis ignored him. Her eyes were on the television screen. "Goodness, she's an unpleasant-looking woman. Was she a suspect?"

"No."

"Well, I think somebody ought to have suspected her of something, Gregor. She looks like she deserves it."

Tommy Moradanyan had his right hand in the bowl of onion dip up to his wrist. As Gregor watched, Tommy pulled it out and started licking on the large white mound that emerged as if it were a lollipop.

"Excellent," he said to Gregor through a mouthful of white. "Really very superior."

Tommy Moradanyan was three.

Bennis was looking at the television set, her thick cloud of wiry black hair escaping in wisps from the barrette she was using to hold it to the top of her head.

"If I were going to commit suicide, I wouldn't use a gun," she said. "I'd do something dramatic like jump off the top of the World Trade Center with a streamer sign attached to my back blaming the whole thing on my dysfunctional childhood."

"I'd use a gun," Gregor said. "Jumping off tall buildings gives you too much time to change your mind on the way down."

"You couldn't jump off the top of the World Trade Center anyway," Bennis said. "I checked it out once for a time travel story I was doing. They've got that observation deck protected up one end and down the other. And you can't even *get* on the roof."

"Are you two talking about suicide?" Donna Moradanyan came into the room with a bowl of cold stuffed grape leaves in her hands. She saw her small son with his hand covered with onion dip and grabbed for the stack of napkins to wipe him off. "Honestly, Tommy," she said. "What will Russ say if he sees you like this?"

"He'll say I have a really excellent appetite," Tommy said positively.

Donna threw the wad of napkins into the nearest wastepaper basket and gave Tommy a stuffed grape leaf.

"The really awful thing is that he's probably right," she said. "Every time he does something incredibly messy, Russ acts like he's giving evidence of genius or something. Do you think that's good parenting?"

"Yes," Gregor said.

"I don't know how to define the word parenting" Bennis said.

"It's just boy stuff," Tommy Moradanyan said wisely.

Donna shot her son a look that said she ought to argue about this—give a lecture on sexism, maybe, or repeat one of those talks on how Cleanliness Is Next to Godliness that Lida Arkmanian liked to throw around—but then she turned her attention to the news again. The picture of Virginia Hanley was just fading behind the anchorwoman's left shoulder. It was being replaced by the picture of two very young girls on an ice skating rink, posing elegantly but uncertainly like Nancy Kerrigan in the diet soda commercial.

"I wish I understood why people do the things they do," Donna said. "I mean, what good did it do this woman to do what she did? Her husband isn't going to love her for it. He probably won't even feel guilty that she did it, because he'll just say that she was crazy. And she didn't even make a big splash in the papers, because with all this stuff about Fountain of Youth, she's just a side issue."

"She would have been more than a side issue if the circumstances had been different," Gregor said. "The problem was that this house she blew herself away in was the next county and a completely different jurisdiction. Nobody connected her to Fountain of Youth in the beginning. Which is a good thing, if you ask me, because if anybody had connected her to Fountain of Youth, we would have been forced to treat her death as only a probable suicide, and then God only knows what would have happened. We'd have been hung up for another two weeks, in all likelihood. I wouldn't be home now. I would be sitting in a motel on the New Haven–Orange border, listening to the staff get ready for the sleepover New Year's Eve party."

"I approve of sleepover New Year's Eve parties," Bennis said. "They keep a lot of drunk people off the roads."

"It works just as well if you can walk home," Donna Moradanyan said. She was still staring at the television set, where the two very young girls had been replaced by an ice hockey game. Big men in thick protective pads were skating back and forth to no purpose. Nobody made a goal.

"It's as if people have lost any sense that there's more than one option in the world," Donna said suddenly, "or maybe I mean two. Put up with it or blow it away. That's all anybody thinks about. Even in the movies."

"Tony Bandero wasn't blowing people away," Bennis pointed out.

Donna waved this into oblivion. "It amounts to the same thing. It's like that Menendez brothers business. Think about it. They could have done a million things about the child abuse. They could have filed suit against their parents. They could have written a book and gone on the talk show circuit. They could have just disappeared. The world was full of options, but what they did was blow their parents away and tons and tons of people thought that made perfect sense. But it didn't make perfect sense."

"You're not making perfect sense," Bennis said. "Why are you worrying about the Menendez brothers?"

"I'm not. I'm just—" Donna shrugged helplessly. "I think I like this case least of all the ones Gregor has been involved in. I like it even less than the first one."

"I don't," Bennis said.

"Buy maybe it's just stimulus overload. If you know what I mean. The Menendez brothers. Virginia Hanley. Bosnia. Tony Bandero. Even Arnold Schwarzenegger in *Terminator II*. It's just the same thing over and over again. I'm really sick of it."

"Tony Bandero and Bosnia in the same breath," Bennis said. "That's a stretch, Donna."

"Gregor knows what I mean," Donna said.

Tommy had his hand in the onion dip again. Donna took it out again, and cleaned it up again, and held onto it this time.

"Russ has been talking about signing up with the DA's office when he passes his bar exam," Donna said. "An assistant DA got killed last week by some guy he was prosecuting on a drug charge."

"Ah," Gregor Demarkian said.

Donna tugged on Tommy's hand and went stomping back across the living room, through the dining room, into the kitchen. Her blond hair bounced in the breeze she made. Tommy had to pump his legs hard just to keep up.

"She's been in a lousy mood all week," Bennis said after she had gone. "I've made a couple of stabs at getting Russ to switch his interest to wills and estates, but I don't think it's working."

— 2 —

The odd thing, Gregor thought later, when the VCR had been hooked up and Donna and Bennis were watching the videotape of a 1950s horror movie called *Them*, was that in getting caught for the murders of Tim and Alissa Bradbury, Detective Tony Bandero had finally gotten what he had always really wanted: national recognition. Ever since the arrest, the newspapers had been full of it. It had been all over the network news, too. Gregor supposed that over the next month, the magazines would get onto it. The local stringer for *People* magazine had already called Gregor's apartment twice, and left three messages on Bennis Hannaford's answering machine. The *Sally Jessy Raphael* people had tried to reach him through the Bureau, which had sensibly refused to accommodate them. *The Philadelphia Inquirer* was having a field day, running headlines like BATTING A THOUSAND and DEMARKIAN UPSTAGES CONN POLICE. At least the references to "the Armenian-American Hercule Poirot" had been kept to the minimum. The *Inquirer* was the publication that had started all that, but in the present circumstances the newspaper was much more concerned to note that the police in its own precincts were far more competent than the police in New Haven, never mind the fact that New Haven had Yale and Philadelphia had only the University of Pennsylvania, which everybody outside the state considered second-rate Ivy League.

Or something.

Gregor sat at Tibor's dining room table, surrounded by paperback copies of Judith Krantz novels and plates of *loukoumia* and thick butter cookies in the shape of stars. Tibor and Russ Donahue sat with him, ignoring the women and Tommy Moradanyan and the giant ants that were marching across the television screen. Tibor was a small, thin man with a receding hairline and a lined and pock-marked face. He looked a good ten years older than Gregor Demarkian but was in fact a couple of years younger. Russ Donahue was a tall man with sandy hair and the face of a Hollywood choirboy. He had been with the Philadelphia police department for the last seven years.

"What tipped me off," Gregor was telling them, "was the business with the balcony, and the way Traci Cardinale talked. The balcony thing was especially important, because there was only one person who could have made that railing fall over, and that was Traci Cardinale herself."

"I still don't see why somebody couldn't have sneaked out on the balcony and done it while nobody was looking, Krekor," Father Tibor said. "It is the first thing I would have thought of if I had been there."

"It was the first thing you were supposed to think of," Gregor said, "but if it had happened that way, somebody would at least have been hurt. That wood fell all over Traci Cardinale's desk, which she was supposedly sitting at, and she didn't get so much as a splinter."

"I take it the balcony had been rigged to fall beforehand," Russ Donahue said.

"Tony came over and did it himself one night when Traci Cardinale was working late," Gregor told him. "The line he fed Traci was that he was in big trouble on this case, he was getting a lot of pressure because Magda Hale was so prominent in New Haven, and now he had been forced to call me in because his superiors didn't think he was doing enough to see the case to a conclusion—"

"Was that true?" Tibor asked.

"No," Gregor said. "It was Tony's own personal idea to get in touch with me. But Traci didn't know that. Tony convinced her I was the big bad enemy, out to show him up and maybe ruin his career. So she let him come in in the middle of the night, when she was the only one there and the rest of the house was blocked off by security doors, and they did a little judicious sawing and puttering so that the railing looked all right, but was actually very easy to destroy. And then, when the time came, Traci destroyed it. And Tony created a media circus around it, and I was supposed to be thrown off the scent."

"Which you weren't," Russ Donahue said.

"What I was was nearly half convinced that Traci Cardinale must have murdered Tim Bradbury," Gregor said, "except that it was obvious that the railing had to have been sawed, and I couldn't see Traci doing it. And the more I looked over those bits of wood, the more I was sure Traci couldn't have done it, not unless she had done it months before. Her hands were perfectly smooth. There were no signs of abrasions or calluses on them. She hadn't been sawing anything."

"But Krekor," Tibor said, "how did you know that the person Traci Cardinale had been helping was Tony Bandero? Why not Simon Roveter? Why not Magda Hale."

"I didn't know it," Gregor said. "I just knew that Traci Cardinale knew Tony Bandero better than she was admitting to, and I found that—curious."

"Yes," Tibor persisted, "but how did you know that?"

"Well," Gregor said, "Traci called everyone at Fountain of Youth, including Magda Hale and Simon Roveter and all the students, by their first names. But she called all the outside people, even rank patrolmen with no status at all, by their last names. Mr. O'Neill. Mrs. Donnegan. Except for Tony Bandero. Tony Bandero, Traci always called Tony."

"That's pretty weak," Russ Donahue said. "I wouldn't want to write something like that up in a report."

"Neither would I, but fortunately I don't have to file reports." Gregor sighed. "As it turned out, I was right. I do feel a little guilty about not doing something about it earlier, though. Traci could have wound up dead."

"She really knew not at all that Tony Bandero was involved in the murder?" Tibor asked.

"She definitely knew nothing at all," Gregor said. "What tipped her off was the death of Stella Mortimer. Stella found that phone number, and she called it, but what she also did was to show it to Traci one afternoon, and Traci recognized it. And the next thing Traci knew, Stella was dead and there didn't seem to be any other reason for it."

"Is she going to testify to all this in court?" Russ asked. "This month's star witness?"

"She says she will," Gregor said. "I'm afraid I gave her a bit of a lecture before I left about how if you suspect someone of poisoning two people you probably shouldn't accept cups of coffee from him while you're asking him if he really did it. She seemed to think the lecture was a bit more than she ought to have to take."

"It probably was," Father Tibor said sadly. "You probably delivered it to her while she was in the hospital. In these things you do not have a wonderful sense of timing, Krekor."

"I don't have any sense of timing at all," Gregor said. "I don't see why I should have. My job isn't social work. In fact, technically I don't have a job at all."

"You should really get your private detective's license," Russ Donahue said. "Not getting it at this point is just an attitude on your part. What would it hurt?"

"It would be too much trouble," Gregor said.

Over on the television set, the army was bringing flame throwers and tanks into the sewers of Los Angeles to rid them of giant ants. Gregor got up and went over to see what

Bennis and Donna and Tommy Moradanyan were doing. Only Tommy had his eyes glued to the television set. Donna was asleep. Bennis was looking idly through that day's issue of the *Inquirer*, checking out Gregor's publicity. There was a fair amount of publicity to check out. Besides the main story on the front page, there was a two-page inside spread with fuzzy pictures from all of Gregor's old cases and a boxed sidebar titled, "Why Cops Go Bad—A Psychologist Reports." It had definitely been a slow news week.

"Someday," Gregor said, "I'm going to wrap up one of these cases on the same day that peace arrives in Northern Ireland or Communist China invades South Korea, and nobody is going to notice."

"Sure they'll notice," Bennis said, without looking up. "You're a lot more fun than Northern Ireland or South Korea."

"If you want Donna Moradanyan to see in the New Year, you'd better wake her up. It's about six minutes to midnight."

Bennis checked her watch and straightened on the couch. Then she shook Donna by the foot and said:

"Donna. Come on. Wake up."

Donna didn't move.

"Maybe we ought to skip waking her up for the New Year," Bennis said. "I mean, what difference does it make, anyway? The New Year is going to come in regardless."

"That's my line of argument," Gregor said. "I'm the one who's always saying that celebrating the New Year makes me feel ridiculous."

Bennis shook Donna Moradanyan's foot again. Donna turned over on her side, facing the back of the couch. Bennis gave up and stretched out on the couch herself, angling her legs so that she didn't squeeze Tommy Moradanyan out.

"Forget it," she said. "Tell Tibor and Russ I'm going to turn on the celebrations any second."

— 3 —

Later, well after midnight, when Tommy Moradanyan had
fallen asleep on the couch next to his mother and it had become obvious that they were not going to wake up until they
were good and ready, Gregor Demarkian and Bennis
Hannaford walked back across Cavanaugh Street together.
Russ was staying to wait for Donna and Tommy. Tibor was
in one of his hyperactive moods where all he really wanted
to do was play hand after hand of solitaire and talk endlessly
about what his life had been like before he left the Soviet
Union—when there had been a Soviet Union, which, to
Gregor, had begun to seem like an eternity ago. Cavanaugh
Street was unusually deserted. It was never a very lively place
late at night. It was too much of a family neighborhood for
that. Even so, there were usually more lights on than this, no
matter how late it got. The problem was that the two people
most likely to leave their lights burning all night were both
away for the holiday. Old George Tekemanian was visiting
his grandson Martin and his three great-grandchildren out
on the Main Line. Lida Arkmanian was out in California
spending the holiday with "a friend." Gregor looked up at
the big line of tall windows that marched from one side to
the other across the front of the third floor of Lida's townhouse, all dark now. Gregor had grown up with Lida
Arkmanian on this very street, when it had been not much
better than a slum. It was only recently that the area had
been gentrified and turned into what *Philadelphia* magazine
had called "the best urban renewal story in America."
Gregor looked at the townhouses and the duplexes and the
shiny storefronts selling everything from Armenian food-
stuffs to expensive glass sculptures that looked like teardrops
having nervous breakdowns. The neighborhood was decorated to within an inch of its life. The entire facade of the
four-story brownstone where Bennis and Gregor both had
floor-through apartments was wrapped up like a Christmas
package in blue foil paper, complete with a big blue satin rib-
bon on the roof. That was Donna Moradanyan's hobby,
wrapping up the brownstone where Gregor and Bennis lived.
Donna Moradanyan lived there, too, on the fourth floor. She

had not, Gregor noted, taken down her Christmas decorations to replace them with decorations for New Year's. It only went to prove his theory that New Year's Eve was not a real holiday. For real holidays, Donna Moradanyan decorated.

Father Tibor Kasparian's apartment was around the back of Holy Trinity Armenian Christian Church. Once Gregor and Bennis were on Cavanaugh Street proper, they couldn't see the lights in its front windows or over its front door. The streetlamps that lined the sidewalk didn't seem to give off enough light. I don't like looking at Cavanaugh Street in the dark, Gregor realized. It makes me sense as if the whole place has died.

"I think everybody is going to be a lot calmer after the wedding is over with," Bennis was saying, "especially Donna, who doesn't want to have a big wedding to begin with. Russ has suggested that they just take Tommy and elope to Bermuda or someplace, but Donna is afraid of her mother."

"Mothers like to give weddings," Gregor said. "Especially Armenian mothers."

"Donna's mother isn't Armenian, Gregor. She grew up on Cavanaugh Street. If you ask me, what she really wants is to have a lot of fancy pictures to send to Peter Desarian." Peter Desarian was Donna's former lover and Tommy Moradanyan's father. "Donna and I keep trying to figure out how she's going to con the *Inquirer* into calling Russ a 'prominent attorney' in the wedding announcements."

Gregor Demarkian had not known Bennis Hannaford growing up. He had met her on the Main Line, during his first case of extracurricular murder after his retirement from the Federal Bureau of Investigation. Walking under the dim light of the streetlamps with her wild black hair and high, wide cheekbones and her enormous blue eyes, she looked at once familiar and exotic. Bennis could have been mistaken for an Armenian more easily than Donna Moradanyan—with her blond athleticness—could have been identified as one. At the same time, she was so obviously what she was born to be: an unadulterated WASP, a Main Line debutante, a daughter of the Philadelphia railroad rich. Sometimes

Gregor wished that that part of her didn't put him off so much.

"Gregor?" Bennis said. "Are you listening to me?"

They were right in front of Lida Arkmanian's townhouse now, in the middle of the block, nowhere near the walk lights or the designated crossing. Gregor looked both ways in spite of the fact that he couldn't hear any traffic anywhere in the city. Then he started to jaywalk. Bennis jaywalked with him, without looking.

"I'm listening," he said. "I just feel like I've been living with Donna Moradanyan's wedding for most of my life."

"She's only been engaged for six months, Gregor."

"Yes, I know, and she's going to be engaged for six months more. Maybe I'll follow Lida Arkmanian's example and take a nice long vacation until I have to show up in a tuxedo jacket."

"At least she's having the wedding here and not out on the Main Line," Bennis said. "Can you imagine what a mess it would have been, with all of us trucking out on the train or carpooling or whatever?"

They had reached the steep front stoop to their brownstone. Gregor got to the top of it and tried his key in the lock, only to find that the door hadn't been locked in the first place. Bennis and Donna never locked the damn thing, no matter how many times he told them how dangerous it was for them not to. At least Bennis locked the door to her own apartment. Half the time, Donna forgot to do that.

"One of these days, we're all going to get burgled," Gregor said, holding the door open for Bennis.

Bennis passed inside without commenting and turned on the light in the hall.

"Gregor," she said, "do you ever think about giving it up, investigating murders and that kind of thing?"

"I don't think about giving it up and I don't think about staying with it. It just happens."

"What if it stopped happening?"

"I don't know. I don't suppose it will unless I want it to. And I don't have anything else right now that I'd rather do."

Bennis climbed the stairs to the second floor with Gregor right behind her. When she got to the landing, she got out her keys and started to fiddle with her door.

"Well," she said. "Happy New Year. I probably won't see you again before I leave for California."

"You'll see me tomorrow," Gregor said. "You'll start to pack and find fifteen things you have to borrow from me, starting with my shirts."

Bennis opened her door and turned the light on in her foyer. "I'm thinking of giving up your shirts," she said. "I'm thinking of taking up with your sweaters instead."

The light on the landing was even dimmer than the lights on the street had been. The pale glow of it shimmererd over the top of Bennis's head, making her hair look lit from within. Gregor Demarkian suddenly got one of the strangest urges of his life.

"Bennis?" he said.

"What is it? Bennis turned toward him.

Gregor leaned forward quickly and gave her a kiss on the tip of her nose.

"Happy New Year," he told her.

Then he turned and went as quickly as he could up the stairs to his own apartment.

About the Author

JANE HADDAM is the author of twelve Gregor Demarkian Holiday mysteries. *Not A Creature Was Stirring*, the first in the series, was nominated for both an Anthony and the Mystery Writers of America Edgar Award. She lives in Litchfield County, Connecticut, with her husband, and two sons, where she is at work on a Birthday mystery, *And One to Die On*.

If you enjoyed FOUNTAIN OF DEATH, you will want to
read the latest Jane Haddam hardcover, AND ONE TO
DIE ON.

Here is a special preview of AND ONE TO DIE ON,
available at your local booksellers in March 1996.

AND ONE
TO DIE ON

A BIRTHDAY MYSTERY

BY

JANE HADDAM

Sometimes, she would stand in front of the mirror and stare at the lines in her face, the deep ravines spreading across her forehead, the fine webs spinning out from the corners of her eyes, the two deep gashes, like ragged cliffs, on either side of her mouth. Sometimes she would see, superimposed on this, a picture of herself at seventeen, her great dark liquid eyes staring out from under thick lashes, her mouth painted into a bow and parted, the way they all did it, then. That was a poster she was remembering, the first poster for the first movie she ever starred in. It was somewhere in this house, with a few hundred other posters, locked away from sight. She had changed a lot in this house, since she came to live here, permanently, in 1938. She had changed the curtains in the living room and the rugs in the bedroom and all the wall decorations except the ones in the foyer. She had even changed the kind of food there was in the pantry and how it was brought there. She had felt imprisoned here, those first years, but she didn't any longer. It felt perfectly natural to be living here, in a house built into the rock, hanging over the sea. It even felt safe. Lately she had been worried, as she hadn't been in decades, that her defenses had been breached.

Now it was nearly midnight on a cold day in late October, and she was coming down the broad, angled stairs to the foyer. She was moving very carefully, because at the age of ninety-nine that was the best she could do. On the wall of the stairwell posters hung in a graduated rank, showing the exaggerated make-up and the overexpressive emotionalism of all American silent movies. TASHEBA KENT and CONRAD DARCAN in BETRAYED. TASHEBA KENT and RUDOLPH VALENTINO in DESERT NIGHTS.

TASHEBA KENT and HAROLD HOLLIS in JACA-RANDA. There were no posters advertising a movie with Tasheba Kent and Cavender Marsh, because by the time Cavender began to star in movies, Tasheba Kent had been retired for a decade.

There was a narrow balcony to the front of the house through the French windows in the living room, and Tasheba went there, stepping out into the wind without worrying about her health. They were always warning her—Cavender, the doctors, her secretary, Miss Dart—that she could catch pneumonia at any time, but she wouldn't live like that, locked up, clutching at every additional second of breath. She pulled one of the lighter chairs out onto the balcony and sat down on it. The house was on an island, separated by only a narrow strip of water from the coast of central Maine. She could see choppy black ocean tipped with white and the black rocks of the shore, looking sharp on the edges and entirely inhospitable.

Years ago, when she and Cav had first come here, there was no dock on the Maine side. She had bought the house in 1917 and never lived in it. She and Cav had had to build the dock and buy the boat the first of the grocery men used. They had had to make arrangements for the *Los Angeles Times* to be flown in and for their favorite foods, like caviar and pâté, to be shipped up from New York. They had caused a lot of fuss, then, when they were supposed to want to hide, and Tash knew that subconsciously they had done it all on purpose.

Tash put her small feet up on the railing and felt the wind in her face. It was cold and wet out here and she liked it. She could hear footsteps in the foyer now, coming through the living room door, on their way to find her, but she had expected those. Cavender woke up frequently in the night. He didn't like it when he found the other side of the bed empty. He'd never liked that. That was how they had gotten into this mess to begin with. Tash wondered sometimes how their lives would have turned out if Cavender hadn't been born into a family so poor that there was only one bed for all six of the boy children.

The approaching footsteps were firm and hard-stepped. Cav had been educated in parochial schools. The nuns had taught him to pick his feet up when he walked.

"Tash?" he asked.

"There's no need to whisper," Tash said. "Geraldine Dart's fast asleep on the third floor, and there's nobody else here but us."

Cav came out on the balcony and looked around. The weather was bad, there was no question about it. The wind was sharp and cold. Any minute now, it was going to start to rain. Cav retreated a little.

"You ought to come in," he said. "It's awful out."

"I don't want to come in. I've been thinking."

"That was silly. I would think you were old enough to know better."

"I was thinking about the party. Are you sure all those people are going to come?"

"Oh, yes."

"Are you sure it's going to be all right? We haven't seen anyone for so long. We've always been so careful."

Cav came out on the balcony again. He reminded Tash of one of those Swiss story clocks, where carved wooden characters came out of swinging wooden doors, over and over again, like jacks-in-the-box in perpetual motion.

"It's been fifty years now since it all happened," Cav said seriously. "I don't think anybody cares anymore."

"I'd still feel safer if we didn't have to go through with it. Are you sure we have to go through with it?"

"Well, Tash, there are other ways of making money than selling all your memorabilia at auction, but I never learned how to go about doing them and I'm too old to start. And so are you."

"I suppose."

"Besides," Cav said. "I'll be glad to get it all out of here. It spooks me sometimes, running into my past the way I do around here. Doesn't it spook you?"

"No," Tash said thoughtfully. "I think I rather like it. In some ways, in this house, it's as if I never got old."

"You got old," Cav told her. "And so did I. And the roof needs a twenty-five-thousand-dollar repair job. And I've already had one heart attack. We need to hire a full-time nurse and you know it, just in case."

"I don't think I'll wait for 'just in case.' I think that on my hundred and third birthday, I will climb up to the widow's walk on this house, and dive off into the sea."

"Come to bed," Cav said. "We have a lot of people coming very soon. If you're not rested, you won't be able to visit with them."

Cav was right, of course. No matter how good she felt most of the time—how clear in her mind, how strong in her muscles—she was going to be one hundred years old at the end of the week, and she tired easily. She took the arm he held out to her and stood up. She looked back at the sea one more time. It wouldn't be a bad way to go, Tash thought, diving off the widow's walk. People would say it was just like her.

"Tell me something," she said. "Are you sorry we did what we did, way back then? Do you ever wish it could have turned out differently?"

"No."

"Never? Not even once?"

"Not even once. Sometimes I still find myself surprised that it worked out the way it did, that it didn't turn out worse. But I never regret it."

"And you don't think anybody cares anymore. You don't think anybody out there is still angry at us."

"There isn't anyone out there left to be angry, Tash. We've outlasted them all."

Tash let herself be helped across the living room to the foyer, across the foyer to the small cubicle elevator at the back. She came down the stairs on foot, but she never went up anymore. When she tried she just collapsed.

She sat down on the little seat in the corner of the elevator car. Cav's children. Her own sister. Aunts and uncles and nieces and nephews. Lawyers and accountants and agents and movie executives. Once everybody in the world had been angry at them. When they had first come out to the island, they'd had to keep the phone off the hook. But Cav was probably right. That was fifty years ago. Almost nobody remembered—and the people who did, like the reporter who was coming for the weekend from *Personality* magazine, thought it was romantic.

Good lord, the kind of trouble you could get yourself into, over nothing more significant than a little light adultery.

The elevator came to a bumping stop.

"Here we are," Cav said. "Let me help you up."

Tash let him help her. Cav was always desperate for proof that he was necessary to her. Tash thought the least she could do was give it to him.

Hannah Kent Graham should have let the maid pack for her. She knew that. She should have written a list of all the clothes she wanted to take, left her suitcases open on her bed, and come out into the living room to do some serious drinking. Hannah Graham almost never did any serious drinking. She almost never did any serious eating, either. What she did do was a lot of very serious surgery. Face lifts, tummy tucks, liposuction, breast augmentation, rhinoplasty: Hannah had had them all, and some of them more than once. She was fifty-seven years old and only five foot three, but she weighed less than ninety pounds and wore clothes more fashionable than half the starlets she saw window-shopping on Rodeo Drive. Anyplace else in the world except here in Beverly Hills, Hannah would have looked decidedly peculiar—reconstructed, not quite biological, made of cellophane skin stretched across plastic bone—but she didn't live anyplace else in the world. She didn't care what hicks in Austin, Texas, thought of her, either. She was the single most successful real estate agent in Los Angeles, and she looked it.

So far, in forty-five minutes, she had managed to pack two silk day dresses, two evening suits, and a dozen pairs of Christian Dior underwear. She was sucking on her Perrier and ice as if it were an opium teat. In a chair in a corner of the room, her latest husband—number six—was sipping a brandy and soda and trying not to laugh.

If this husband had been like the three that came before him—beach boys all, picked up in Malibu, notable only for the size of the bulges in their pants—Hannah would have been ready to brain him, but John Graham was actually a serious person. He was almost as old as Hannah herself, at least fifty, and he was a very successful lawyer. He was not, however, a divorce lawyer. Hannah was not that stupid. John handled contract negotiations and long-term development deals for movie stars who really wanted to direct.

Hannah threw a jade green evening dress into the suitbag and backed up to look it over.

"What I don't understand about all this," she said, "is why I'm going out there to attend a one hundredth birthday party for that poisonous old bitch. I mean, why do I want to bother?"

"Personally, I think you want to confront your father. Isn't that what your therapist said?"

"My therapist is a jerk. I don't even know my father. He disappeared into the sunset with that bitch when I was three months old."

"That's my point."

"She murdered my mother," Hannah said. "There isn't any other way to put it."

"Sure there is," John told her. "Especially since she was in Paris or someplace at the exact moment your mother was being killed on the Côte d'Azur. It was your father the police thought killed your mother."

"It comes to the same thing, John. That bitch drove him to it. He went away with her afterwards. He left me to be brought up by dear old Aunt Bessie, the world paradigm for the dysfunctional personality."

"There's your father again. That's it exactly. What you really want to do, whether you realize it or not, is brain your old man. I hope you aren't taking a gun along on this weekend."

"I'm thinking of taking cyanide. I also think I'm sick of therapy-speak. You know what all this is going to mean, don't you? The auction and all the rest of it? It's all going to come out again. The magazines are going to have a field day. *People. Us. Personality.* Isn't *that* going to be fun?"

"You're going to find it very good for business," John said placidly. "People are going to see you as a very romantic figure. It'll do you nothing but good, Hannah. You just watch."

The really disgusting thing, Hannah thought, was that John was probably right. The really important people wouldn't be impressed—they probably wouldn't even notice—but the second stringers would be all hot to trot. The agency would be inundated with people looking for *anything at all* in Beverly Hills for under a million dollars, who really only wanted to see her close up. If this was the kind of thing I wanted to do with my life, Hannah thought, I would have become an actress.

The jade green evening dress was much too much for a weekend on an island off the coast of Maine. Even if they dressed for dinner there, they wouldn't go in for washed silk and rhinestones. What would they go in for? Hannah put the jade green evening dress back in the closet and took out a plainer one in dark blue. Then she put that one back, too. It made her look like she weighed at least a hundred and five.

"What do you think they have to auction off?" she

asked John. "Do you think they have anything of my mother's?"

"I don't know. They might."

"Aunt Bessie always said there wasn't anything of hers left after it was all over, that everything she had was in their house in France and it was never shipped back here for me to have. Maybe he kept it."

"Maybe he did."

"Would you let him, if you were her? Reminders of the murdered wife all around your house?"

"You make a lot of assumptions, Hannah. You assume she's the dominant partner in the relationship. You assume that if he has your mother's things, they must be lying around in his house."

"*Her* house. It was always her house. She bought it before she ever met him."

"Her house. Whatever. Maybe he put those things in an attic somewhere, or a basement. Maybe he keeps them locked up in a hope chest in a closet. They don't have to be where your aunt is tripping over them all the time."

"Don't remind me that she's my aunt, John. It makes me ill."

"I think you better forget about all this packing and go have something to drink. Just leave it all here for the maid to finish with in the morning, and we can sleep in the guest room."

"You only like to sleep in the guest room because there's a mirror on the ceiling."

"Sure. I like to see your bony little ass bopping up and down like a Mexican jumping bean."

Hannah made a face at him and headed out of the bedroom toward the living room. She had to go down a hall carpeted in pale grey and across an entryway of polished fieldstone. Like most houses costing over five million dollars in Beverly Hills, hers looked like the set for a TV miniseries of a Jackie Collins novel. The living room had a conversation pit with its own fireplace. It also had a twenty-two-foot-long wet bar made of teak with a brass footrail. Hannah went around to the back of this and found a bottle of Smirnoff vodka and a glass. Vodka was supposed to be better for your skin than darker liquors.

Hannah poured vodka into her glass straight and drank it down straight. It burned her throat, but it made her feel instantly better.

"You know," she said to John, who had followed her out to get a refill for himself, "maybe this won't be so terrible after all. Maybe I'll be able to create an enormous scene, big enough to cause major headlines, and then maybe I'll threaten to sue."

"Sue?"

"To stop the auction. You're good at lawsuits, John, help me think. Maybe I can claim that everything they have really belongs to my mother. Or maybe I can claim that the whole auction is a way of trading in on the name of my mother. Think about it, John. There must be something."

John filled his glass with ice and poured a double shot of brandy in it. This time, he didn't seem any more interested in mixers than Hannah was.

"Hannah," he said. "Give it up. Go to Maine. Scream and yell at your father. Tell your aunt she deserves to rot in hell. Then come home. Trust me. If you try to do anything else, you'll only get yourself in trouble."

Hannah poured herself another glass of vodka and swigged it down, the way she had the first.

"Crap," she said miserably. "You're probably right."

For Carlton Ji, journalism was not so much a career as it was a new kind of computer game, except without the computer, which suited Carlton just fine. Two of his older brothers had gone into computer work, and a third—Winston the Medical Doctor, as Carlton's mother always put it—did a lot of programming on the side. For Carlton, however, keyboards and memory banks and microchips were all a lot of fuss and nonsense. If he tried to work one of the "simple" programs his brothers were always bringing him, he ended up doing something odd to the machine, so that it shut down and wouldn't work anymore. If he tried to write his first drafts on the word processor at work, he found he couldn't get them to print out on the printer or even to come back onto the screen. They disappeared, that was all, and Carlton had learned to write his articles out in longhand instead. It was frustrating. Computers made life easier, if you knew how to use them. Carlton could see that. Besides, there wasn't a human being of any sex or color in the United States today who really believed there was any such thing as an Asian-American man who was computer illiterate.

Fortunately for Carlton Ji, his computer at *Personality* magazine had a mouse, which just needed to be picked up in the hand and moved around. It was by using the mouse that he had found out what he had found out about the death of Lilith Brayne. He didn't have anything conclusive, of course. If there had been anything definitive lying around, somebody else would have picked it up years ago. What he had was what one of his brothers called "a computer coincidence." The coincidence had been there all along, of course, but it had remained unnoticed until a computer program threw all the elements up on a screen. The trick was that the elements might never have appeared together if there hadn't been a program to force them together, because they weren't the kind of elements a human brain would ordinarily think of combining. Computers were stupid. They did exactly what you told them to do, even if it made no sense.

Carlton Ji wasn't sure what he had done to make the computer do what it did, but one day there he was, staring at a list of seemingly unrelated items on the terminal screen, and it hit him.

"FOUND AT THE SCENE," the screen flashed at him, and then:

GOLD COMPACT
GOLD KEY RING

GOLD CIGARETTE CASE
EBONY AND IVORY CIGARETTE HOLDER
BLACK FEATHER BOA
DIAMOND AND SAPPHIRE DINNER RING

Then the screen wiped itself clean and started, "TASHEBA KENT IN PARIS." This list was even longer than the previous one, because the researcher had keyed in everything she could find, no matter how unimportant. These included:

SILVER GREY ROLLS ROYCE WITH SILVER-PLATED TRIM
DIAMOND AND RUBY DINNER RING
BLACK BEADED EVENING DRESS
AMBER AND EBONY HOOKAH
BLACK FEATHER BOA
VIVIENNE CRI SHOES WITH RHINESTONE BUCKLES

If the black feather boa hadn't been in the same position each time—second from the bottom—Carlton might not have noticed it. But he did notice it, and when he went to the paper files to check it out, the point became downright peculiar.

"It was either the same black feather boa or an identical one," Carlton told Jasper Fein, the editor from Duluth House he was hoping to interest in a new book on the death of Lilith Brayne. Like a lot of other reporters from *Personality* magazine, and reporters from *Time* and *Newsweek* and *People*, too, Carlton's dream was to get a really spectacular book into print. The kind of thing that sold a million copies in hardcover. The kind of thing that would get his face on the cover of the *Sunday Times Magazine*, or maybe even into *Vanity Fair*. Other reporters had done it, and reporters with a lot less going for them than Carlton Ji.

"You've got to look at the pictures," Carlton told Jasper Fein, "and then you have to read the reports in order. The police in Cap d'Antibes found a black feather boa among Lilith Brayne's things just after she died. That was on Tuesday night—early Wednesday morning, really, around two-thirty or three o'clock. Then later on Wednesday morning, around ten, they interviewed Tasheba Kent in Paris, and *she* was wearing a black feather boa."

Jasper Fein shook his head. "You've lost me, Carlton. So there were two feather boas. So what?"

"So what happened to the first feather boa?"

"What *happened* to it?"

"That's right," Carlton said triumphantly. "Because after the black feather boa was seen around Tasheba Kent's neck at ten o'clock on Wednesday morning, no black feather boa was ever found in Lilith Brayne's things in the South of France again. That feather boa just disappeared without a trace."

Jasper Fein frowned. "Maybe the police just didn't consider it important. Maybe it's not listed because they didn't see any reason to list it."

"They listed a lipstick brush," Carlton objected. "They listed a pair of tweezers."

"Twice?"

"That's right, twice. Once at the scene and once again for the magistrate at the inquest."

"And the only thing that was missing was this black feather boa."

"That's right."

Jasper Fein drummed his fingers against the tablecloth. They were having lunch in the Pool Room at the Four Seasons—not the best room in the restaurant, not the room where Jasper would have taken one of his authors who had already been on the bestseller lists, but the Four Seasons nonetheless. Carlton had no idea what lunch was going to cost, because his copy of the menu hadn't had any prices on it.

"Okay," Jasper conceded. "This is beginning to sound interesting."

Carlton Ji beamed. "It certainly sounds interesting to me," he said, "and I'm in a unique position to do something about it. I'm supposed to go up to Maine and spend four days on that Godforsaken island where they live now, doing a story for the magazine."

"Love among the geriactric set?"

"I can take any angle I want, actually. My editor just thinks it's a great idea to have Tasheba Kent in the magazine. Hollywood glamour. Silent movies. Love and death. It's a natural."

"Did you say those feather boas were identical?"

"They were as far as I could tell from the photographs, and there are a lot of photographs, and most of them are pretty good. The descriptions in the police reports are identical, too."

"Hmm. It's odd, isn't it? I wonder what it's all about."

"Maybe I'll have a chance to find out when I go to Maine. Maybe I can get someone up there to talk to me."

"Maybe you can," Jasper said, "but don't be worried if you don't. They're old people now. Tasheba Kent must be, my God—"

"One hundred," Carlton said.

"Really?"

"Among the other things that are going on during this weekend I'm supposed to attend is a hundreth birthday party for Tasheba Kent."

"There's the angle for *Personality* magazine. That's the kind of thing you want to play up over there. Not all this stuff about the death of Lilith Brayne."

"To tell you the truth," Carlton said, "I'm going to have to play up the death of Lilith Brayne. My editor's going to insist on it."

Jasper Fein looked ready to ask Carlton how that could, in fact, be the truth, when Carlton had said only a few moments before that his editor would take any angle he wanted to give her. Jasper took a sip of his chablis instead, and Carlton relaxed a little. At least they understood each other. At least Jasper realized that Carlton was going to hang onto his ownership of this idea. Now they could start to talk business for real, and Carlton had a chance of ending up with what he wanted.

Carlton wasn't going to talk money now, though. He wasn't going to talk details. He was going to wait until he got back from Maine. Then he'd have more to bargain with.

BANTAM MYSTERY COLLECTION

____ 57258-X **THE LAST SUPPERS** Davidson • • • • • • • • • • • • • • $5.50

____ 56859-0 **A FAR AND DEADLY CRY** Peitso • • • • • • • • • $4.99

____ 57235-0 **MURDER AT MONTICELLO** Brown • • • • • • • • • $5.99

____ 29484-9 **RUFFLY SPEAKING** Conant • • • • • • • • • $4.99

____ 29684-1 **FEMMES FATAL** Cannell • • • • • • • • • $4.99

____ 56936-8 **BLEEDING HEARTS** Haddam • • • • • • • • • $4.99

____ 56532-X **MORTAL MEMORY** Cook • • • • • • • • • • • $5.99

____ 56020-4 **THE LESSON OF HER DEATH** Deaver • • • • • $5.99

____ 56239-8 **REST IN PIECES** Brown • • • • • • • • • • • • • $5.50

____ 56537-0 **SCANDAL IN FAIR HAVEN** Hart • • • • • • • $4.99

____ 56272-X **ONE LAST KISS** Kelman • • • • • • • • • • • $5.99

____ 57399-3 **A GRAVE TALENT** King • • • • • • • • • • • • $5.50

____ 57251-2 **PLAYING FOR THE ASHES** George • • • • • • • $6.50

____ 57172-9 **THE RED SCREAM** Walker • • • • • • • • • • $5.50

____ 56954-6 **FAMILY STALKER** Katz • • • • • • • • • • • • $4.99

____ 56805-1 **THE CURIOUS EAT THEMSELVES** Straley • • • • • $5.50

____ 56840-X **THE SEDUCTION** Wallace • • • • • • • • • • • $5.50

____ 56877-9 **WILD KAT** Kijewski • • • • • • • • • • • • • $5.50

____ 56931-7 **DEATH IN THE COUNTRY** Green • • • • • • • • $4.99

____ 56172-3 **BURNING TIME** Glass • • • • • • • • • • • • • $3.99

- -

Ask for these books at your local bookstore or use this page to order.

Please send me the books I have checked above. I am enclosing $_____ (add $2.50 to cover postage and handling). Send check or money order, no cash or C.O.D.'s, please.

Name _____

Address_____

City/State/Zip _____

Send order to: Bantam Books, Dept. MC, 2451 S. Wolf Rd., Des Plaines, IL 60018
Allow four to six weeks for delivery.
Prices and availability subject to change without notice.   MC 12/95

ELIZABETH GEORGE

"George is a master . . . an outstanding practitioner of the modern English mystery."—*Chicago Tribune*

A GREAT DELIVERANCE _____ 27802-9 $6.50/$8.99 in Canada

Winner of the 1988 Anthony and Agatha Awards for Best First Novel.
"Spellbinding . . . A truly fascinating story that is part psychological suspense and part detective story."—*Chicago Sun-Times*

PAYMENT IN BLOOD _____ 28436-3 $6.50/$8.99

"Satisfying indeed. George has another hit on her hands."—*The Washington Post*

WELL-SCHOOLED IN MURDER _____ 28734-6 $6.50/$8.99

"[This book] puts the author in the running with the genre's masters."—*People*

A SUITABLE VENGEANCE _____ 29560-8 $6.50/$8.99

"Both unusual and extremely satisfying ."—*The Toronto Sun*

FOR THE SAKE OF ELENA _____ 56127-8 $6.50/$7.99

"George is . . . a born storyteller who spins a web of enchantment that captures the reader and will not let him go."—*The San Diego Union*

MISSING JOSEPH _____ 56604-0 $5.99/$7.99

"A totally satisfying mystery experience."—*The Denver Post*

PLAYING FOR THE ASHES _____ 57251-2 $6.50/$8.99

"Compelling...infinitely engrossing..."—*People*

Ask for these books at your local bookstore or use this page to order.

Please send me the books I have checked above. I am enclosing $_____ (add $2.50 to cover postage and handling). Send check or money order, no cash or C.O.D.'s, please.

Name _____

Address _____

City/State/Zip _____

Send order to: Bantam Books, Dept. EG, 2451 S. Wolf Rd., Des Plaines, IL 60018
Allow four to six weeks for delivery.
Prices and availability subject to change without notice.   EG 11/95